White Wings

Dan Montague

White Wings

A DUTTON BOOK

DUTTON
Published by the Penguin Group
Penguin Putnam Inc., 375 Hudson Street, New York, New York 10014, U.S.A.
Penguin Books Ltd, 27 Wrights Lane, London W8 5TZ, England
Penguin Books Australia Ltd, Ringwood, Victoria, Australia
Penguin Books Canada Ltd, 10 Alcorn Avenue, Toronto, Ontario, Canada M4V 3B2
Penguin Books (N.Z.) Ltd, 182–190 Wairau Road, Auckland 10, New Zealand

Penguin Books Ltd, Registered Offices: Harmondsworth, Middlesex, England

First published by Dutton, a member of Penguin Putnam Inc.

First Printing, July, 1997
10   9   8   7   6   5   4   3   2   1

 REGISTERED TRADEMARK—MARCA REGISTRADA

Montague, Dan.
    White wings / Dan Montague.
        p.   cm.
    ISBN 0-525-94303-X
    I. Title.
    PS3563.05372W48   1997
    813'.54—dc21   96-29874
                                                                CIP

Printed in the United States of America
Set in Caslon 540
Designed by Eve L. Kirch

PUBLISHER'S NOTE

For Zoë

Ζώη μοῦ, δαζ αγαπϖ

—From *Maid of Athens* by Lord Byron

Acknowledgments

It was my good fortune that Carolyn Jenks agreed to be my agent and it was her knowledge of the industry and perseverance that brought *White Wings* to the attention of Al Silverman, a skillful editor and a patient guide.

I am indebted to the staff of the Abbot Public Library in Marblehead, Massachusetts, for their help in researching the material for this book, and to the creators of Mystic Seaport in Mystic, Connecticut, for their wisdom in preserving great sailing vessels including N. G. Herreshoff's Buzzards Bay 15 on which this novel is based.

While I love to sail, I had to turn to my son, Daniel Montague, III, who is a true sailor and boat builder, for technical assistance in the art of boat restoration and sailing.

I thank my readers, daughters Melanie Carpenter and Martha Bodine and granddaughter, Cregan Montague, for reviewing draft after draft of this novel until, with their guidance, we produced a final copy, and Shoko Hirao for her help with the Japanese words and phrases.

Lastly, I could not have written *White Wings* without the help of Zoë Montague, my wife, who read every word of every draft and was always ready with encouragement and guidance, just as she has been throughout our forty-six years of marriage.

Dear Rebecca—

My mother taught me this song when I was a little girl and I'm passing it on to you. It was written by Banks Winters in 1884.

Love,
Mom.

White Wings

White Wings, They nev-er grow wea-ry, They car-ry me

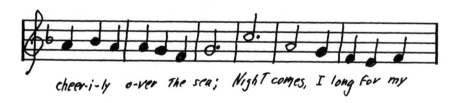

cheer-i-ly o-ver the sea; Night comes, I long for my

dear-ie, I'll spread out my white wings and sail home To Thee!

Prologue—June 25, 1973

On the rain-swept granite rocks beneath Marblehead's historic Fort Sewall a woman in foul-weather gear braced herself against the storm. It was night and she held a navy surplus battle lantern whose beam disappeared in the slanting rain.

Lightning flashed. It happened so quickly, she wasn't sure that what she'd seen was a sail. Then it struck again, a long, undulating flash of lightning. "There!" she shouted into the wind. "Thank God! It is a sail." Moments later, driven by huge breaking waves, she could see a gray blur of motion coming at her like a ghost out of the night. Running before the wind, pulled by its jib sail, its mainsail in tatters, the small sailboat held an unwavering course toward Fort Sewall where its skipper would turn into the shelter of the harbor. It was *White Wings*. She was coming home.

Suddenly the woman realized something was wrong. The boat wasn't turning. *White Wings*, riding the wind on the crest of a breaker, was being driven straight toward the rocks. Then, it was too late to turn. The huge wave pitched the boat over the first line of rocks, plunging her bow down into a foaming pool. Slicing through the roar of the wind and waves was the sound of wood scraping against granite, planks cracking and fracturing. The next wave struck, flipping her stern-over-bow, snapping the mast like a matchstick. *White Wings* lay in the pool, her hull rising and falling with each successive wave, her sails stretched across the rocks like broken wings.

PART ONE

~

The Channel

~

OCTOBER 1994

1

Saturday morning I slept in. No alarm to jar me awake. I slept until I was done sleeping and then awoke. Or maybe it was the late October sunrise shining in my eyes that woke me, or a squawking seagull flying past my window, or the halyards slapping aluminum masts on sailboats gently rocking in the harbor—whatever, it was peaceful. The rest of the week I'm a slave to the clock, slamming down the alarm at six a.m., then off to work as an art teacher in the local high school. But weekends I sleep in. I love weekends.

In the first stirrings of wakefulness, when the body's still asleep but the mind is waking up, dreams linger briefly before drifting off. Some I'm glad to be rid of: where I get lost, where someone's chasing me, where I walk into my classroom naked or start a lecture and can't find my notes. Some I cling to, like finding money under a rock or having sex with a beautiful woman. But last night there was something intriguing about my dream I wanted to recall before it was gone completely.

Gradually, fragments of the dream filtered through the mist clogging my mind. I was in a room, not my own, opening a box filled with photo store envelopes each containing a set of black-and-white snapshots. Picture after picture of a man in a sailboat. And a woman. Both strangers to me. I felt like a voyeur peeking into the intimate lives of others.

The pictures were all of the same two people, taken separately, never together, as if they had passed the camera back and forth between them. The young woman in her early twenties had laughing eyes and short, curly hair. Her one-piece bathing suit with wide shoulder straps and a brief skirt, discreet by today's standards, still revealed her full breasts and slim, athletic hips and legs. The man, about her age, in swim trunks, had dark hair and sharp features, and was tall with a slight yet muscular build. Several pictures showed him at the tiller, some sitting, some half standing, others pulling hard on the mainsheet. In all of them, apparently on command, he had glanced up at the camera, eyes squinting against the sun and with his partially opened mouth in a take-my-picture smile. The photos of his partner caught her standing at the mast, perfect as a *Vogue* model, arm locked around the stay, waving back at him, or hiking out, her long graceful legs stretched across the cockpit. She was laughing and the wind and spray were in her hair.

Straining to bring my dream pictures into focus, I looked at the boat's foredeck, the positioning of the mast, and the coaming around the cockpit. They reminded me of pictures I'd seen in a book of classic sailboats, a book I'd relished as a teenager. Like the woman's old-fashioned bathing suit, the boat was from an earlier time, maybe fifty, sixty years ago. I remembered my favorite boat in the book. A Buzzards Bay 15. I even remembered who'd built it. N. G. Herreshoff. Thinking about it, I decided the boat in my dream was the same as the boat in the book. Why not, I figured. It was my favorite boat and it was my dream.

Finally, the details of the dream passed and I was fully awake. I went to the bathroom, brushed my teeth, then showered and shaved. Standing before the mirror, I conducted a personal inventory. Twenty-seven and already I was beginning to slump beneath my driver's license height of six feet. Must remember to stand up straight, especially at school. My brown hair hadn't receded any noticeable amount since yesterday and still had that full Kennedy bounce even though I had no claim to that family. I like my blue eyes but the bags under them seemed a little bigger each morning, maybe because my cheeks were getting fuller and I was packing more strain into my face. Trying my award-winning smile that endeared me to old ladies but, apparently, was doing nothing for my love life, I stretched the bags into smile lines around my eyes and my cheeks into dimples. I need to do that more often, I decided. Hides my aging. I had liked my chest and shoulders ever since I outgrew adolescence. They were broad and full, carrying my 175 pounds with ease. Satisfied, I went to the kitchenette and started the coffeemaker.

While it hissed and dribbled, I looked out my front window at the harbor. The sun was rising above the fog bank that hung over the outer islands and shrouded the opposite shore with a translucent mist. Through this soft gauze of fog, the sun touched the treetops, igniting the leaves with brilliant fall hues of rust, gold, and yellow. You're lucky to be living here, Matthew Adams, I told myself.

And it was luck. When I moved to Marblehead, Massachusetts, after teaching in Fall River for four years, I wanted to live near the harbor, but rentals were too expensive for someone on a teacher's salary, even a department head, which I was. One day last August when I was apartment hunting and looking longingly at a condo by the harbor, a woman coming out of an adjoining unit asked if I would be interested in subleasing hers for four months. She'd been transferred and was willing to let me have it at half what she was paying. I jumped at the chance. Now, two and a half months later, I still had the rest of October and November before I had to move.

The aroma of coffee interrupted my self-congratulations, and I poured myself a cup. Returning to the window, I tripped over a half-empty carton still not unpacked from my move to Marblehead and filled with photographs from five years of college in Amherst and my teaching years in Fall River. Looking into the open box at the packages of photos, I thought about my recent dream.

So that's it, I said to myself. I jumbled up the memory of these photo envelopes with the longing I had as a kid for the Herreshoff boat and came up with a dream about sailing with a beautiful woman. Fine with me. Hope I dream it again.

Still, it was strange. I wasn't the man in the dream. Nor could I explain the two people whose faces remained etched in my mind.

Again I was at the window, sipping my coffee, looking at the harbor and wishing, as I did every morning, that one of the sailboats was mine. I noticed there were more vacant moorings. What had been a forest of masts when I arrived in August had gradually diminished to a scattering of sailboats as yacht owners had their boats pulled in preparation for winter. I watched a skiff, lashed like a miniature tug to the side of a forty-foot yacht, inch its graceful burden toward the Marblehead Trading Company crane. And it immediately occurred to me that this might be a good time to buy a boat. I wasn't after a forty-foot yacht. That I certainly couldn't afford, but a small daysailer might be possible. Somewhere, I thought, there must be a money-strapped sailor who can't afford to keep his boat through the winter months.

I had been around boats since I was a kid. At summer camp on Cape Cod when I was eleven, twelve, and thirteen, I'd learned to sail a dinghy. In high school I helped my dad build a double-ender sailboat with centerboard, which we sailed on lakes in western Mass and Vermont. He let me sail it, but it was his boat. Then, during my four years teaching in Fall River, I refined my sailing skills, but always on someone else's boat. Now I wanted one of my own.

Do it, I said to myself. Take the plunge. Finding my copy of the weekly *Marblehead Reporter*, I checked the classifieds. There were listings for furniture, cars, houses, firewood, etc., etc., but no boats. Then I noticed the yard sales scheduled for Saturday. One on Pleasant Street actually had a boat for sale.

I dressed quickly in my hiking boots, a pair of tan Dockers, and a blue sweatshirt and drove my Jeep Cherokee to the address. My spirits were soaring. I was going to buy a boat.

Calm down, I told myself. Don't buy the first thing that comes along. No fiberglass, no plywood hulls. Look for one with character and no dry rot. The most you can do is a thousand dollars. If it needs work, that's okay. You can do it yourself. You've got the whole winter to put it in shape.

On Pleasant Street, I parked behind a line of cars and walked half a block to a large white house with a wide yard fronted by a wrought iron fence. Two tall oak trees dominated the yard. Beside the front walk was a large sign, FAIR WINDS INN. A porch stretched from one side of the house to the other, with a formidable door in the center and two floor-to-ceiling windows on each side. On the second-story level were five tall windows above the porch roof, and above them a series of balusters topping the ancient structure like a queen's crown.

A plaque by the front door showed the house was built in 1823, not old by Marblehead standards; some of the houses date from the 1600s. On the left side of the house a driveway led back to a double garage at the rear of the lot. I walked up the drive and joined about fifteen people near the garage entrance. A mother and daughter were holding one dress after another against their shoulders, a young woman was sorting through boxes of books, a middle-aged woman was checking glasses and plates for chips, and a hefty man in his fifties was testing the comfort of a lawn chair that shifted precariously under his weight.

"What'll ya take for the chair?" he asked the fellow in charge, who was dressed in a black silk shirt and black pleated cotton pants and seemed overwhelmed by the customers the sale had attracted.

"That's two dollars," he said.

"Huh? I'll give y'a buck."

The man in black sighed and said, "Take it. It's yours." The shopper handed him a dollar bill, folded the chair, and headed for his car.

I went up to the guy in charge. "The ad says you have a boat for sale."

He pointed behind him. "It's over there behind the dress rack."

I squeezed past the women looking at dresses and saw a wooden dory turned upside down on two sawhorses. A three-strand line circled the gunwale. Patches of faded blue suggested its former color. The boat clearly had character and at one time had been a snappy little craft, but now the lapstrake panels on the side and bottom that were supposed to overlap one another to form a tight fit were sprung and warped.

The yard sale man approached. "I'm not a sailor, but a man was just here who said you could cover that with fiberglass and have a nice little boat."

"No," I said, disappointed, "that's not what I'm looking for."

"Well, have a look around. There might be something else you like."

"Thanks," I said and began drifting among the tables filled with household and clothing items with some yard and workshop tools thrown in. There were a few nice pieces, like depression glass and an art deco bedroom set that appeared to date from the thirties. I wandered into the garage where a large oriental rug lay partially unrolled on a workbench. Not bad, I thought. The family must have had money once upon a time.

In the darkness on the other side of the garage against the wall, my eye caught the outline of a long hull covered with a tarpaulin. Well, I thought, what do we have here? I crossed the garage for a better look just as the silk-shirt man came up.

"That's not for sale. Just the rug in here and the stuff outside."

"Mind if I have a look at the boat?"

"Go ahead, but don't touch anything. Nothing on that side's for sale." He shrugged and walked out of the garage.

A lightbulb with a pull chain hung from the ceiling. After the man left, I turned it on. The boat sat on a trailer with flat tires. Its tarpaulin was covered with dust and looked like it'd been there for years. I lifted a corner of the canvas and flopped it back, raising a cloud of dust. What I saw astonished me. The long bow trailing back to a shallow keel looked like a Buzzards Bay 15. And the length was about right. Mesmerized, I pulled the covering back still further and saw the elongated oval coaming surrounding the cockpit. There was no doubt about it. A Buzzards Bay 15.

A wave of lightheadedness passed over me and I seized the edge of the boat for support. My knees began to buckle, so I rested them against the trailer wheel. Squeezing my eyes shut tight, I shook my head. Gradually it began to clear. Fainting is not something I do. What is wrong with me? I wondered. Then my thought returned to the unbelievable prize against which I was leaning. Incredibly, I was looking at the boat I had known only in pictures, a boat I thought had long since passed from the scene. And more than that, I was touching the very boat about which I'd dreamed last night. This was too much. Maybe the shock of it caused my dizziness.

Recovering, I stood and ran my fingers over the deck, feeling the flaking paint. I climbed onto the wheel of the trailer and leaned into the cockpit where I tapped three or four frames. They were solid. No rot. I felt along the edge of the centerboard box and found a buckled bottom plank. Near the bow, the planking was severely fractured, leaving gaping holes. I winced, feeling the boat's pain in my own ribs. Standing back, I surveyed what I could see of the boat with the tarpaulin half off. The mast was sheared off about six inches above the deck. Looking up at the ceiling, I saw its remains wrapped in a torn sail suspended from the overhead beams.

"I told you, that boat's not for sale," the man called from the garage door. He was annoyed.

"So you did," I replied. "I was just curious. Is it your boat?"

"No," he snapped. "Belongs to the lady that owns the inn. What's in here is hers. What's outside is mine and a few other neighbors'."

"Think she might be willing to sell the boat?"

"No. I told you it's not for sale. Now, please turn off the light and leave the garage."

What a jerk, I thought as I pulled the light chain and followed him out of the garage. "Mind if I ask the lady herself about the boat?"

"It won't do you any good, but do what you want. She's not here today, though."

"Will she be here tomorrow?"

"Look," he said—now he was really pissed—"I've got a yard sale to run. How do I know when she'll be back? She comes and goes. Who knows?"

I decided to risk his wrath a little further and ask him another question. I was beginning to enjoy tormenting him. "What's the name of the lady who owns the inn?" I asked.

"Hayakawa," he replied without looking at me. "Mrs. Hayakawa."

"Thanks," I said, then remembered I hadn't pulled the tarpaulin back over the boat. As soon as he drifted to another part of the yard, I slipped back into the garage.

I walked to the bow of the boat and placed my hand against the cool, smooth wood of its side. "I've found you," I whispered. And then, recalling my dream, "Or, did you find me?"

2

The next morning, I decided to look my best when I went calling on Mrs. Hayakawa. "Mrs. Hayakawa," I said aloud to the mirror as I was shaving, "my name is Matthew Adams." I performed what I thought was a Japanese bow to my image. "I'm head of the art department at Marblehead High School. I was here for the yard sale yesterday and saw your boat in the garage. It's a Herreshoff, isn't it?" No, I'd better not say that. She may not know it's a collector's item. Might boost the price out of range.

I arrived at eleven o'clock in case she was a late riser. On my second knock the door opened. "Hello," I said to a tall, attractive Caucasian woman in her fifties. She had short gray hair and, tilting her head slightly, regarded me with brown eyes over the top of half-glasses that sat on the bridge of her nose. She was wearing a loose-fitting plaid shirt and black jeans. "I'm looking for Mrs. Hayakawa," I said.

"I'm Mrs. Hayakawa."

Surprised and momentarily shaken by this change in my expectations, I couldn't find the words to begin my speech. While I hesitated, she continued. "It's too early to check in, but I'm sure we'll have a vacancy later this afternoon."

"No," I said, adding stupidly, "I have a place to stay. I live here in Marblehead."

"Oh," she said, eying me cautiously. I could see the door starting to close.

I hurried on. "My name is Matthew Adams and I'm an art teacher in the high school here." This seemed to reassure her and the door stopped closing. "I was here at the yard sale yesterday and saw the boat in the garage."

"You mean the little dory?"

"No, the sailboat inside the garage," I said, flashing my winning smile, a killer for women her age. "I wondered if you'd like to sell it?"

"No, I don't think so," she said politely, removing her glasses, which fell to her chest and dangled from a cord around her neck. "It's been in our family a long time. I couldn't part with it."

"I guess you know it's severely damaged. It would be very expensive to . . ."

"I'm aware it's damaged. Obviously." Her tone held a warning not to push the issue. "But that's not the point."

"I'm sorry." Now I was sorry. "I didn't mean to be offensive."

"You see," her voice moderating, "it was my mother's boat. She sailed it up to the year she died."

Again I asked forgiveness and added, "It's a beautiful boat and I can understand why she didn't want it sold."

"Well, I don't really think you do understand, but that's all right."

"Just out of curiosity, though, could you tell me how it got so damaged?"

She looked at me sharply and said, "On the rocks, in a storm. It slipped its moorings."

"Oh," I said, appalled. "Your mother must have been heart-broken."

"Mr. Adams, I don't even know you and you're asking about things that are none of your business. I have other things to do. Good-bye." Again she started to close the door.

Hell, I'm not going to get the boat anyway. I might as well tell her I think it's a Herreshoff. "Mrs. Hayakawa," I said, feeling uneasy with my aggressiveness, "I'll be honest with you. Your sailboat's a Herreshoff. I'm sure of it. It's a collector's item."

"That may be," she said, her voice now hard, "but that has nothing to do with why the boat was important to my mother or to me." Then, with a firm clunk, the heavy oak door closed abruptly.

"Rats!" I said softly, staring at the polished oak. So much for my winning smile. Turning, I crossed the porch and was on the steps when I heard the door open.

"Mr. Adams." I stopped. Looked around. She was standing in the doorway, her head slightly tipped to the right and her shoulders slumped, the picture of apology. "That wasn't fair of me."

"I'm afraid I got what I deserved. I'm usually not that pushy."

We looked at each other for a moment across the wide porch, then she spoke. "You seem to know a lot about boats for an art teacher." She smiled. I returned the smile but stayed on the other side of the porch.

"I love sailing," I said, "and I love boats, especially wooden boats." I've got to keep her talking, I thought. "Yesterday, at the yard sale, I tried to look at the boat, but the man handling the sale practically booted me out of the garage."

"Good for Arnold." She laughed and a softness returned to her eyes. She stepped out from the doorway but continued to lean against its frame. Now her face reflected the comfortable ease of her clothing. She carried herself with a grace that allowed her to be casual without compromising dignity. "That's just what I told him to do. People swarm like hornets at a yard sale and they'll rob you blind if they get half a chance."

"I was in the garage looking at the oriental rug when I saw your boat under the tarpaulin. He said I could have a look if I didn't touch anything. I'm afraid I got carried away. When he left, I pulled the tarpaulin back . . . and, Mrs. Hakaya . . ."

"Hayakawa," she said with an understanding smile.

"Mrs. Hayakawa," I stammered, "I grew up looking at pictures of that boat, or one like it, and I never thought I'd see one for real. It's the most beautiful boat I've ever seen."

"And this is why you're being such a bother?" Another smile.

"Well, yes." When she shrugged her shoulders, I knew I had a chance. "I don't suppose," I said tentatively, "now that the yard sale is over, I could have one last look at the boat." Then, hurriedly, "I know you don't want to sell it, and I'm not asking to buy it. Just look at it."

She cocked her head to the side, taking measure of me. "Yeah. I'll bet." She pushed open the door behind her. "Come on in.

We'll go through the house and out the back door. You can look, but I'm still not selling."

"Oh, I know," I said, trying to conceal my excitement.

We entered a front hall that I could see extended to the rear of the house. On the left, just beyond a door, were stairs to the second floor. On the right side of the hall was a double door open to a large sitting room. The ceilings were at least nine feet high and the floors wide pine boards that showed the foot wear of many decades. Several pieces of heavy leather-upholstered furniture clashed with the period of the house.

I stopped to look at the room. "This is remarkable," I exclaimed. "I can't tell if I'm in the nineteen-twenties or the nineteenth century."

Mrs. Hayakawa turned and regarded the room. "Yes. I guess you could say that. You see, we—our family, that is—used to have a hotel here in Marblehead and this furniture was in the sitting room off the lobby. It fit then." She paused for a moment, with a smile that lamented a time gone by. "But that was years ago."

She led me down the hall to a door that went into a kitchen, and out a back door to the garage.

"Where was the hotel?" I asked.

"On Lee Street. It burned down in 'fifty-seven. There're condominiums there now."

"Good heavens," I said, helping her swing open the garage doors. "That's where I live." Thinking of the unimaginative architecture, I added, "What a shame they replaced the hotel with those dull buildings."

"Well, I guess it had to be. The hotel was part of another era and could never support itself today. Even then, it was losing money." She went to the boat and turned on the light. "Why am I telling you all this?" she said as if I had enticed her into revealing family secrets.

"I'm really not trying to pry." My words drifted off as my mind turned to the boat. "Mind if I pull the cover back?"

She gave me a teasing smile. "You'll have a hard time seeing it if you don't."

I caught the front corner of the tarpaulin and threw it over the bow, then went to the other side and pulled it off the entire boat onto the floor. There she was. The Herreshoff. I stopped, put my palms together at my chin and gazed at the boat. Her lines were as beautiful as I remembered from the pictures. Reverently I approached her side, stroking the smooth planking, barely touching it with my fingers.

"So that's the story of the hotel and here is the boat," she said curtly.

Hardly hearing her, I moved up the side of the boat to the bow where the side was crushed. I knelt and ran my fingers over the splintered edges of broken planking and into the gaping hole beneath the deck. Two frames were twisted and fractured. The deck had been torn away from the sheer plank. I put my arm into the hole, passed cobwebs, and felt bits of gravel and mussel shells still in the bottom. It smelled of the ocean. Closing my eyes, I let myself be drawn into its world. As if in a dream, I heard the distant sound of wind and sea. It grew louder until it was a deafening roar. Further and further I drifted into the swirling blackness. I could feel the boat pitching in violent, driving waves. Lightning cracked and for an instant the darkness was transformed into angry white foam and black water. Our mainsail, torn and useless, flapped help-lessly on the swinging boom. The jib, like a wind sock, kept us stern to the wind. Thrown about by a sea gone mad, I realized I wasn't *in* the boat. I had *become* the boat.

Another crack of lightning and I saw the jagged rock in our path. Suddenly an enormous swell rose up beneath us, lifting the hull over the rock but sending the bow diving into a black hole beyond. Instantly engulfed in water, we were thrown upside down as our stern came crashing over, snapping the mast. We hit the rock wall with the force of a wrecking ball, screaming as sharp planes of granite knifed into our side. With each new wave we were sucked back and slammed again at the unyielding wall.

Through the roar of the pounding surf I heard a distant voice. "Matthew? Matthew?" It called from another shore. "Are you all right?"

The noise subsided. The fog about me lifted. Gradually my mind cleared. I was still kneeling on the floor, my head leaning against the broken planks. "I think so," I answered haltingly. I touched my forehead and felt blood. "I guess I scratched myself."

"You were there so long I thought you'd passed out." She knelt beside me and took my elbow. "Here, lean back against this box. Don't try to get up for a minute."

I did as she asked. My breath came in short gasps. My mouth was dry.

"I . . . I'm all right. I don't really know what happened."

"Your forehead's bleeding. Can you make it back to the house? I'll get something for the cut."

Slowly I got up, Mrs. Hayakawa still holding my elbow. "I think I'm okay now," I said, and we started for her back door.

She dabbed hydrogen peroxide on my scratch and prepared a cup of tea. "You know, I'm concerned about you." We were sitting at her kitchen table. She had drawn her chair up beside mine and looked at me intently. "Don't take offense, Matthew, but have you ever had anything like a petit mal seizure? It's a kind of mild epilepsy."

"No. At least not that I know of."

"You left for a while. It was like you weren't there."

"How long did it last?" I asked, my own concern now matching hers.

"Probably not more than thirty seconds. Your head went down once, hard against the side of the boat, but that was the only movement. You seemed frozen."

Looking into her kind eyes, I frowned. I wanted to tell her where I'd been and what had happened, but I couldn't. I didn't understand it myself. It was like a dream, but it wasn't a dream. It was real. Never before had I experienced anything like it, being transported out of myself. I don't even believe in such things. But it did happen. When I touched the boat and felt its wounded side, the boat and I became one, and together we crashed onto the rocks.

3

I groped for the alarm and pushed the off button. Six o'clock. Shit. And Monday, too. I sighed and stretched. Starting to get up, I remembered the boat and immediately flopped back onto the pillow. Again, for the hundredth time, I asked myself, did it really happen? And I answered, as I had a hundred times before, it must have. Mrs. Hayakawa said I was out for thirty seconds. There had to be a rational explanation: fainting, *déjà vu*, the overactive imagination my mother claimed I had? Well, what the hell, I said, swinging my legs to the floor and sitting on the edge of the bed, it's a new day. Probably never happen again. Time for school.

Soon I was back in my classroom beginning to work my way through the Monday schedule: an art appreciation course, basic principles of drawing, a study hall, and an advanced drawing-from-life class. Being busy took my mind off yesterday's episode, yet my fingers continued to gravitate to the Band-Aid on my forehead.

Lunchtime. Instantly my classroom emptied as kids raced to the cafeteria or slipped off campus to Dunkin' Donuts, some for a jolt of sugar and some for a cigarette, leaving their chairs askew and papers on the floor. I gazed at the scene, like a battlefield after a war: empty, eerily quiet, and desperately lonely. I was sitting at my desk, holding a homemade ham and Swiss cheese sandwich in my left hand and a pencil in my right, correcting test papers as I ate. Again I looked at the vacant room. Not like a battlefield, I thought. Like my life: empty, quiet, and lonely.

The social life I'd had in Fall River had been passable but unproductive. I dated several women but didn't become seriously involved until the summer before last when I was teaching summer school, I ran into Regina Shelton on the dock at the Fall River Sailing Marina. I'd known her previously when she dated one of my sailing buddies. Regina, about five-two with a slight, sexy body, was dressed in a white short-sleeved blouse and tan slacks, her long blond hair flowing down her back. She had delicate features and pale skin protected from the sun by a long-visored sailing cap. The cuffs of her slacks were rolled up and her feet were bare. She asked if I wanted to go sailing.

In short order the two of us were under way on her father's thirty-two-foot Catalina. Before the trip was over I'd learned she was no longer dating my friend and was planning to spend the summer sailing the Catalina. She asked me to be her first mate, and every minute I wasn't in the classroom I was with Regina sailing the waters of Mount Hope Bay. Each weekend we'd sail through Narragansett Bay to Newport and party with her friends from one boat to the next until I thought I'd drop. And when I dropped, it was into Regina's bunk. It was a heady time for a small-town guy from North Adams, Massachusetts. I felt like I'd walked into a movie. At one party I met her father, who took an interest in me and my love of sailing. When he asked if I'd ever considered moving to a career more lucrative than teaching, I wondered if he was looking at me as a potential son-in-law.

The new school year had started when my romance with Regina ended abruptly. With the end of the sailing season, her yachting friends took off for winter sailing in Florida and the Bahamas and she moved to Coral Gables, where her mother had a Pearson 34. The cold truth of my relationship with Regina, that I was little more than a first mate and party buddy, sent me spiraling into depression. I was physically exhausted from a full teaching load and trying to keep up with Regina. The first weekend after she left, I slept for twenty-four hours. In the days that followed, feeling somewhat renewed, I began to enjoy the relaxed quiet of my own apartment and the challenge of teaching kids to see colors and shapes they didn't know were there. By January, however, the long nights and short days brought a return of loneliness and, with it, feelings of discouragement with my job and its lack of direction. Then one day in March the fickle winds of spring lifted my spirits with a fifty-five-degree day, and I resolved to take charge of my life by finding a better job in a new town. My search paid off and eventually I signed a contract with Marblehead High School to be head of the art department.

Last summer I spent with my parents in North Adams, helping Dad and Mom in their woodworking shop. I'm their only child, and they were glad to have me for a few weeks. Dad's fifty-three and Mom three years younger. They were married in 1966 and I was born the next year. He'd been an engineer in the early days of Digital Equipment Corporation in Maynard, Massachusetts, and Mom taught fifth grade in the same town. When I was eight they'd saved enough money to follow their dream, and dropped out of the world of high tech to open their shop in North Adams. Dad's about my height but stockier, and his hands are callused and strong from working with tools. I got my blue eyes from him and someday will probably have his gray hair. He's an easy man to be around because he likes what he's doing and he knows he's good at it. His contentment shows in his face. Over the years he's become a skilled cabinetmaker and has developed a market niche in replicating Shaker furniture, the graceful chairs, tables, and cabinets designed and built by the Shaker religious sect in the nineteenth century. It was the proximity to Shaker country that attracted Dad to North Adams, and not any connection to our family name.

Mom doesn't look fifty. Her hair is still brown and her figure trim. Three mornings a week she works out at the Y with several of her friends. A sharp dresser and an attractive woman, she's recognized in the town as a good business person. She keeps the books and runs the sales end of the business. Through ads placed in *Design Times*, she's doubled sales and built a customer list that extends across the country.

North Adams is all right. It's home and a place to go between jobs. And it was nice being with Mom and Dad. But there wasn't much to do. The friends I'd known in high school were married or had long since moved away. Occasionally I'd meet someone on the street I knew. We'd agree to get together soon, each knowing we wouldn't. Working with Dad in the shop was my salvation. I like woodworking and I'm good at it. But when August rolled around, I was anxious to find a place in Marblehead and get started with my new life.

Taking a bite of my sandwich, I realized I'd been sitting at my desk daydreaming for ten minutes and hadn't corrected a single paper. What is it with me? I wondered. Here I am, living in the perfect town with the perfect apartment and feeling as lonely and down as I did in Fall River, maybe more so. It's like I stayed in the same place and just shifted the scenery. And my job was basically the same: planning courses, conducting classes, grading work, and staying out of trouble.

I'd made a few acquaintances among the faculty but these didn't carry over to nonschool hours. Twice I'd gone to the pub at the town landing and sat awkwardly at the bar while tight clusters of apparently old friends laughed and joked at the tables around me. I felt out of it. Desperate to meet someone, I tried going to the local Methodist church, the denomination in which I'd grown up. The first time, I attended the family service at nine-thirty and was heartened to see people my age. At the coffee hour following the service, however, I discovered they were parents of young children with an agenda totally foreign to me. The next Sunday I went to the eleven o'clock service, where I was warmly received by people my parents' age. I could have gone to North Adams and been warmly received by my own parents.

I continued to sit at my desk, sandwich halfway to my mouth, pencil poised on the paper but not writing. I realized I was lonely to the point of tears. Is this what it means, I asked myself, to be clinically depressed? Whatever it is, I know I'm not making it and it's got nothing to do with where I live.

With moisture gathering in my eyes and tightness in my throat, suddenly it hit me. Christ, I thought, I'm going crazy! I made up that dream about the boat and then imagined I felt it crash on the rocks. I'm hallucinating because I'm not making it in the real world. Then, remembering Mrs. Hayakawa and the tenderness with which she'd washed my face and applied the Band-Aid to my forehead, I thought, Ugh! Did I make up that whole boat thing just to get an old lady my mother's age to feel sorry for me? Disgusted,

I took out my handkerchief, looked at the door to be sure no one was watching, and wiped my eyes.

I need to get hold of myself, I decided. Taking a large bite of my sandwich, I glanced at the October schedule pinned on the bulletin board. Columbus Day was coming up the following Monday, a chance to get away for a three-day weekend. Should I go home to North Adams? The foliage would be in its full glory and I could count on Mom to pamper her only child.

No, I thought, that's not it.

How about a date with the lovely Miss Jane Smithers who teaches music? Now that's more like it. The image of Miss Smithers drifted gracefully across my mind's stage, lingering for a moment to turn and look at me. A soft breeze caressed her long brown hair and caught her colorful, filmy India-cotton skirt, pressing it back against her thighs. As she turned to walk toward me, her breasts swayed gently. This was the image of Miss Smithers I'd often taken to my lonely bed at night.

I'd met her the second day of school and tried several times, unsuccessfully, to strike up a conversation. I wondered why women I find attractive are not attracted to me, while the ones who are, aren't what I'm looking for. I guess if they're attracted to me, I think something's wrong with them. I wrestled a few moments with this conundrum until, bored with the thought, I turned back to fantasizing about Miss Smithers.

Why just a date? Why not the whole three-day weekend? Imagine, Miss Smithers and me on Cape Cod, in an old inn, three days and two nights, in a jacuzzi, sipping champagne, exploring her beautiful breasts. I'm not only lonely, I'm horny.

Resolved to get a grip on myself, beginning with my social life, I folded the remains of my sandwich in its Baggie and headed for the faculty lounge.

Fate was on my side. There she was standing by the window drinking a Coke and looking at the golden maples on Pleasant Street across from the high school. I came up beside her. She was wearing a plaid wool skirt and a loose-fitting sweater that accentuated the swell of her breasts. I looked down, catching my breath.

Continuing to look out the window, she said, "Beautiful, aren't they?"

"Yes." The trees, you fool. She's talking about the trees. "They're lovely."

"Oh, hi, Matthew," she said, turning toward me. "I didn't realize it was you." Then, returning her gaze to the trees across the street, she said in a voice soft and dreamy as a warm day in autumn, "I'd like to be out there, walking along, kicking the leaves."

Is that a suggestion? I hoped. "Well, let's go. Right now. We still have twenty minutes left." Ah, I thought, what an impetuous fool I am.

"No, I can't," she sighed. "I've got to go over some notes before class." Then she looked up at me with her large auburn eyes and said, "But thanks for asking."

I gulped and was terrified she could see my Adam's apple bob up and down. "Well, I have another idea. How would you like to go out for dinner Friday night and later go for a long walk kicking leaves all over Marblehead?"

She smiled that old put-off smile with which I was so familiar and said, "It sounds really marvelous, but, Matthew, I think you should know I'm in a relationship that's very close."

"Oh," I said, suddenly deflated. "It really would have been marvelous, and thanks for telling me about your friend. He's a lucky guy."

"Matthew, you're a dear." As she turned toward the door, she twiddled her fingers. "See you."

I walked back to my classroom, shut the door, and finished my ham and cheese sandwich.

I'm fairly resilient and usually bounce back from discouragement quickly, but today my dark mood lingered. Once I had assigned the matter of the "boat experience"—as I now termed it—to a depression caused by extreme loneliness, I thought I should feel less disturbed. I didn't. As far as my strikeout with Miss Smithers was concerned, I'd given it my best shot. Talking with her, however, had only increased the sense of loneliness that hung like a heavy coat over my shoulders. That evening, when I finished lesson plans for the next day, I opened a bottle of Sam Adams, relaxed in a sling chair by the window, and looked out at the harbor.

In the half-light of evening, the dark trees and houses of Marblehead Neck were silhouetted against a deep blue-green sky. At the end of the point, the iridescent light of the navigational tower glowed a sharp green, warning returning sailors of the massive granite rocks beneath it. The view was captivating and, after two beers, I was feeling somewhat better. Gradually an idea began to take shape.

I called my dad in North Adams and found him just finishing dinner. After bringing each other up to date on what was happening in our lives, I talking only about school, I asked him if he remembered that book on sailboats I liked as a kid.

"The one by Bray? *Watercraft*?"

"That's it. Wasn't there a Buzzards Bay 15 in that book?"

"Yeah, I think so." And then he confirmed what I thought I had remembered. "You know, a lot of the boats in that book are in the small boat shack at Mystic Seaport."

"That's what I thought. I've got a long weekend coming up. Thought maybe I'd go down there and do some sketching."

"We'd love to have you come home for a visit, but I don't blame you for wanting to see those boats."

So, it was settled. I'd go to Mystic, Connecticut, for a night or two and spend some time in the museum, sketching boats. Who knew, I might even meet someone visiting Mystic as lonely as I.

The more I thought about the trip, the more I realized my real motive was to find a boat like the one I'd seen in Mrs. Hayakawa's garage. I telephoned her and told her I was planning to go to Mystic Seaport to find out more about her boat.

"Oh, Matthew," she sighed, sounding exasperated, "please don't keep pushing me about the boat. I wish you'd just forget about it."

I assured her once again I had no intention of buying the boat. It was just an excuse for going to Connecticut. I told her I needed to get away for the long weekend. Then I asked if she had a picture of the boat I could borrow to take with me. The reluctance in her voice was clear but she said she'd search her closets. And, much to my surprise, she invited me to drop by Tuesday evening.

At seven o'clock the next night, I knocked on the inn's door. Soon the door opened. Mrs. Hayakawa was dressed in dark gray wool slacks and a black turtleneck sweater set off with a strand of pearls. Looking at me over the top of her glasses, she greeted me warmly.

"Come in, Matthew," she said pleasantly, then stopped me beneath the hall light to examine my forehead. The scratch was healing, so I hadn't bothered to replace her Band-Aid. Touching my temple with the fingers of her right hand, she gently turned my head to the light. I found the tenderness of this gesture unnerving. But maybe she was just being motherly.

"Looks okay. How're you feeling?"

"Fine. No ill effects I'm aware of," I said, laughing.

"Good. Let's go inside." Opening the door in front of the stairway, she said, "I keep the rooms on this side of the house just for me, and my daughter when she visits. My guests are allowed to use the living room and dining room. That's where I serve them breakfast. All the upstairs rooms are for guests."

We entered a large room that served as a sitting room and dining area and included a kitchenette. Beyond this was a narrow hallway leading back to the inn's kitchen. There were three doors off the hall, which I assumed were to two bedrooms and probably a bathroom. A wing-backed sofa, which appeared to be an antique, sat against one wall. Two matching chairs flanked an intricately carved cherry table between the two front windows. A bouquet of fall flowers on the table added color to the room. Next to the doorway where we had entered was a large old-fashioned rolltop desk with the top rolled back. The slots were filled with neatly arranged records, envelopes, and paper. Against the wall by the hallway was a bookcase, the top shelf of which was lined with framed photographs. The room expressed a comfortable orderliness much like that of Mrs. Hayakawa herself.

"I hope you still have room for dessert," she was saying as I continued to look around, already feeling at ease. On a coffee table in front of the sofa was a lemon chess pie, two cups with saucers, cream and sugar, and a teapot tucked beneath a cozy.

"My favorite pie," I said. "And yes, I do have room." For dinner I had had warmed-up pasta with bolognese sauce but was out of my usual dessert, frozen yogurt. "This is very nice of you."

"Well, it's nice to have company," she said as she uncovered the teapot. "Would you like some?"

"Thank you."

"By the way. Please call me Taylor. Hayakawa's such a mouthful."

I smiled. "Thanks. I will."

Pouring the tea, she said, "Looking through Mom's pictures made me feel lonely, so I thought it would be fun to share dessert with you."

I walked to the bookcase and gazed at the line of photos, most of which were portraits. Looking at the picture of a young soldier, I asked, "Isn't this a British uniform?"

"That's my father, James DeWolf. He was a pilot in the RAF during World War Two."

Surprised, I said, "I didn't realize you were English. You have no accent."

"I'm not. I was born and raised right here in Marblehead." She joined me at the bookcase and picked up the picture of her father. "He's not British either. He grew up in Lynn and was a hotshot pilot in the thirties, so I'm told. When the war started in Europe, he enlisted in the RAF. I never knew him. He was killed in 1941."

She picked up another picture, of an attractive lady in her fifties.

"Your grandmother?" I asked.

"No," she said. "I'm afraid these are not in any chronological order. This is Mom taken a couple of years before she died. Isn't she lovely?"

I examined the photo. The woman looked to be about the same age as Taylor, but I wouldn't have recognized them as mother and daughter. Their features were somewhat the same, the mother's face and chin slimmer, the daughter's somewhat fuller, the mother's nose longer and narrower, the daughter's a bit wider with a slight bump at the bridge. It was their expressions, however, that made them different. I looked at Taylor and then at the photo. She saw what I was doing and smiled. Where her mother appeared defiant, Taylor seemed compliant. In her mother's eyes was a touch of the rebel, in Taylor's only proper conservatism. And one other thing about her mother. There was an elusiveness that made me feel, if I looked away and back again, she might not be there.

"Yes, she's very lovely. Must have been a knockout when she was younger. Did she remarry?"

"Never did, not that she couldn't have. She had plenty of offers. She worked for Gram and Gramp in the hotel and there were lots of men who stayed there during the summers." She set the frame back on the shelf and we returned to the coffee table. "How about some pie?"

It was as good as it looked, the tart sweetness melting in my mouth.

"I hope you don't mind my asking, but I'm curious about your last name. Hayakawa isn't exactly an old Marblehead name."

She smiled. "I thought you'd get around to that. The short answer is, Tadeo Hayakawa and I were students at Tufts University in the early sixties. We fell in love and got married right after graduation. He was gung ho to be an American. Even wanted to set up an importing business for Japanese-made marine equipment right here in Marblehead. But when we returned to Japan, his family had other ideas. They set him up in business over there and before long he reverted to the ways of Japan. Being a wife in Japan's not the same as here. The husband's the boss and your job is to stay home and treat him like a king. I stuck it out for nine years, but when Mom died, when Rebecca was six, I came home to Marblehead. We've been divorced for years."

I felt uneasy having her tell me this. True, I was curious, but I was also afraid she would feel I was trespassing too far into her private life, and slam the door in my face. On the other hand, maybe she just wanted someone to talk with as much as I did. So, taking a chance, I kept going. "You mentioned Rebecca. Your daughter?"

"Yes," she said. "She's twenty-seven now. Works for the Markham Hotel in Boston." She looked at me with a sad smile and said, "That's a lot of family for one night, how about some more pie?"

I couldn't refuse. She cut a generous slice and placed it on my plate. On my third bite, I asked if she'd found any photographs of the boat.

"I found one of my mother on the boat but you can't see much of it. Then I remembered that Aunt Aggie has a bunch of them. She's not really an aunt, but I've always called her Aunt Aggie. She and

Mom were best friends, known each other all their lives. Aggie's about, let's see—" Her right index finger tapped her left thumb as she figured the years in her head. "Both born in 'twenty-one, so that makes Aggie . . . seventy-three. Wait till you meet her, though. She's a young seventy-three."

I hesitated, then asked, "Do you think she'd loan me a couple of pictures to take to the museum?"

"You'd have to ask her." Then she stopped and looked me straight in the eye. It was a hard look. Oh, oh, I thought, now I've gone too far.

"Why do you really want to go to the boat museum?" she said. "Does this boat mean that much to you?"

"It does," I said honestly. "And I'm not sure why. I know I want a sailboat—that's one of the reasons I moved to Marblehead. And I want it to be one of the classic wooden boats. But it's more than that." I set my fork down and leaned back against the sofa. "Friday night, the night before I came to the yard sale and saw your boat, I dreamed about it." She looked at me as I spoke, her forehead slightly furrowed. "I don't mean 'dream' in a vague sense, like 'I dreamed I'd find the perfect boat.' " I looked at her intently and continued, my voice faltering. "I dreamed about the very boat that sits in your garage."

Now she leaned back, her left hand going to her chin as she pondered what I was saying. Without speaking, she nodded for me to continue.

"I dreamed I was shuffling through a box of old photographs and came across several of a young man and woman in a boat." I paused. "It was your boat. The man, about my age, was intent on sailing the boat and you could tell by his expression in each of the pictures how much fun he was having." I smiled as I remembered the pictures. "The woman was tall and beautiful. In one picture she was hiking out on a close haul. In another she was standing at the mast, laughing, the wind blowing her hair. She was waving to the person taking the picture."

Taylor's face went blank. Her mouth opened slightly. For a moment she stared at me. Then she reached beneath a book on the table beside the sofa and extracted a snapshot. She held the photograph in front of me.

"Do you mean like this?"

I studied the photo. It was the picture in my dream. The woman, her arm around the stay, was leaning against the mast, sunlight highlighting her hair as it was caught and lifted by the wind. I felt the breath go out of me. My head felt light and for a moment I thought I was slipping away as I had the other day, but slowly it passed. My hand went up and took the picture from Taylor. I brought it closer, studying it. Then I spoke.

"Yes," I said, closing my eyes. "Exactly like that."

For several moments we sat quietly without speaking. Then Taylor leaned forward and put her hand on mine.

"Matthew," her voice soft, "if you hadn't described the picture before I showed it to you, I'd be skeptical." She shook her head, still having trouble comprehending what had happened. "This is very strange, but there's no doubt. You dreamed about photographs of my parents, pictures taken in the boat."

Still regaining control of myself, I nodded, her hand comforting as it gently patted mine.

"This is my mother," she said, looking at the photograph, "Rebecca DeWolf. And it must have been my father taking the picture, probably the summer of 1940, before he enlisted in the RAF. Mom was about nineteen."

I looked again at the picture. Her mother was stunning: tall with the long slender legs of a swimmer, graceful neck, confident chin, straight nose, high cheekbones, and wide-set eyes. The left strap of her bathing suit had slipped from her shoulder, revealing the swell of her breast. The sly look she was giving the man taking the picture suggested she'd pulled it down just for him.

"Did she take any pictures of your father that day?" I asked, remembering the man at the tiller in my dream.

"Not that I know of," Taylor said, then realized why I'd asked. "Oh, that's right. You dreamed about him, too."

"Yes," I said, handing the picture back to her. "Aggie gave you this one. Maybe she has one of your father in the boat, too."

"I doubt it. I'm sure she would have given it to me if she did."

It seemed strange she'd never asked, but I decided not to push it further. Instead, I let myself succumb to the comfortable intimacy of sitting side by side with Taylor, her hand resting on mine. The warmth of our closeness wasn't sexual, at least not as far as I was concerned. After all, she was my mother's age. But I did notice for the first time the perfume she was wearing. I could understand it if the situation were reversed, a man her age and a woman mine. Even as I thought this, I knew it was politically incorrect, but hell, this wasn't a theoretical situation. I felt uneasy sitting next to a woman twice my age who was very attractive in a restrained sort of way.

Then I realized why I was troubled. I didn't want this intimacy to be sexual. I wanted her to be her age, the age of my mother. I wanted to tell her about what happened when I passed out. Like a child, I wanted to ease the burden of a frightening experience by sharing it with my mother.

I sat quietly for several moments, looking down at the crumbs left on my pie plate. Taylor tilted her head toward my face and asked, "Are you all right, Matthew?"

"Yes," my voice uncertain.

"What is it?" she said softly.

I turned my face toward hers and my fear was eased by the gentleness of her smile.

"I want to tell you something," I began, "and I'm afraid you'll think I'm crazy. I mean, literally crazy. Sunday, when I passed out, when you thought I might be having an epileptic attack, I . . ." I paused, searching for a way to explain what had happened. "When I touched the boat . . . put my hand through the hole in its side . . . felt its broken frames and torn planking . . . I could hear the waves . . . feel the boat thrown up onto the rocks . . . hear the screaming of the wood against the rocks as its side was pierced. I was there, a part of the boat, until I heard you calling me." I laughed in a self-effacing way and said, "See what I mean? Sounds crazy, doesn't it?"

"No. Not crazy," she said softly. "I knew something was happening. You were there but not there." She patted my hand again. "I've never experienced anything like that myself, and yet, I've come close sometimes." She leaned back against the sofa so she could look at me better.

"After Rebecca was born, when I lived in Japan, I started going to church. We lived in Yokohama where there was an Anglican church with both a Japanese and an English-American congregation. I told Tad I wanted to take our daughter to church to expose her to Christianity, but what I really wanted was to be with Western people. Our marriage had become more and more Japanese in the sense that I was the stay-at-home servant to my husband. When I was pregnant, I discovered his evening business appointments with his partners always included young girls. I shouldn't have been surprised," she sighed. "This is how it's done in Japan. I was just naive. We had been so close when we were at Tufts I thought our marriage could withstand the double standard that sometimes exists in Japan. When I confronted Tad, he laughed at me and said, 'Look at you, big and fat with a baby,' and walked out. So he kept fooling around with his little girls while I stayed home. At first I was hurt, but it wasn't long before I was just damn mad at him leaving me at home while he had fun." She gave a little throw-away laugh and said, "But that was twenty-eight years ago."

"Are you still mad at him?" I asked.

"I'm angry, yes, but more at myself for wasting all those years." She paused to adjust her glasses and take a deep breath. "I didn't mean to get into all of that. I was telling you about joining Christ Church on the Bluff in Yokohama. You can see why I wanted to be around some Americans." I nodded. "In any case, this was and is a very unusual church. It was built about 1920 by the Mission to Seamen organization and looked like an English stone church transplanted to Japan. It was really quite beautiful. To the right of the front door was a brass plaque which said, 'Destroyed by earthquake, 1923—Destroyed by firebombs, 1945.' The plaque spoke to the faith and resiliency of the congregation, especially those Japanese who welcomed the Americans after the war. When we said the general confession at Morning Prayer, I always prayed to be forgiven as an American who in some way helped to drop the firebombs.

"One Sunday, as we knelt for the Eucharist, we had a slight earthquake, maybe a number three, not much. The priest stopped for a moment as the candles flickered and the chandelier swayed.

He looked up to heaven and waited for another jolt. When none came, he resumed the prayers. As for myself, I was thinking about the massive 1923 quake when everything was leveled." She stopped for a moment. "I guess I'm wandering."

"No," I said, "not at all. Please go on."

When she began again, her words were precise and purposeful. "What I really want to say is this. For decades the walls of that little church had absorbed the prayers and the longings and the fears and the joys of some deeply spiritual people. They had endured the earthquakes and the firebombings and stayed together as a congregation. And when I knelt in that church, I could feel their presence." She took a deep breath, then sighed. "I don't know if I've said it right."

"I think you said it just right."

"Maybe when circumstances or situations are right, when a person or a group of people experience and express the deepest human feelings over a long period of time, these feelings cling to the walls around them, penetrate them and become embedded." Taylor removed her glasses and rubbed her eyes. "Or maybe we're both crazy."

We laughed together.

I got up, walked to the end table, and picked up the picture which Taylor had replaced. I looked at her mother on the boat and said, "What I don't understand is, with that boat in your garage for years and lots of people looking at it and touching it, why should I be the one who experienced its wreck?"

I left Marblehead Saturday morning, driving south through Swampscott, Lynn, and Revere, past Logan International Airport and into the Sumner Tunnel to Boston. I made a quick turn by the meat and cheese shops in the North End, where Italian is still the preferred language. Then up the ramp next to Quincy Market, jammed with people of all nationalities buying fruits, vegetables, and fish at below bargain prices. This put me on the elevated central artery that funnels all north-south traffic through Boston. Weekdays the traffic creeps along the artery, but this morning I moved rapidly past the huge towers of International Place on the right and the majestic arch and dome of the Boston Harbor Hotel on the left. Before long I was on the expressway heading south where I eventually picked up Interstate 95.

Surely this fall had to be one of the prettiest on record. When it rained, it rained at night, and the days were warm and sunny. The trees were in full color and seemed to stretch endlessly on either side of the road. I sailed through Providence, Rhode Island, below the white marble dome of the state capitol and on into Connecticut. In less than three hours I was pulling into Mystic. I passed the historic seaport area, with its tall square-rigger masts visible over the rooftops, and headed into town to get some lunch and collect my thoughts. I found a parking place on Pearl Street and walked back around the corner to the Draw Bridge Inne on West Main where I ordered a reuben sandwich and a Bud Lite.

Seated at the window watching people pass by, I noticed a number of good-looking women. I guess I was hungry for more than food.

For the past three days I had tried to put the "boat experience" out of my mind. Dreaming about the boat and the very same picture Taylor had showed me, plus reliving the boat's crash on the rocks, was bizarre. I tried to convince myself my mind was just playing tricks on me, but I knew it was more than that. For the first time in my life, I began to wonder if I might be turning into some kind of mystic. In spite of the fact I didn't feel like a guru and was as sane as a high school teacher can be, I knew my mind was functioning separately from my will in this particular area. Maybe this was only the beginning. Maybe it would spread to other parts of my life. Fear settled in my stomach like a stone. Leaving half the reuben on the plate, I paid my bill and left the restaurant.

Walking leisurely, I made my way down West Main toward the drawbridge over the Mystic River. The shops were mainly boutiques smelling of sweet-scented candles and potpourri which seem to draw tourists like moths to a flame, galleries with paintings of ships and sand dunes, and clothing stores to outfit the young, the rich, and the restless for mountains or sailboats. The drawbridge was steel with huge blocks of concrete mounted as a counterbalance on the top of a superstructure. I walked to the center of the span and looked up the Mystic River toward the historic village about a quarter of a mile on the right bank. In plain view, even at that distance, were two square-riggers which I learned later were the *Charles W. Morgan*, a whaling bark built in 1841, and the *Joseph Conrad*, a training ship launched in 1882. Tucked somewhere among the many old buildings of the village was the small boat shack that housed the Herreshoff collection where I would spend most of my time.

I noticed I wasn't hurrying to visit the village and was relieved that I still had to find a place to stay. Sooner or later, however, I would have to go to the museum and look for the boat. What would happen when I found it? Would I have another episode like the one in the garage? I could see myself alone in the museum, my body lying on the floor while my mind sailed away on one of Herreshoff's yachts. I shuddered and gripped the railings of the bridge.

Beneath me the ebb tide was running fast, cold and swirling. As

I looked up, my eye caught a strange sight in the middle of the river. About a hundred yards away something was flopping in the water. At first I thought it was a cormorant drying its wings. As it drew nearer it looked like a wounded seagull. It would flap its wings ten or twelve times like a person doing the butterfly stroke, then rest with only its head above water. It was frantically trying to reach shore before being swept out into the ocean. When it was about twenty-five yards away I realized it was a pigeon. Again and again it repeated the process of resting and then spasmodically slapping its wings against the water. I wanted to shout at it to take courage and keep trying to make the other bank, but as it reached the bridge, it stopped trying and surrendered to the outgoing tide.

That poor pigeon, I thought. What kind of a freak accident made it land in the water? And then it hit me. Like the pigeon who had no business being in the Mystic River, I had no business getting into mysticism. And, like the pigeon, I too could feel an overpowering tide pulling me into unknown waters.

I returned to my Jeep, drove to the information center, and asked about lodging. In the brochure rack I found a Days Inn folder. A phone call produced a room for two nights at a moderate price. I drove to the motel, checked in, and put my gear in the room. Unable to think of any further excuses, I went to Mystic Seaport Village where I paid fifteen dollars for admission and was given a lapel sticker good for two days. I decided to walk around for a while, visit a few of the exhibits, get my bearings, and eventually sneak up on the small boat shack with its Herreshoff boats.

Carrying my sketch pad, I walked along the waterfront, stopping at Shaefer's Spouter Tavern, which advertised Gray's Ales at five cents a glass. What a bargain! But inside I found a TV monitor describing a nineteenth-century tavern, and no ale. I continued on down the dirt road, feeling I had returned to the mid-1800s. I visited a one-room church, an old-fashioned drugstore, and a ship carver's shop. When I came to the cooperage, a woman in period clothing was showing a group of children how a barrel is made and had just assembled all the slats within the hoops. One youngster gave the barrel a kick, the hoops slid off, and all the slats opened up like petals on a flower. I laughed and thought I might as well be back in my classroom.

A movie was being filmed at the pier where the *Charles W. Morgan* was moored. Over and over again a wagon pulled by a white horse and carrying bundles and boxes was driven up to the gangway, where actors dressed like longshoremen of the mid-nineteenth century unloaded it and carried the objects up and into the ship. The sails were unfurled and flags were flying. A man in a stovepipe hat and black tails counted each parcel as it came aboard.

Staying clear of cables and boxes of equipment, I watched the camera crew and director go about their business. A woman passed me carrying a tray of coffee from the snack bar and approached the director. She was several inches shorter than I and dressed in army fatigues two sizes too big. At first I mistook her for a young man because her hair was tucked under her army field cap. I heard the director say thanks and tell her to wait by the equipment. "I might have something for you in a minute," he said with a condescending smile. She crossed back over the cables and stood beside me.

"What are you shooting?" I asked.

"It's a PBS movie," she said in a disgruntled voice. I glanced at her and decided the person hidden beneath the Desert Storm camouflage was somewhere between eighteen and thirty.

"When will it be on TV?"

"Next spring."

She wasn't big on conversation. I tried again. "I've always wondered," I ventured, "how is it possible to do a whole movie or TV show when it takes an hour to shoot just thirty seconds?"

She took off her cap and shook out her hair. A bundle of dark red curls exploded. Looking at me like an impatient adult talking to a child, she said, "It gets done."

"Oh," I said. Then, as I was starting to ask what her job was, she turned and walked away. I said to myself, well, that's show biz, and set off for the boat shop a little further up the quay where they actually built wooden boats.

Beyond the counter that separated the tourists from the craftsmen, one of the pros was building a small pulling boat. The floor of the shop was yellow with wood shavings and smelled of freshly cut cedar and oak. It filled my lungs and made me long to begin rebuilding Taylor's boat. I asked directions to the boat shack and he pointed the way.

The shack was exactly that: a long, narrow clapboard barn with a tall door slightly mishung on huge hinges. I hesitated as I reached for the door handle. This was the moment I had both waited for and dreaded. Gradually I pulled the door open and looked inside. It took a moment for my eyes to adjust from bright sunlight to dim interior. The building was a little over thirty feet wide and a hundred feet long. Ten or twelve boats were lined up against the side and rear walls, separated by a rail barrier from a ten-foot aisle down the middle. To my right, three Herreshoff boats rested in the dim shadows under the sloping ceiling. So far so good. No lightness in my head. No irregular breathing. And no one else in the building to disturb my encounter with the boat.

I glanced down the row of three and thought the third most nearly resembled Taylor's boat, but decided to take my time. I stopped at the first boat, a Buzzards Bay 12^1/$_2$-footer called *Nettle*. The description plate said it was built in 1914, but it looked in mint condition. In the darkness beneath the hull I could see a shallow keel. The bow stem curved back below a short forward deck which almost disappeared along the sides. Cockpit coaming started from a point forward of the mast and continued aft to the stern. Without a centerboard box, there was plenty of room in the cockpit. The masts on all three boats had been cut off at about two feet to accommodate the shack's low ceiling.

Next was *Alerion III*, the largest of the three boats and certainly one of the most beautiful boats I'd ever seen. The plaque said it was designed in 1914 by N. G. Herreshoff at the age of sixty-four, the culmination of years of yachtbuilding experience. Resting on its cradle it looked like a rocket ready for launching. The cockpit was nestled between a long forward deck and shorter stern deck. Graceful dark wood coaming began at a forward compartment hatch and circled the cockpit to the afterdeck. Later I learned this boat had been Herreshoff's personal joy and was kept in Bermuda for his vacation pleasure.

I had been careful not to look at the last boat in line, but could resist the temptation no longer. I turned slowly and there it was: the very same design as Taylor's boat. This one was called *Fiddler*. I walked to the opposite side of the aisle so I could observe the full length of the boat. Because the portion below the waterline was painted dark green, I could visualize the boat resting on the water like a rose petal with only the center touching and the bow and stern lifting above the water. This illusion of suspension above the water was created by a waterline of fifteen feet and an overall length on deck of twenty-five. The long forward deck, which began at the midpoint of the boat, gently rose to the forepeak. The cockpit, circled by a varnished coaming that revealed the grain in the wood, ran aft from the midpoint to a stern deck that was about four or five feet long. There was about three feet of hull and keel below the waterline. Even as it sat there anchored to the floor, the boat was so graceful it appeared to be in motion.

I crossed the room and leaning over the railing, touched the painted deck. I let my fingers run down the side of the boat, feeling a slight ridge where the side planks were joined. I waited. Nothing happened. I felt fine. No sounds. No cold winds sweeping over me. I was tempted to believe that I had made up the experience in Taylor's garage. In no time my fears were gone. I folded back the cover page on my sketch pad and began drawing.

I made several sketches, some off the right side of the bow, some from the side, and some from the stern quarter. Then I imagined her heeled on her starboard and then her port sides. I visualized her under full sail, her mast piercing the shack roof and reaching into the blue sky. From time to time people entered the barn, ambled about, and departed. Sometimes they'd look over my shoulder and go "uh-huh." I filled several pages with sketches of *Fiddler* in every position imaginable, until I actually grew tired of drawing. Then I packed up my gear and walked outside. The autumn sun was low and I was getting hungry.

On the way to the gate, I passed some of the TV crew members loading equipment into a truck. Among them was the redhead in army fatigues throwing boxes into the truck and giving orders. I waited until the last of the material was loaded and then approached.

"Oh, you again," she said.

"Hi! Done for the day?"

"Yeah. Done, thank God." She glanced at me, then tipped her head to the side and studied me intently.

"Hmm!" she murmured approvingly. "You with anybody?"

"No," I said, a little nonplussed.

"Good," and then, as if it were a foregone conclusion, "Let's have dinner together."

It wasn't a request. It was an order. I thought about it for a second or two, then gave in to my curiosity. "Okay," I said, "sounds good to me."

"It's now quarter to five," she announced. "Pick me up at the Signal Hill Inn at six." She turned to walk away.

"Hey!" I called. "What's your name?"

Without turning around, she called, "Miranda Seagle."

I hollered, "Mine's Matthew Adams." She was following the truck behind a building and I'm not sure she heard me. This could be interesting, I thought.

5

At six sharp I walked into the small lobby of the Signal Hill Inn. The house phone was across from the desk in front of a large brick fireplace over which hung a painting of a whaling boat bearing down on its victim. I picked up the phone and asked the clerk to dial Miranda Seagle's room. After five rings she answered. "Miranda?" I asked.

"Yeah. Be right down."

A door next to the fireplace flew open. Miranda swept into the lobby and, without waiting for me to catch up, headed for the outside door. She had changed from her army fatigues to a white blouse, open at the neck, beneath a bright red cardigan. Black designer jeans hugged her round bottom and high heels added three inches to her height. As we crossed the parking lot she asked, "What'd you say your name was?"

"Matthew Adams," I said with an intonation that made it sound like a question. Then, still off balance, I added, "I'm a teacher."

She shot me a look. "Oh. In that case we'll go dutch."

"What if I'd said investment banker?" I asked, running to keep pace.

"Then you'd be taking me."

Before we reached her '94 Miata, crouching sleek and black at the corner of the lot, she bleeped open the locks with her security remote.

"I guess you're driving," I said.

"Yeah. You mind?"

This was getting to be fun. I decided to relax. Did I have a choice?

"Fine. Where're we going?"

"Bravo Bravo. Good drinks. Good food. Medium priced." She spun out of the long circular drive and onto the street with more macho than a teenager reaching for adulthood. A half mile of determined silence brought us to the restaurant. Parking on the street, we entered the quiet restaurant and were seated by a gracious hostess at a table for two next to the front windows. The walls were done in forest green and a small bar set back at one side indicated this was primarily an eating and not a drinking establishment. On our table a discreet flower arrangement in a slender vase, and linen tablecloth and napkins, made me glad we were going dutch.

Miranda, who hadn't looked directly at me since I'd met her, drummed her fingers and stared at a waiter several tables away. I began to wonder if, in addition to my current delusional problems, I'd also become invisible.

"Nice place—lousy service," she snapped.

"Give 'em a break. We just sat down."

She clenched and unclenched her fist, glanced at me once, then looked out the window.

"You're in a great mood," I said.

"You're fucking-A right."

"Look, Miranda, you're the one who wanted to go to dinner with me, but I'll be damned if I see why. You might as well be sitting here alone."

She looked at me for the first time, then leaned back and looped her right arm over the back of the chair. For several seconds we held each other's gaze. Miranda was round. Her face was round and her shoulders round. Round breasts rose appealingly beneath her sweater. Tight, round curls of her dark red hair flared into a round aura about her head. Brown eyes beneath dark brows accented her fair skin, and a trace of freckles was visible through her makeup. I liked the way she looked, but I wasn't sure I liked being with her.

She broke the silence. "Why are you here?"

I thought for a while, my eyes locked on hers, then said, "I had this fantasy about this weekend. There was this woman, a nice dinner, champagne, a jacuzzi, a big bed. It didn't happen. I came here anyway to sketch a boat in the Seaport museum. I ran into you and you suggested dinner together. So, I figured, maybe all is not lost."

"Sorry, buddy," she said in a slow, low voice, "I don't have a jacuzzi."

I smiled. "Why don't you call me Matthew. My name is Matthew Adams. Remember?"

Giving a disinterested toss of her head, she curled her lip.

"Why are you so bitchy tonight?" I asked. "Or are you like this all the time?"

"I'm like this a lot. But right now I'm especially teed off with the fucking director and this crummy job."

The waiter appeared clutching menus and beaming down at us. "Care for anything from the bar?"

"Amstel Light," Miranda said without hesitation and without taking her eyes off me.

"Humm," I muttered thoughtfully, "make it two."

"You've heard of Manny Seagle, the Hollywood director?"

"My God. Your father?"

"Huh," she uttered in a way that could mean either yes or no.

"No wonder you're in this business."

"Well, it helps a lot being named Seagle, but you'll notice I didn't actually say he was my father. Most people just assume it, so I let them. Like you did. It helped me get in the door of Phillips Productions. But I got the job because of recommendations from the dean of the Motion Picture and TV Department at Berkeley. My father's name really is Manny Seagle, but he manages a shoe store for his brother-in-law in Muncie."

I laughed.

"I graduated last June," she continued, "and got this job as assistant production coordinator, which sounds great. Right?" I nodded. "You saw what it is. I make sure the right stuff gets there at the right time and gets put back after we shoot. Big deal." She turned to look for the waiter and our drinks, then whipped her head back in my direction. "And this asshole director treats me like a kid. So that's why I'm bitchy."

"Yeah," I sympathized. "I heard him tell you to wait by the truck like a good little girl."

"That's what I mean."

"So, you based on the West Coast?"

"No." She sighed regretfully. "New York."

"What's it like living in the big city?"

Her face and shoulders drooped. "Well, it's not Muncie and it's not Berkeley."

"What's it like, really? I've always lived in small towns."

She thought for a moment and said, "I can't tell if people really know more than I do or just act that way. They're all so damned self-contained, especially in this business. And blasé. Like being scared shitless or really liking something is beneath them. So I play it tough and act tough and they stay away from me and I stay away from them." She picked up the menu and studied it. I did the same.

The waiter returned with our beer, carefully pouring it into tall glasses. It was not a place to drink from the bottle. He recited the house specials. Miranda ordered sole and I asked for salmon. "Here's to you," I said lifting my glass.

She raised hers halfway and mumbled, "Same to you."

Taking a large gulp of beer, she said, "Ohhh, that's good," then added, "So what's with you? You said you're a teacher?"

I told her I was an art teacher and described the school and Marblehead. Sailing, I said, was big in my life, and I hoped to get a boat by next summer. She told me about wanting to be a director and how certain she was of her ability. Our entrees arrived and we attacked our fish like sharks in a feeding frenzy. Halfway through the meal, with the initial edge of hunger somewhat abated, I paused to wonder why I was here. At least Miranda was nice to look at and probably, somewhere under her fighting armor, was a person worth knowing. In any case, it was better than eating alone.

"What time is it?" she asked. "My watch isn't working."

"Seven-thirty. Why?"

"There's a PBS special I want to catch at eight. Phillips Productions made a bid for it and lost. I want to see what the competition did." The waiter drifted by to ask if we wanted dessert. I was about to say no when Miranda jumped in. "We've always got time for dessert." She ordered apple pie a la mode and I asked for pecan pie a la mode.

In the car on the way back to the inn, she asked if I'd like to come up and watch the show with her. "Give me your artistic criticism," she said in a voice that was only half sarcastic. I looked at her, surprised. Her hardened expression was melting and she was beginning to seem like a young woman from Muncie.

"I never thought of myself as a TV critic, but I'll give it a try."

The room was large, with a window that looked out on the now darkened Pequotsepos Cove. Dominating the room was a four-poster bed with canopy and valance. It clashed so drastically with Miranda's personality that I said, laughing, "Isn't that sweet?"

"Forget it," she said, but I noticed she was smiling as she opened a tall maple cabinet, revealing the TV. She took a seat in an armchair by the window and I sat on the bed, propping up two pillows to lean against. With remote in hand, she flipped on the TV and found the right channel. "I really do want your opinion," she said. "I know I'll be prejudiced. These people are good but they get artsy and lose the common touch."

The show, about sex education in public schools, presented case-by-case evidence that argued in favor of sex education and the distribution of condoms as an effective way to reduce both pregnancies and the spread of AIDS. I found the show interesting but not one I would have watched on a Saturday night. Still, being here in Miranda's room watching this show was better than being alone in Marblehead.

After fifteen minutes the show began to wear on us. Miranda, curling her lip in disgust and receiving a grunt of agreement from me, suggested we raid the minibar. Hopping up, she darted across the room to a cabinet door under the TV. "How about an after-dinner brandy?" she called.

"Sounds good to me."

She poured the little bottles into brandy snifters and came over to the bed. "Here," she said. "Now, budge over some and hand me those two pillows." I hunched up and moved over a couple of feet while she climbed onto the bed beside me. This time she clinked her glass with mine and we toasted sex education.

"God, this is boring," she wailed and touched the mute button on the remote. "I want to leave the picture on so I won't miss the credits at the end." We lay there on the bed, leaning up against the headboard sipping our brandy, and watched statistics and people move silently across the screen. "Tell me about the town you grew up in," Miranda asked with a sincerity I hadn't heard earlier.

I told her about North Adams, about the Berkshires in fall foliage, about skiing and ice skating, about fishing in the river in the summer, about the spring flowers, and about my family and our workshop and store. She told me about Muncie and her high school where she'd studied dramatics and theater production. She had three brothers and, as the youngest in the family, had to fight a constant battle for her rights.

When the credits came on the screen at the end of the show, she studied the names and found one she knew from Berkeley. Then she switched from TV to radio, finding some late evening jazz from a New Haven station.

We lay there for maybe five minutes listening to the music. My eyes were closed. I felt her little finger almost imperceptibly begin to touch my little finger. Then her warm, moist palm slipped over the back of my hand and she whispered, "Matthew, this is one hell of a big bed. I'll get lost in it. Stay here tonight."

My eyes popped open. Did she say what I thought she said?

"Well?"

"Yes," I said with maybe too much enthusiasm. Then, sitting up in front of her, I stared into her eyes. "On one condition. You'll let me run my fingers through those wonderful curls of yours."

She laughed and leaned her head toward me. As I combed her curls with my fingers, she lay her head against my chest and purred like a mountain lion. Then she tumbled me over and pinned my shoulders to the mattress.

"Say uncle. Say uncle," she demanded.

"I give up," I pleaded.

"Oh, don't give up, not yet anyway." As I lay on my back looking up at her, she began unbuttoning my shirt. Then I unbuttoned her blouse. Lord, this was too much. I hadn't had sex for more than a year. We tumbled and rolled around the bed until we managed to get each other completely undressed. Exhilarated beyond measure, I knelt on the bed and, picking up Miranda in the cradle of my arms, threw her up into the air. She fell back onto the bed and we both collapsed in laughter. I wrapped her in my arms, pulling the full length of her sweet, warm, naked body against me.

"I'd almost forgotten," I said softly, "how nice it is to press my body against another body." She purred agreement.

"Oh oh," she said, sitting up. "Speaking of sex education, just where is your condom, young man?"

"Oh no! Oh shit!" I moaned. "I haven't carried them in months." I put my head into the pillow and hammered the mattress with my fists.

"Well, don't despair. Like the trusty Girl Scout that I am, I've come prepared." She jumped up and ran to the bathroom. Seconds later she bounded back into the room, her breasts bouncing delightfully. In her hand was a slim plastic package. "Now you just be a good boy and lie down."

I did. Opening the package, she knelt over me to begin fitting the condom in place. As she touched me, months of remembered temptation pressed through my groin—the sexy women I'd seen at lunchtime from the restaurant window, Miss Smithers' gently swaying breasts beneath her loose-fitting blouses, the seventeen-year-old women in my classes with supple bodies and seductive looks. So, as Miranda began to unroll the condom, I erupted.

"Oh no!" I cried, putting my hands over my face.

"Does this happen often?" Miranda asked.

"Often? Hell, I haven't had sex in so long I can't remember."

She got up, went to the bathroom, and returned with a hand towel. Carefully and with a smile that showed she loved her work, she wiped my stomach and chest.

"You know what your problem is? Sexual deprivation." Then she took me by the hand and led me into the shower. "You just let me handle it, so to speak, and I'll make it all right." And she did. With hot water streaming over us, she washed me all over and then gave me the soap to lather and wash her. By and by we finished, dried each other, and dashed to the bed.

The next couple of hours we steered a rolling sea of passion, from quiet troughs to wild crests, while the canopy over the bed flapped like a sail in a storm. Our hands and our tongues explored each other's bodies—the roundness, the curves, the firmness, the indentations, the crevasses, the openings. We tasted our mingled sweat. The musky smell of sex filled our nostrils. I was the artist sculpting her breasts and hips, her shoulders and legs. She was the director moving the show to climax after climax.

Finally, spent and exhausted, we lay on the damp sheets, her head on my shoulder and her leg thrown over my stomach. The fingers of my right hand slowly kneaded her curls while my left stroked her breast as it lay against my chest. We were tired but not sleepy, so I began to ramble on about Taylor's boat. Starting with the yard sale, I told her about the dream and the pictures. I described every detail of the "boat experience," how my mind became linked with the soul of the boat, if that's what it was. I explained why I'd come to Mystic and how I'd found the very same model among the Herreshoff boats in the boat shack. When I related the disquieting scene of the pigeon being swept out to sea and how I empathized with it, she said she was sorry for the pigeon but not for me.

"Gee, thanks a lot," I said.

"No." She sat up and faced me. "Why should I feel sorry for you? It's no big deal. So you're a channel, or you and the boat together are a channel. Hell, people have been channeling since the beginning of time. Not everybody's a channel, true, but the idea of channeling's nothing special. You're not getting swept out into some kind of a weird ocean. You're just channeling."

"How do you know so much about this? Has it ever happened to you?"

"No, but it happened all the time to my great-grandmother in Russia. People used to bring her stuff, articles of clothing or a lock of hair belonging to someone who'd died or was missing, and she'd touch it and try to make contact with the person—and most of the time she did. My mother told me about it."

"Well, that's fine, but I don't believe in that stuff."

"Hah!" She laughed. "It doesn't matter if you believe in it, you're doing it. It's got nothing to do with belief or faith. It just is."

"So, I should just go on back to Marblehead, touch the boat, and see what it has to say?"

"If you really want that boat and want to rebuild it, I guess that's what you're going to have to do." I looked up at her as she sat on the bed beside me. She smiled. "It's all right. It's really all right."

Feeling a load of fear and worry slide from my mind, I began to smile too. Then we were both laughing and reaching for each other. I pulled her down and into my arms and kissed her on the lips for the first time that night. We made love once more and fell asleep in each other's arms.

I awakened to a lobster-red Miranda, fresh from a hot shower, standing nude beside the bed, handing me a cup of coffee she'd made in the coffeemaker attached to the wall in the bathroom.

"Stay where you are. No sense in both of us getting up."

I rose on one elbow. "Thanks for the coffee. What's the time?"

"Six o'clock. We TV people start early." She got a towel from the bathroom and began vigorously drying her hair. When she noticed me watching, she said uh-uh and turned toward the mirror. The back view was as nice as the front. "Don't even think about it," she called over her shoulder. "Duty calls." Deftly she pulled on her underwear and fatigues, applied makeup, and headed for the door.

"You might as well check out of your motel and save the money," she said, reaching for the doorknob. "I ought to be done about three. Come by for me." And she was gone.

Taking my time getting up, I watched TV, brushed my teeth with her toothpaste and my finger, and showered. I looked at myself in the mirror with a satisfied smile, thinking how incredible last night was. Not just the sex, but the fact she'd listened to me without ridicule when I told her about my "boat experience." So I channeled? Like her grandmother. So what? Still I wondered, what was it I was supposed to be channeling? And why?

I went to the Two Sisters Deli I'd seen on Pearl Street for a warmed blueberry muffin with a side of bacon and a mug of coffee, then drove to the Days Inn, picked up my bag, and checked out. My sketches were finished, so there was no need to return to the boat shack. Instead I went to the Mystic Seaport Bookstore and looked up books about Herreshoff boats. They were all in the thirty-dollar range. I noted their titles and decided to check them out later from the public library in Marblehead.

Inquiring about plans for boats displayed in the museum, I was referred to the Ships Plans Collection in Rossie Mill just up the street. This was more than I'd hoped for. I asked the receptionist about plans for *Fiddler*, and she handed me a large manila envelope.

"That'll be twenty dollars, but why don't you look them over first and see if they're what you want."

In an adjoining conference room I opened the plans. Bold letters at the top of each of two pages warned that under no circumstances were these plans to be used to build a duplicate of the original Herreshoff model. It said nothing about restoring. A legend listed the boat's components including wood types and their sizes, information vital to the restoration.

Twenty dollars, I thought. A lot of dough, but I need the plans. Good thing I'm bunking with Miranda tonight. I can use some of the money I would have used for the motel room. I folded up the plans and paid the receptionist.

By then it was almost one and I was hungry. I returned to the Seaport, flashed my entrance button, good for two days, and headed for the snack bar. This took me past the quay where Phillips Productions should have been shooting, but there wasn't the slightest trace of a TV crew or its equipment. Adjacent to the quay, in a building that housed the Mystic Press, I found a man cleaning up after demonstrating the printing press used in the mid-1800s.

"The TV crew that was here yesterday—do you know where they're shooting today?"

He looked up from the large rectangular printer's block he was wiping and said, "They packed up about noon and took off."

"Are they shooting somewhere else in the village?"

"Don't think so. I saw the trucks leave through the service entrance."

I thanked him and hurried out the gate to my Jeep. In minutes I was walking into the Signal Hill Inn. I asked the clerk at the desk to dial Miranda's room, but she said Miranda had checked out.

"Are you sure?"

"Yes. Are you Mr. Adams?"

"Yes."

"Well, she left a message for you."

She handed me a hotel envelope with my name on it. Sitting down in front of the fireplace, I opened it.

Dear Matthew,

   Sorry to miss you. We finished early and are returning to New York to shoot the remaining scenes in the studio. I'll never feel lost in a big bed when you're there with me. Come and keep me warm the next time you're in New York.

Love, Miranda

P.S. My phone number is 212-555-3749—Call me.

Driving back to Marblehead disappointed, I vowed to take a trip to New York to see Miranda. She'd been a lot of fun. I was even beginning to like her brassiness. And she'd taught me something—channeling's not a scary thing. It's like a gift. Maybe in time, I thought, I'll accept it as nonchalantly as she does.

At least, I no longer felt like I was going crazy.

By the time I reached Providence, my disappointment and my fears had drifted away with the passing miles and I found myself figuring how to get the boat and begin repairs as soon as possible. Taylor was becoming friendlier and, even if she wouldn't sell me the boat, perhaps she'd let me repair it. Maybe I could become a part owner. In any case, I planned to spend all day Monday, Columbus Day, painting a large watercolor picture of the boat to give to her as a gift.

To repair the boat through the coming winter, I would need a heated building. Taylor's garage was too cluttered and drafty. Finding a workshop big enough to accommodate the boat would take time, but repairing the trailer and getting it moved would be easy. My Jeep already had a trailer hitch.

Once I found a workshop, I'd need power tools, at least a table saw and a band saw. Carting the wood back and forth to the high school workshop would be too much trouble, and renting the equipment for several months too expensive. So, power tools were clearly a problem.

When I reached Attleboro just inside Massachusetts, I was so hungry I stopped at McDonald's. As I ate my Big Mac, I estimated the cost of the restoration. The oak for the frames and the cedar for the planking could cost as much as five hundred dollars. At least another five hundred would be needed for bronze fittings, screws, and paint. The rigging still wrapped around the mast was in doubtful shape, so I'd need stays, shrouds, and bronze turn-buckles. This and a dozen other items I'd probably forgotten would cost another five hundred. And finally, to rebuild the mast and have new sails made would cost at least two thousand dollars. Added up, it came to three thousand five hundred dollars and maybe more. Who was I kidding? I didn't have that kind of money. I would have to either stretch the repairs over two or three years or get a partner to help with the funding.

Then there was the other pressing matter. I needed a place to live starting December first, and it'd have to be cheap or I wouldn't have the money to repair the boat.

Back in the car, with a second cup of coffee sitting in the cup holder between the seats, I pondered the last outstanding matter. Taylor hadn't told me the truth about the wreck. The mast hanging from the garage ceiling still had torn sections of sail attached. It looked as if the people who salvaged the boat off the rocks had folded the boom and gaff against the mast and wrapped what was left of the sail around it, tying it with the sheet. If the boat had slipped its moorings during a storm, it would not have had its sails raised.

Was it possible Taylor's mother died in the wreck? And if so, could this have something to do with the emotions I was chan-neling from the boat? In any case, my curiosity was piqued.

I wanted information about the boat, the wreck, and Taylor's mother, Rebecca DeWolf.

I remembered that Taylor had suggested I ask the woman she called Aunt Aggie for pictures of the boat. She'd said Aggie had been a close friend of her mother's all her life. Her name was Agnes Sparr and she lived on Gregory Street. Maybe she could answer some of my questions.

I called Agnes Sparr as soon as I arrived in Marblehead, a little after five, identifying myself as Matthew Adams, a friend of Mrs.

Hayakawa. "She said you might have pictures of the boat belonging to Rebecca DeWolf."

Her voice was strong and her response precise. "Of course I have pictures of *White Wings*, but why is that of interest to you?"

"*White Wings?*" I asked.

"Yes. The boat you're asking about."

"Oh. I didn't know her name."

"Why are you interested?"

"I'm painting a picture of the boat for Mrs. Hayakawa and I'd hoped to see some actual photographs of it under sail."

"Taylor's right. I've got some pictures."

"Would it be possible for me to come by to see them? I live just up the street."

"I think so, but let me call you back in a few minutes. What did you say your name was?"

"Matthew Adams," I said and gave her my phone number.

Having obviously checked me out with Taylor Hayakawa, she called back and said it would be fine for me to come by about seven o'clock.

I walked, portfolio in hand, down Lee Street to Gregory and then to her house. The sun had set, but the sky was still a pale greenish blue over the harbor. A few white-hulled boats remained at their moorings and rocked gently on the outgoing tide. Mrs. Sparr's house was perched on a corner lot on the east side of the street just as it started downhill. The house was square with shingled siding that had weathered gray. Beginning at the second floor, a mansard roof of dark gray asphalt shingles swept up and inward, forming a graceful cap to the house. Because of the sloping hill, the south side of the foundation was about nine feet high and had a large double door cut into it as an entrance to the basement. I walked up the front steps to a varnished oak door and knocked.

If she was expecting me at seven, she was in no hurry to get to the door. Finally an outside light flicked on, a lock turned, and the door slowly opened.

"Mr. Adams?" she asked. I nodded. "Come in, please."

Agnes Sparr, as Taylor had said, looked younger than her seventy-three years. She was dressed in dungarees, a flannel shirt, and hiking boots. Her white hair was cut in a short bob and combed back over the wire rims of her glasses. The only true measure of her age was a slight stoop in the shoulders, and fingers that were curved and knotted by arthritis.

"Come into the sitting room," she said, leading the way through a hall and into a room on the right. She reached her chair, strategically located across from the television, and sat down, gesturing to another chair for me. The TV was off and in the background somewhere a Mozart piano concerto was playing. The room had a high ceiling, perhaps nine feet, and was cluttered with chairs, tables, bookcases, cardboard boxes, and stacks of newspapers, as though the contents of two rooms had been crammed into one. A table lamp and a floor lamp provided the light.

"Thank you for seeing me on such short notice, Mrs. Sparr."

"It's Miss Sparr, Mr. Adams," she said. "I've never been married." She had a face I would like to paint. It was calm yet strong. The lines around her mouth and eyes seemed to fit easily into her smile. "So you're interested in seeing pictures of *White Wings*?"

"That's right. I just got back from Mystic Seaport, where I made sketches of *Fiddler*, a Herreshoff Buzzards Bay 15, which is the same class as *White Wings*. I brought them along, if you'd like to see them."

As I was speaking, Miss Sparr was watching me with a searching, penetrating look that seemed to reach inside me. When I finished there was an awkward silence while she continued to gaze at me, tipping her head first to one side, then to the other.

"It's almost as if I know you, Mr. Adams. Something about your eyes and your hands, like someone I knew years ago."

If I could have thought of something to say, I would have. She squinted again, then shook her head. "Of course, that's foolishness. Anyone I had known years ago would be either dead or as old as I. Still . . ." Her voice drifted off but her words resonated uneasily in my head.

I handed her the sketches, and she leafed through them disinterestedly. "You draw very well. Taylor tells me you're an art teacher in the high school."

"Yes, I am. These sketches, of course, are just my imagination of how *White Wings* would look under sail. That's why I hope you might have some photographs of the real thing."

"Why do you want to paint *White Wings?*" she asked, leaning her head slightly as if inviting me to share a secret.

"I would like to give it as a gift to Taylor, ah, I mean, Mrs. Hayakawa."

"And why would you like to give her such a gift?"

I looked at her askance and said, "Miss Sparr, you're onto me, aren't you? You know already. I want that boat. I want to restore it so it can sail again as it once did. The frames and planking are in marvelous shape. There's no rot, only damage, and I can repair that."

"I know what you want. Taylor told me. So you think she'll sell you the boat?"

"I don't know, but even if she won't, maybe she'll let me restore it. It's truly a work of art and it's a shame to have it sitting in that garage all broken up."

"I agree with you." She smiled for the first time. "Taylor seems to think you might be capable of doing the job."

"Did she say that?" I asked, amazed.

"She did. Are you?"

"My father's a cabinetmaker and I've worked with him in his shop. We built a boat together once. He and my mother live in North Adams. Taylor could call him."

"I might suggest that to her." Then she reached to the table beside her chair and picked up several photographs. They were in gray cardboard folders, the kind that stand up when opened for placing on a shelf. "I believe this is what you came for," she said, handing them to me.

I looked through them quietly, not surprised to find the same scenes I had seen in my dream. I thought about what Miranda had told me. Channeling. I remained composed, but the excitement at seeing *White Wings* under sail was overwhelming. I noticed, though, the photos included only Taylor's mother. There were none of her father.

After I'd studied them for some time, I said, "Miss Sparr, Taylor tells me you were a close friend of Mrs. DeWolf's all her life."

"Please call me Aggie. Nobody calls me Miss Sparr. And I'll call you Matthew, if I may?" When I nodded, she looked up at a corner of the room as if reaching into the past. "Yes, we were friends. We started kindergarten here in Marblehead and continued through all the grades together. After high school we remained close. Saw each other almost every day until she died."

"Aggie," I said hesitantly, "I haven't said anything to Taylor about this, but she said the night the boat was wrecked, it had slipped its moorings. But the way the torn sail is wrapped around the mast hanging in her garage, it's pretty obvious it was under sail."

She looked at me intently. "Taylor said you might mention this, and if you did I should tell the truth." She paused and took a deep breath. "Becky was sailing *White Wings* that evening and apparently was swept overboard in the storm. At the time you asked Taylor about it, she hardly knew you and didn't feel at ease speaking about it. She wasn't deliberately lying to you."

I felt good that Taylor now at least trusted me. "Can you tell me any more about the accident?"

Aggie folded her hands in her lap and began. "It was June twenty-fifth, 1973. It hardly seems twenty-one years ago. Becky had a ritual she followed every June twenty-fifth. I think it had something to do with keeping alive the memory of Taylor's father. Some event the two of them had shared together. She'd sail *White Wings* out by herself beyond the harbor and spend the afternoon, then return just before the wind dropped off in the evening. If it was raining, she'd go out dressed in a slicker. If there was no wind, she'd bob around becalmed until it picked up. And if a storm threatened, she'd go out anyway. It didn't matter. And that's what happened. She went out and she never came back. Only *White Wings* returned. It crashed on the rocks below Fort Sewall, almost as if it were trying to make port alone." She finished speaking and sat quietly, lost in her memories.

Finally she spoke. "So you want to restore *White Wings*?" I nodded. "If Taylor agrees, you'll need a place to work. That garage of hers is a mess and drafty as all get out." I nodded again. "Now, assuming you are able to work out some sort of deal with Taylor, you can bring the boat over here and use the workshop in the basement. My father used to build boats down there."

I couldn't believe my ears. I felt like a kid who'd just been given the best present in his life. Then I remembered how high the boat sat on its trailer platform and my hopes began to fall. "I don't think it'll fit through the door. It's wide enough but is it high enough?"

"It'll fit," she said confidently. "It fit before so I expect it'll fit again."

"You had *White Wings* in your basement?" I asked, amazed.

"Yes. We hid it there, but that's a long story for another time."

I positioned my easel so the sun from the window wouldn't fall directly on the paper, then lightly sketched the outline of my subject with pencil and began applying a background wash for the ocean and sky. I let that dry for about half an hour before dry brushing the various watercolors into shapes of boat, sails, and people. Working quickly, I unfurled the sails of *White Wings* on the paper. I heeled the boat hard to port, raising the starboard high and lifting the long sweep of the bow above the waves. I sent the keel slicing like a knife through green water. The jib I sheeted in tight and I close-hauled the mainsail. In the cockpit I stationed the man in my dream photos holding the tiller in his left hand and the sheet in his right, with his face turned away from view toward the sail. And Rebecca, beautiful young Rebecca, I placed by the mast, wind in her hair and her face lifted toward the sky.

By six o'clock the painting was done and the paper drying. I walked up to Crocker Park on the granite cliff above the harbor, glad to stretch the tension out of my shoulders, and sat until sunset looking at the boats.

The minute school was over the next day, I went to a framing shop on Washington Street and bought matting and a frame. By five o'clock the matting was cut and the framing complete. At noon, when I had called Taylor to see if she would be in that evening, she'd invited me for dinner at six. I looked forward to the company and to eating someone else's cooking.

On my way to Taylor's, I stopped at Shubie's liquor store and picked up a chilled bottle of chardonnay, then drove to her house. With the bottle in one hand and the painting, wrapped in butcher paper and measuring two feet by three, in the other, I knocked on her door with the butt of the bottle. She opened it, laughing at my awkward burden, and invited me in.

One look at Taylor and I realized I was underdressed for the evening. My jeans, white shirt, and Irish sweater were no match for Taylor's ensemble. She wore a mid-calf silk jumper with paisley patterns in varying shades of purple over a long-sleeved cream-colored blouse open at the neck. She was stunning.

"Hi," I said. "What a beautiful dress."

"Thank you, Matthew."

I gave her the wine, which she said would be perfect for the swordfish we'd be having. We went into her sitting room, where I reversed a straight chair and leaned the still wrapped painting against its back. Near the front window was a small dining table elegantly set with china, silver, and even candles. Taylor poured two glasses of the wine I'd brought and handed one to me.

"Here's to your painting," she said, raising her glass.

"You'd better have a look at it first. You may not like it." I set down my glass and unwrapped the painting. Taylor folded her arms, still holding her glass in one hand, and gazed at it. She tried another angle, taking two steps to the right and backing up a little. Then she came up close.

"It's remarkable," she said. "You catch the feeling of being under sail." She took a step backward and cocked her head to one side. "And most of all, you've captured the free spirit of my mother."

"What a strange choice of words," I said.

"Captured her free spirit?" She laughed. "Yes, I guess it is. Like an oxymoron." Then, looking at me, she added, "Unless, of course, you really are capable of capturing free spirits."

"But then they'd no longer be free."

"Not necessarily," she said. "I think some people find their freedom in having been captured by the right person." Was she speaking about her mother or about people in general?

Raising her glass, she repeated her toast. "To your painting!"

"No, to *your* painting and to *White Wings* herself. May she sail again."

Later, during dinner, I asked her what she meant by her mother's free spirit. Taylor thought for a while, fork suspended over her fish, then said, "She was a person unto herself, strong willed, not wanting to be dependent on anyone. One part of her was businesslike and organized, which was a good thing. As Gramp and Gram Butler got older, Rebecca practically ran the hotel. And then there was the fire in 'fifty-seven that destroyed the hotel. It was awful. I was having my fifteenth birthday party when suddenly fire broke out in the back stairwell and swept up to the fourth floor. My grandparents had just left the party and gone up to their room. Firemen were running everywhere, getting people out of the hotel and trying to reach Gram and Gramp, but the fourth floor was all flames. When it was all over, they were gone and Mom was left alone with me. She was, let's see, thirty-six then, and I was fifteen. With the insurance money, we bought this house and turned it into an inn.

"Mom was pretty strict. I had to toe the line and do my part. In school she expected me to excel and I did." She paused for a moment to take a bite, thinking while she chewed.

"But there was another side, too. She was always kind of moody. As a teenager I resented it, thinking she used her dark moods to make me feel guilty, as if I caused them. Now that I'm grown and, like Mom, have raised a daughter myself without the help of a husband, I understand those moods of despair and loneliness. And I understand how your children can throw your sadness back at you, blaming you for raining on their parade." She considered this for a moment, then continued. "Mom had it even tougher than I did, though: a war widow, a young mother with a baby, aging parents, and a hotel to take care of."

Taylor paused, her face pensive. "On rare occasions the moodiness eased, like a fog lifting. I only caught glimpses of these moments. Sometimes I'd come upon her sitting alone on the hotel balcony, her face softened by a dreamy smile. Sometimes I'd see it when we went walking by the ocean, she looking into the distance for minutes on end, forgetting I was with her. And always it happened when she'd sail away for an afternoon alone on *White Wings*. I watched her once with binoculars after she'd raised the sails and taken the tiller in hand. Her expression was different." Taylor gestured toward the painting. "It was something like that," she said, pointing to the woman standing at the mast. "See her chin, lifted. I know she's smiling and there's joy in her eyes, even if the details in the painting can't be that specific. And you know why?" she said, looking at me. "She's found what she wants in life, the person she wants to be with."

"And that's the expression you'd see through the binoculars, even though she was alone?"

"Yes." She paused, dropping her eyes. "I don't think she was alone at those times. I think he was with her."

We sat quietly for several moments. Finally I broke the silence. "And you never knew your father?"

"No, he was killed five months before I was born." She sighed. "I don't think she ever got over it. Looking at his picture, it's hard to believe he was the one who had set her free by capturing her heart." She looked across the room at the picture of her father in his RAF uniform. "It must be the formalness of the picture. So military. Not expressing his real personality." Then, returning her gaze to me, she went on. "It was those moments when I watched her sail away on *White Wings*, I knew she was with him. At other times she'd look at me with that same wistful look, as though she was seeing him in me. Then she'd take me in her arms and hug me so hard I thought I'd break."

"Well, he was in you," I offered. "She must have seen him in your eyes or your expressions."

"But it's strange. I look at that picture of him and I feel no connection. I don't think I've ever told this to anyone before, but growing up I was sure I was adopted. I know a lot of kids worry about this, but for me it was like a truth I tried to suppress."

"Did you ever ask your mother?"

"No. I knew somehow that such a question would have been out of bounds."

"But now, aren't records like that open to people under the Freedom of Information Act?"

"It doesn't matter," she said, waving her hand. "Just a childish fear. If I really wanted to, I know how I could find out. All I'd have to do is ask Aunt Aggie. She knows everything about Mom. Maybe I'm still afraid of what I would find out."

I felt the air grow uncomfortable with the heaviness of the conversation. Apparently Taylor felt the same. "That's enough of that. Would you pour us some more wine?"

I reached for the bottle. "The swordfish is delicious."

"I enjoy cooking, but with Rebecca gone, my daughter I mean, it's hard to get interested in cooking just for one. So I was glad you could come."

We finished dinner and I rose to help Taylor carry dishes to the kitchenette sink. She snuffed out the candles and looked at me through the lingering smoke.

"Matthew, I know what's on your mind."

"You do?" I was picking up dessert plates and coffee cups. "Oh. Yes," I said, setting them back down. "I guess you do."

"The painting is a wonderful gift and I think you'd have done it even if you didn't want *White Wings*. But you do want the boat." I looked at the painting and nodded. "Let's sit down for a minute longer and you tell me what you have in mind."

This was it. What I'd waited for. I sat down. Without looking at her, I began. "I'd like to see *White Wings* in the water again and I'd like to be the one to restore her." I lifted my eyes, meeting hers.

"I guess you know now I'd never sell her."

"I know. I understand. I'm not asking to buy her, but, maybe, together we could rebuild her."

We didn't speak for a while. Suddenly, Taylor stood up. "I've got an idea." She headed for the door that led to the inn's kitchen. Along the way she reached into a closet and got a flashlight. "Come on. This is too big a decision to make alone."

Puzzled, I followed her through the kitchen to the back door. My God, I thought, she's going to the garage. We followed the beam of the flashlight across the driveway, unlocked the big door of the garage, and swung it open. Immediately she went to the boat and pulled the light chain over it. A dull glow illuminated the hulking tarpaulin.

"Help me uncover her." We each took a corner of the tarp and pulled it backward from the bow. I stopped when the forward section was exposed and looked questioningly at Taylor. "No," she said. "All the way."

Stepping over boxes and squeezing between the hull and the wall of the garage, I pulled the tarpaulin all the way to the stern and let it drop on the floor. Then I came around the bow and stood beside Taylor. For several moments we looked at *White Wings* resting on the carriage like a graceful phoenix asleep on its nest.

We walked to her side, Taylor taking my hand in hers and touching the boat with her other hand. I raised my free hand and placed it too against the hull.

"Ask her, Matthew," Taylor whispered. "Ask her what we should do."

I closed my eyes. A shiver ran through my body. I thought of Miranda and her words of reassurance. "It's only channeling. Nothing to be afraid of." I waited. Taylor's hand was warm in mine, the side of *White Wings* cool. I waited for the swirling winds of another dimension. Nothing.

Then, as if from a distance, like a homebound vessel inching into view over the horizon, growing, taking shape as it drew near, a profound calmness came to me. My breathing became deep and regular. A sense of serenity entered my partially closed eyes, filling my head and lifting my mind. Gradually the calmness turned to joy, then the joy to exhilaration. A breeze caught my sail and sent me skimming across the water. Suddenly I was free, set free. Alive again. One with the wind, the sky, and the sea.

Presently the scene blurred. Waters receded. Again I was standing with Taylor, our hands touching. We didn't speak. I let go of her hand and put my arm around her waist and she put hers around mine.

"I didn't want it to end," I said softly. "I wanted to sail on forever. It was beautiful."

"Then it's settled," she said. "Let's begin the restoration."

Taylor agreed we should move *White Wings* to Aggie's basement workshop. I would estimate the cost of restoration and then we'd talk about funding and ownership. The best deal for me would be to match my labor and expertise against Taylor's funds and then share the ownership, but she might not go along with this.

It took me the rest of the week working after school to repair the trailer. The tires were shot and replacements were hard to find. Finally on Sunday morning the trailer was hooked to my Jeep, and Taylor and I drove it through empty streets to Aggie's house. Aggie joined us in her driveway on the south side of the house and the three of us slowly circled the boat, getting our first good look at it in the light of day.

The damage was far more severe than any of us had realized. In Taylor's dark garage we had seen the broken frames on the starboard side but had not been aware of the compression fractures of the same frames on the port side. Also, the rudder was cracked lengthwise and the rudder post pulled loose on top. Bolts through the keel into the keelson were dislodged and the hood ends of at least half the planks were ripped out of the stem. All of this was in addition to the gaping hole in the starboard side, the buckled planks next to the centerboard box, and the section of deck separated from the sheer plank.

"Matthew," Aggie said, narrowing her eyes on the damaged

boat. "You're going to need to get her off the trailer and onto some jack stands. You can't work on the keel while it's on the trailer."

"Jack stands?" Taylor asked.

I started to explain, but Aggie broke in. "The steel braces you've seen propping up boats when they're on land."

"Oh," Taylor said.

"Aggie, you sound like an old salt," I said with surprise.

"I ought to," she said curtly.

As Aggie rounded the boat examining the hull, Taylor quietly told me, "Aggie's a lobsterman, Matthew, or was until she retired five years ago. Worked on boats all her life except during the war."

"Thanks," I whispered to Taylor, then said to Aggie, "You're right about the jack stands."

"I got some on the north side of the house. I'll give you a hand moving the boat off the trailer and onto the stands. But let's eat first." She headed through her basement to stairs that led up to her kitchen, Taylor and I following.

We sat around the kitchen table while Aggie prepared a breakfast of waffles, maple syrup, and bacon as a celebration for our decision to begin work on *White Wings*. Into an old electric waffle iron she poured batter that puffed and steamed as it lifted the lid and oozed out the edges. When it stopped steaming, she lifted the lid, revealing the golden brown waffles. I lost count of the number I ate.

Over a second cup of coffee, Aggie asked Taylor, "Ever wonder how *White Wings* got in your garage?"

Taylor thought for a moment. "Why, no. It's just always been there. Since I came home from Japan after Mom died."

"I put it there. After I got it off the rocks."

"You salvaged *White Wings*?" I asked, surprised.

"With a little help." Then she drew into herself as though she'd said more than she wanted to.

"Tell us what happened, Aggie," Taylor pleaded.

A sadness fell across Aggie's face. She sighed. "I guess I would like to tell you. Get it off my chest." Her words came slowly as she wrenched them from her memory. "Twenty-one years ago. It doesn't seem that long. Seeing *White Wings* out there on the trailer's brought it all back. It's not just that I watched *White Wings* go on the rocks, it was losing Becky."

"Oh, Aggie, I'm sorry," Taylor said. "I never should have asked."

"It's okay. I'm ready to talk about it." She took a sip of coffee, then began.

"When the storm hit and Becky didn't get back, it was night by then. I called the Coast Guard and went up to Fort Sewall to watch for her return. The storm was still raging. Thunder and lightning. It was awful. Sometimes I'd hear the big Coast Guard helicopter working out over the water, but I never saw it through the rain.

"Then, sometime after midnight, I saw *White Wings*. Her mainsail was torn and flapping, but she was pulled ahead of the wind by her jib. At first I rejoiced. Thank God, I thought, Becky's made it. But the boat didn't turn into the harbor. Just kept heading for the rocks below me. I waved my light and screamed. Didn't matter. Then a big breaker caught the little boat, lifted her high over the first line of rocks and sent her crashing into the next line. Another wave lifted her stern and threw it over the bow, snapping the mast. I ran down the hill and got as close to the rocks as I could, but still the boat was fifty feet away. I flashed my light around and called for Becky. I felt helpless. Finally I ran back up the hill to the first house I saw and hammered on the door. I told them to get the rescue squad. Pretty soon there were men with wet suits and lines climbing over the rocks, and the helicopter was overhead with its big lights. They never found Becky.

"As it grew light, I went home and tried to call you in Japan, Taylor, but all I got was somebody speaking Japanese. I decided to try later. Then it occurred to me I could save what was left of the boat. I called Angelo Tarpello, who had a marine construction company, and persuaded him to put a crane on one of his barges and get over to Fort Sewall. I went there to wait for him.

"That's when I saw Karl Kramer."

"Kramer," Taylor said, pondering the name. "Sounds familiar."

"Yeah. Captain Kramer. The ex-harbormaster."

"Oh, I remember him. He was at my fifteenth birthday party, the night the hotel burned down. There was something about him, something kind of slimy. The way he looked at Mom. You two didn't like him much."

"Hah!" Aggie laughed sarcastically. "You got that right."

What's this about, I wondered, but didn't want to interrupt.

Aggie continued. "Well, the storm had passed and the tide was out, leaving *White Wings* high and dry. Kramer had anchored his big power boat off the rocks and had rowed in in his dinghy. He was climbing over *White Wings*, lashing a heavy line around her hull. I yelled at him to get off the boat. He just looked at me and laughed. I started out across the rocks for the boat, which took a while because they were slippery with seaweed. When I got to it, he'd gone back to his boat, hauling the line behind him. To make a long story short, we yelled back and forth, he telling me that he'd pull my lobstering license if I touched that line and I telling him I could drop a word or two that could get him fired as harbormaster. Anyway, I untied the line and about that time Tarpello arrived. We lifted the boat off the rocks and carried it to Parker's Landing, then onto the trailer. I towed it to your garage, Taylor, and locked the door."

"And there it's sat all these years," Taylor said.

"Well, why did this Kramer want to yank *White Wings* off the rocks?" I asked. "There wouldn't have been anything left of her."

"That's right," Aggie said. "We argued for months about it. He claimed he wanted to get rid of it because it was an eyesore. But I think he did it to get back at Becky, even though she was gone. He couldn't hurt her anymore, so he went after her boat. He knew how much it meant to her."

"God!" I said. "That's sick."

"Sick, yes," Aggie groaned. "Kramer's a sick man."

"If you don't mind my asking," I went on, "what was it between him and Becky?"

"I think I know," Taylor said. "The stories I heard were that he wanted to marry Mom after high school and she threw him over."

"That's close," Aggie said, "but it's more than that." She slid back her chair and stood up slowly. "It's another long story. Let's not get into it now. We got a boat to put in the basement."

I brought the stands around from the side of the house while Aggie and Taylor cleaned up the breakfast dishes. Then the two women came down to the basement and, under Aggie's guidance, the three of us spent the rest of the morning maneuvering the boat off the trailer and onto the jack stands.

The following week I crawled over, under, and around *White*

Wings surveying the extent of the damage and determining the amount of lumber, fittings, and paint needed for the restoration. This completed, I began calling lumberyards and mills across New England to locate the oak and cedar for the hull and the spruce for the mast. No yard and few mills had the freshly cut white oak that was needed. Finally a call to the Elwell Yard in Bristol, Maine, produced all the lumber necessary and I could choose it myself. The cost of materials, plus new sails, would be more than five thousand dollars.

I noticed a curious thing while examining the boat. A section of nylon line about three feet long was attached to the bow cleat. This in itself wasn't strange. What was unusual was the way it was laid to the cleat. The proper way is to start about three feet from the end of a line and lay in back and forth from one side of the cleat to the other in figure eights until you near the end of the line, then invert the last two bends so they are below the previous turn. This locks it in place until it is ready for easy dislodging. But this piece of line was laid to the cleat in reverse order. The wrapping back and forth began at the end of the line with the final bends inverted to lock the line in place. The line then ran out for about three feet to where it had been cut with a knife. I studied it for a while and concluded it had been made either by an idiot who knew nothing about sailing or by someone who had a very specific purpose in mind. Oh, well. Whoever laid that line to the cleat had done it twenty-one years ago, so it made no difference now. Twenty-one years ago, I thought. I was only six. I had lived most of my life while that old piece of line was wrapped to that cleat. I released it and threw it over a peg.

The end of the week, Aggie came down to the basement where I was working and, without knowing I needed a place to live, suggested I move into her apartment on the second floor. The tenant was moving out November tenth and I could move in anytime after that.

"Aggie, you've saved my life," I said, throwing my arms around her and giving her a kiss.

She turned her head aside, saying, "Go on now. This is a business deal. I'm not giving you the place. The rent's seven hundred a month and the security deposit's five hundred."

"Oh," I said. "I've got a problem, then. I've subleased the condo through November. If I pay half a month's rent for November, I won't have five hundred dollars for the security deposit."

Aggie thought for a moment, then said, "I'll make you a deal. I'll skip the half month's rent in November and the security deposit if you'll shovel the walks in the winter, mow the lawn in the summer, and take out my garbage every week."

"You're on, Aggie." I tried to give her another kiss, but she ducked and went up the stairs shaking her head.

Taylor invited Aggie and me to go with her to Fort Sewall for the annual Halloween visit of the pirates to Marblehead and then to have a late dinner at her home. I asked her about the pirates but all she'd say was, "You'll find out." She said her daughter, Rebecca, would meet us there. I agreed to drive.

I looked forward to meeting Rebecca. I wasn't so hooked on Miranda that I was unwilling to broaden my options. Besides, Miranda hadn't returned my calls.

Like most New Englanders, I love Halloween. Driving to Aggie's, I passed several groups of little children on their rounds; little ghosts, ghouls, goblins, and werewolves, under the watchful eyes of bored older brothers or sisters. Unafraid, the little ones would march up to porches on which a rag-stuffed figure sat grotesquely on a dilapidated chair, and knock on doors swathed in cobwebs creeping with plastic spiders. "Trick-or-treat," they'd call.

This was the part of Halloween I remembered, but soon I was to learn that Marblehead does it one better. Pirates invade the town.

In 1734 the citizens of Marblehead built Fort Sewall on a point of land at the head of the harbor to protect the town from pirate attacks. But now on Halloween, present-day citizens dressed as pirates succeed in capturing the fort and setting up camp. The ancient iron doors to the subterranean powder magazines are opened and swarthy pirates with eye patches and bawdy women with wart-marked faces greet children brave enough to enter their dens. Outside, in the fort's parade ground, pirates, eighteenth-century citizens, and shackled soldiers mill about a huge bonfire.

I picked up Aggie in my Jeep a little after eight and then Taylor, dropping them off at the road leading up to the fort so Aggie wouldn't have far to walk. Then I circled eight blocks before finding a parking place. This must really be some party, I thought. As I walked back to the fort, a chill northeast wind snapped at my face. Fall was giving way to winter. I found Taylor and Aggie keeping warm by the bonfire. Joining them, I watched a commotion taking place at the iron-gated entrance to one of the powder magazines. Two pirates were dragging a young woman out of the tavern, pulling her toward a large wooden cage.

Taylor tapped Aggie's shoulder and pointed at the wench with pockmarked face, straggly hair, and a loose blouse. Aggie smiled and nodded. I imagined they knew her.

"All right, you saucy little thief, we've got you now," one of the pirates snorted. "You picked one too many pockets. It's jail for you."

"Take your grimy hands offa me, you filthy scum," the wench shouted back at him, as he shoved her into the cage.

We laughed and moved on to make room for other people. We went through the iron gate into a room where a pirate king, bedecked with saber and two pistols, offered us a pen to sign on as pirates for their next trip to sea. In another room a woman sitting by a treasure chest handed each of us chocolate coins wrapped in gold foil. A fortune teller invited us to sit on a bench in front of a table onto which she dumped her assortment of tiny bones.

"Ah," she said to me, "I see romance in your future and—wait. What is this?" She examined the detritus further. "There's an ocean voyage soon to come."

"Hey." I laughed. "We'll launch *White Wings* after all."

While Aggie excused herself because of the press of the crowd, Taylor and I joined a group of people moving further back into the passageways. Angling this way and that, we finally climbed some steps that led to a rear door. Outside again, we encountered a giant iron pot heating over a wood fire. A woman in bonnet, long dress, and heavy wool shawl handed each of us a cup of hot cider.

"That hits the spot," Taylor said and I agreed. The weather was decidedly colder and the wind had picked up.

"Will Aggie be all right by herself?" I asked.

"Don't worry about that old gal," Taylor said. "She's pretty hardy. I asked her to look for Rebecca and bring her up here to the back of the fort." Taylor led me away from the crowd to the top of the earthworks. "There's something I want to show you." Behind us the bonfire cast dancing shadows of the brigands. The sound of a drum, flute, and fiddle filled the air. We began circling the walkway until we were opposite the light tower across the harbor that marked the headland of Marblehead Neck. I turned up my collar against the cold wind blowing in from the ocean. Forty feet below us, the sea roared as huge swells rolled in against the granite cliff, filling a hundred hidden crevasses with white surging water. Then, as the black water withdrew in cascading waterfalls, the waves regrouped for another onslaught against the rocks.

Taylor stopped and pointed down. "Here is where they found the boat." I looked down at several jagged rocks that emerged and sank as the waves rolled across them. "Aggie told me it was wedged between those two rocks," she said, directing my attention to two outcroppings of granite larger than the rest. Looking down at the dark water rising and falling among the rocks, I shuddered.

"Do you think she was in the boat when it crashed on the rocks?"

"There's no way to tell." She sighed. "All we know is, her body was never found." Taylor was silent for several moments as she looked out to sea. "Aggie and I disagree about how she died."

"What does Aggie think?" I asked.

"She thinks she was swept over the side. This happened to Aggie once. She was alone in a sailboat, lost her footing, and fell in. Fortunately, another boat was nearby and picked her up, but she said she'd about had it by the time the boat got there. She thinks something like that happened to Mom."

"And what do you think?"

"Probably Aggie's right, but sometimes I think she may have just eased herself over the side and slipped into the water."

"On purpose?" I turned and stared at her.

"Sometimes I think so. She was alone, you know. Rebecca and I were in Japan. We were having troubles of our own, but after a while I stopped writing Mom about them. Her letters back were so depressed that our troubles only brought her down further. I know she worried about us, and when you're seven thousand miles away there's not much you can do."

"But wasn't Aggie there for her?"

"She was, and she would have laid down her life for Mom. She wrote me in March of the year Mom died that she too was worried about her. She talked about Mom's dark moods. I knew about them too. I still have this idea that Mom longed to be with my father, that life without him wasn't worth living. I know she saw him in me, but with me away, every connection was gone. Except for *White Wings*. Maybe she decided to join him that night in the storm."

"What a sad thought."

"Maybe and maybe not. Sometimes even death seems like a reprieve."

Off to our right I heard Aggie calling to us. "Hello there. Look what I found." Out of the shadows Aggie walked toward us, accompanied by the wench whom we'd watched being jailed.

Taylor smiled. "Matthew, I'd like you to meet my daughter."

"Rebecca?" I asked, amazed. Her face, covered with the stage makeup of smeared dirt and pockmarks, was obscured by her tangled black wig. My eyes dropped to her wide-necked blouse that had slipped fetchingly off one shoulder. I was anxious to see her without the makeup.

"Glad to meet you," she said. "Want to join the pirates?"

"I already signed on," I said, "down at the fort."

"No, I mean the group of us who do the Marblehead pirates. It's a lot of fun."

"It looks like it. I'll check into it for next year."

"Are we ready to go?" Rebecca asked. "I'm starved."

"Why don't you three start walking down the road?" I offered. "I'll get the car and meet you."

Shortly we entered Taylor's quarters in Fair Winds Inn. Rebecca went to her bedroom to change out of costume while Taylor made some final preparations for her dinner of pasta with clam sauce and salad. At Taylor's direction, I made drinks: white wine for me, scotch for Taylor, and a martini with olive for Aggie. While Taylor busied herself in the kitchenette, Aggie and I relaxed on the sofa.

"So, did you see the spot?" Aggie asked.

"Where the boat was found?"

"Yes."

"I saw it," I said. "Scary."

"I thought that's why Taylor took you up there." We sipped our drinks. "You make a good martini."

"Thanks. Taylor said the two of you don't agree on how she died."

"True enough. Taylor's mistaken about her mother committing suicide. That wasn't in her character."

"What about the depressions?"

"Children don't understand parents. They think they sit around and worry about them. Taylor was depressed, living with a husband who ignored her, and assumed her mother was overcome with frustration at not being able to help her. Of course, Becky was upset and sorry for her, but not to the point of jumping in the ocean. And she did miss Taylor's father, but she hadn't lost the spirit to live." She thought for a moment, then added, "I never should have written that letter about Becky's dark moods. It just fed Taylor's worries."

"You know everything about her, don't you, Aggie? Becky, I mean."

She smiled slightly. "Yes, I do."

"Why don't you tell Taylor the whole story? There's more, isn't there?"

"She's never asked. I don't think she's ready to find out."

"Will you tell me?"

"Hmm. Maybe someday when I know you better."

Taylor, drying her hands on an apron, joined us. "Now, where's that scotch?"

The three of us talked about how good the simmering clam sauce smelled, the approaching cold weather, and the pirate event. After a few minutes Rebecca's door opened. She came down the hall briskly, stopping as she entered the room. "Finally, I'm ready. Where's the food?"

God, I thought, she's as beautiful as I'd hoped. Oriental splendor and grace in a tall, slender body. She wore black stirrup pants and a blue silk blouse open at the neck with long, full sleeves buttoned at the cuffs. She had on low-heeled patent leather shoes. Her hair, a deep brunette, was combed back and clipped at the neck, then cascaded to her waist. High cheekbones and dark eyebrows gave an exotic flair to her face. As she walked into the room, the contours of her breasts sent light shimmering across the silk of her blouse. Her eyes met mine. She smiled. Instantly I knew I could lose myself forever in that smile.

I swallowed hard to control my voice. "What a change!" I said.

"I hope so, but being a wench once in a while is fun."

"Can I get you a drink?" I asked.

"Yes. Wine would be fine."

"And, Matthew," Taylor asked, "please get me another scotch. Aggie? Another martini?"

"No thanks. Two and I'd be asleep."

"Let me help you, Matthew," Rebecca said, following me to the kitchenette. "I hear you're a teacher here in Marblehead." As she spoke, she lowered her head and looked at me with wide-set, almost almond-shaped eyes. I felt a quiver all the way down my body.

"That's right. Art. And you?"

"I'm manager of international sales at the Markham Hotel in Boston."

"That's impressive. You must travel a lot?"

"I do," she said, relaxing against the bar. "And right now, I'm exhausted. It's not as romantic as it sounds, traveling around the world. It's hard work and sometimes a little boring. Got back Friday from France, a travel show in Deauville, and I'm still strung out on jet lag. But I wouldn't have missed the pirate event for anything."

"It looked like a lot of fun." I handed her the glass of wine. For an instant our fingers touched. She didn't seem to notice. "Where do you go next?" I asked as we returned to the sitting area.

"In November I'm off to London for the World Travel Market and then I continue on around the world to Tokyo for the World Travel Fair. Since I speak Japanese, I spend most of my time there." Taylor listened with the expression of a proud parent.

"Matthew not only teaches art," Taylor said, "he's the artist who painted *White Wings*."

The painting now hung over the sofa on which Aggie sat. She turned to gaze over her shoulder.

"It looks nice there, Taylor."

"It's really very good," Rebecca said thoughtfully. "That boat means so much to us and there it sits in the garage. You've given it life again."

"Well, actually, Rebecca, Matthew is doing more than the painting. He's going to restore the boat."

She looked at me dubiously and then at her mother. Forcing a smile, she said, "I see." And then with special emphasis, "Grandmother gave me that boat and I've always hoped we could get it repaired."

The room fell silent. After an awkward moment, Taylor spoke.

"Rebecca," she said, choosing her words carefully, "you were a very small child when your grandmother was alive. She never actually said she was giving you the boat."

Her daughter sank into a chair, her face turning to stone. "I know how old I was, Mother. I was five when we visited Marblehead. Gram took me sailing in *White Wings* and promised she'd give me the boat when I grew up." This was said with the voice of a spoiled little girl. I felt my attraction to her plummeting. "When we moved back to Marblehead, I used to go out to the garage and sit by the boat knowing it would be mine one day."

I could see where this conversation was going and I didn't like it. Aggie was getting tense, too.

Taylor said, evenly, "Darling, I know how much that boat has meant to you, but I don't think it was ever Gram's intention to give it to you."

"Mother, you weren't in the boat with us. You don't know what she said. I've been waiting for the time when I can sail it again."

"Look, Rebecca," her voice now harsh, "this is getting ridiculous. That boat's been in the garage for twenty years and this is the first time you've even thought of sailing it."

"Ah. Now you're reading my thoughts. That's really great, Mother."

"All right. That's enough. It's time we changed the subject. We're all tired and it's late. How about dinner?" Rebecca remained slouched in her chair. Suddenly she sat up and shot a look of challenge at her mother. "Have you given the boat to this man, Mother?"

"No. He has agreed to restore it, but we haven't discussed ownership."

Rebecca rose to her feet and stood over Taylor. When she spoke, her voice was like ice. "You amaze me, Mother. First, you decide for yourself that the boat is not mine and then you give it away." Turning toward me, she said, "And who are you, anyway? I don't know you. You weren't even around when I was here a month ago. How have you managed to insinuate yourself into our family in one month and steal *White Wings* from me?"

At first I was just afraid my plans for the boat would come to naught, but now I was beginning to get mad. "I don't like being accused of stealing. And anyway, nobody's stolen the boat. It's sitting in Aggie's basement and we're estimating the cost of repairs."

"Hah! So you have taken it," her words shooting like darts across the room. "Way to go, Mother. You'll never see *White Wings* again. And do you know how valuable that boat is? Well, I guarantee he does, and now he's got it." With that she stalked to her bedroom, slamming the door.

I looked at Taylor. Taylor looked at me. Aggie, pulling herself up from the sofa, said, "Maybe we ought to postpone the dinner. What do you think, Taylor? It'll keep, won't it?"

"Well, yes," Taylor said, "but it's not fair to let her tantrum spoil your evening."

"Nothing's spoiled," Aggie said. "Rebecca's just tired from her travels. Also, it sounds like she really thought the boat was hers. Maybe we were all a bit hasty. Maybe we should have included her."

"I'm terribly sorry for all of this," Taylor said. Then, wringing her hands, she added, "I don't know. You're probably right, Aggie. We should have included her." And turning toward me, "Matthew, please don't think badly of Rebecca. I'm sure we can get this ironed out."

"I got a little angry too, and that didn't help. I'm sorry."

"Well, we're all sorry," Aggie said. "Drive me home, Matthew. It's way past this old woman's bedtime."

The clock on my classroom wall crept toward two-thirty. I was exhausted from insomnia after the fiasco at Taylor's house. My students were tired from Halloween parties and playing Halloween tag with the police. The art appreciation class dragged on. Even the colored dots on Seurat's *Sunday Afternoon on the Grande Jatte* refused to meld into a visual whole. One wise guy raised a limp hand and asked, "What's the pointillism of art appreciation?" I smiled and thanked him for remembering the name of Seurat's technique. Finally, the bell saved us all.

I returned to the condo and did something I rarely do. I took a nap. The telephone jarred me out of my slumber a little after four or I might have slept into the evening. It was Taylor.

"Well, Matthew, what can I say? It was an awful evening and it didn't get any better after you left."

"What do you mean?"

"I tried to talk with her through the bedroom door and she threw a book at it. At least I think it was a book."

"Is there anything I can do?"

"God, no! That would be the worst thing I could think of. She's not very fond of you right now."

"Is she still there?"

"No, she left this morning without even saying good-bye." Then she added quickly, "Matthew, it may not seem like it now, but she's usually not like this. There must be a problem at work that's bothering her. She doesn't talk about her job, but I can tell when things aren't going well. I can see the strain in her face. Maybe it was the jet lag. I don't know. Or maybe it's partially my fault. She had a tough time as a kid."

"You mean in Japan?"

"Yes. She hardly ever saw her father and there were maids to take care of her every wish. When she was five, we enrolled her in the Yokohama Jogakiun, an exclusive girls' school. The other children treated her like a mixed breed, which, of course, she was. She'd come home in tears. Her Japanese grandparents were wonderful, though. I think they were as disgusted as I was with their son because he'd turned into a playboy and wasn't doing all that well at work. They treated her like a little princess whenever they'd see her. At least, after the divorce, her grandparents felt so guilty they set up a trust fund for her that's fairly substantial."

I just listened. Taylor needed to talk.

"When we came home to Marblehead right after Mom's death, Rebecca had to endure that loss, as did I. But then children don't think of that. Just of themselves. When she started school here, she was a mixed-breed again and some of the kids teased her about that. Actually, I think they were jealous because she was so cute."

"She certainly is beautiful now." Even in her rage, last night, that beauty had shown through.

"You noticed? Most men do."

"Yeah, I'm sure they do."

"Sooo. Where do we go from here? What do we do about the boat?"

There was a pause. "You still on?" I asked.

"Yes. I hate to say this, but I think it best if we do nothing for a while. I wouldn't start dismantling the damaged parts and I certainly wouldn't buy any materials. We'll leave the boat where it is, if that's all right with Aggie. I'm sure it will be."

"Maybe I can at least take measurements for the sail and build a steam box."

"What's that?"

"A steam box? I'll need to bend the planks to fit the curve of the hull. The steam box makes the wood pliable."

"Well, just don't lay out any money for the boat. I think Rebecca will come around in time, but it won't be soon."

We said good-bye and I hung up the phone very disappointed. I hadn't realized how much I'd counted on starting the restoration. Part of me blamed Taylor. Why didn't she include Rebecca in the discussions earlier? If she had, maybe Rebecca would have been willing to share the cost of materials. But that wasn't fair. I'd been pushing her relentlessly to give me the boat ever since I first saw it. Oh well, I thought, make the best of it—do what you can without spending money, and hope Rebecca comes around.

A call to Miranda, I decided, would brighten my day, but I'd have to wait until evening. To pass the time, I did lesson plans, fixed dinner, and waited for the little hand to reach seven. She should be home by then. I dialed.

Ring. Ring. Ring. "Hello. I'm not available right now. Please leave your name, number, and when you called and I'll think about returning your call."

"Miranda. This is Matthew. It's Tuesday evening. Please do a little more than just think about calling me back." And then I gave her my number. God, what an exasperating woman.

In the days that followed, I found solace in the classroom. Evenings, I kept busy bringing work home from school, going for walks, and making sketches for the steam box. When the weekend came, I bought the lumber I'd need for the box and took it to Aggie's basement. Then I remembered that Aggie had said I could move in anytime after the tenth, so I went to Shaw's supermarket and picked up several cartons. There was no rush, but starting to pack up gave me something to do. The next Saturday I rented a U-Haul trailer and carted my furniture and the cartons down the street and up the stairs to my new home.

Actually, with the whole second floor, I had more room than in the condo, though no harbor view. There was a kitchen–dining room on the back right and a small storeroom or study plus a bathroom on the back left. The bedroom overlooked the street on the left front with a living room to the right. A sliding door off the dining room opened onto a deck that stretched all the way across the back. By Saturday evening everything was in place and Aggie invited me down for dinner. Ah, I thought, a home-cooked meal.

She asked me to fix one of my outstanding martinis and to
have one myself. I declined the martini but took a beer. As I carefully dripped five drops of vermouth into a glass of gin, she dialed
Marblehead House of Pizza. "How do you like it?" she called.

"Home-cooked."

"What?"

"Any way you want it is fine with me."

She ordered a large with anchovies and mushrooms. "You'll
have to go get it in twenty minutes." Aggie had sold her pickup
truck when she stopped lobstering and had never bought another
car. "We're number thirty-five. You see, I can only get House of
Pizza pizza when I've got someone to pick it up. They make the
best, but they don't deliver."

As we sat down in the living room to wait, Aggie asked, "What's
the latest with my godchild?"

"Rebecca?"

"Yes. She was baptized in Japan, but I was her godmother in
absentia. You know, she wasn't herself the other night. She's really
a caring person."

I shrugged. "Right now I'll have to take your word for it. As far
as I know, she's in Boston and hasn't contacted her mother."

"Well, let it ride for a while."

"If we wait another week, she'll be on her way to London and
Tokyo. We probably won't see her until Christmas."

"Look, Matthew, the boat's been there for twenty-one years.
What's wrong with waiting a little longer?"

"I want to get started. That's what's wrong with it."

She spoke softly. "Easy, easy. You must be patient."

"I'm sorry. I'm just anxious."

"Where're you going to put the boat when it's restored?"

"I haven't thought about that. I suppose we'll have to rent one
of the moorings in the harbor."

"It's not that easy, young man. The waiting list for those can be
years long."

"How do I find out?"

"If I were you, I'd start by talking with the harbormaster. His
office is just down the street in the boatyard behind the Marblehead Yacht Club."

One more barrier, I thought. What else will get in the way?

I picked up the pizza. Aggie was right. The best I've ever tasted.

The next morning, Sunday, I headed for the harbormaster's office. I walked a short distance down to the commercial pier used by the lobster and fishing boats for loading gear and bait and for unloading their catch, then past five or six monstrous fiberglass sailboats sitting high above the road on jack stands or in wooden cradles, protected from the upcoming wintry weather by blue tarps. I entered the boatyard and found the harbormaster's office. It was closed. Posted hours were Monday through Friday, 8:00 A.M. to 5:00 P.M. Another day of waiting.

Immediately after school on Monday, I dashed back to the apartment, parked the Jeep, and went a second time to the harbormaster's office. This time the door opened. A receptionist sat at a desk surrounded by several pieces of computer equipment. The office was large and included two smaller desks against the far wall and a worktable. Charts of the harbor covered the walls along with announcements of CPR classes and small boat handling courses. To the right was a closed door leading to an inner office that I assumed belonged to the harbormaster. At the worktable an older man sat splicing a line using a spikelike tool called a fid, if my memory served me. He looked as if central casting had sent him there to create a nautical atmosphere.

"Can I help you?" the woman asked.

"Yes. Can you tell me how I go about getting a mooring in the harbor for a sailboat?"

"Well, I can tell you right off there's a nine-year waiting list."

"Nine years?" I groaned. "I thought it would be bad, but not that bad. What are the chances of tying up to one of the piers?"

"At the town piers there are rings, but those are for dinghies and there's a waiting list for those, too. There're some boatyard piers, but I'll tell you the cost for any length of time would be prohibitive."

My despair must have been visible because the old man sitting at the table said, "You're new around here, aren't you, son?" He continued probing the line with his fid, lifting the strands and splicing the loose ends back through to make a loop. He didn't look up at me.

"Fairly new. Came here in August. I teach at the high school."

"Came to Marblehead 'cause you want to sail. Right?"

I walked over to the table. "That was part of it."

"Have a seat." He looked up at me for the first time. His face was square with a slightly curved bald pate on top and a wide, hard jaw across the bottom. The squareness was accentuated by a series of parallel lines beginning with two deep furrows across his forehead, then followed by a line of dark eyebrows and ending with a straight, wide mouth set between tight lips. When he spoke, his lips hardly moved. Brown eyes were barely visible between narrowed lids. His cheeks stretched around his wide mouth in such a way that I couldn't tell if he was smiling or grimacing. He wore a heavy wool knit sweater with a denim shirt poking out of the collar. I estimated his age between seventy and eighty. His gruff voice fit his character. "Tell me about your boat."

I sat down. "Well, right now it's a wreck. I'm restoring it."

"Wood?"

"Yeah. It's a Buzzards Bay 15 by Herreshoff."

He stopped splicing and looked directly at me. "You don't say. Not many of those around." His gaze returned to the line and spike in his hands.

"I know."

"You doin' the work yourself?"

"Yeah."

"That's gonna take some craftsmanship."

"I know. I think I can do it."

He looked up at me doubtfully, then dropped his eyes back to the splicing. After a while he spoke again. "Where'd you find a Buzzards Bay 15?"

"Here in town. Belongs to a lady. She's had it in her garage for years. Boat's in real bad shape. No rot, though."

He seemed to ponder that for several moments, then, keeping his concentration on his work, asked, "Is it *White Wings?*"

My eyes opened wide with surprise. "Yes. It is."

"Thought so."

"How'd you know?"

"I know 'bout every boat in town."

"You're not Captain Kramer, are you?"

"Yup," he said looking up at me. "Name's Karl Kramer. What's yours?"

"Matthew. Matthew Adams."

"How'd you hear about me, Matthew?" Again his eyes returned to his work.

"Taylor Hayakawa mentioned your name."

He looked up briefly. "What'd she say?"

"Just that she knew you." If Taylor and Aggie had something against this man, I didn't want to get into it.

"So," he said, laying down his line and fid, "watcha gonna do for a moorin' when you get this boat in shape?"

"I don't know. That's why I came here."

The receptionist spoke up. "There's no waiting list for the west harbor."

"Hmm," I thought aloud, "what's wrong with it?"

"Nothing, really," she said. "It's just on the other side of Marblehead, near Salem, and not as convenient as this side. Do you want an application form?"

"Yes. I'd better reserve one. Hope to have the boat restored by next summer."

"Where're you workin' on it?" Kramer asked.

"Agnes Sparr's house."

"Hah," he grunted. "Mighta known."

I looked at him, wondering what that meant.

"Well, thanks for your help," I said to Kramer and the woman.

Then, with a smile that barely cracked his granite face, he said, "Good luck on the restoration. *White Wings* is a beautiful boat."

So that's Captain Kramer, I thought. Not a bad guy. Maybe a little gruff, but he was nice to me.

10

The next evening, Tuesday, as I was returning from a parent-teachers meeting, I parked my Jeep in the short driveway and was heading up the back steps when Aggie called to me from her kitchen door.

"Tomorrow's garbage pickup, Matthew. When you can, come down and I'll show you what to do." I said I'd be down in a minute. "Oh," she added, "and bring your trash down with you."

I hadn't seen Aggie since my meeting with Kramer the day before and decided not to mention it. She didn't like him, so why upset her? I consolidated my trash, consisting mainly of moving cartons and packing paper, into two big boxes and left them on the back porch. Aggie showed me where her wastebaskets were and her plastic trash barrels, and I figured out the rest.

"You can put the barrels out by the driveway."

I was emptying her kitchen wastebasket when I glanced at Aggie standing at the sink drying the few dishes she had used for her solitary dinner. She was dressed in a blue work shirt and dungarees as if she'd just finished a long day tending her lobster pots. I knew, though, she'd been raking leaves because I'd seen the leaf piles in the backyard. Her shoulders were slightly stooped as she stood over the sink, yet I was impressed by the dignity of her bearing and the concentration she brought to the task of drying a plate. She neither smiled nor frowned. Whatever she was feeling or thinking was hidden behind a mask of resignation to a life of

simple routine. Still, there was a contentedness in that acceptance that showed in lines of kindness around her eyes and mouth. Aggie was an attractive woman.

"Aggie," I said as I returned the empty wastebasket to its place in the kitchen closet, "will you be my grandmother?"

She gave me a smile. "Sure. When do I start?"

I laughed. "Really, though, I'm surprised you're not a grandmother with a dozen grandchildren."

"Matthew," she said, shaking her head, "you're sweet to say that, but it wasn't the life I chose."

Still curious, I asked, "Did you ever marry?"

She sighed and, giving me a look of forbearance, said, "Why don't you finish taking out the garbage and come back in. You can join me for a nightcap."

Ten minutes later I was sitting with her in the living room drinking a beer while she warmed a brandy snifter in the palm of her hand.

"Matthew," she said slowly, "I like you. You have a quality that few people have. You're a good listener, so you're easy to talk to."

I smiled. "Thank you."

"But there's also a disadvantage to that quality. Sometimes people will say too much and then feel uneasy, vulnerable."

I frowned.

"I know," she said, responding to my expression. "I don't think you would ever take advantage of the confidences people share with you."

"No, I wouldn't." I'd never thought about it before, but I didn't think it was something I'd do.

After a few moments of thought, she continued. "You've become a friend of Taylor and probably will be a friend of Rebecca after she calms down, and you're going to be restoring Becky's boat. So I want you to know where I fit into this family.

"I've told you Becky and I grew up together. Even from kindergarten, when my mother would bring me to the hotel or her mother would bring her here to play. We had our spats, but we were best friends through school and as grownups. When we were eleven or twelve, as girls do, I had a crush on Becky. Later, as teenagers, when other girls were getting interested in boys, I still had a crush on her."

She doesn't have to tell me this, I thought. It makes no difference to me.

As if sensing my thoughts, she said, "I know you may not want to hear all this, but I want you to have the whole picture." She took a deep breath and went on.

"Apart from Becky, I had no friends. Didn't seem to fit in with any group. I clung to the dream that one day she would realize how pure my love for her was and she would be mine. Then, when we were seniors, she fell in love with Karl Kramer. Yes, one and the same. He was Captain Kramer even then—captain of the football team—and Becky was captain of the cheerleaders. The details you'll have to fill in for yourself," she said in a voice so low I could hardly hear her, "but let's just say that I thought my world had come to an end when she fell for Karl."

Aggie stopped talking and looked into her glass as if it were a crystal ball in which she could see replayed scenes of her youth. For a full minute we sat there together, quietly, in the circle of light from her floor lamp. I didn't know what to say, just felt this sadness for Aggie, a sadness I couldn't put into words.

Finally I asked, "What happened between her and Kramer?"

It was as though she didn't hear me. She was still deep in her world of long ago.

"I didn't talk with Becky until the end of our senior year. We made up, finally, and became friends again. I was always her closest friend and she mine. I'd lost none of my feeling for her, but she never loved me in the way I loved her."

"I'm glad you did become friends again."

"Thank you, Matthew." She sighed.

I said good night and climbed the back steps to my apartment. On the landing I stopped and looked down the street at a tiny corner of the harbor. So that's the source of Aggie's dislike of Kramer, I thought, a jealousy that goes back to their days in high school. Just think, it started when they were ten years younger than I am now.

No, I decided, shaking my head. Aggie's too much of a person for that. It's got to be more.

11

The water in the teakettle came to a boil and steam began hissing from the spout into the tube leading to one end of the steam box. The box, made of pine, was eight feet long and ten inches on a side. The end into which the tube entered was sealed. The other end had a door with three small vent holes to allow the steam to escape. Gradually the steam built up in the box and began to drift out the vents at the other end. I'd laid a six-foot piece of one-by-four cedar in the box as a test both of the tightness of the box and to see how long the steaming required.

While the wood was steaming I surveyed the improvements I'd made in the basement workshop. Two floodlights were mounted in the ceiling over the boat and another over the workbench. Aggie's father's band saw and table saw both had new blades, were cleaned up and oiled. The two big boxes of assorted tools, screws, and general junk that I'd found under the bench had been emptied and culled, with the usable pieces hung on brackets behind the bench or arranged in clear plastic boxes. Aggie's furnace had a heat vent and fan that blew air into the basement and provided enough warmth to make it suitable for working. It was going to be a good place to work during the winter—if, that is, we could get Rebecca's cooperation.

After several minutes I removed the cedar and bent it against five wooden blocks I'd screwed into the top of the workbench in the shape of a long arc. But it was not yet sufficiently pliable to make the bend, so I put it back in the box for several more minutes. This time it bent to the arc in good fashion.

I'd been living in Aggie's apartment now for two weeks and spending most evenings in the basement. Once the lights were in and it was cleaned up, it felt cozy and comfortable. In the center of it all was *White Wings*, sitting on jack stands, looking like a wounded sailor waiting for a doctor to make her well. Walking around her hull, I would run my hand along her side, caressing her, unafraid of a repeat of my strange experience. In fact, were it to happen, I wouldn't have minded. If *White Wings* had something further to say, I was ready to listen. I even found myself talking aloud to her. "Well, old friend, how do you like the floodlights?" Sometimes I asked her advice. "How long should I make the steam box?" And when I was sweeping the basement, "Sorry about the dust." Hah, I laughed to myself, she's more than an old friend. She's my partner.

The following Thursday I drove to North Adams for Thanksgiving with Mom and Dad. Aggie had invited me to join her and Taylor for the feast, but it'd been four months since I'd seen my folks, and Thanksgiving was a good time to be with family. Mom cooked the traditional turkey with her special oyster dressing, and the pumpkin pie was made from scratch, topped with whipped cream. The tourism season had been good to them because of the balmy fall days, and they were ending the year well in the black.

After dinner Dad and I cleaned up the kitchen, then the three of us went for a walk along the Hoosac River. I told them about the boat and the restoration plans as well as the problem we were having with Rebecca. They wished me well, but it was my problem which we all knew I'd have to solve myself.

The next day Dad was back at work in his shop. He employs a man and woman who are both skilled cabinetmakers, but he'd given them the whole four-day weekend off. Dad was putting the finishing touches on a breakfront. I stood there, the plans for *White Wings* rolled under my arm, watching him sand and fit drawers. Finally he noticed me.

"Good morning," he said, straightening up from his crouched position by one of the drawers. "This goes out first of the week, so I'm pushing to get it done. How do you like it?"

"It's beautiful." The wood was gnarled cherry and so highly

polished that it seemed you could look inside the wood at the swirling grain.

"Got your plans there?" Dad asked.

"Yeah. I'd like you to take a look at them if you've got a minute."

We spread them out on a workbench and Dad and I leaned over them. I said I wasn't sure how far back to cut the broken planks nor the best way to attach the replacement planks to the frames. He told me exactly how to do it, as I knew he would. But what I liked best was standing there beside him, my shoulder pressed against his as we examined the plans. Dad's like an anchor to my best memories of growing up, and an example of what I hope to become.

I also borrowed his spare drawknife, several screwdrivers of various sizes, and a power drill set.

Friday night we ate leftover Thanksgiving dinner. Mom just set everything in the middle of the table and we picked at the turkey until only the carcass was left. I drove home Saturday under threatening skies, and by the time I reached 128, the beltway around Boston, it was raining. I didn't really want to go home to an empty apartment, so I stopped at Home Depot, off Route 114, to browse.

Parking the Jeep in the lot, I got soaking wet as I ran through the downpour to the store. Hardware and building supply stores are fun, the bigger the better. I roamed the aisles with no intention of buying anything until I came upon a rain suit made of serviceable plastic with hood, jacket, and overalls. Just the thing for an all-weather sailor, and only $19.98. I bought it and donned the jacket and hood for my race to the car.

When I parked beside Aggie's house, the sky was heavy with dark clouds and the rain was coming down in buckets. I love a storm, so I raced up to my apartment and put on the entire rain suit, waterproof overalls included, and a pair of rubber boots I already had. Shielded against the elements, I plunged through the driving rain down to the commercial pier, two blocks away, where the lobstermen tie up their dinghies.

Still half a block from the pier, I could hear the surge of waves against the rocks. Reaching the ramp to the floating dock, I looked down at a rolling sea. Tides in Marblehead have an average nine-foot swing, and when it is low tide, as it was now, the ramp down to the dock assumes a precipitous angle. The dock is in two linked sections each about forty feet long and fifteen feet wide. It is concrete on top of Styrofoam—very serviceable and very heavy. Yet the swells driving in from the northern end of the harbor lifted first one section and then the other as the black water rolled beneath. The dock groaned against its mooring lines and screeched beneath the wheels at the base of the ramp. Several dinghies had been hauled onto the dock, but there were about six still chained to rings at the side. The waves were dashing them against one another and slamming them into the side of the dock.

A man in boots, rain jacket, and sou'wester was pulling on the chain of one of the dinghies in an attempt to hoist it aboard the dock. He rode the rolling dock with ease, anticipating its every heave. As it rose and fell beneath him, his upper body remained vertical while his legs and hips swiveled with the dock. Then he fell.

Gripping the ramp's wet railing, I inched my way down the steep slope to the plateform. The man had braced himself against the overturned hull of a dinghy and was pulling himself upright. When he saw me he called, "You there! Wanna lend me a hand?"

Once on the dock, I groped my way toward him using the dinghies already there for support. When I reached him, I took his arm to help him stand, but he pulled it away abruptly.

"Not me. I'm all right. Help me get these damn boats up."

We went to the edge, where I knelt and began tugging on a boat chain. Each time the plateform rolled, the black water rushed up at me and I feared I would tumble into it. Then the side would lift, throwing me backward. Finally the bow came up against the dock and, together, we hoisted it up so it was resting on the edge. Then each of us grabbed a gunwale and slid the dinghy onto the plateform.

"These damn fishermen were supposed to have these boats on the dock by noon today," he yelled over the storm. "We posted the nor'easter warnin' yesterday. We oughta just leave 'em in the water and let 'em get crushed by the dock. Goddamn 'em." I could see him limping as we moved from one boat to the next.

It was Karl Kramer.

After we'd hauled five of the six boats onto the dock, he gestured to the last dinghy. "Skip that son of a bitch. The painter's too damn short. We'd have to twist it around and bring it up stern first and I'm not up to that. Screw it." With that, he started to climb the ramp, gripping the rail and pulling himself up. I followed. At the top he turned to me and said, "If you're still up to it, you can help me hoist the ramp."

If I was up to it? I hadn't had so much fun since I'd come to Marblehead. "Sure. Let's do it," I said with the eagerness of a kid.

Kramer looked at me warily. "Stay here. I'll bring my truck down."

He disappeared into the rain behind the big yachts halfway up the hill, moored for the winter on their jack stands. In a minute I saw his pickup turn onto Commercial Street, then his brake lights go on, and he backed down to park at the head of the ramp. A tubular steel yoke about twelve feet high, like an inverted U, was positioned with one leg on each side of the ramp. One block with tackle was secured to the top of the yoke, from which hung an assortment of lines to a second block tied to the railing beside the ramp. Kramer set about releasing this block and untangling the lines.

"See this block," he said, handing it to me. "I wancha to take it down, pullin' out the line as you go, and attach it to the bottom of the ramp."

I took the block, climbed down the ramp, and secured it as he had said. He watched me complete the job and gave me a thumbs-up. In the meantime he took the line coming through the block still hooked to the top of the yoke and ran it through a pulley anchored to a rock some distance back. This he tied to his bumper. Slowly he pulled forward in the pickup until all the lines were taut. Then he motioned me to come to his open window on the driver's side.

"Tell you what I wancha to do. Go back down the ramp. At the bottom you'll see two lines that secure the ramp to the dock. Untie these lines and get the hell back up here in a hurry before the ramp starts swingin' free. Got it?"

"Gotcha." As I started down the ramp for a third time, I saw the boat we had left in the water. The stern had swung around and was trapped under the plateform, swamped. As the dock dropped after each passing wave, it fell onto the boat. Screw it, Kramer had said, and screwed it was. Poor owner.

The wheels at the bottom of the ramp, which permit it to roll forward and back with the changes in the tide, were instead scraping sideways as the dock rolled. The lines were wet and crusted with salt. I noticed that first one and then the other would loosen as the dock shifted from side to side. Squatting on the deck to keep from falling, I worked the knots free, changing from one line to the other as they loosened. With my hands practically frozen, I let the lines go and dashed up the ramp. Kramer motioned me to the cab window.

"I'm going to go forward. It'll lift the ramp. You stay here and watch. When the ramp's just above level, gimme a wave."

I wanted to say "Aye, aye, sir," but I didn't dare. Because of the mechanical advantage of the six lines, he'd driven well up the hill before I waved at him to stop. He pulled on the brake and walked back down to the pulley hooked to the brace and secured the line. The ramp was up.

"Thanks for your help," he said. "It was more of a job than I'd thought."

"Glad I could help."

"Can I buy you a beer? I was goin' down to the Barnacle."

"Sure," I said, delighted but keeping my enthusiasm in check. We got back in the pickup and headed through the old part of town toward the restaurant. "That boat we couldn't get up was stuck under the dock when I went back down," I said.

"Well, that's tough, but it's not our job to pull 'em up on the dock."

"Whoever owned those five boats we pulled up, then, are lucky that you were the one who came down here."

He took a rag off the dashboard and wiped the steam off the windshield. "Yeah, well, they got it hard enough tryin' to make a livin' with the way fishin's goin' these days. I know whose boats they are and I'll give 'em hell the next time I see 'em for not getting 'em out."

It was only a little after five and the dinner crowd had not yet arrived, so we were able to park in front of the Barnacle. It's a bar and restaurant located right on the water's edge and just a block from Fort Sewall. We entered and stripped off our wet coats. I also took off my rain overalls since they seemed a bit out of place for the restaurant. Following Kramer in, I could see what a big man he was. His shoulders were broad and he stood well over six feet. His long hands dangled out of the sleeves of his sweater. Hard to believe he was over seventy years old. There was a small table by the window with a good view of the harbor and the storm blowing in from the northeast. We sat and Kramer ordered a double shot of rum, I a Sam Adams ale.

"You're the guy restorin' *White Wings*," Kramer said. "Didn't recognize you till you took off the hood."

"Right," I said. "How come you were down there hoisting the ramp?"

He looked out the window and rubbed his big hands together like he was drying them. "I help out at the harbormaster's office when I can. Couple of the men were away for the Thanksgiving weekend, so I said I'd pull the ramp." Then, looking at me, "How's the restoration goin'?"

"Haven't really started yet."

"I'd like to come by and have a look at *White Wings*. It's been a long time since I've seen her."

Given Aggie's feelings about Kramer, I doubted she'd want him in her house. "Yeah, maybe we could do that sometime."

Detecting my ambivalence, he said, "Guess Aggie wouldn't like that, huh?" Our drinks arrived. He downed the rum and ordered another double. I took a swig of the ale. "Yeah," he said thoughtfully, "she and Taylor don't like me."

"They haven't really talked about you that much," I said guardedly. Then I thought, here's my chance to find out about him and Becky. "Becky must have liked you, though. Taylor said she had you over a few times."

"She did," he said. And then, with what may have been a smile on his tight lips, "Up to a point." His rum arrived. This time he sipped it. "We were gonna get married once."

"Really?" I said with genuine surprise.

"In high school. We talked about gettin' married as soon as we graduated. We started goin' together in the fall, football season. By the time of the last game on Thanksgiving, we were so much in love we couldn't think about anythin' else. Yeah, we were gonna get married soon as we finished school."

He stopped, drank some more rum, and looked out the window. When he turned back to me, his face had grown bleak. "I guess maybe it's what happened to me in that last game. I ran out to catch a pass and was hit from the front and back at the same time. Couldn't get up. They carted me off the field to the hospital. When I came outa surgery, they told me I'd injured both my knees, be on crutches the rest of my life."

"Ugh," I muttered.

He looked up at me and I could see his eyelids had gone lax as the rum moved into his body.

"Yeah. Ugh," he said, sneering and smiling at the same time. "I was in the hospital recoverin' and doin' physical therapy for two months. Becky was okay. She'd come every day and help with my schoolwork so I'd be able to graduate. In February I was back in school on crutches, but things started goin' bad between us. Hell, I'd been a star, and now I couldn't even get from one class to the other on time. I'd see her walkin' down the hall talkin' to some other guy, and I'd go nuts. She'd say it was nothin', but I'd start yellin' at her. Finally it got too much for both of us and we broke up."

"Is that why she used to ask you over? She felt guilty?"

He laughed. "Guilty? Hell, Becky never felt guilty. Naw, she was a hellcat. Never regretted anythin' she did." He held up his glass and asked, "How about another?"

"Fine by me, but let me get this round."

"Naw." His voice was slightly slurred. "You helped me out back there at the dock and I 'preciate it." He motioned to the waitress, pointing to his glass and my bottle. We watched the storm banging the waves against the rocks outside the window. It was nice to be in a warm place looking out. Our drinks arrived.

"I watched you down there on the dock," I said. "Your knees seem to be okay now."

"Oh, I get around all right. I'm just not too steady. It's more arthritis now than anythin' else."

"How long was it before you were able to walk without crutches?"

"I got some braces right after graduation and learned to walk with 'em. Even started working as coolie on my dad's boat."

"No kidding." I wondered what a coolie was.

"Yeah. I could sit on the rail and pull the lobster pots into the boat as they came up on the winch. Then I'd take out the lobsters and plug 'em." So that's what a coolie does, I thought. "I wasn't as good as if I had two good legs, but at least I was workin' and that made me feel better."

Taking a chance, I asked, "So you still had some feelings for Becky?"

He looked at me with one eyebrow slightly raised and said, "Yeah. She married this other guy but I figured it wouldn't last more'n a year. I was gonna be there when it fell apart."

I was still curious about the hold he had over her. "So what happened?"

"Well, it didn't work that way. He went off to war and got hisself killed. I met Harriet and got married."

"So you gave up on Becky?"

Kramer looked me hard in the eye. "I never gave up on Becky. I always wanted her."

"She must have felt *something* toward you."

"No, it was because of *White Wings* she invited me."

"*White Wings*?"

"Huh," he scoffed. "She was afraid I'd tell the truth."

"Truth about what?"

"That I helped her hide *White Wings* in Aggie's basement the night she stole it."

12

Sunday morning, as soon as I heard Aggie in the kitchen, I went down the back steps and knocked on her back door.

"Good morning, Matt—"

"What's this about Becky stealing *White Wings*?"

She looked at me for a moment. "Hmm," she said, "why don't you come in?"

I followed her into the kitchen and she returned to her coffee-making. Without looking at me, she said, "Sooo, you've been talking to Kramer."

"Well, is it true?"

"Not exactly."

"Not exactly? He said he helped you and Becky hide the boat in your basement after she'd stolen it. No wonder you knew *White Wings* would fit down there."

"Yes. That's why I knew it would fit." She was pouring water into the top of her coffeemaker. "It's also true we were hiding the boat. But Becky hadn't stolen it, no matter what Kramer says."

I slumped down in one of her kitchen chairs. "Aggie, I think it's time you told me the whole story."

Aggie turned from the kitchen counter and said, "You are an excitable young man, Matthew Adams."

"Well, is Kramer lying?"

"No, though I wouldn't put it past him." She dried her hands on her apron and sat down. "In this case, he's just misinformed." She looked at me calmly, a slight smile involuntarily showing itself at the edges of her mouth. I was damned if I was going to ask another question. Moments passed. I could see she was enjoying this standoff. Finally she lowered her eyes and said, "She wasn't stealing the boat. She was keeping it for its rightful owner until he came back."

"Then why hide it in your basement?"

"Look. The answer is, because someone else thought they owned it." She got up and removed two mugs from her cupboard. "Coffee?"

"Yes, thank you."

She filled the two mugs and returned to the table. "I guess the time has come to make a clean breast of this. I see that now." She sighed. "Good old Kramer has lifted the lid and there's no way to explain this piecemeal. But I'm not going to tell you until I've had a chance to clear it with Taylor. Rebecca's going to have to be a part of this too, and that might be difficult to arrange."

"Finally," I said, relaxing.

"Rebecca won't be back for two more weeks, so you're just going to have to find something else to think about until then."

I sipped some of the hot coffee. "Why do we have to wait for her?"

She looked at me, annoyed. "Because this is family business and, frankly, it has nothing to do with you. If Taylor wants to include you, fine. But at this point, I think you should rein in your aggressiveness."

I took my reprimand in silence and began to cool down. After a minute I said, "You're right. I'm sorry."

She nodded. "What else did Kramer say?"

"He said he and Becky were supposed to get married after graduation but they broke up. Said he always wanted her even after he married Harriet."

"Yes, I guess that is true. But he wasn't always a nice man."

"He seemed like a pretty nice guy last night." I told her about helping Kramer with the boats and the ramp in the storm. "He could have let those boats get crushed by the dock, but he felt sorry for the guys who own them."

"Well, there's that side of him, too."

"You really don't like him, do you?"

"No, and if I were you, I'd be careful what I said around him."

I returned to my apartment feeling out of sorts. Whatever it was between Aggie and Kramer, it had nothing to do with me. *White Wings*, however, was another matter. Did this mean that Kramer could throw a monkey wrench into the restoration? Probably not. It was fifty years ago they hid the boat. Or stole it. Well, I was just going to have to wait until Rebecca got back to find out.

It was still raining, the morning was dark and gloomy, and my apartment was a mess. The bed was unmade, my dinner dishes were in the sink, last week's issues of the *Boston Globe* were strewn about the living room, and books and school papers covered my desk. And my boat—well, it felt like mine—couldn't be touched for at least two weeks.

And I was lonely. I thought about Miranda. She was fun to be with, but I doubted it would ever be more than that. Right now, though, someone fun to be with sounded good. I decided to give her a call.

"Hello. I'm not available right now. Please leave your name, number, and when you called and I'll think about returning your call."

"Damn it, Miranda, I don't want your machine. This is Matthew Adams, of the warm bed fame, if you remember. I want to see you. Please give me a call."

The middle of the week, when I returned home from school, the message light was blinking on my machine. "Hi Matthew. Sorry I didn't get back to you before. We've been shooting in Jamaica for the last few weeks. Not hard to take in this weather. I'll be in and out for the next several weeks, but would like to see you. Give me a call."

That night I called and once again got her machine. I left my message. "Hi Miranda's machine, this is Matthew's machine. If you're as nice as your owner, I'd like to get to know you. Give me your address so I'll know where to come when I'm in New York."

The following week, I got her message. "Hi. Pretty corny, Matthew." And then she left her address. I was making some progress, but it would have been nice to talk to her in person.

The weekend before Rebecca was to return, I invited Taylor

and Aggie to my apartment for dinner. Aggie declined due to a bothersome cold, and I promised to bring dinner to her on a tray. It was a Saturday night, so I had the afternoon to cook. I made a lamb curry with garlic and fresh ginger plus a dozen other ingredients. It tasted as good as it smelled. Taylor asked me to marry her and be her wife.

Aggie, when I took her tray down, said that in spite of her cold she could still taste the exotic spicing.

After dinner, Taylor said Aggie had told her about my conversation with Kramer and his contention that Becky had stolen *White Wings*. "That's the most preposterous thing I've ever heard, believe me, Matthew. Where does that man get off saying such a thing?"

"Aggie didn't exactly deny it, though. She admitted they'd hidden the boat in her basement."

"She told me that too, but she's never said why."

"How come you've never pressed her?"

She sighed. "I guess I've been afraid to. It's all tied up with my fear that I was adopted. It's irrational, I know. Here I am a grown woman, and I'm afraid to look at the possibility my parents aren't who I thought they were. What difference can it make now? They've been dead for years and I'm a parent myself."

I nodded sympathetically.

"And now that goddamn Kramer is telling people stories about my mother after he's had a few. That really annoys me." She brought her open hand down hard on the table, shaking the wineglasses. "What's more, I don't even know if they're true or not."

"Aggie said he was misled."

"Yeah, but there's more, I'm sure." She sighed. "Maybe it's time for me to get the whole story, even if it hurts. Rebecca, too, ought to know about her grandparents. And as far as I'm concerned, since the boat's involved, you can sit in on it also."

"I'd like that, but don't you think you ought to clear that with Rebecca first? We didn't part on the best of terms."

"God, Matthew. You're absolutely right. I almost did it again. Leaving her out."

I went to the refrigerator to get two chocolate mousse cakes I'd bought that morning at Delphine's French Pastry Shop. I served them with hazelnut coffee. Taylor closed her eyes and let the mousse melt in her mouth.

"Speaking of Rebecca," I said, "how am I going to make peace with her?"

"I think the best thing is for me to call her when she gets back and bring her up to date on what's happened, then see where we go from there."

Taylor did call her at the end of the week. "Her mood was entirely different," she reported. "The trip was a success and Rebecca wrote contracts with four tour companies in London and three in Tokyo. Her manager was pleased." Then Taylor's voice changed to a more confidential tone. "I think there might be more. She sounded so happy, I've a hunch her love life has taken a turn for the better."

I wasn't sure I wanted to hear that. I asked, "Did you say anything about me or the boat?"

"She brought it up herself."

"No kidding?"

"Said she was sorry about her outburst that night and she'd like a chance to apologize to you and Aggie."

"That's wonderful. God, I'd like to get started on that boat."

"Then I told her what Kramer said. She'd forgotten who he was until I reminded her. She was outraged. Couldn't believe a person would spread such lies."

"Did you tell her Aggie wants to set the whole record straight?"

"Yes, and if there's something we need to know, she wants to hear it. Brave girl. Braver than I." She laughed. "I've talked with Aggie about all of this, and she's invited the three of us for brunch next Sunday."

The day before the brunch, I bought Aggie a Christmas tree and helped her decorate it. She dug out an old crèche for the center of the table and together we placed pine boughs around the windows. All in all it looked very festive for Sunday morning.

Before Taylor and Rebecca arrived, I had come downstairs to see if Aggie needed any help. She was dressed in her usual dungarees but with a bright red blouse on which she'd pinned a sprig of holly. I had on a pair of black wool slacks I'd bought for the occasion and my white shirt and Irish sweater.

"You look sharp, Aggie, ready for Saint Nick."

"Hah! Just thought I'd get presentable for a change." At that moment the doorbell rang. "Want to get that, Matthew?"

I opened the door to Taylor and Rebecca. "Merry Christmas!" I said.

"And to you the same, Matthew," Taylor said, slipping her coat off and handing it to me. She wore a dark blue pleated skirt and an ivory-colored blouse with miniature sleigh bells pinned to the lapel.

Rebecca waited for me to close the door, then said, "Merry Christmas, Matthew." She looked at me with a smile that said she was no longer angry.

"Merry Christmas, Rebecca," I said, looking into her soft eyes, hoping I might find more than reconciliation. Again I was swept away by her beauty. Her hair was rolled into a bun and tied with a red ribbon. She wore a tailored jacket of silk brocade and a straight black skirt. How I would love to paint her, I thought. Her narrow cheeks, her high cheekbones, her full lips.

Taylor and Rebecca admired the decorations while our hostess disappeared into the kitchen, returning with a tray of mimosas each of which had a Santa Claus swizzle stick. "Got these in Miami forty years ago," she said proudly, "and I've been saving them for just the right occasion."

"Aunt Aggie," Rebecca laughed, "you are something else."

Aggie lifted her glass. "Merry Christmas to all of you."

"And to you," we responded.

We settled down in our chairs and I was about to start some small talk about the weather when Aggie spoke up.

"So," she said, as if calling a meeting to order, "it's time we got a few things straightened out. This being the season of good will, it's a good time to make amends. And I for one want to apologize for bringing *White Wings* to my basement without first discussing the matter with you, Rebecca."

"Oh, don't, Aggie," Rebecca said. "I'm the one that blew up and made a fool of myself. I apologize to all of you and especially to you, Matthew. At the same time, I think you should have talked with me first. Whether I was right or wrong, I did grow up with the impression that Gram wanted me to have the boat, so there was some reason for me getting upset."

"I can tell you something about that," Aggie said, "and I say this as Becky's closest friend and, I might add, confidante." She made sure she had our full attention. "Becky wouldn't have given the boat to anyone because it wasn't hers to give."

Aggie waited for this to sink in, then continued. "She may have said, 'Take care of this boat,' or 'Save this boat,' but she'd never have said, 'This boat is yours.' "

Turning to Taylor, she said, "*White Wings* belonged to your father and Becky never gave up hope of finding him. When he left for the war, he asked her to keep it for him. After he was reported missing in action, she clung to that boat as she had clung to him in the few months they were together. When she sailed *White Wings*, she felt he was with her. I remember her telling me once that she could feel the pull of his hand on the tiller beside hers. And you must understand, this was not just a dream for Becky, she believed it. Over the years, the boat became more than a symbol that he still lived, it became the talisman that would ensure his return one day. On her fiftieth birthday, Becky said to me that if she should die before I did, I was to see to it the boat was saved for him, because she knew he would return."

No one spoke, no one moved. Finally Rebecca said in a halting voice, "Now that I think of it, Gram may well have said to me, 'Save this boat if anything ever happens to me.' "

"That sounds a lot more like Becky," Aggie said.

"Do you really think, Aggie, my father was alive?" Taylor asked.

"Who knows? People reported as missing in action sometimes turned up later. Not that she didn't search for him. You'll see all of this when I give you her letters and photos and news clippings."

"How old would he be today?" I asked.

"Well, he was five years older than Becky, so that would make him seventy-nine."

"And when the boat was wrecked," Rebecca said as if thinking aloud, "the symbol of his being alive ended up on those rocks beneath Fort Sewall."

"It was wrecked but not destroyed," I said. "We can restore it.

As I worked around *White Wings* in the basement," then, to let Rebecca know I hadn't actually been working on the boat, I added, "putting up lights and cleaning up the workbench, I felt the boat waiting for someone to restore her. She's not dead. She's very much alive, just broken."

"I like that, Matthew," Rebecca said. "I like the way you put it, 'just broken.' But can we really fix her? After all these years can she really be restored?"

"Absolutely. She's in good shape. If she were a person, she would be suffering only from broken bones and pulled muscles, not gangrene or cancer. And bones can be fixed."

"Speaking of things fixed, our brunch is ready," Aggie announced.

We moved to her dining room where the table was set with Christmas place mats. Aggie brought a steaming pie tin from the kitchen and set it on a trivet. "Hope you all like ham and mushroom quiche." The top of the quiche was garnished in Christmas colors with slices of red peppers and green sprigs of fresh basil.

Midway through brunch, Taylor said to Aggie, "You mentioned letters and photos and news clippings. Are they ones Mother saved?"

"Yes. She gave them to me shortly before you returned from Japan."

"And that's just before she died," Taylor said.

"That's right. It was almost as though she had a premonition something might happen to her. She said she didn't want these things sitting around for other people to see and didn't want you to find them in a drawer somewhere until you were ready to know more about your father. That's why she gave them to me."

We all looked at Taylor.

"I'm ready now and I'm glad you're all here as support. I know that whatever I find out is not going to change anything in the present."

"There're two big boxes in the basement filled with stuff. We can bring them up and you can take your time here in the living room going through them. If you have questions I'll be here to answer them. And, Taylor, you can sort out the things you want to take home. Matthew, come with me to the basement and I'll show you where the boxes are."

"I'd like to go down with you," Rebecca said. "I haven't seen *White Wings* in years." Then, somewhat chagrined, "Despite all the fuss I made."

"I'll come too," Taylor said. "I'd like to see the workshop."

As we started down, I picked up the plans and cost estimates I'd brought from my apartment in case Rebecca had some questions. When I flipped on the lights, the workshop looked perfect. The bench was clean, the tools were arranged behind it on brackets, the two saws gleamed in the overhead lights, and in the center of it all was *White Wings*.

"Oh, the poor thing," Rebecca said. "I'd forgotten how damaged she was."

"You can really see her now, sitting out like this with the lights on," Taylor said.

I laid the plans on the bench and showed Rebecca how I was going to make the repairs. Starting with the hole in the starboard side, I pointed out how far back I'd have to cut the planks and how I'd replace the damaged frames. Rebecca followed with interest, asking questions about the kind of wood we'd use and how we'd bend it to fit the frames. I noticed she was saying "we" instead of "you." I liked that. She noticed how the deck had pulled away from the sheer plank and clamp and wondered how I would go about repairing that. When we came to the bow stem where some of the planks had been ripped loose from the stem, she sighed. "Oh, Matthew, it looks like there's too much. The poor thing is so broken up."

I was standing directly in front of the boat now. As I ran my hand down the stem to the section from which the planks had pulled loose, I felt a lightness pass over me. Then my field of vision was quickly suffused by an aura of drifting, shifting light that closed in on my center of focus until I saw nothing. My feet no longer touched the concrete floor but seemed to float in a void. All my senses concentrated in my fingers, which had transformed themselves into the oak of the boat's stem. There was the roar of wind and waves, the crashing of the bow into the water, the keening of the rigging, and the wild flapping of torn sails. Suddenly there was a flash and a thunderous crack like a lightning strike. Pain pierced my fingers, surged through my body, and lodged in my chest. I fell.

Like a voice echoing through a tunnel I heard the words, "He's all right, Rebecca. He's all right. Just let him settle there."

"He is not. He's fainted. Look, he's white as a ghost. We'd better call a doctor." I felt her arms around my shoulders as she gently supported me where I'd fallen.

Again Taylor's voice. "Just keep holding him. He'll come around in a minute. This has happened before."

"Is it epilepsy?" Rebecca asked.

"No, it's not that. We don't know what it is," Taylor said. "But whatever it is, it's something between him and the boat."

The next voice I heard was my own. "I'm . . . I'm okay now."

I opened my eyes and saw that my head was cradled in Rebecca's arms. I closed them again and let myself rest there. Then I felt Taylor helping Rebecca lift me onto a box and lean me back against the workbench. Soon Rebecca was holding a glass of water to my lips. I drank.

"You poor guy," she was saying. Then, "Oh, he's cut his finger."

I touched my bleeding finger with my other hand. Then I remembered the flash of light and the loud crack. I started to get up.

"No, Matthew," Taylor said. "Wait a few minutes."

"I've got to get up," I said, struggling. I got to my feet and, with Rebecca supporting my elbow, lurched to the bow of the boat. Touching the stem and leaving a faint track of blood, I ran my wounded finger down the timeworn piece of oak until it slipped into a small round hole. By now both my consciousness and my equilibrium were returning. I could stand without Rebecca's help, yet she continued to hover beside me looking confused and frightened.

"Let him do what he wants, Rebecca," Taylor said, touching her arm.

"Really. I'm okay now," I said, trying to reassure her. "But I'll need your help." From under the workbench I pulled out a long, thin steel rod that Aggie's father had saved just in case he'd ever need a long, thin steel rod. I silently thanked him and brought it back to the bow. Inserting it through the hole my finger had found in the stem, I asked Rebecca to continue guiding it through the hole. I went to the starboard side, stuck my head through the boat's hull where it was fractured, and grasped the end of the rod. Pulling it through the hole in the stem and making sure it was straight, I drew it further into the hull until the tip butted against one of the frames. And sure enough, there was a small hole in the forward side of the frame.

Setting the end of the rod in this hole so I wouldn't lose its location, I called to Rebecca, "Okay, please bring me the saber saw off the back of the workbench."

"Uh-huh," she said. "What's a saber saw?"

"That one," Aggie said, pointing.

"Also, the flashlight standing up at the back."

"Flashlights I know." Rebecca laughed, her mood lightening.

I climbed up into the cockpit with the saw and had Rebecca shine the light through the fracture in the boat's side. Carefully I began to cut the frame above the hole in the shape of a V. When the two cuts met, I popped out the piece of wood I'd sawed free. At the bottom of the V-shaped piece was a blunt, round hunk of metal.

I crawled out of the hull and cockpit and stood before the others, holding out my hand.

"What it is?" Taylor asked.

"I'm afraid it's a bullet."

At first she looked puzzled. Then pain contorted her face.

"Oh God, no," she cried.

"Easy," I said, putting my arm around her. "It may mean nothing at all. She's an old boat. It may have happened long before Becky sailed her."

She looked directly into my eyes, her hands gripping my shoulders.

"That's not what happened, Matthew, and you of all people know it. You touched that boat and it spoke to you. Whatever happened on the night Mother died, this bullet is part of it."

PART TWO

~

Becky DeWolf

~

July 1939

13

I lay on my back on the chaise longue and filled my navel with suntan lotion. Dipping my first finger into the creamy pool, I drew circles around my stomach and made little roads up to my chest. I was on the sundeck off my bedroom on the top floor of the Harborside Hotel, owned and operated by my mother and father and situated, appropriately, on the side of Marblehead Harbor. During the summer, between graduating from high school and beginning North Shore Business College in Salem, I was a waitress in the hotel. Not much of a job, but a job nonetheless. I'd finished the Saturday luncheon period and, with Clara and Estelle, the other waitresses, prepared the dining room for dinner. Now I had three hours all to myself.

A hot July sun shone over the privacy wall between my deck and my parents', warming my body and anointing my forehead with a sheen of perspiration. Since no Peeping Toms could disturb my solitude, I slipped my arms out of my robe and let it fall to the deck. My bathing suit had stenciled its imprint in white on my body. Refilling my navel reservoir, I extended the roads and circles of suntan lotion to my shoulder strap marks and my breasts, waist, and hips. How luxurious I felt lying there on my private deck in the afternoon sun while seagulls soared overhead.

From the Odyssey Yacht Club below me and about a block to the left, the sounds of an orchestra, popping champagne corks, and people's laughter mingled with the call of the gulls. I propped myself up on my elbows for a look at yet another wedding reception, the third in as many weeks. A blue and white striped tent had been erected in the parking lot, and more than two hundred people, women in colorful silk dresses and straw hats and men in white jackets, held champagne glasses and little plates of hors d'oeuvres as they talked and laughed with one another. On the other side of the lot, attendants were busy parking a line of long black Buicks, Packards, and Chryslers. Some event, I thought.

I settled back on the chaise and closed my eyes. I'd seen some of those wedding guests at our check-in desk. They were elegantly dressed and seemed to regard our lobby with the disdain of royalty. I was sure the ones my age had never seen the inside of a public school or waited on tables. God, it would be fun to be that rich.

Oh well, I was lucky my folks had the hotel and I had a job.

Graduation was such a climactic experience that the last few weeks had been a letdown. Working six days a week didn't help either. And the hours for waitressing are depressing, spread out from seven in the morning to nine at night with three hours off before lunch and three before dinner. The problem is you're free when your friends are working, and working when they're going out having a good time. And there's another problem with working and living in a hotel. You're constantly associating with people who are wealthier and appear to be living carefree lives. I suppose they aren't, but it looks that way. They seem so cosmopolitan and suave and they're always dressed like they stepped out of *Vogue* magazine. Occasionally a man would mistake me for a guest and invite me to the bar for a drink. I'd politely decline, but it hurts inside to know you're not their equal, you're their servant.

Well, I thought, I'll be starting business college in September. I wish it were Wellesley or Radcliffe where I'd be living in a dorm with other girls.

I leaned up on my elbows again and looked out across the causeway toward the ocean. On the horizon was a four-stack ocean liner heading for Europe. I imagined the people standing at the rail watching the Boston skyline disappear, anticipating a night of dining and dancing in the ship's palatial ballroom. Someday, I dreamed. Someday.

The day was warm, the air still. I could feel the toasty fingers of the sun against my bare skin. I began thinking about the good times I'd had with the guy I'd dated the beginning of senior year, Karl Kramer. It ended badly, but started hot and heavy in the front seat of his dad's Chevy. I lathered my fingers in the smooth cream from my navel and brought them to my breasts, moving around and around until my nipples were hard to the touch.

At first the sound was like a dentist's drill you hear through the waiting room door. Then it was a distant motorcycle. Suddenly it burst upon me with a roar and I opened my eyes to see an airplane sailing past my deck no more than a hundred feet away. I sat up on my elbows and stared into the goggled eyes of the pilot sitting in the open cockpit of his biplane. Beneath the wings were two enormous pontoons. As suddenly as he had arrived he sped away, pointing the nose of the craft into the sky. Up, up it went, gradually losing speed until it crested, then dropped off to the left and fell back to earth in a dive along the same track it had ascended. With his engine roaring, he shot past my deck in the opposite direction. This time he waved. As I waved back, I suddenly realized I was naked. Jumping up and grabbing for my robe, I watched him disappear over the Odyssey Yacht Club, heading toward the mouth of the harbor. In less than thirty seconds he was back again, approaching in a shallow dive. Just as he reached the club, he pulled the nose upward, his engine screaming, and performed a magnificent loop. At its top, his forward motion seemed to stop and he hung upside down in space. Then the airplane dropped to earth, gaining speed until it pulled out of its dive over the heads of the cheering wedding guests. Banking wide to the left, he circled the harbor and disappeared.

"Wow!" I said aloud.

The whine of the airplane's engine grew more distant and then stopped altogether. Moments later I could hear it again, sputtering and gunning as it came into view around the yacht club, taxiing on the water. As it passed the club, the pilot waved to the guests while they cheered and applauded. He continued past the club and nudged the aircraft up to the hotel dock. To my surprise, my father was there on the dock, greeting him and throwing him a line. Quickly as I could, I pulled on a pair of shorts and a halter and ran to the elevator. On the way down, I slipped on my sandals. Oh hell,

I thought, what does my hair look like? Using my fingers as a comb, I stroked back the wayward strands. As I ran past the desk to the lobby door, my mother called, "His name is James DeWolf." We both laughed.

As soon as I could see the dock, I slowed to a walk. Casually, I strolled down the brick path to the dock and approached my father, Graham Butler, who was securing bumpers to the pontoons of the airplane and adding extra lines.

Dad's presence always calms me. He's big, about six feet tall, with a full face and a husky build. At forty-seven, his once dark brown hair is turning gray. He's a cuddly sort of man, although I'd never say that to his face, and as a child I loved to sit on his lap. He and two other men bought the hotel after the Great War just before he married Mom. In the mid-twenties, with business booming, he bought out his partners and he and Mom became sole owners of a first-class forty-room hotel. Then came the crash. For the last nine years they've managed to keep their heads above water only by endless hours of hard work and the loyalty of a few guests who return year after year.

"That should hold it," Dad was saying. "It's a floating dock, so the tide won't make any difference." Then, turning to me, he said, "Hi, Becky. I'd like you to meet Mr. DeWolf."

The pilot stood on the lower wing extending over the end of the dock. He wore a brown flying suit zipped up the front which had an assortment of pockets at the chest, hips, and legs. A yellow scarf was tied around his neck and tucked into the suit. His goggles were pushed up over his leather helmet, revealing a face younger than I'd anticipated. As he turned to me, he pulled off his helmet and smiled broadly. A shock of blond hair pointed in several directions at once until he raked it back with his right hand.

"Hi, Becky," he said buoyantly.

I waved up at him. "It's nice to meet you, Mr. DeWolf."

"Call me Jimmy. I won't know you're talking to me if you call me Mr. DeWolf." He reached into the forward cockpit and removed a suitcase, then walked back down the wing, jumping onto the dock.

"Mr. DeWolf is spending the night with us," Dad said. "Why don't you take him up and see that he gets properly checked in?"

We started up the path, Jimmy swinging his bag. "I'm here for the wedding reception at the O.Y.C. I was working this morning and couldn't make the wedding."

"You surely gave them a treat with the loop you did. Everybody cheered."

"Yeah, I thought that would add a little life to the party."

"Are you friends with the bride or groom?"

"Both now. First the groom, Hugh, and then when he met Alexandra, her too."

Striding beside him up the walk I could see he was taller than I, but he couldn't be much older, certainly no more than his early twenties. Why doesn't he just ask me to go to the reception with him? I could get ready in a flash.

"So, you're spending the night with us?"

"That's right. It's going to be some party and I wouldn't dare try to fly home tonight."

"Where's home?"

"Actually it's next door. I live in Lynn, but I keep the Waco at Boston Airport."

"The Waco?"

"Yeah," he said, stopping and turning to look back at his light blue plane. "Isn't it beautiful? It's a Waco UPF-7. I had the pontoons put on. May be the only one around that can land on water."

"Why water? Why not land?"

"Most of the parties I go to are on the water, like at the Cape or up in Maine. If I land at an airport, then I have to get a ride to the party."

I looked at the open cockpits and asked, "What do you do when it rains?"

"Get wet. But a lot blows past you 'cause of the propeller blast."

We entered the lobby and I led him to the desk. "This is Mr. DeWolf, Mom. Dad said to take good care of him."

"That I will," she said with a smile.

Martha Butler, my mom, is most comfortable behind the reception desk. Actually, she manages not only the front desk but the hotel staff, and does the buying for the kitchen and bar as well. She and Dad are the same age but Mom looks a few years younger, at least when she's smiling. Her once trim figure is a little fuller now, but her hair is still a vibrant brown with natural highlights that catch the sun. When she's not smiling, I can see in her face the strain of long hours struggling to make ends meet. Now she was smiling.

"Hi, Jimmy," she said and, much to my surprise, "How're your dad and mom?"

"Fine, Mrs. Butler."

"Well, give them my best. Here"—she slid a registration form across the desk—"if you'd just fill this out." Then she turned to me. "Jimmy's father owns DeWolf Distributing Company. We buy all our bar goods from him."

"Oh," I acknowledged with eyebrows raised.

Mom handed Jimmy the key to 308. "Is this just for one night, Jimmy?"

"Yes. That's the plan."

"Becky, why don't you show Jimmy the room?"

"That's okay," Jimmy said. "I can find it." He picked up his bag. "Tell you what I'd really like. Could you have a gin and tonic sent up to the room?"

"Sure," Mom said, "and it's on the house." Jimmy left and Mom asked me if I would mix the drink and take it up to him.

"Are you kidding? Of course I will," I said happily. "So his father is *the* Mr. DeWolf. No wonder Jimmy has his own airplane."

"He's supposed to be using it for a business he's starting."

"From what he told me, he's using it to fly to beach parties."

"Well, that too, I expect."

"Isn't he just about the handsomest man you've ever seen?"

"Looks like a movie star, doesn't he?"

"Yeah." I sighed dreamily. I could see him again push his thick blond hair back, square his broad shoulders, and tighten the belt of his flying suit until I was sure I could reach around his waist with only one arm. He was just the right height that, if I pressed my body against his, I'd be able to bury my head in the hollow of his neck.

"He's way out of our league," Mom said. "You better take him the drink he ordered."

I went to mix the gin and tonic. When I knocked on 308, he

came to the door dressed in a robe, looking like a blond Cary Grant.

"Here's your drink."

"Oh, I didn't mean you had to bring it. I thought there would be a bellboy."

"That's all right. You're a friend of the family."

There was an awkward pause until I realized he didn't know if he should tip me.

"Enjoy the party," I said quickly and backed away toward the stairs.

"Well, thanks for the drink," he called.

"You're welcome."

I went up to my room on the floor above and looked at the clock. One hour to go before I had to be back in the dining room. I borrowed my father's binoculars from his room and returned to my deck. Sitting so that I would not be seen, I peered over my railing at the reception party. How grand they all looked. There was the usual crowd around the bar and a line at the hors d'oeuvres table. Some were dancing in front of the orchestra stand, but mostly they were gathered in small groups, talking and waving at friends.

After fifteen minutes I saw Jimmy arrive. He was dressed in a white coat with dark blue pants, a blue bow tie, and white shoes. No sooner did he move into the crowd than people flocked to him. A man brought him a drink and a girl held a plate of food for him while he talked animatedly. Soon he left this group and walked to the bride, standing in her long satin gown by a bank of flowers. He embraced her, kissing her on the lips. So that's Alexandra, I thought. Lucky girl. Then the groom approached making a naughty-naughty gesture with his finger at Jimmy. They hugged. Lucky Hugh.

I watched the festivities until my eyes blurred and my shoulders ached from crouching over the railing, then changed into my waitress uniform.

The next morning at the end of the breakfast period, he strolled into the dining room dressed in the same dark pants, with his white shirt open at the neck. I pounced on him before the other waitresses had a chance to come near his table.

"Good morning," I said cheerily. "May I take your order?"

"Oh hi, Becky," his eyes only partially open. "Just a cup of coffee for now." Then he looked up at me and said, "So, they've got you waiting tables?"

"That's right. I live here and work here too."

"Good for you." His mind seemed elsewhere.

"How was the reception?"

"Very drunk."

"In that case, I'll get your coffee *posthaste*."

"Thanks."

As I was pouring his coffee, I saw a police officer talking with Dad in the lobby. Dad gestured for him to remain there and came into the dining room heading toward Jimmy. I was putting the coffee cup on the table when Dad said, "Jimmy. Sorry to bother you, but there's a policeman out here who wants to talk with you."

"Now?" Jimmy said, annoyed.

"I think it would be better to see him in the lobby than in here."

"All right," he said with a groan.

As if my job required it, I went to the hostess's desk by the door and sorted menus.

"James DeWolf?" the officer asked.

"That's me." Jimmy stood with his weight on one foot and his hands in his pockets, the picture of petulance.

"Is that your airplane tied up at the dock?"

"It is."

"Well, young man, I'm afraid I have a citation for you."

"What for?" Jimmy said with genuine surprise.

The officer took out a pad and flipped to a page marked with his pencil. "Flying below a thousand feet over an urban area, performing acrobatics below fifteen hundred feet, and generally disturbing the peace."

"That's crazy. I was over the water where there's no limit and the loop was over the water too."

"Mr. DeWolf, my job is to serve you with this citation. No use in arguing with me. You're to be in district court in Salem on July the twenty-eighth when you can explain all this to the judge. Good-bye, sir." He walked away leaving Jimmy fuming.

"Of all the goddamn stupid things." He stomped back into the dining room, muttering, "What a jerkwater town. You'd think they'd appreciate a little excitement." Halfway to his table he stopped, looked at me, and said, "Skip the coffee. I'm going outside."

I watched him walk down the path to his airplane, hands dug deeply into his pockets and shoulders hunched over. He checked the lines tied to the dock, then climbed into the rear cockpit and sat, his head barely showing.

He stayed there for several minutes without moving. I wondered if he'd fallen asleep.

The breakfast period over, we closed the doors and started cleaning up. I told Clara, one of the other waitresses, I had something I wanted to do and asked her to take over for me.

"Sure, honey." She laughed. "And see if he's got a brother."

On a tray I placed a small pot of coffee, cup and saucer, cream and sugar and spoon. Also a glass of water and a Bromo-Seltzer. Checking my hair in the glass window separating the lobby from the dining room, I picked up the tray and headed for the dock.

I stood next to the fuselage and called, "Mr. DeWolf. This is room service, or should I say, plane service. I have your coffee. I've also brought Bromo-Seltzer, if you prefer."

No response. Finally I heard movement inside the cockpit and his head poked up. "What'd you say?"

I held up the tray and smiled. "Coffee? Do you want it up there or down here on the picnic table?"

He groaned, then climbed down and sat at the table. Setting the tray on the table, I poured his coffee, then stepped back and stood behind him. He took a sip. Then another. Suddenly he turned to me.

"Will you *please* sit down."

I sat.

"That's better."

He blew on his coffee and took another sip, a smile beginning at the edge of his mouth and eyes.

Then, face toward the harbor but eyes turned to me, he said, "Come fly with me, Becky."

14

"Clear!" Jimmy yelled and pushed the starter button. The propeller made several halting turns and then, with a burst of exhaust, the engine roared to life. The plane had been turned around so it was pointing north, toward the harbor mouth. Dad was on the dock holding the tip of the wing until Jimmy gave the high sign. I was strapped into the front seat, wearing helmet and goggles, a leather jacket and slacks. Behind my seat was a picnic basket with food, my bathing suit, and a towel. Waving goodbye from the end of the dock was Mom, who had willingly agreed to take my place at lunch. Gradually, as Jimmy eased the throttle forward, we moved away from the dock. My first airplane ride!

The front cockpit of the Waco UPF-7 has a duplicate set of controls and a wide seat capable of seating two people. In front of me was an assortment of dials and knobs, and on the floor a stick and foot pedals. I could see the foot pedals moving in and out alternatively and the stick being pulled back slightly. Jimmy had warned me not to touch the controls because he was handling them from the rear cockpit. We taxied past the Odyssey Yacht Club, the town pier at State Street, and finally Fort Sewall. People stood on the docks and hillsides watching and waving. I waved back. I felt exuberant. There was a gentle northwest wind and the sea was relatively calm. Once past the outermost moorings, Jimmy turned toward the lighthouse point, then, after going a couple hundred yards, back toward the northwest. Over the idling engine he called, "Are you ready?"

"You bet!" I yelled.

"Put your goggles down."

"I got 'em down."

"Here we go."

I saw the throttle move forward and heard the engine roar. The stick came back toward me, the tail dipped slightly, and I felt myself pushed back into the seat as we raced over the water. Faster and faster we went, bouncing slightly as the waves hit the pontoons. Then the stick came back farther, the nose rose, and we were airborne with the wind whipping past my windshield, over my head. As I leaned sideways, a blast of rushing air hit my helmet. Looking over the edge of the cockpit, I watched the water and islands fall away beneath us. I turned around to look at Jimmy but couldn't see him, so I held my hand high and gave a thumbs-up signal to show how happy I was.

The plane climbed so rapidly I could hardly believe it. Soon we were over the harbor between Marblehead and Salem, banking back toward Marblehead. I could see Abbot Hall on the hill in the center of town and then the Odyssey Yacht Club and Harborside Hotel. Mom and Dad were both on the veranda waving as we flew over. Jimmy banked to the right and instantly we were flying over Aggie's house. I looked at the altimeter and saw we were at a thousand feet.

The towns of Swampscott and Lynn and Revere passed beneath us on the right side and Nahant Island on the left. Since we were over water, we had come down to five hundred feet. After ten minutes or so, we climbed back up to fifteen hundred feet and, keeping a heading of southwest, we flew over Boston Airport. Beyond the airport to the right was Boston itself with the sun reflecting on the gold dome of the capitol on Beacon Hill. Near the water I saw the tall customs house, Faneuil Hall, and Quincy Market. The harbor was filled with small boats and several two- and three-masted schooners tied up to the warehouse quays. When we flew over Commonwealth Pier, an ocean liner was being nudged in to the quay by three tugboats.

Then Jimmy banked left and I saw the compass move to the

southeast. Soon we were completely over water and coming down to five hundred feet. I watched Quincy leave us on the right side of the plane and could see the whole of Cape Cod on the horizon as a giant arch. The expanse of water was enormous, broken only occasionally by a sail or a fishing boat.

After twenty minutes over the open water, I looked down on Provincetown and the tall Pilgrim's Memorial Tower. I was feeling great, no nausea, just relaxed. Here Jimmy banked to the right and we passed over the huge tract of sand dunes where I had heard F. Scott Fitzgerald and other authors summered in small shacks. Soon the sand gave way to forests which stretched across the cape from one side to the other. In five minutes we were circling a small lake nestled in the trees. Suddenly I thought we were falling out of the sky. The nose began to point down and to the right, but the left wing dipped and the plane slipped downward rapidly to the left. The trees came up around us on all sides with the lake only twenty feet below. Just as we leveled off, I let out a yelp as the stick came back between my legs. The nose came up and the pontoons touched the water, sending a spray into the air behind us. We stopped quickly and Jimmy cut the engine.

"Still up there?" he called.

"Right here," I said. "Your plane just did an indecent thing."

"Oh? What was that?"

"The stick came back on me where it shouldn't have. At least you could have told me it was going to happen."

"Sorry. Next time you'll know." He was climbing out of his cockpit and pulling off his helmet. In his hand was a line with a small anchor tied to it. He dropped the anchor into the water and tied the line to a wing strut.

"How'd you like it?" he asked.

"It was wonderful. The world's so different from up there."

"I know," he said, pensively looking at the sky, "it is. Feel okay?"

"I feel great. It was a lot smoother than I thought it'd be."

"It's not always that smooth. Sometimes you really get tossed around."

"What happened when we were landing? I thought we were going to crash."

"I sideslipped so we'd lose altitude fast and get into this little lake."

"It was on purpose, then?"

"Uh-huh." He looked around. "Like the setting here?" The small lake was a mirror, circled by tall rushes and thick evergreens. I stood in the cockpit and looked in all directions over the top of the upper wing. There was one broken-down dock with a canoe tied to it and, just visible in the trees, the porch of a cabin. No other signs of life.

"Jimmy, this is beautiful. What a hideaway."

"It is, isn't it?" He was standing on the lower wing just behind my cockpit and looking at the shoreline. His hand rested on my shoulder.

"So peaceful," I said. Then, "Hungry?"

"I could eat a horse. What's for lunch?"

"The cook made us roast beef sandwiches and potato salad. Sound good?"

"Swell. But first, the champagne."

"You're kidding," I said.

"No. Brought it back from the party last night. Bring the lunch down here and we'll sit on the pontoon and dangle our feet in the water."

"Just a minute. I'll put my bathing suit on and be right down."

I heard him climb back into his cockpit and assumed he was doing the same thing. I shed my jacket, blouse, and bra, and slipped out of my slacks and underpants. Here I was sitting naked in the front cockpit and Jimmy was only three feet away in the rear seat, probably naked too. I looked at my long legs, narrow hips, and medium-sized breasts and wondered if I'd measure up to the girls he went around with. Hoping for the best, I wiggled into my suit. As I reached around for the picnic basket, I saw Jimmy's legs climbing out of his cockpit and realized there was no partition between the seats.

"Ye gods!" I exclaimed. "You can see right through."

"Don't worry," he said with a sly smile. "I didn't look."

Soon we were sitting on the pontoon in our bathing suits, dangling our feet in the water. The lunch, two glasses from the OYC, and a bottle of champagne were between us in the basket, which Jimmy had tied to the pontoon strut. "Now this is heaven," I said.

"Hmmm. Yes," Jimmy said. He worked at the cork on the champagne bottle until it popped, flying high into the air behind the plane. Immediately the wine foamed out of the bottle and down his hand until only two thirds was left. He laughed. "Wonder how they do this on the airliners?"

I held the glasses while he poured.

"Here's to a beautiful airplane!" I proposed, lifting my glass.

"And here's to a beautiful girl," Jimmy toasted, his eyes serious.

"Beautiful!" I laughed. "I don't know about that."

"Well, you are."

Blushing, I tried to change the subject. "Come here often?" I asked.

"Whenever I can," he said, shifting his gaze from me to the lake. "It's great for swimming. Not as cold as the ocean." I was pretty sure he didn't come alone. "Finish that glass and we'll have a swim."

We downed the champagne and carefully set our glasses in the lunch basket. I crawled forward on the pontoon until I was out from under the wing, and stood. Diving in, I swam out from the plane, turning to watch Jimmy slide off the pontoon and swim toward me.

I headed out into the lake, doing the crawl. The water was perfect. It felt good to stretch my arms and legs and feel the pull of my muscles against the water's resistance. Jimmy followed but couldn't match my pace. I circled and headed back toward the plane, meeting him halfway.

"If you want, you can dive off the edge of my cockpit," he offered. "The water's plenty deep."

"Okay," I said and returned to the plane.

I climbed onto the pontoon and up into his cockpit. Standing on the seat, I stretched my arms over my head, locking my fingers and looking at the sky, then down at Jimmy. I felt a tingle of excitement as I saw his eyes moving up and down my body. Climbing onto the edge of the cockpit, I stood straight up and dove. I surfaced just in front of Jimmy. He took my face in his hands and said,

"You're beautiful. I could watch you dive all day." I could feel his breath against my face.

"You're nice," I said, then raised my arms above my head and sank out of sight. I swam underwater to the plane and came up next to the pontoon. "Let's eat."

Halfway through lunch, I asked about his court hearing.

"Oh, that," he said offhandedly. "Nothing to worry about. I'll just tell my dad and he'll take care of it."

"No kidding?"

"Sure," he said with a hint of arrogance. "He helped the governor get elected. All he has to do is make a phone call."

I raised my glass, still with a little champagne left in it, and said, "Here's to your dad."

Jimmy took a sip and nodded. "He's okay. Could be a lot worse."

Sore subject, I thought. Better stay clear of it.

We said nothing for a while, then he spoke. "Dad likes to throw his weight around." And to justify himself, "But I'm doing all right on my own. I made a deal with him. Instead of his sending me to college, I told him I wanted an airplane. One I could use for business. He figured I'd flunk out of college anyway because my grades were pretty poor in prep school, so he agreed. Part of the deal was for him to pay for my flight training. I went to the Ryan School of Aeronautics in San Diego. Spent two years out there. Did well, too." His expression begged my approval. "Now I've got a commercial license and I'm qualified to fly transports."

"Wow! I'm impressed." I meant it, too. "Do you mean you can fly those big two- and three-engine airplanes that land at Boston?"

"I already have. That was part of our training."

"So, are you going to do that?"

He looked at me, a confident smile on his face. "I'm doing better than that. I'm starting the DeWolf Flying Service," he said, sketching the words in the air with his hand as if painting a sign.

"You mean your own company?"

"Yup, and I've already started. I told you I couldn't get to Marblehead in time for the wedding yesterday. Well, I had my first job. My dad had gotten a rush order of Moët champagne for a party in Portland, Maine, and I flew up six cases. I covered expenses plus a little profit."

"Congratulations!" I said, winning another smile from Jimmy.

"You see, that's what I plan to do. With my Waco, here, I can fly rush orders that have to get someplace by a certain time. I can carry parts for boats that break down at sea or do fish spotting for the big fishing companies. I can take two people on fishing or hunting trips out into the wilds of Maine. The possibilities are endless."

I was beginning to think there was more to Jimmy than I'd first seen. "But what'll you do in the winter?" I asked. "Doesn't it all freeze up?"

"Oh, I have a set of wheels for the Waco. And if I get customers for winter hunting trips, I can put skis over the wheels."

I laughed. "Sure beats waiting tables."

"Well, I don't expect you're going to wait tables all your life. All those rich guys that come to the hotel," he said with a grin, "one of 'em's going to ask you to marry him."

"Of course," I said, affecting a blasé voice. "Turned three down yesterday."

Jimmy laughed and slipped off the pontoon into the water. "Come on, I want to show you a neat place I found on shore."

"Sorry," I said in my best matron voice. "We have to wait an hour before going swimming."

"Becky, get in the water," he ordered.

"Yes sir," I said, and joined him. We swam to an opening in the rushes where a stream flowed into the lake. On one side was a sandbank.

"Time to stretch out on the sand and rest for an hour," he said, smiling. "Then we don't have to worry about getting cramps when we swim back to the plane." He lay down and beckoned me to lie down beside him. Here it comes, I thought. Time to pay for my plane ride. I stood over him looking down, my shadow falling across his body. His shoulders were broad but not as muscular as Karl's. His waist and hips were narrow and I could see a bulge in the swimming trunks. He'd tucked his right hand under his head and laid his left arm straight out. Drops of water glistened on his chest. How easy it would be to kneel, straddle his legs, and cover his body with mine.

Instead I said, "You know, Mr. DeWolf, I'll lie down and I'll even put my head on your outstretched arm, but that's all I plan to do."

"Suit yourself," he said easily. He didn't sound like he was laying a trap for seduction, so I relaxed beside him. I could feel my right arm against his side, the back of my hand against his wet trunks, and his moist thigh pressed against mine. The sun warmed my stomach but I had to close my eyes against the bright blue of the sky.

In a dreamy voice he said, "I've always wanted to fly. I was ten when Lindbergh flew the Atlantic. He was my hero." He closed his eyes, lost in his childhood memories. "Dad used to take me to barnstorming shows and I'd watch the Gypsy Moths and Tiger Moths dogfight in the air and do loops and barrel rolls with smoke streaming out of their tails. I went up once when I was fifteen in a Flying Jenny. The pilot let me hold the stick for a short while. I knew right then I'd be a pilot someday."

Suddenly I realized I was rubbing my little toe against his little toe. I didn't mean it to be suggestive and he didn't seem to take it that way. It fit naturally with our being alone, lying side by side on that little piece of sand by a lake deep in the woods.

I turned my head toward him so that my cheek rested on his upper arm. "I'll paint DeWolf Flying Service on the side of your Waco if you'd like."

He sat up and leaned on his left elbow, letting my head flop back on the sand. "Would you do that, Becky?"

"Sure. I'd love to."

He turned his body toward me, shading my eyes with his head, and stroked my hair with his right hand. The sun behind his blond head created a yellow halo. "You *are* a sweetheart," he said softly, bringing his lips to mine. We kissed.

It was now or never and I decided it had better be now or I was a goner. I sat up, easing him to one side, and stood. "I should be getting back. I've still got the dinner hour to do."

"Aw, come on Becky, lie back down. We've got plenty of time." The bulge in his swim trunks was noticeably larger and he made no attempt to hide it.

"Too much of a rush, young man, and it wouldn't be fair to Mom to stick her with dinner too."

Reaching down to pull him up, I said, "Wouldn't it be neat to have a tent here and a little campfire to cook dinner on?"

"Would you like to do that sometime?" he said. "I mean sleep over, here?"

I took his two hands in mine and, standing with my face next to his, said, "I think I would, Jimmy, but first I'd like to get to know you a little better."

"Let's see what we can do about that," he said and gave me a quick kiss. Then he turned and ran into the water, calling over his shoulder, "Race you to the plane."

15

Climbing down from the forward cockpit, I stood on the pontoon as Jimmy brought the plane next to the hotel dock. When it was a foot away, I jumped onto the dock and he gunned the engine, moving the Waco out into the boat channel that runs between the shoreline and the boat moorings. As he taxied away, the prop wash caught his yellow scarf, sending it fluttering into the water. He gestured with his hands to forget it, then waved and blew me a kiss. I touched my lips to my palm and blew my kiss to him. With the lunch basket in my left hand, I watched him until he disappeared around the yacht club.

At the end of the dock was a boat hook which I used to retrieve the scarf as it drifted by. The bell in Abbot Hall tower was ringing six o'clock as I turned and ran up the path to the hotel.

Monday was my day off, but there were no phone calls for me nor airplanes pulling up to the dock. I moped about my room until ten. All I could think about was Jimmy. I could feel his hands on my face when we were just inches apart in the water. I saw him lying on the sand with his arm outstretched asking me to lie down beside him. I could taste his lips as he bent over me on the sand and kissed me. Why didn't he call? By Wednesday, when I'd heard nothing, I started to lose hope. Clara and Estelle, who thought there was a real romance getting under way between Jimmy and me, tried to lift my spirits. They said he was probably busy making money and would call as soon as he could. By Thursday afternoon I was sure it was over. Then Mom called me from the reception desk. "There's a phone call for you, Becky."

I rushed to the desk.

"Hi, Becky? This is Jimmy."

I slid around the corner to talk in private. I felt tongue-tied. "Well, hello, stranger," I said limply. "I thought you'd forgotten all about me."

"How could I forget you? No, I've been busy getting letters out."

"Good for you, but—"

"I know," he interrupted, "and I'm sorry. Look, I've got to be in Salem tomorrow for the hearing—yeah, I know—it's a long story and I'll tell you about it. Can you come with me?"

"I've got to work. What time is it?"

"Ten o'clock."

"Well, come by at nine-thirty and I'll see if I can get off."

"Christ, Becky, your folks own the hotel. Just do it."

"It's not like that, Jimmy. I'll see. Come by at nine-thirty."

I could tell by the way he hung up he was annoyed. Now I wondered if he'd come at all.

He didn't fly. He drove. At nine-thirty sharp a 1939 Buick convertible coupe with the top down pulled into the parking area and Jimmy got out. I did manage to get off work and was waiting for him in the lobby, dressed in a light blue cotton dress with short sleeves and a zipper down the front. I carried a white purse on a long strap over my shoulder. Jimmy had dressed for the hearing in brown slacks, a tan sport coat, white shirt, and a dark brown knit tie. I met him on the steps and we walked to the car.

"So, you did get off?" His tone was abrupt.

"So you see."

"Good. I appreciate you coming with me." I was glad to hear that.

"So, what happened about the hearing?"

"It's simple. Dad refused to call anybody. Said if I was going to horse around in my plane, I'd have to pay the consequences. I told him I'd done nothing wrong, that it was just some jerkwater cop who wanted to make a name for himself, but he wouldn't listen."

I looked at him as he drove. What a little boy's face he has when he's mad, I thought. "Did you get a lawyer?" I asked.

"Screw the lawyers. I've got to pay for this myself so I'm not hiring any goddamned lawyer. I'll just explain to the judge that the minimum altitude limit doesn't apply because I was over water." We drove for a few blocks in silence. "Maybe you'll bring me good luck."

"Lord, Jimmy, don't say that. If they fine you then it'll be my fault for not bringing you luck."

"I didn't mean it that way." His voice softened. "I'm just glad you're here." He looked at me and smiled that big, warm smile of his. Right then I felt I'd follow him anywhere.

We parked at the Salem courthouse and before long were sitting on a bench in one of the courtrooms. James DeWolf was the fifth name called. Jimmy went up to the rail and the judge read the charge, asking him how he pled.

"Not guilty, Your Honor." He then went into an explanation of the law regarding minimum altitudes, saying there was no minimum over water unless there were boats present and then it was five hundred feet. "And Your Honor, I was never below five hundred feet the whole time."

I was no expert on heights but I knew darned well I looked straight across at Jimmy from my balcony and that's not five hundred feet.

"What about the charge of disturbing the peace?" the judge continued. "Understand you did some acrobatics. That sounds like noise to me."

"Yes, sir, I did one loop and I guess it was a little noisy."

"Okay. We'll drop the charges of flying too low and fine you fifty dollars for disturbing the peace." Wham went his gavel. "Next case."

"But . . ."

"No buts. Pay the clerk the money," said the judge, pointing toward a woman sitting at the end of the rail.

Jimmy shrugged and walked over to the clerk, taking out his checkbook. He wrote the check and came back to where I was sitting. "Let's get out of here." I got up and followed him out of the courtroom and out of the building.

"Shit!" he said. "Now I've got to get fifty dollars into my account damned quick."

"You mean you haven't got it?" I asked, dumbfounded. "You wrote a bad check to a clerk of the court?"

"Don't worry, Becky, it's okay. I've got a trust fund and I get my monthly payment tomorrow. It'll more than cover the fifty bucks." He stopped and, taking hold of my shoulders, turned me toward him. He brought his face close to mine and said, "It's okay. Now let's go to lunch."

"And pay with what?" I asked suspiciously.

He laughed. "You are a Depression child, aren't you? Always worried about money and jobs and working." He pulled my arm through his and led me toward the car. "I've plenty of money in my pocket. Don't worry."

We drove in silence for a block and then Jimmy burst out laughing. "Wanna know something else? The minimum altitude for loops is fifteen hundred feet and the judge didn't know it. He really could have nailed me."

I shook my head, dismayed.

We came to the Hawthorne Hotel in Salem and parked on a side street. The dining room was much larger than ours but no more elegant. We were seated by the window. Jimmy ordered a bottle of wine with a name that sounded impressive but meant nothing to me and proceeded to go through the ritual of tasting it after the waiter did the uncorking.

"I'm glad that's over. The hearing, I mean. Fifty bucks isn't so bad to add a little life to an otherwise dull wedding reception."

"I thought you had a good time."

"Yeah, it wasn't all bad. The champagne helped a lot."

"What do you mean?"

"That party was one of the toughest times of my life."

"Really? Why?"

"Oh, they were impressed as hell about my arriving in the Waco and doing the loop, but they expect me to do things like that. I'm the clown that livens up the party."

"Oh, come on, Jimmy, I can't believe they feel that way."

"And you know what else? I'm beginning to feel like a little kid around them. Hugh, the guy that got married, is starting med school next fall. Another guy you don't know is going to Columbia Law School. Shirley, one of the girls, is going to Europe to study at the Sorbonne. And about half the people there got married last month after college graduation. Jeff—hell, Jeff was my drinking buddy. He's going to be a vice president in his dad's real estate company." He took a sip of the wine and looked out the window. "And me, I do loops in an airplane so everybody'll laugh and have a good time."

I reached across the table, taking his hand in mine and leaning toward him. He looked up and our eyes met. "How many can fly an airplane like you do? How many can pilot an airliner with thirty or forty passengers on board? How many have started their own company? I think you're great, and you can make me laugh anytime you want."

He took his other hand and placed it over mine. And there it was, that smile of his. "Becky, you're about the nicest thing that's ever happened to me. I mean that."

"You'd better mean it, because if you don't, you're going to have to stop melting me with your smiles."

He laughed. "I mean it."

"So, when do I start painting 'DeWolf Flying Service' on the Waco?"

"Whenever you say."

"Got a pen?" I asked, taking a to-do list out of my purse and turning it over. He handed me a pen. "Here's what I think. The 'DeWolf' should be in a flowing script, big letters, with 'Flying Service' in smaller block letters underneath. Like it?"

"Hey, that's great. We could put one on each side of the fuselage. Tell you what. I'll pull it out of the water—I keep it at the amphibious ramp at Boston Airport—and we'll do it there. I'll get the paint and the brushes. When are you free?"

"I'm never free," I said slyly.

"Ohhh. It'll cost me then?" he said, raising one eyebrow.

"Yeah. The cost is meaning it when you say I'm the best thing that's ever happened to you."

"You're on. When do we start?"

"Monday morning. I'll drive down. Where do I meet you?"

"At the seaplane hangar on the north side of the airport."

*   *   *

Sunday I was eating lunch with Mom and Dad in the hotel kitchen before the dining room opened.

"So, I've seen Jimmy DeWolf around here a couple of times," Dad was saying.

I smiled. "Isn't that the truth!"

"You getting serious?" he asked.

"Well, I wouldn't mind if we did, but I'm not sure how far this will go."

Mom asked, "Isn't he kind of a wild kid? I hear he couldn't settle down enough to go to college."

I could feel myself getting defensive. The two of them must have planned this conversation. "He spent two years at a school for aviation in California and got himself certified to fly airliners. That sounds pretty responsible to me."

"Becky," Mom went on, "I'm not trying to start an argument. It's just that he comes from a very rich family that are way above our social class." She set down her fork and looked at me intently. "Seriously, would you feel comfortable going to some of the social functions he's expected to attend?"

"Like what?"

"Well, I don't know. Probably receptions for the governor or formal balls at the Ritz-Carlton."

"Sounds pretty nice to me," I said defiantly.

"Calm down now, Becky," Dad urged. "Nobody's going to tell you what to do."

"You're right about that," I said with my chin raised.

He continued, "It's just that we don't want you to get hurt."

"Look," I said with a sigh, "I'm eighteen years old, I've graduated from high school and I'm a mature young woman. A lot of kids in my class are already married." Then, for emphasis, I said, "I'm grown up. I can take care of myself."

"Well, sweetheart," Dad said, "I hope so because we want only the best for you."

"And Becky," Mother said taking my hand, "please be careful. He runs with a fast crowd."

I looked at her, mentally counting to ten, then answered, "I will, Mother."

* * *

Monday morning Dad let me drive the Studebaker to East Boston. I parked behind the hangar located near the water on the north side of the airport. Dressed in shorts and blouse and sandals, with a bandanna around my head, I drew some whistles from the mechanics in the hangar. The Waco was pulled up onto the ramp and Jimmy, standing on a platform beside the engine, waved and hollered, "Here, put these on." He threw me a pair of overalls. "It'll keep the paint off your clothes and their eyes off your legs."

I liked that. He was jealous, or maybe just being solicitous.

Jimmy jumped down from the platform. "I've missed you."

"Me too," I said. "What're you doing?"

"Changing spark plugs." He had a wrench in his right hand. He laid it down on the platform and began wiping his hands on a rag. "I've got the paint here and the brushes."

"I thought I'd sketch it out first with a soft pencil until we get it like we want it."

"Good idea, but be careful. The fuselage is just painted fabric and the tip of the pencil could go right through it."

I'd had about as much work talk as I could stand. I walked up to Jimmy, putting my hand behind his head and massaging the back of his neck. Bringing my face close to his, I asked, "Have you really missed me?"

His eyes flicked over to the mechanics in the hangar, then back at me. "God, Becky, they'll see you."

I pulled his head even closer to mine. "Well, have you?"

"Yes! Yes, I have."

"Good." I laughed. "Keep it up." I released him and put on the overalls.

For the next two hours I sketched and painted the name on the fuselage and Jimmy worked on the engine. When I finished one side, I stepped back and looked at it. Not bad, I thought.

"Hey, Jimmy, come and look at my handiwork."

He jumped down and, wiping his hands on the rag, walked around the wing to where I was working just behind the cockpit. He slipped his arm around me, glancing at the hangar to be sure no one was looking. "Becky, that is beautiful. 'DeWolf Flying Service.' By God, it looks like we're in business."

"It does look good, doesn't it?"

"And you know what I like most?" He tightened his arm around my shoulder. "You and me working together. I've never known a girl who wanted to work with me on my plane."

I slipped my arm around his waist. Out of the corner of my eye I caught sight of a woman striding toward us. She looked to be about twenty-five and wore tan slacks and a white blouse. Long dark hair fell down her back, and her ample breasts bounced with each determined step. Her jaw was set and her eyes flashing. She came around the tail of the plane and stopped within slapping distance of Jimmy.

"There you are, you goddamn son of a bitch! I thought I'd find you here."

"Felicia!" Jimmy said, stepping back and dropping his arm from my shoulder. "What are you doing here?"

"You bastard. Why didn't you tell me you stole that mailing list from your father?"

"Stole it?" Jimmy said defensively. "I didn't steal it. Hell, it's my dad's. How could I steal it?"

"Well, he says you stole it—that you had no right to mail your letters to his friends and business associates."

"Come on, Felicia, cool off," Jimmy said in a labored voice. "I can straighten it out with Dad."

"Oh yeah, that's fine for you. You always take care of good ol' Jimmy. But what about me? I got fired." Jimmy flinched. "Yeah, fired by your father for helping you."

"I'm really sorry, Felicia. But I don't see why he fired you. You didn't address that stuff on company time. We did it at your place." Jimmy's expression did an abrupt oh-oh, and he attempted to recover by hurrying on. "He can't fire you for that."

"Oh, yeah? Well, he did. Said I took the list from the files and took them home. Which, of course, I did." And then she screamed at him, "Because you told me it was okay, you louse."

I looked at Felicia and asked calmly, "And when did you two work on this mailing list?"

"Ha!" She laughed in my face. "Each night for the last week, and, honey, we worked pretty late, too." Then to Jimmy, "Who's this? Your new girlfriend?" His face turned pink. "You bastard," she said emphatically, "I got the mailing out for you and the famous DeWolf Flying Service, and now you dump me."

Jimmy glanced at me with an expression of total innocence and said to Felicia, "You know perfectly well we just had a working agreement."

"Humph! Working agreement my ass." Then she broke into tears. "After all I did for you, too. And now I'm out of work. Have you got any idea how hard it is to get a job?" She stomped off, stopping by the tail and yelling to me through her tears, "Has he flown you down to the lake on Cape Cod yet?" Then she turned and ran.

We stood side by side for a moment. Then I unhooked the overalls and let them drop to the ground. Stepping out of them, I glared at Jimmy. "You really are a louse, aren't you?"

I cried most of the way home. When I wasn't crying, I was calling Jimmy every cuss word I knew. That asshole, I said to myself, was screwing Felicia all last week while I was home wondering why he hadn't called. And then, when he calls, I follow him like a loyal puppy to the Salem courthouse. And today, "Oh Becky, I've missed you sooo much." Yeah, help me work on my plane and I'll pay you with a tumble in bed just like I did with Felicia.

But I was just as mad at myself. What a stoop to fall for that line of his, "You're the greatest thing that ever happened to me."

Then, into my mind floated pictures of myself flying in his airplane, looking down at the tops of buildings in Boston, feeling the excitement of sideslipping into the lake. I could still feel his arm around my waist, my face in his hands, his wet body pressing against my side. I could see myself again riding in his Buick, his hand touching my knee as he shifted into third, the wind blowing through my hair, and envy on the faces of girls we'd pass. I want that, I thought. I'm tired of waiting tables. I want to go to the kind of parties Jimmy goes to. I want to have fun and I want to have it with Jimmy. Jimmy with the handsome face and blond hair and big smile. I want him to love me and nobody else. What I don't want is for him to be the jerk he's being.

In Swampscott I had to stop because I couldn't see the road through my tears.

I decided not to go back to the hotel and have Mom or Dad see me. They'd know for sure I'd been crying and, whether they said it or not, they'd be thinking, "We told you so." I needed to talk to somebody, but who? Then I thought of Aggie. It was a little after noon, so she should be at the commercial pier helping her dad unload lobsters.

I'd known Aggie since we were little kids. We grew up best friends. But last October, on my birthday, we had a blowup. She had this big surprise planned for my birthday and I forgot. Actually, I'd been looking forward to it until Karl Kramer, the captain of our football team, asked me to go dancing at the Fo'cas'le Ballroom the same night. I was so excited I forgot all about Aggie and her surprise. On the afternoon of my birthday, Karl drove me home to the hotel and said he'd be back in a couple of hours to pick me up. When I walked into the lobby there was Aggie, all dressed up and waiting for me. Oh no, I thought. Now I've done it. I begged her forgiveness and asked her to change the surprise to another night. She was furious and ran out of the hotel. Later Mother told me that Aggie had bought tickets to a play in Boston and was even planning to take me out for dinner. I felt awful. I tried to apologize but she wouldn't talk to me for weeks.

Finally I admitted to myself that she wanted more than just a friendship and was jealous of my boyfriends. There wasn't much I was willing to do about that. When we got our yearbooks, however, I asked her to sign mine. She hesitated at first, then wrote, "Your friend forever, Aggie." I hugged her and told her how much her friendship meant to me. I wrote in hers, "To a true friend who's always there when I need her, Becky." This eased things between us and we started getting together again for an occasional movie or a sundae at Howard's.

Now I knew it was Aggie's shoulder I wanted to cry on.

I parked a block away and walked to the pier past several trucks belonging to lobstermen. From the top of the ramp I looked down at three lobster boats, tied stern to, unloading boxes of lobsters onto the dock. The middle boat was *Bright Star*, belonging to Aggie's father. There was Aggie unloading the last five boxes. I hailed her and waved.

A rubber apron covered her overalls, and her pant legs were tucked into rubber boots. The sleeves of her work shirt were rolled up. Aggie looked every bit a lobsterman even to her deeply tanned face and strong arms. Her brown hair was bobbed and, though she tried to hide her good looks, her subtle beauty shone through. She gave me one of her quick, self-conscious smiles and waved back.

"Don't just stand there, come on down."

The tide was out, so the ramp to the dock was steep. Twelve boxes brimming with brownish green lobsters were stacked behind *Bright Star.* Mr. Sparr was hosing down the deck. He was dressed like Aggie, but didn't look at all like her. In his late fifties, he had a long, big-boned face and gray hair that curled tightly. A long mustache hung down around the corners of his mouth, in which a half-smoked cigarette was tucked. Aggie's looks came from her mother, who died when Aggie was sixteen.

"Good haul, Mr. Sparr," I said.

"Not bad," he said with a shrug, closing one eye against the smoke from his cigarette. "Not as good as it used to be."

"Don't believe him," Aggie said. "He's never satisfied. How you doing?"

"Okay, I guess. Need a hand?"

"Yeah. Help me get these up the ramp and then we'll go get some lunch. You eaten yet?"

"No. Lunch sounds good."

We stacked one box on another and, with Aggie pulling on a long steel hook and me pushing, slid the boxes across the wet dock, lifted them one at a time onto the ramp, and pushed them up the steep incline to the top of the quay. I didn't realize a box holding about thirty lobsters could weigh so much. By the time we finished, I was exhausted. Aggie's dad yelled at us to go ahead on home and he'd take care of weighing out the lobsters.

It was only two blocks to Aggie's house, so we walked. I opened a can of Campbell's chicken soup and heated it on the stove while she took a shower. Then we sat on her back porch and had soup, bakery bread, and coffee.

Aggie had changed from her wet, smelly blue jeans and blue work shirt to a clean pair of blue jeans and a pressed work shirt. Her hair was still wet from the shower. She had a strong, taut face.

"You don't look so hot," she said. "What's wrong?"

So I told her.

"Want my advice?" she said. "Forget Jimmy. He'll only cause you pain."

Her bluntness took me aback. I decided to let it pass. "The trouble is, I don't want to forget him."

"Do you love him?" Her voice was cold and matter-of-fact.

"God, Aggie, will you show a little compassion? I had a hell of a morning. I don't know what I feel right now."

"Sorry."

We sat in silence for a while, gazing in different directions. Then I picked up my napkin, dabbed at my mouth, and started to get up.

"I'm sorry I came by, Aggie. Sorry I bothered you with this."

Aggie jumped up and, circling the table, put her arms around me. "No. Don't go, Becky." She hugged me. "I'm such a bitch sometimes. I do want to hear about this. I am glad you came to me."

"Aggie," I said with tears in my eyes for the second time in two hours, "you're my friend. I've got nobody else I can talk to. I need your friendship."

"You've got it, baby. Please forgive me." We held each other for a full minute, then relaxed our arms and returned to our seats.

"You asked if I love him," I said. "I'm not sure. I love the way he looks. I love his enthusiasm about flying. He's exciting to be with. He's got a beautiful car. He's also spoiled and selfish and irresponsible. The thing is, he seems to need a girl hanging around him most of the time to give him reassurance."

I sighed. "I think Felicia was willing to do anything, including going to bed, just to be around him."

"Are you?"

"I haven't yet."

"Uh-huh! And as soon as you do, you'll be like all the rest. Now you're different. You're a challenge."

On Wednesday a hand-delivered letter was dropped in our mailbox. It was addressed to me. I took it up to my room to read it.

Dear Becky,

I have an appointment with the OYC this morning about the DeWolf Flying Service so I thought I would drop this note by to you. I think you were mean to walk off without giving me a chance to explain about Felicia and the letters we mailed out. The fact that you assumed the worst shows what a low opinion you have of me. After the fun we had on the Cape, I would think you could show a little trust, at least enough to give me a chance to explain. Sure I dated Felicia and I'll admit we were very close a few times. And I did take her to the little lake twice, but hell, Becky, she was my girlfriend. All that happened before I met you. So last week, when we were mailing out the letters at her house, I used that time to break up. It was hard for her and that's why she came storming down to the airport. That, and the fact Dad fired her. That stuff about stealing the mailing list from Dad is bullshit. The only possible reason he could object to my mailing announcement letters to his friends and associates is his lack of confidence in my new company.

So I think you did me dirt when you walked off on me. I would appreciate an apology.

Regards, Jimmy

I set the letter down and stared blankly into space for about two minutes, then picked it up and read it again. I couldn't believe anyone could be so egotistical and insensitive.

But it's hard to be mad at a letter so blatantly stupid. He's such a kid, I thought. I lay down on the chaise and began to analyze the situation. At least he cares enough about me to write this ridiculous letter and to hand-deliver it. And it sounds like he wants us to get back together—which, in his terms, means an apology from me. So, I guess it's up to me if I want to make something of this.

But do I want to? Do I care that much about Jimmy?

This thought rolled around my mind for several minutes, bouncing against my feelings. I knew I didn't love Jimmy yet, but I loved the things I could do with him. And if it ever came to making love, he had a sexy body.

At the same time he was unreliable, deceitful, and probably downright dishonest, all attributes that flash caution signals. But I wanted to try.

I'm probably nuts, I decided, but I'm going to give him a whirl. Then I laid out my plan.

Friday morning I begged off waiting tables for breakfast and drove to Boston Airport. Before I left, I called the hangar and asked one of the mechanics if DeWolf's Waco was still on the ramp. It was. I parked and peeked around the fence to be sure Jimmy wasn't there, and then walked to the plane. In the front cockpit I found the overalls rolled up and the paint and brushes on the floor. Two hours later I finished painting "DeWolf Flying Service" on the other side of the fuselage. Then I climbed into the cockpit and wrote Jimmy a note.

Dear Jimmy,

I promised I'd paint the name on the plane and I have. If you're still interested in seeing me, give me a call and we'll set up a time to talk.

Regards, Becky

I went home, waited tables for the luncheon period, and called the catering department at the Ritz in Boston. I told the salesgirl who answered the phone that I wanted to give my mother and father a twenty-fifth wedding anniversary present by paying their way to a special event at the Ritz. "Can you tell me," I asked, "what important functions are scheduled for August?"

She wanted to know what kind of things and I said large parties that people would pay to attend like charity balls. She told me there was a Jewish refugee relief organization having a fund-raising dinner on August third, and the Consolidated Charities of Greater Boston was holding a ball on the eleventh.

"That's the one," I said. "Do you have a name I can call for reservations?" She gave me a name and telephone number. I thanked her and immediately called the number. I asked if there was still room for another couple at the dance and how much was the contribution. She said I could be a sponsor for a thousand dollars (I gasped) or a contributing supporter for five hundred (I gasped again). I asked what I would have to contribute for a couple just to get in.

"Oh," she said disparagingly. "That would be fifty dollars. And what is the name, please?"

"I'll get back to you. Thanks."

Jimmy called that evening in the middle of the dinner period, wouldn't you know. I took the call anyway.

"Hello."

"Hi, Becky."

"So you went to your plane."

"Yeah. Thanks for painting the rest of the sign."

"You're welcome. I said I would."

"I know. Thanks." Pause. "You want to talk?"

"I think that would be a good idea." Long pause. "Still there, Jimmy?"

"You're not going to apologize, are you?"

"No. Are you?"

"Me? What for?"

No, I told myself. Don't get into it. I paused, then said, "Well, I did finish painting the sign."

"So you did." Pause. "Okay, guess we ought to talk."

"Do you really want to, or should we forget the whole thing?"

"You mean about Felicia?"

"No!"—I started to add "stupid" but thought better of it—"I mean you and me. Forget this whole business of you and me together."

"Gosh, no, Becky. I don't want to forget about us."

"Then let's talk."

"Okay, I'll pick you up tomorrow morning at nine."

"Make it ten. I've got to serve breakfast."

"Oh, okay."

"Car. Not airplane."

The next morning it was raining. Top up, we drove to Redd's Pond below Marblehead's Old Burial Hill. From the car window we watched four mallard ducks swimming in the rain.

"Look at that," I said. "One male and three females."

"How do you know?"

"The plumage. The colorful one is the male. The plain brown ones are female."

"Lucky duck." He laughed.

"Oh, I don't know. Too many females might get him in trouble."

"Huh," he muttered as if he had been hit. Then he put his arm around my shoulder and pulled me to him. I went.

"I've missed you, Becky."

"Oh-oh," I said accusingly. "The last time you said that, you weren't missing me much. What have you been up to the last few days?"

"Nothing. Honest. And you might not believe this, but I was missing you even when I was working on the mailing."

"Uh-huh," I said, turning and looking him in the eye. "Seriously. Do you really mean that? Jimmy, do you really like me?"

He pressed his hand against my cheek, gently massaging my ear with the tip of his fingers. His other arm pulled me even closer and we kissed. His lips were soft and moist. After a moment, he moved his head back slightly and smiled. I wanted to smile too, but couldn't. I had to hear him say it.

"Jimmy, do you like me?"

"Jesus, Becky, you are insistent. Yes, yes, yes, I like you. There, now, are you happy?"

I hunched up so my knees were in his lap, took his face in my two hands, and kissed him so hard our teeth clicked.

"Wow!" he exclaimed.

"Now," I demanded, "tell me why you like me."

"Oh, boy!" he moaned. "All right. I like you because you're beautiful," pause. "Because you're fun to be with, and . . . because you like to help me with my plane."

"You're almost right, Jimmy. I am beautiful and I am fun to be with. But from now on I'm going to do more for you than little odd jobs or standing around while you work on your plane." He drew back guardedly. "I'm going to be your partner."

"Partner? What do you mean? You can't fly."

"No, but let me put it this way." I sat back in the seat. "How's business going?"

Surprised, he said, "It's going."

"Any new business lined up?"

"Not yet. But wait a minute, what's this got to do with us?"

"A lot." I continued my questioning. "Have you been by to see the fishing companies yet? Or the yacht clubs, other than the OYC?"

"No, but I've made some phone calls."

"Good." I smiled, then switched back to my serious face. "Another thing. Your company, don't you need a business permit and insurance to carry passengers and freight?"

Jimmy looked at me distrustfully. "What the hell business is this of yours? Christ, I let you paint a sign on my plane and it sounds like you're taking over."

"Maybe I should. It's pretty damned clear you don't know the first thing about running a company."

"Well, thanks a lot, lady. And just what the hell do you know about flying an airplane?" He pulled his hands away and squirmed behind the wheel.

"Absolutely nothing. But listen. I've been thinking about this a lot. How much business are you going to lose if nobody's there to take your phone calls while you're out flying? If you're working on your plane, who's going to take care of getting a business permit if you need one? Who's going to call on customers and show them flashy pictures of the Waco and tell them all the services the company can give them, while you're changing sparkplugs? Do you see what I mean?"

He sat looking out the windshield, blinking his eyes about every five seconds. He actually appeared to be thinking.

"Hmmm, I see what you mean. And I assume the person who is going to do all this is you."

"That's right. That's why I'm going to be your partner."

"So you'd go to the fishing companies and the yacht clubs?"

"Yes, and do follow-up calls on people you mailed letters to."

"Hmmm." Sounded like he was thinking again.

"I hope you're serious about making the DeWolf Flying Service a success," I said, "because I sure as hell am."

He turned and smiled, sticking his face toward mine for a kiss.

Bringing my finger up to his lips, I said, "And one more thing."

He pulled back, tilting his head warily.

"You said I was fun to be with, and I am."

"Uh-huh."

"Well, on August eleventh, you're taking me to the Consolidated Charities Ball at the Ritz."

"I am ?"

"Yes. You are. It's black tie, so wear your tux." I swiveled my hips until I pressed against him and again brought my knees into his lap. Then I gave him a long, deep kiss that I hoped he'd remember when they told him the minimum contribution was fifty dollars.

17

I love to dream I'm flying. Not in a plane. Like a bird. I know just how to do it. I start by running and with each stride take longer and longer steps. Then I fix my mind on the belief I can fly and, holding that thought, lift my head and soar into the sky over the town and the countryside.

It's like that for me now. I've fixed my mind on making something happen, and it's happening.

Getting Jimmy to agree to take me to the ball was the final touch. What fun Aggie and I had buying the gown!

"What I want," I told her, "is a gown that makes me look about twenty-five, shows off my figure, and creates an aura of dignified mystery and sophistication." I did a couple of quick twirls, flaring my cotton skirt well above my knees.

Aggie watched admiringly and laughed. "Well, you've got the looks and the body. Have you got the money?"

"Hope so. I took all my savings out of the bank. I'm willing to go for broke on this."

We visited several dress shops on Tremont Street in Boston, finally settling on one where a woman with a French accent assured us she had just the gown. Silk, in oyster white with a pattern of large red orchids, its halter top was cut sufficiently low to offer an enticing view and the back even lower. The skirt was tight around the hips and cut very narrow with a slit up one side to making walking possible. Long white gloves set off the ensemble.

Together they cost more than I spend on all my clothes for an entire year. Mom would kill me if she knew.

Then I tried on several pairs of shoes in four different stores until we found just the right ones, white with very high heels.

"But won't these make you taller than Jimmy?"

I laughed. "Hope so."

Aggie insisted we visit the cosmetics section of Jordan Marsh. "It's time you learned how to do makeup." I sat on a stool while a middle-aged woman in a white smock applied this and rubbed on that, plucked eyebrows and applied eyebrow pencil and eye shadow, touched up eyelashes, applied just the right shade of lipstick, and highlighted my cheekbones with a hint of rouge.

When the woman removed the towel from my shoulders, Aggie stepped back to have a look. "God, Becky. You're a dream."

I turned to the mirror. "Is that me?"

It was and I looked just as good as I hoped I would. No longer a teenager struggling for that grown-up look but a young woman, vibrant and alluring, yet with a suggestion that I was holding back even more than I was revealing.

The woman totaled the bill and handed it to me.

"I can't do this. It's a fortune."

But Aggie snatched it up and paid it, stuffing the jars and tubes into my purse. "This is my treat. Call it an early birthday present."

August eleventh arrived, and Jimmy and I pulled up in front of the Ritz in his Buick. The uniformed doorman opened my door and, taking my elbow, assisted me from the car. I waited at the curb while Jimmy turned the car over to the parking attendant. Not bad, I thought, arriving at the Ritz in a Buick convertible, standing at the entrance while the elite of Boston pass by me into the hotel.

Jimmy came around the front of the car, stopped for a moment, then took my hands in his and looked at me. "Becky, you look sensational." I could tell he really meant it.

With my arm through his, he led me across the carpeted entrance to the door, held open by another doorman, and into the hotel foyer. We passed two or three clusters of people in formal dress, laughing and greeting one another, and headed up the curved staircase leading to the second level and the ballroom. Three elderly women sat at a desk by the entrance checking off names of guests. As Jimmy talked with them, I held my head high and gazed confidently at other women also waiting for husbands and dates to check in.

Then Jimmy came and took my arm and we entered the ballroom, he looking handsome in his tux, I in my silk gown which slipped sensuously against my legs with each step. The glances from people we passed confirmed what I felt, that we were a striking couple.

The ballroom was two stories high, and tall windows were hung with royal blue draperies trimmed in gold braid. At the far end of the room was an orchestra stand where one of Boston's favorites, the Eddie Rich Band, was playing "Deep Purple." Round tables spread with fine linen were placed about the room, although most people were standing or dancing. Potted palms, flanking the bandstand and in the corners of the ballroom, added a rich touch. We'd not gone twenty feet before a waitress in a black uniform and white apron appeared bearing champagne. At the other end of the room was a sumptuous table filled with mounds of shrimp, trays of oysters on the half shell, an entire smoked salmon, and various cheeses and crackers and cut vegetables. In the center of the table was an ice sculpture portraying a guardian angel. The wall beside the main door held billboard displays of the many institutions served by Consolidated Charities.

The orchestra began "Canadian Sunset," and Jimmy asked me to dance.

We set our glasses on the tray of a passing waitress and moved onto the floor. He was a good dancer, holding me tightly with his right hand firmly in the small of my back. We danced to the rhythm of the foxtrot, Jimmy nodding to people he knew, I swept away by the excitement of the evening and the intimacy of our bodies gliding together.

As the music ended, he gestured toward a couple standing near the windows. "Hey, there's Mike, with Carol. Let's go say hello." We left the dance floor and wended our way through the tables.

"Becky, I'd like you to meet Mike Worzecki and Carol McNash. This is Becky Butler." We said hello and Carol and I complimented each others' dresses. She was five inches shorter than I and was dressed in a rose-colored gown with narrow shoulder straps. She wore her wavy hair shoulder length and had a cute figure. Mike was stocky with a high forehead.

"Mike's a pilot too, Becky," Jimmy said.

"Oh, do you fly professionally?" I asked.

"No." He laughed. "I'm in the fruit business with my father, but we do own a plane."

"Mike and I fly together sometimes," Jimmy said. "Pretend that we're dogfighting like they do in the air shows."

Mike grew serious. "We may be doing it for real, the way things are going these days." When I looked at him blankly, he said, "I mean, it doesn't look so good for Poland, does it?"

"No," Jimmy said. "Hitler's panzers are lined up on the border."

"That's what I mean," said Mike.

"Well, let's hope," Carol said to end the subject. She touched my arm and asked me to go with her to the ladies' room.

"Sure," I said, and to Jimmy, "See you guys later."

After we'd left, Carol whispered to me, "That's all he talks about lately."

"Are you two serious?"

"Not engaged yet, but, yes, we are serious. I pray we don't get involved if there's a war. I'm afraid Mike might try to enlist in the air corps."

When we returned, the subject had changed from war to fighter planes, Spitfires and Messerschmitt-109s.

"Come on, you two," Carol interrupted. "We came here to dance." She took Mike's arm and I took Jimmy's and we pulled them to the dance floor just as the band started "Take the A Train." Jimmy was as good with upbeat music as with slow dance. The other dancers parted somewhat and we found ourselves in a circle of admirers putting on a floor show. When the song finished, they applauded and we laughed and bowed. Carol and Mike drifted off to talk with another couple. Jimmy and I walked to the hors d'oeuvre table.

"Carol's afraid Mike's going to enlist in the air corps," I said.

"Wouldn't surprise me. If England gets in it, I think he'd try to join the RAF."

We each took a small plate and filled it with steamed shrimp which we dipped in sauce. "Hey," Jimmy said, "would you like a drink before we start getting into the food?"

"Another drink?" I said. "I've already had one champagne."

"Then it's time for more. We've got the whole night ahead of us."

"Okay, but I think I'll stick to champagne." Holding the plate in my right hand, I hugged his arm with mine. "Oh, Jimmy, I'm having so much fun. Thanks a million for bringing me."

He looked at me with his boyish smile. "The pleasure's mine."

"You know what I like most?"

"No."

"Being with you." I squeezed his arm again and gave him a quick kiss on the cheek. He beamed.

"Ever had a scotch and soda?" he asked.

"No. Is it okay after champagne?"

"Sure, but be careful," he said, leering. "Scotch lowers a girl's inhibitions."

"I'll be careful and *you* better stay away from the raw oysters."

He laughed and we continued toward the bar. Suddenly he made an abrupt about-face in front of me.

"My God," he whispered. "My parents are over there."

"So, what's wrong with that?" I asked, surprised. "Aren't you supposed to be here?"

"Not that. It's just that I didn't know they were coming." He started to sneak a look over his shoulder, then changed his mind. "Did they see me? Can you tell?"

I leaned my head to the right and looked past his ear. "Well, if your mother's the one in black and gold," I said gleefully, "she's pointing toward us and pulling on your dad's sleeve to look. He's turning this way."

"Oh shit!"

"What's wrong?"

"We're still not on the best of terms." He sighed. "In fact, he's mad as hell at me about the mailing list."

"Hmmm. So, taking the mailing list was no big deal, huh?"

Through his teeth he snarled, "Damn it, Becky, not now."

"You better think of something quick. Here they come." His mother was walking toward us, her husband in tow.

"Jimmy dear, I had no idea you would be here."

Jimmy turned toward his mother, a look of surprise on his face.

"Why, Mom, Dad," his smile strained. "I didn't know you were coming."

"Not coming?" his dad snapped. "You know I'm vice chairman of Consolidated Charities. Of course I'd be coming."

"Oh, I forgot."

"Humph," Mr. DeWolf muttered. "Why the sudden interest in charity?"

"Well . . . I . . ." he stammered.

"I asked him to bring me," I said.

"Uh . . . yeah," Jimmy said, recovering. "Mom, Dad, this is Becky Butler. Becky, my parents, George and Florence DeWolf."

"How nice to meet you, Becky," his mother said.

"I'm pleased to meet you, too. My mother and father have a hotel in Marblehead, the Harborside, and do business with you, Mr. DeWolf."

"Oh, that Butler," he said. "Well, it is a pleasure to meet you." For a fraction of a second his eyes dropped to my breasts for a quick appraisal of his son's date.

"I was just on my way to the bar to get us a drink," Jimmy said. "Can I get anything for you?"

"We're set for now," his dad answered. "I've got to give a talk later, so I'm taking it slow." As Jimmy left, his dad said, "Enjoy the drinks. They're compliments of DeWolf Distributing."

"That's very generous of you, Mr. DeWolf," I said.

"It's good business." Mr. DeWolf was an inch shorter than Jimmy but about fifty pounds heavier, and it looked as though most of it was muscle. His face was full, with a no-nonsense tightness to his jaw. His light brown hair was Brylcreemed against his head and, in his tux, he was a handsome man. Mrs. DeWolf was all mother and looked like a person who kept the cookie jar full when her children were young. Wearing a metallic gold gown with a black jacket tailored to conceal a few extra pounds, she seemed genuinely warm yet quick to defer to her husband.

"It's always nice to meet Jimmy's young friends," Mrs. De-Wolf said.

"I'm more than a friend, Mrs. DeWolf," I said with a boldness that surprised me. Then, looking Mr. DeWolf straight in the eye, I said, "I'm his business partner."

"His what?" he growled.

"His business partner. The DeWolf Flying Service."

"I know what he calls it." His lip curled as he said it. "I fired that goddamn secretary in my office for stealing my mailing list."

His tone frightened me and I felt my confidence slip. "I'm sorry about that," I said weakly. "If there's anything we can do to correct that, we'd like to try."

"No! Just leave it alone. And for God's sake," his voice rose, "no more letters to my mailing list."

Florence, touching his arm, looked guardedly from side to side, embarrassed by his loud words.

I took a deep breath and tried to smile at Florence. "You'd be proud of your son, Mrs. DeWolf. He's an excellent pilot, as I'm sure you know. I had no trouble obtaining a business license for the company. We've done well in the last two weeks."

Without looking at me, George asked in a sarcastic voice, "Yeah, but are you making any money?"

"Yes," I said, regaining some of my confidence. "Jimmy had two charters to bring people from Long Island to Marblehead. We delivered emergency medicine to a hospital in Belfast, Maine. And yesterday he flew an engine part to a disabled fishing boat adrift fifty miles out of Gloucester."

He looked at me with eyebrows raised. "Hmmm. Are these your doings or Jimmy's?"

"We make a good team, sir."

"You do, huh," he said, looking away.

"We have two fishing-trip charters coming up next week. You probably know the four men: Chief of Police O'Boyle and Vice Mayor Harriman on the first trip, and Mr. Terrini who owns the restaurants and Monsignor Sheehan on the second."

His eyes narrowed again. "They were on my mailing list, weren't they?"

"I'm afraid they were, sir."

"And they responded to Jimmy's letter?" his voice surprised.

"That's right."

"I'll tell you one thing, young lady," he said gruffly. "You sound like you've got a head on your shoulders, and if you weren't working with Jimmy, I'd call those friends of mine and warn them not to risk the trip."

At that moment Jimmy arrived with our drinks. His dad turned to him and said, "I've been talking to your new partner."

Jimmy looked at his dad, his parent-pleasing smile fading to incredulity. "Partner?" His eyes shifted to me, questioning. "Becky?"

"That's right," his dad said with a smile, instantly aware he had found the chink in the armor of our partnership.

Jimmy laughed nervously, switching his eyes back and forth between his father and me. "Partner, huh? Well, we had talked about a partnership."

"Good," his dad said, changing his tone and surprising both of us. "Becky could be a real help for you."

"Yeah?" Jimmy said. Then, abruptly turning, he seized my elbow. "Well, see you later. Come on, Becky, let's dance."

"It's been nice meeting you," I called over my shoulder as Jimmy tugged on my arm.

Balancing our drinks in one hand, we danced our way out of earshot. Then Jimmy snarled, "And just what the hell was that all about?" I was quiet, deciding it best to let him blow off. He started again, "Were you talking about my business?"

"Yes," I said defiantly, "our business, the DeWolf Flying Service." We had danced ourselves into a corner where Jimmy finished his scotch in one gulp and set the glass on a table. I set my still filled glass down, too.

"*Our* business, huh?" He was practically standing on my toes, his face hard against mine. "What did you say?"

"I said *we* were doing very well," my nose almost touching his. I'd be damned if I'd back off an inch.

"When I told him about the charter trips coming up and the people you're taking, he said, 'Weren't they on my mailing list?' and I said yes. He was amazed they'd responded to you."

"Christ!" Jimmy said, shaking his head and turning his anger from me to his dad. "He never gives me any credit." He backed up a few inches.

I decided not to tell him the rest about his wanting to call and warn them.

"So now you've met my dad."

"It was an experience." I smiled and kept smiling until the corners of Jimmy mouth turned up slightly. "Your mom's nice."

"She's okay," he said, putting his arm around me. "Let's dance."

For the rest of the evening we successfully avoided his parents. Jimmy loved to dance and I loved being in his arms sweeping around the dance floor. When he introduced me to his friends, I could see he liked showing me off, and I could tell from their expressions that they thought me attractive. And Mom said I wouldn't fit in. Hah! Two or three of the girls, a bit older than I, regarded me coolly, and I wondered if they were former girlfriends of Jimmy's. I just held my head high and squeezed his arm. He was mine now. Jimmy had a few too many scotch and sodas and I began to worry about his driving, so I suggested we go for a walk in the Public Garden.

We went down the winding stairs, out the front door, and across Arlington Street into the Public Garden. The moon was half full and, as we crossed the iron bridge over the pond, it reflected in the water. Some ducks made V-shaped ripples in the water as they moved silently toward a small island. We stopped midway across the bridge and I put my arm around him.

"Jimmy," I said, turning my face to his, "this has been the best evening of my life."

"Same here." He smiled and looked at me. "You're a knockout. I was proud to have you as my date."

"I was proud, too." Then, risking it, I added, "How about as your partner?"

He sighed, half closing his eyes, and said, "Yeah, that too." I couldn't tell if he was pretending or really bothered by my persistence.

I lifted his chin with the tip of my finger and brought my lips next to his. "Really? Okay?"

His answer was buried in our kiss, a long deep kiss.

"Let's go home, Becky." He pressed his body against mine.

"Let's," I said. "I think it's time."

We practically ran back to the Ritz. It seemed to take forever for the attendant to get the car. When it arrived, we jumped in and I slid over next to Jimmy.

"You've wondered where I live? I'll show you."

My head was against his chest, and his arm around my neck. Gradually his hand moved down and into the top of my gown. When he began to massage my breast, I caught my breath and swallowed hard. Oh God, don't stop. I began rubbing my hand up and down his thigh until I was touching the edge of the swelling at his crotch. When the car stopped, I didn't know where we were and cared less. He led me up some stairs to a second-floor apartment and into the bedroom. In seconds we were naked and on the bed, our arms and legs wrapped around each other.

In a moment of sanity, I said, "Don't come inside me, Jimmy. Don't. I don't want to get pregnant."

"Oh baby, who cares? We're going to get married anyway, aren't we?"

"We are? Do you mean that?" I leaned back to look at him.

"Becky, I want you so much." He rolled me onto my back, covered me with his body.

"I know you do now," I said, barely able to whisper through my passion. "But what about later?"

He answered in a husky voice, "Forever, Becky. Forever."

18

We were married twelve weeks later on November fourth in Old North Church, Marblehead. Aggie, holding fast to her opinion I shouldn't be marrying Jimmy, was maid of honor. Jimmy's younger brother, Alan, came home from Yale to be best man. There were four bridesmaids and four ushers plus a five-year-old cousin of Jimmy's who was ring bearer. We had tried to alter Mother's wedding gown, but it was too short and we had to get a new one. We chose a white satin with a square neck and long sleeves. The veil, attached to a tiara, flowed out into a five-foot train. It was all I had ever hoped my wedding would be: beautiful music, flowers and candles everywhere, and a church packed with relatives and friends of both families.

Jimmy had given me a diamond engagement ring one week after the ball and asked when I wanted to get married. Why put it off? I thought. I've found the one I want to marry and we love each other. I said we ought to wait for two or three months just to keep our parents happy but no longer. When I showed Mother the ring and said we were getting married as soon as possible, I think she thought I was pregnant. At first I couldn't be sure I wasn't, but thank God, three weeks later I got my period.

Mr. DeWolf—I still had trouble calling him George—was pleased Jimmy wanted to get married and especially to me. Gradually he had come to like me because I didn't cower every time he approached, and because I'd gotten Jimmy interested in working, a feat that had eluded him since his son was a teenager. Also, I think he liked the way I looked. Florence wished I were a little older but was willing to accept me as the best Jimmy had found. During the three months of our engagement, they took me into their family, inviting me to Sunday dinner each week along with Jimmy. In the past, he had made his weekly pilgrimage out of a sense of duty, but now, going together, it was a chance to improve his relationship with his father.

I had started business college the day after Labor Day, taking evening courses in accounting and business law. After the partnership agreement was drawn up, I quit waitressing at the hotel and worked with Jimmy full-time. When we became engaged, whatever fears he may have had about sharing control of his company vanished.

By the end of October, between charter trips for fishing and hunting, making emergency shipments of equipment and engine parts, picking up a sailor with acute appendicitis from a freighter off Cape Cod, and flying sightseeing trips to the Berkshires for fall foliage, we had more business than we could handle.

The first night of our honeymoon we drove as far as Boston and stayed at the Ritz. Jimmy said, "Thank God we don't have to use rubbers anymore," which I had required after that first night in his apartment.

"Sorry," I said, "no babies for a while. As for you pulling out in time, I can't trust you or myself." He was upset, but acquiesced.

We found some Glenn Miller music on the radio, opened a bottle of champagne from the reception, stripped off our clothes, and, with occasional sips of champagne, danced lasciviously in front of a full-length mirror until, giggling, we fell into bed and made love.

The next morning we took the train to New York and spent a week going to shows, shopping, dining, making love, resting, and making love some more. We returned on the twelfth and I moved into Jimmy's apartment, my new home. The apartment was one of twenty-eight units in a large brick and stone building on Lynn Shore Drive in Lynn. It had five rooms, with living room windows facing the ocean. Jimmy had practically no furniture, but thanks to his dad, we had gift certificates at both a furniture and a house-wares store.

We had rented an office for the DeWolf Flying Service in East Boston just outside the airport on the second floor of a building that also housed a law firm and a freight forwarder. On the Monday before Thanksgiving, I was sitting at our only desk looking at our books, which were up to date, when Jimmy came in with coffee and doughnuts.

"Nothing to do?" I asked.

"Not till noon when I have lunch with Fred Barton. Want to see if I can get some of his air freight business." He opened the box of doughnuts and slid my cup of coffee across the desk to me.

"I've been thinking." I paused until Jimmy sat down. "What are our chances of buying another plane? A cabin plane that carries about five people?"

"Hmmm," Jimmy muttered, frowning.

"Winter's coming. We can't sell charters unless we find people adventurous enough to fly in an open cockpit. And we can only carry two passengers. I think we'd get more charters if we could carry four or five."

"Got anything in mind?"

I opened an aviation magazine to a page I'd marked. "What do you think of this?" It was a Stinson Reliant, big and sleek with a high wing, a radial engine, and more power and speed than the Waco.

"Looks kind of tame."

"It is. But maybe that's what we need for charters. Bet it's warm in winter."

"Yeah. Probably is."

"I think we ought to look at giving up the pontoons. Switching back and forth to wheels takes too much down time when we could be using the plane for income. We can't keep limiting our-selves to business that's on or just next to the water."

"Yeah, but that's our niche in the market. How many companies can serve the little towns up and down the coast that have no airports?"

"That's true, but when you add it up, how much business is there if we're limited to just that market?"

Jimmy looked at the article and picture of the Stinson for a while, then tossed the magazine onto the desk. "How do we get the down payment, especially for a plane like this?"

"Well," I said cautiously, "we could sell the Waco."

"Sell the Waco? Not on your life." He began pacing the floor of our small office. "That'd be like giving up an arm. Hell, Becky, the Waco's part of me."

"Okay, okay, but just think about it." I drank some coffee. "Maybe there's some other way to get the money."

"Don't get any ideas of going to Dad. I don't want him thinking I can't make it on my own."

"I didn't mean to ask him to give us the money. Just loan us the money at the going interest rate or at least co-sign a loan. We'd make all the payments and he wouldn't be out a thing."

"What is this?" He was angry now. "Some damned accounting idea you've learned?"

"No." I tried to cool him down. "But doesn't it just make sense to you?"

"No, it doesn't. That Waco has put us in business and it's making us money." He grabbed up his jacket and headed for the door. "You just keep doing the books and making the sales calls and I'll fly the airplane."

I slumped into my chair. Christ, but Jimmy could be frustrating at times. No business sense. Stupid pride. Still a kid playing with his Waco. He wouldn't be making a dime if it weren't for me.

At the end of the day he came by the office and picked me up. My anger had cooled and I think his had too, but we drove in silence not knowing how to come back together.

A block from home he said, "I got some business from Fred Barton. I'm going to make runs every other day to Manchester and Augusta flying canceled checks."

"Congratulations," I said, leaning over and kissing his cheek. No mention was made of the fact he'd have to replace the pontoons with the wheels.

Back in October the Worzeckis had heard from an aunt in Poland that both grandparents had been killed when Nazi planes hit the railroad yard in their little town. Poland was conquered in no time, cut to pieces by Hitler's and Stalin's armies. Mike immediately contacted the British consul general in Boston to find out how he could enlist. They referred him to the recruiting office in Montreal. The RAF recruiters accepted his flying experience in private planes as equivalent to basic training and swore him in. He was to join a group of Canadian volunteers the end of November and go to England for fighter training.

Mike and Carol invited us and a group of Mike's friends to a good-bye party. Carol and I watched Mike and Jimmy excitedly comparing British and German fighter planes, as if they knew what they were talking about.

"It scares me," Carol whispered. "When I close my eyes all I see are those newsreel pictures of fighter planes going down in smoke."

"I know," I said with a slight shudder. "It scares me too."

Then, bracing herself with a forced smile, she showed me her engagement ring.

"Oh, it's beautiful," I said. "Will you get married before he leaves?"

"I want to, but he says it's better to wait a few months until the war's over." She hid her face in her handkerchief and began to cry. "Becky, I'm so scared. I'm afraid I'll lose him." She spoke between sobs. "He's like a kid with this flying. And now that his grandparents have been killed, all he talks about is getting back at the Germans."

I put my arm around her and patted her hand. I could think of nothing to say.

We had Thanksgiving at the DeWolfs'. Their home, two blocks from Jimmy's apartment, was farther back from the ocean, but because it was situated on a hill, its dining room windows had a splendid view of the water. It was a rambling three-story Victorian with clapboard siding, a wide front porch, and a turret on the right side. Jimmy's brother, Alan, was home from Yale and had brought a pretty girl named Sarah. They were three years older than I, but being a married woman, it seemed like I was a little older. They talked about school and Jimmy and I talked about our flying business.

"How's it going?" George asked.

"Pretty good," Jimmy answered. "I've got a regular flight every other business day to Augusta and Manchester to pick up canceled checks for Boston banks."

"Good for you. That scheduled stuff is a lot better than being dependent on day-to-day business."

"We're still getting some of that too. All in all, it looks good."

Jimmy was confident and it showed in the relaxed way he talked with his dad.

Saturday morning we were awakened at four-thirty by the telephone. I ran to the dining room and answered it, thinking something bad had happened to one of our parents. It was for Jimmy—the operations department of King Fisheries. I called him to the phone and sat beside him as he talked with Harry King, son of the owner.

Jimmy listened for a while, then said, "Yeah, I guess I could, but the charge will be triple the usual fee." Pause. "Well, hell, Harry, first it's the weekend and second it's practically winter and third it's seventy-five miles out in the ocean." Pause. "I've got to put the pontoons back on and that will take a couple of hours and then I've got to gas up. I could be ready to go about eight o'clock." Pause. "Get the part down to the north hangar by seven. What is it?" Pause. "A drive shaft? How much does it weigh?" Pause. "Three hundred pounds and ten feet long? Shit, Harry. Well, yeah, we can handle it, but we'll have to tie it underneath on the pontoon struts. What's the weather out there?" Pause. "Okay. See you at seven o'clock." He hung up.

Jubilantly, he announced, "Are we going to make ourselves a piece of change! Come on. Let's get dressed. I'll need your help."

"What'd he say about the weather?"

"Not bad. Two-foot seas."

"Can the Waco handle that okay?"

"Piece of cake. Let's get going."

The sky was overcast with the beginnings of a gray dawn when we got to the airport. We jacked up the Waco and removed the wheels, then brought the pontoons on a flat cart from a storeroom in the hangar. With the two of us pushing and shoving we maneuvered the pontoons into position and bolted them onto the struts. When Harry's men brought the drive shaft at seven, they helped us secure it fore and aft between the struts below the plane's belly.

"Any more on the weather?" Jimmy asked.

"The *Regina* radioed just before I left. No change. Still two-foot seas. I brought a chart."

"Let's have a look," Jimmy said as they spread the chart on a workbench. The *Regina*'s location was already plotted. She was dead in the water seventy-five miles northeast of Gloucester. "What's the drift out there?"

"Northwest at three knots. If we figure an hour's flying time from now, it puts it right about here," Harry said, marking the chart with his pencil.

Jimmy called the tower, filed his flight plan, and gassed the plane, then all of us rolled it down the ramp into the water. Donning his fleece-lined flying suit and life jacket, he climbed into the cockpit. The engine roared and I watched him fly away into a gray sky.

"If you don't mind," I told Harry, "I'd like to come down to your office and follow this on your radio."

I drove the Buick behind the King Fisheries truck down to the Boston Fish Pier. Their office was on the second floor over their processing and packaging area. From the window I could see two seventy-five-foot King Fisheries boats tied up to the quay below us unloading their catch. Harry ushered me into the operations office where a radio operator was sitting at a console of dials and knobs. A microphone was in his hand and a speaker sat on top of the console. He was talking to fishing boats other than the *Regina* that were on their way into port. After an hour, the *Regina* called in.

"We got the biplane off our port bow. It's circling. We'll put a boat in the water to go make the pickup."

"How's the weather holding up?" the radioman asked.

"Downhill. The wind's come up some and the sea's a little rougher."

Harry took the microphone. "Captain. This is Harry King. If it looks too rough, wave him off."

"Well, I wouldn't want to try it," the captain replied.

"Uh, captain, I've got the pilot's wife here with me."

"Oh. It's not too bad. He was checking it out when he circled and he apparently thinks it's okay to land. He's gone downwind to make his approach."

"Becky, would you like a cup of coffee?" Harry asked.

I was sitting on the edge of my chair. "Thanks," I said with all my attention focused on the radio.

Harry nodded to another man to get the coffee.

The radio scratched static for about two minutes and then came to life. "He's coming in now. Coming in on our lee side where we've broken down the waves somewhat. He's looking good. Rear of the pontoons clipping the tops of the waves. Now he's—oh my God, he flipped. The plane flipped right over on its nose. It's upside down."

I lost my breath and rocked forward in the chair. Harry caught my shoulders. I could feel myself fainting. The man bringing the coffee braced me up as Harry grabbed the microphone.

"Captain, get the boat out there."

"It's already on its way. The plane's about fifty yards off our port beam. One of the men is stripping down. He's got a line around his waist."

The words were a blur. A light seemed to blaze into my closed eyes. My hands were shaking.

"He's diving into the water, beneath the cockpit. . . . I think he's got him. They're pulling him back to the boat. Yeah, there's two of them."

I stood. Walked to the radio desk. Harry put his arm around me. "Just hang in there, Becky. We'll know in a minute."

Static, only static.

"Here," Harry said, picking up the cup, "take a drink of coffee."

The static continued. "What the hell is happening?" I cried.

A voice broke the static. "Boat's alongside now and they're lifting him aboard."

Harry was on the radio again. "Captain, call the Coast Guard and tell them to come out and pick up a casualty. Tell 'em to get their cutter moving right away."

"Will do, sir." He changed frequency and we heard nothing for a while. Then he was back. "Got 'em, sir. They're on their way.

We've got the pilot in the cabin now. He's unconscious. Got a bad bruise on his head."

I squeezed Harry's arm. "How long before he'll be in?"

"It'll probably take the Coast Guard eight hours each way. About three o'clock tomorrow morning. Look, I'll drive you home."

"No, take me to his parents' house in Lynn. I'll wait there."

"Jake, follow me in the truck and bring me back."

As I walked out the door of the operations room, supported on Harry's arm, I heard the radio crackle with one last message.

"The plane's gone down."

19

Even a rose dies one petal at a time. Our dream died instantly. I was sitting on the right side of the Buick's front seat as Harry drove me to the DeWolfs'. It had started raining and the wipers slogged a steady swipe, swipe, swipe across the windshield. My eyes were turned toward the side window but I saw nothing.

In an instant Jimmy had crashed. Again and again I saw it in my imagination. One moment he was gliding in over the waves, his hand on the stick ready to flare the Waco and settle it on the rough seas. The next moment he was upside down, trapped in the cockpit, belted to the seat. Thank God for that brave man who dove into freezing water and pulled him out.

It had been an hour since the crash. I projected the worst possibilities. Maybe he's dead by now. Maybe he's injured and will never recover. A blow to the head, the captain had said. I could see his blond hair damp and matted with blood, his beautiful face twisted and swollen. Please God, let him be all right. Let him recover.

It was about noon when we parked in the DeWolfs' driveway. Harry jumped out and came around to open my door. With his jacket held over my head, we dashed to the porch. I asked him if I could call the radio operator as soon as I got inside. He urged me to call as often as I wished. As he turned to go to the truck that had followed us into the driveway, Mrs. DeWolf came to the door.

"What's all the commotion?" Then, seeing me and the Buick

without Jimmy, she asked, "What's wrong? Has something happened to Jimmy?"

I led her into the house and told her to sit down.

"Jimmy's okay," I lied. "The Waco went down when it was landing next to a fishing boat, but they got him out and he's on the boat now. A Coast Guard cutter is on its way to pick him up."

Tears came to her eyes as they locked on mine. "And he's all right?" Her voice faltered.

"He's unconscious, but they said he seemed to be okay. He's had a bump on the head."

"Oh, my God. My poor Jimmy," she cried.

"I'd better tell Dad to come home." I went to the phone and called Mr. DeWolf's office. His secretary said he'd already finished for the day, it being Saturday, and was on his way home. Then I dialed King Fisheries and asked for the radio operator.

"What's the latest from the *Regina* on my husband?"

"Mrs. DeWolf, he's still unconscious but they say his heartbeat's strong and his breathing's steady. I'll call you if there's any change."

"Hope you don't mind, but I'd like to check in with you every so often."

"Please do."

When Dad DeWolf arrived I told him all I knew and the three of us began a long vigil. Our many calls to the radio operator offered nothing new. The cutter was due to arrive at the *Regina* about seven-fifteen that evening. A doctor was on board, so we should be able to get more news at that time. It was still the Thanksgiving weekend and Alan and his girlfriend, Sarah, hadn't left yet. They offered to make dinner.

At eight o'clock, Harry called. The Coast Guard doctor had just radioed that Jimmy was still unconscious, that he had an apparent concussion, but his vital signs were all strong and indications were encouraging. The cutter should dock at the Coast Guard pier in Boston at three a.m. and we could meet it. Dad called the family doctor and arranged to have Jimmy admitted to Mass General. A Coast Guard ambulance would transport him.

The wait resumed. We picked at the dinner Sarah cooked. I catnapped on the sofa, waking every hour or so to call King Fisheries.

The radioman had kindly volunteered to stay the night and had remained in radio contact with the Coast Guard cutter. There was no change in Jimmy's condition. At two in the morning we all piled into the Buick, and Alan drove us to the Coast Guard pier. We waited some more. Finally the lights of the vessel came into view and within minutes it was tying up to the pier. The ambulance was there and the medics rushed aboard to bring the wire mesh stretcher bearing Jimmy down the gangway.

I gasped when I saw him. His face was horribly swollen. Mother DeWolf cried out and placed her hand on his cheek. I touched his arm beneath the straps. "It'll be okay, Jimmy," I said. "You're going to be okay." There was no response.

"Sorry, ma'am," the medic said, nudging us aside as he carried the stretcher to the ambulance. "We need to get him to the hospital."

"I'm coming with you," I said, and jumped into the ambulance before they had a chance to tell me I couldn't.

After five dark and cloudy days the sun broke through, flooding Jimmy's hospital room with light. A propitious omen, I hoped. Maybe this would be the day he'd regain consciousness. The swelling in his face had receded and he looked like Jimmy again, although the right side of his temple was bandaged. I was sitting by his bed casually glancing at a *Cosmopolitan* when I happened to look up. His eyes, open, were fixed on me. Without speaking, I smiled. Ever so slightly, he returned my smile.

"What happened?" His voice was weak, but the sound of it brought tears of joy to my eyes. "Where am I?"

Bending over him, I kissed his cheek. "You're in Mass General, darling."

"Did I crash?"

"Yes. Landing next to the *Regina*."

"Oh . . . yeah, the *Regina*."

I took his hand and burst out crying. "Oh God, Jimmy, you are all right. Thank God you're all right."

When I finished sobbing, he asked, "How long have I been here?"

"Five days. I've missed you, darling. I love you very much."

"Uh. And the Waco?" The dreaded question.

"It's gone, darling. We're just lucky to have you."

He closed his eyes. After a moment he said, "Shit," and drifted off to sleep again.

Six days later, much to the displeasure of his mother who wanted him at home, we moved him to the bedroom in our apartment and onto a rented hospital bed. He was instructed to stay in bed and keep his head slightly elevated. I stayed with him, but spent much of the time on the phone straightening out insurance matters. We would receive something for the total loss of the plane, but owing to a large deductible, it wouldn't come close to a down payment on another aircraft. Also, I had to coordinate with King Fisheries on their insurance claim for the loss of the drive shaft Jimmy was delivering that went down with the Waco. These concerns kept my mind busy while I was preparing Jimmy's meals, giving him his medicine, and seeing to his general comfort.

After a week at home, as his strength returned, he became restless. I bought him *Aviation Weekly*, *Esquire*, *Life*, *Collier's*, and *The Saturday Evening Post*, all of which he quickly devoured. When he started listening to soap operas, *Ma Perkins* and *Young Doctor Malone*, I knew it was time to get him out of the house. After an appointment at his doctor's office, I drove him to the airport. We sat in the car near the runway fence and watched planes land and take off.

"Want a cup of coffee?" I asked.

"Sure," he said with no enthusiasm.

I returned with the coffee to find him leaning against the fence. It was a sunny day but chilled by a brisk December wind. "Do you want to stand out here or get in the car?"

"In the car. I'm cold." I started the engine and turned on the heater. We sat for several minutes in silence watching the planes and drinking our coffee. Then, abruptly, he said, "Let's get out of here."

On the way home I said, "Tell me what you're thinking."

For a long time he said nothing. Finally he spoke. "I've lost everything. The plane's gone—and that means DeWolf Flying Service is gone—and we haven't got enough money to buy another. The plane was instead of college, so now I don't have an education or a plane. Shit, Becky. We've got nothing." He sank into his seat.

I put my hand on his leg and said, "We haven't lost everything. You're alive. That's the most important thing. And I love you."

"Humph," he mumbled, squirming further into his seat.

"We won't be able to get another plane for a while, but the way I figure it, with both of us working and with your trust fund, we can save enough for a down payment in eight months. And the way we were getting business with the Waco, we'd have no trouble getting it again."

"Ha," he muttered. "Who the hell is going to hire a pilot who crashed his plane?"

A month and a half later he got a job with Northeastern Airlines as pilot-in-training. His first three months would be probationary, and after that he would be flying DC-3s as second pilot. So Jimmy, who had ridiculed his former classmates from the Ryan School who got jobs lumbering along in clumsy transports while he did loops in the Waco UPF-7, was now a transport pilot himself, or almost. As for me, I got a job as secretary for the lawyer in the office on the first floor of the building where our office had been.

Jimmy's schedule was fairly consistent. Flying the Boston-Montreal run, and twice a week staying overnight in Montreal. Occasionally he was called in to make flights to New York or Washington, D.C. It wasn't bad, because he usually had three full days off in a row. Sometimes these days off fell on weekdays when I was working, and sometimes he had to work on the weekends, but it was tolerable. I continued with my business courses, but skipped class on nights he was at home.

When our days off overlapped, we'd take a ski train to New Hampshire for a weekend or hustle down to New York on Northeastern Airlines for a Broadway show. Jimmy was unusually attentive and considerate, which for some reason gave me the confidence to be even more abandoned in our lovemaking. And we were saving money. When away, Jimmy was on an expense account, and when I was alone I spent very little. We were able to put my salary, the insurance money, and the trust fund income in the bank and watch it grow. We couldn't save enough for the down payment in eight months like I'd hoped, but we would in twelve.

I picked up Jimmy at the airport on the nights he returned from Montreal. Usually I sat in the car in the parking lot, keeping the engine running with the heater on. One night toward the end of March, after I'd waited half an hour beyond the time he usually landed, I went to the Northeastern counter in the terminal building and asked for an ETA. A woman behind the counter said the flight was due at any minute, so I walked outside to the gate. I could see the landing lights of the DC-3 taxiing toward the terminal. With a roar of the port engine, the airplane turned and came to a stop near the gate. The ground crew wheeled out the baggage carts and opened the baggage compartment. An attendant opened the passenger door and three steps were folded down. Twenty-five or thirty passengers deplaned, waved at friends or relatives meeting them, and hurried toward the gate. When all the passengers were out, the crew deplaned: the pilot first, the two stewardesses, and then Jimmy. He looked so snappy in his uniform I decided to stand quietly by the gate and enjoy the sight of him coming toward me. At that moment, one of the stewardesses grabbed his hand and put her arm through his. They looked into each other's eyes and laughed as if at some private joke, while she squeezed his arm against her breast. It lasted only an instant and they dropped hands. As they came through the gate I stepped out and said, "Hi, Jimmy. Welcome home." I tried for a light tone in my voice, but I knew there was an edge to it.

"Oh, hi, Becky," he said as if nothing were wrong. "I don't think you know all these people. You know Clarence, of course. Best first pilot Northeastern has." He laughed. "And this is Jackie Christiansen and Cynthia Smith, our stewardesses."

"Hello, everybody," I said, giving Jackie the once-over, since it was her breast that Jimmy's arm had been pressed against. We said our good-byes and Jimmy and I started for the car. He drove.

"Good flight?" I asked.

"Yeah, just fine. Hey, want to eat at that place in Revere?"

"Fine by me." After a moment I said, "So, who's Jackie Christiansen?"

"You just met her. She was the one walking behind the other one."

"I watched you get off the plane. You seemed to have some very private joke going between you when she clutched your hand."

"Oh ho!" he said dramatically. "Do I detect a little jealousy here?"

"You're damned right you do. That was a lot more than just a playful good-bye."

"Oh, for Christ's sake, Becky, don't be ridiculous. We were . . . just laughing about that guy who was so fat he took up two seats. You saw him get off, didn't you?" I didn't remember any fat guy.

Jimmy slowed the car and pulled to the curb. Sliding over to my side, because I was as close to the window as I could get, he put his arm around me. With his other hand he turned my face toward him. "Come on now, I love you. There's nobody else and there never will be. She's just one of the people I work with." Then he brought his lips to mine.

As he moved back behind the wheel and pulled out into the road, I looked at him sternly. "Damn it, Jimmy, you'd better mean that—that you love me and there's nobody else."

He sighed. "I don't know what more to say. I love you, and there is nobody else."

I wanted to believe him, but the look on his face told me otherwise.

The last week of April, I went with Jimmy to an air show in Dayton, Ohio. All the latest aircraft were on display, including military, and there were flyovers by the air corps, stunt flying, and dogfights with World War I planes.

Together we looked at the Stinson Reliant and the Beechcraft, both of which would have been ideal for the DeWolf Flying Service, but Jimmy showed only mild interest in the prospect of buying a new plane. Instead he stood by the fence and watched flybys of the latest military aircraft. The new four-engine B17s thundered overhead at five hundred feet, bristling with machine guns. Six P40s came in low across the field in formation and flashed past us going at least 250 miles per hour.

The day after we returned from Dayton, as I drove him to the airport, I noticed how glum he was. "What's wrong, darling? You look like you've got the weight of the world on your shoulders."

"I don't know. I think it's the job. Same thing every day. Boston to Montreal. Montreal to Boston. Same route. Same landing patterns. Same hotels. It's not like it was with the Waco, Becky. Each day was different."

"Yeah, but it won't be long. We'll be back to having our own company soon."

Two weeks later, on May tenth, Germany invaded Holland and Belgium, and thousands of British troops were cut off on a narrow beach called Dunkirk. Winston Churchill, the prime minister, sent hundreds of boats of all sizes and descriptions to rescue the troops, and the RAF to protect them from German warplanes. Jimmy figured that finally Mike Worzecki would be getting his chance to do battle with German fighters. It was only a few days later that Carol McNash called to say Mike had been killed in the air battle over Dunkirk.

The next day I took the afternoon off and spent it with her.

"He loved to fly," Carol said. "Sometimes I think he loved it more than life itself." She was looking at her engagement ring, twisting it around her finger. "I still wish we'd gotten married. At least we'd have had a few days together."

I couldn't find words to console her, so I just cried with her.

Jimmy's reaction to Mike's death was strange. I knew he was thinking about him, but he withdrew into himself and said nothing.

Two days later, I picked up Jimmy at the airport after his return from Montreal. I stood by the gate and watched him deplane. Clarence gave him a hug and both Jackie and Cynthia kissed him good-bye. He walked backward for a ways, laughing and waving to them, then turned and strode briskly toward the gate. He was carrying a bottle of champagne. My joy at seeing him quickly dissolved. I sensed what he was going to say.

"Hi, darling. Say hello to Lieutenant DeWolf, Royal Air Force."

20

I glared at his grinning, pleased-with-himself face until I could stand it no longer. I began pummeling his chest with my fists, then broke into tears and ran to the car. Jumping in, I started the engine, backed out of the parking place, and jammed it into first. By then Jimmy had reached the car and stood in its path with one hand on the hood and the bottle of champagne in the other.

"Christ's sakes, Becky. Slow down. You'll kill somebody." He came around to the driver's door and opened it. I slid across the seat, pulling my arms around myself, and stared at the floor. Nobody spoke. Finally Jimmy said, "Will you just let me explain?" I shot a look at him, my jaw grinding my teeth, then stared back at the floor. "Come on, Becky, let's talk."

"Yeah," I said through clenched teeth. "Now you want to talk. Why didn't you talk to me before you went up to Canada and signed your life away?"

"Aw shit!" he groaned. "I haven't signed my life away. I just enlisted."

"Right. And how long did Mike last once the fighting started? One day? Two days?" I shook my head and turned away. "You didn't tell me what you were doing because you knew I'd throw a fit."

He laughed derisively. "You're right about that."

I grabbed the door handle and yanked it open. "You don't care what I think. Only what *you* want." I jumped out. "Then go on, get yourself killed."

As I ran toward the terminal, I could hear him calling, "Becky, damn it. Come back here."

"Go to hell," I yelled across the parking lot and climbed into a waiting cab. "Get moving," I ordered. Apparently the driver had been watching us, because he put it in gear and gunned the engine. As we left the terminal, I saw Jimmy standing by the Buick, shaking his head disgustedly.

"Where to?" the cabby asked.

"Marblehead."

"You got the dough? It ain't cheap, lady."

"Yes. Just get me there. I'll tell you where in Marblehead when we get there." I swore at Jimmy for the next thirteen miles, then I told the driver how to find Aggie's house. I stormed in through her back door and found her in the kitchen doing the dinner dishes.

Angry and half crying, I shouted, "You know what that god-damned bastard did?"

Aggie, wide-eyed, shook her head.

"He's enlisted in the RAF." I began pacing the floor, wringing my hands. "He's tired of flying transports," I said sarcastically. "It's boring." I burst into tears. "So he's gonna go fly Spitfires." I sat at the kitchen table, then got up again. "Hell, my job is boring too, but I've stuck it out so we can get our business going again."

Aggie took me by the shoulders and eased me into the chair.

"His friend Mike got killed over Dunkirk last week. Seven months after he enlisted. How long do you think Jimmy'll last?"

Aggie set a glass of rum in front of me, no ice. I took a gulp. It burned my throat, felt good. She set the bottle on the table.

"Soo," I sighed, "that's it. All our plans gone up in smoke, and Jimmy's leaving for England."

"When does he go?" Aggie asked, sitting down beside me and putting her arm around me.

"I don't know. I was so mad I didn't talk to him."

"Let me get you something to eat," Aggie offered.

"No, the rum's fine."

"I'll get it anyway." She did, heating a piece of meatloaf and some rice and setting it in front of me. I continued to sip the rum. It helped.

"Look," Aggie said, "I've got to go down to the pier and load some bait boxes onto the boat, then get it moored for the night. Why don't you come with me?"

"Oh, I don't know," I said dejectedly. "I probably should go home."

"Well, that you're not going to do, at least not right now. You need to take it easy for a while."

I took a few bites, then set my fork down. "I'm sorry. Not hungry, I guess. Really, Aggie, I'd better go."

"Naw. Let him worry about you for a while."

I thought about it for five seconds and decided she was right. "Okay, let's go to the boat."

Aggie, in blue work clothes and a turtleneck sweater, found me a jacket, picked up the bottle of rum, and strode before me down to the commercial pier where *Bright Star* was tied, stern to.

"Rats. No bait yet. Where is that guy? He should have been here an hour ago." The lobster bait was mackerel delivered in the evening for the next morning's trips. "Oh well. We'll take a spin while we're waiting."

She started the engine, turned on the running lights, and told me to let go the two stern lines. I jumped aboard and we headed out.

In the wheelhouse Aggie stood on the right side by the wheel and I on the left. Between us was a hatch to a cabin below the forward deck where extra lines, tools, rags, and old dog-eared copies of various magazines were tossed helter-skelter on two bunks. A toilet was on the port side just inside the hatch. Next to Aggie on the gunwale was a steel pulley for hoisting lobster pots. Behind us were stacked several lobster boxes like the ones I had helped her push up the gangway. The remaining deck was empty now, but would be filled when she and her father pulled a line of pots for rebaiting before dropping them again into the ocean.

The night was moonless but clear, the sky filled with a thousand stars. As we passed our hotel, I saw guests on the dock but didn't recognize anyone. I searched for Mom and Dad through the big windows of the dining room, where dinner was still being served.

No sight of them and I certainly didn't want to stop and say hello. We passed the yacht club where a Saturday night party was in full swing, then the State Street pier, Fort Sewall, and out into the open water. To our right, the iridescent green glow of the light-house marked the end of the Neck.

Aggie throttled back and said, "I'm going to do two things. One is foolish and the other illegal." First she turned off the engine. Suddenly we were engulfed in silence, with only the ripple of water at the prow as the boat drifted to a stop. "That's the foolish part. Let's just hope it'll start again." She laughed. "Just kidding. It will. I hope." She turned a full 360 degrees, looking in all directions while she said, "Quiet, isn't it?" Then she turned off the running lights. "That's the illegal part." She poured some rum into two glasses and handed one to me. "Come to the stern. I want to show you the stars with no other lights around."

In the harbor, where I'd seen a thousand stars, now I saw a million. The Milky Way was so dense with stars that it washed a pale glow from one horizon to the other. The lights back in town and on Marblehead Neck flickered dimly among the trees as a gentle breeze moved the branches. Farther out into the ocean, black islands rose above the waves like the humped backs of floating whales. In the water around the boat, night zephyrs fractured the reflection of stars, sending them dancing from wave to wave. The tolling of the bell in Abbot Hall rolled across the harbor announcing to those who cared that it was ten o'clock. Then silence returned. Silence and stars.

Aggie pointed at a constellation. "See that?"

"Yeah, that one I know." Raising my glass, I said, "Here's to the Big Dipper!" We drank.

"Move your eye now toward the southeast. See that really bright star there?"

"I think so." Pointing, I asked, "That one?"

"That's Antares in the constellation Scorpio."

"Oh."

"Exactly one year ago, you and I were getting ready to graduate the following week."

"Uh-huh."

"Antares was in the exact same spot as it is now. Same azimuth and the same altitude above the horizon. Between then and now it's sailed across most of the heavens but it's come back to the exact same spot as a year ago."

I cocked my head and looked at her, puzzled.

"One year exactly," she said in a husky voice, a soft smile on her face.

"I'll drink to that," I laughed. We each took a drink.

"A lot's happened. You and I are friends again." She seemed to be in a sentimental mood. "You met Jimmy and went for a plane ride. You got married. Started a company. You're learning accounting and business law. Jimmy crashed his plane and didn't die. He got a job with Northeastern Airlines. And now he's enlisted in the RAF."

We sipped our rum.

"All this happened in one year," Aggie went on, "and Antares came back to the exact same spot. The things that occurred in your life this last year didn't change its course one fraction of a degree."

Maybe, I thought, if I drank a little more rum I'd understand what she was talking about. I did. A chilling breeze picked up suddenly, coming from another direction. I zipped up my jacket and put my arm around Aggie's waist to share the warmth of our bodies. She was still pointing at Antares.

"Neither Hitler nor Churchill nor Roosevelt changed it."

"Not even Roosevelt?" I asked with mock seriousness.

"No, not even Eleanor." We laughed. "And a year from now, exactly now, good old trusty Antares will be in the exact same spot. Or two years or ten or a hundred, after we're all long gone, it'll be in the exact same spot in the sky at this exact same time of the year."

"Sooo?" I asked.

"Well . . . I don't really know."

I tipped my head and looked at her. "You don't know? Great. You've been philosophizing for ten minutes, and all you can say is, 'I don't really know'? "

She shook her head. "Well, no, but somehow I find it comforting. It may not mean a damn thing, but I like to think about it anyway."

"Aggie, you're crazy." I took a drink.

"And another thing." Aggie took a drink too.

"Oh no, not more philosophy?"

"Just one." She hugged me. "I know the stars pretty well. I can look up at the sky any time of the year and recognize planets and stars and constellations, and I'm never alone. They're like old friends."

"I hope I'm like that, too."

"You are." Her arm tightened around my waist again.

The boat began to rock gently in a freshening breeze. I looked toward the open ocean and could no longer make out the island whales I'd seen earlier. Instead, a gray haziness drifted across the water.

"Too much rum, Aggie," I said. "It's starting to look fuzzy out there."

She turned and looked. "Not fuzz. Fog."

I gazed at it for several moments. "It's like a dream floating toward us," I said. The mist hung close to the water, while above it the stars shone as brightly as ever. Moving quickly and silently, fingers of fog reached toward us, touching the bow, enfolding the cabin. The stars dimmed and disappeared. We became entombed. In the distance, the deep belching moan of a fog horn began sounding at regular intervals. The rocking of the boat seemed to lift us out of the water, suspending us in gray space. We held each other, transfixed.

Suddenly two eyes, side by side, green and red, burned their way through the fog. I pulled at Aggie's shoulder so she'd look in that direction. She gasped. Immediately the two lights became one red light, and a great piece of white canvas parted the fog and swooshed past our boat. We jumped backward, but there was no collision, only the sound of a hull cutting through water. Then it was gone, a white stern light disappearing into the fog.

"Was that a dream?" I asked, still caught in the spell of the moment.

"No. A sailboat and it damn near hit us." She ran to the wheelhouse and turned on the running lights. I followed.

"It was like a great white sea bird flying out of the fog."

"She never saw us. She was blinded by her sail."

"No, I think a phantom was at the tiller and he sensed our presence."

"And I think you're a little drunk."

"I hope so. Do you know the boat?"

"Yeah. She's new in the harbor. Only seen her a couple of times. She's named *White Wings*."

21

I awoke in the Sparrs' guest bedroom to the sound of Mr. Sparr calling up to Aggie from the kitchen. "Get up. We gotta get goin'." My eyes felt as if the fluid in the eyeballs had turned to lead, and the struggle to open them was so exhausting I closed them again. Some time later I awoke again. The heaviness had shifted from my eyes to my temples and was pinning my head to the pillow. But my eyes worked. The dull gray rectangle on the wall gradually became a window. Finally, superhuman will combined with the pressure of a bursting bladder got me out of bed and into the bathroom. I was up.

Downstairs I found a note from Aggie saying coffee was on the stove ready for heating, and eggs and bacon, if I wanted them, were in the refrigerator. I didn't want even to think about eggs and bacon, but I did heat the coffee. Aggie wrote she'd be back by one and would drive me home. The kitchen clock said ten-fifteen.

With time on my hands, I headed up the street to our hotel. Last night's fog had lifted and become low-hanging clouds which were breaking up from the warmth of the sun. I appreciated the five-block walk. It helped clear my head. I found Mom and Dad sitting on the veranda, relaxing with a late morning cup of coffee and reading the *Sunday Globe.*

Dad looked up, surprised. "Hi, Becky. What brings you here?"

Mom regarded me carefully, then said with concern, "Darling, you don't look so good."

"Oh, I'm all right." I sat heavily in a chair next to her. "Guess what? Jimmy enlisted in the RAF."

"The RAF?" Mom asked.

"The Royal Air Force. He's going to England and fight the Germans."

She brought her hand to her mouth and gasped.

Dad closed his eyes and uttered a deep sigh. "I don't believe this."

"Yeah. I agree," I said.

He shook his head. "So you'll be alone." Then, after several moments, "What are you planning to do?"

"I'll keep my job, I guess, at least for a while, but I'd like to find something here in Marblehead and move back."

They agreed that would be a good idea and said I could have my old room back.

"No. If I come back, I'll get an apartment." I searched for an excuse. "Wouldn't want to give up the furniture. And besides, Mom, I'm a married woman and want my own place."

"Oh, Becky," Mom said, "you're not even nineteen. Let us help to take care of you a little longer."

"We'll see, Mom." I didn't feel like a discussion right then.

They were having an early lunch in the dining room and invited me to join them. I accepted, discovering I was hungry after all. When we finished, I returned alone to the veranda. I found a lounge chair and sat in the sun reading the paper and watching the boats sail past. Toward one o'clock I walked down to the dock, where I could flag Aggie and her father as they came in from lobstering. The dock was T-shaped, and on the inside of the right side of the T a sailboat was tied. I sat cross-legged to wait for Aggie, and let my eyes wander over the boat. Its lines were simple and graceful. The hull was white and the deck a faded yellow. Around the cockpit the mahogany coaming was varnished a deep red. In the forward part of the cockpit was a centerboard well, and benches ran down each side. A tiller, like the extended arm of a graceful ballerina, was attached to a rudder post that disappeared into the floor. The sails were furled under a canvas cover. Across a narrow stern transom, in flowing script, were the words *White Wings*.

"Well, what do you know?" I said aloud. Wonder if she's owned by a guest at the hotel. At the bow was a small bronze fixture with two lights on either wide of a divider. So, I thought, the green and red eyes that came at us out of the fog. It doesn't look like a phantom now. More like an enormous feather resting on the water. Curious, I walked back up to the hotel and asked Dad who owned the boat.

"Oh, *White Wings*? She belongs to the Reverend Mr. Harrington over at St. Paul's Church. He's the new curate. We're letting him keep her here until he can arrange a mooring."

"I saw the boat last night when Aggie and I were out for a spin. He was heading in, trying to outrun the fog, I guess. Funny time to be out in a small boat."

"You know sailors, Becky. If the wind's up and you got some free time, why not go sailing?"

"I guess so."

I went back to the dock when I saw *Bright Star* coming into the harbor and rode with Aggie and her father to the pier. I helped her unload the boxes of lobsters and push them up the ramp, then we washed up and she drove me to Lynn.

Jimmy was in the apartment talking to a friend on the phone. I waited in the living room for him to hang up. Soon he ambled in and took a seat. We sat for some time, not looking at each other. I thumbed through a copy of *Collier's* and he cleaned his fingernails on his left hand with a fingernail on his right.

"When do you go?" I finally asked.

"Two weeks. June twentieth." He switched hands.

"What happens then?" My voice was soft but not yet forgiving.

"Well, I meet with a group of volunteers in Montreal and we sail for England. I get some basic military training and then in about a month start fighter training."

"How long is that?"

"About three months, I think."

"So that means you should be in the sky fighting Germans about the end of September or the middle of October."

"Yeah, I guess so."

I waited a minute, then asked, "Jimmy, can you see why I was so upset last night?"

"Not really, but I'm getting used to it," he said with resignation. "Guess you like to run things, and when I do what I think is right, you blow up."

I looked at him with discouraged amazement and walked into the bedroom, slamming the door. Ten minutes later he was knocking on the door. "Becky? . . . Becky? May I come in?"

"It's open." I was lying face down on the bed.

He sat on the edge. When he spoke, his voice was apologetic. "You see, I thought you'd be proud of me."

I sat up and locked my arms around my knees. "It's not that I'm not proud of you. I am. You're a good pilot and you'd make a good fighter pilot, but why you, Jimmy? Why you? We've got a good thing going here. We have fun together. I thought we loved each other. We've got a nice place to live. Good jobs. We're saving money and we've got plans for the future. Don't you see, that's all gone now."

"No it's not. Sure, I'll be away for a while, but I'm still earning money and I'll still take care of you. I'm not running out on you. A few months, maybe a year, and I'll be back. We'll have money saved and get the plane we want. Be back in business."

Jimmy was sitting next to me and I leaned over and rested my head against his shoulder. "It's not that," I said as tears filled my eyes. "I'm afraid. I keep thinking about Mike. I don't want to lose you, darling."

He put his arm around my shoulder. "I keep thinking about him, too. Maybe that's one reason I'm going."

Jimmy was scheduled to leave Monday morning. His dad threw him a party on the Saturday before and it lasted far into the night. Jimmy had more than he should to drink and fell asleep the minute we got home.

I tucked him in, then put on my robe and sat in front of our open bedroom window. A cool breeze lifted the curtains. The moon was rising over the ocean, laying a glistening carpet of gold across the water. What will happen? I wondered. A few months, he said. Maybe a year. Then I remembered what Aggie had said about the stars and constellations. They come back to the same spot like old friends. Here was the moon rising again in the night sky, undaunted by my fear and Jimmy's imminent departure.

"Hello, old friend!" I said, smiling.

22

We sat at a table in the airport coffee shop, Mom and Dad DeWolf, Jimmy and I, watching rain fall from dark billowy clouds and streak the window. The departure of the Northeastern flight to Montreal was delayed due to weather. We sat staring at rivulets of water inching, shifting, joining one another and cascading down the glass. Nothing moved on the black asphalt ramp beyond the gate. The DC3 sat poised like a giant sleeping beast with its head pointed at the thunderclouds tumbling in from the ocean.

"Did you remember your toothbrush and toothpaste?" his mother asked.

"Yes, Mother," Jimmy sighed.

"If you didn't, they sell them here at that little stand over there. I saw them as we came in."

"He said he remembered, Florence," Dad DeWolf said.

"Oh," Mother said and opened her purse to search for something she never found. She closed her purse.

The coffee shop was crowded with other people waiting to leave or to say goodbye. From time to time people returned to the counter to replenish cups with steaming coffee, plates with gooey Danish rolls. Jimmy and I said nothing.

Last night, as I lay in bed beside him, the reality of his leaving crashed down upon me. He was off to war. Turning toward the wall, I squeezed my eyes tightly shut to barricade myself from the mounting fear of losing him, of never seeing him again. Suddenly I found myself convulsed with anger at him for leaving me alone, possibly never to come back. I began to cry uncontrollably. Try as I might, I couldn't stop.

Gradually, I became aware of Jimmy's hand rubbing my back, of his voice comforting me. Like a spring unsnapping, I turned and flung myself on top of him, straddling him, kissing him brutally on the lips at the same time as I was hammering his shoulders with my fists. He wrapped his arms around my back and pulled me against him to stop me from striking him. We struggled with one another, our stomachs and chests sliding, grinding, greased by our sweat. The rhythm of our movement grew in intensity. My breathing became heavy and urgent. Sliding back and forth against his moist, hard penis, I groped for it and shoved it inside me. Then, riding him, I banged down harder and harder. My crying turned to groans, guttural sounds like a dog's growl. He put his hands on my hips, pulling me down against him. Faster and faster we moved, he thrusting upward, I driving downward, until our orgasms shook and rattled our bodies into submission. I collapsed against him, my cheek against his wet chest. We lay like that for a long time. Finally, I managed to speak.

"Damn you, Jimmy," I said hoarsely. "Sometimes I love you so much I hate you."

"Same here," he said, his voice drained of energy.

Then I got up, went to the bathroom, and thoroughly douched myself. The last thing I wanted was to get pregnant.

The rain continued to beat against the window of the coffee shop. Jimmy sat impatiently, bobbing his right knee up and down reflexively. "I'm going over to operations and get a weather report," he said. He scraped his chair back and was gone.

"I wish he wasn't ever going to get on that airplane," his mother said. "I wish it would rain till kingdom come."

George looked dismayed with his wife. "Face it, Florence. He's going. This is just a thunderstorm. It'll pass."

"I know. It's just . . ."

"When do you go up to Maine, Mom?" I asked, trying to find a subject other than Jimmy's departure. The DeWolfs had a summer house on a point in Christmas Cove. Jimmy and I had visited once for a long weekend last fall. The scenery was exquisite, the sailing great, and the fires in the fireplace on cool nights cozy.

"This week. I'll go ahead on my own and open up the place, then George will come up when he can. Becky, you know Alan and Sarah are coming up next week and staying for a while. Why don't you come too?"

"I'd love to," I said sincerely. "But I've got my job. I can't just take a vacation when I want to."

"Well, why don't you ask anyway? I'm worried about you being alone now that Jimmy'll be gone."

"I'll see what I can do." I took her hand and said, "I mean that, Mom."

Jimmy returned with a look of satisfaction. "Look out there," he said, pointing to a patch of light gray sky. "It's starting to break up. Another fifteen minutes and they're going to start boarding."

People sitting near us overheard him and the news spread. They began standing and moving toward the door leading to the gate.

"Don't worry about that line," Jimmy said. "I'm flying up front with the crew." He led us to the door to operations, marked "Employees Only."

"Well, this is it," he said with finality. His mother kissed him and his dad patted him on the back.

"Write us as soon as you get there, so we'll know you're all right," Mom said through her tears.

George squared his shoulders and announced, "I'm proud of you, son." Then they stepped back, giving us space for our good-byes.

He put his face to mine but I couldn't see him through my tears. We kissed quickly and he turned, leaving through the operations door. Mom DeWolf found a handkerchief in her purse for her tears. Dad offered me his.

The following Saturday I was driving the Buick, top down, to Maine. I hadn't bothered asking for vacation time. I just quit. When Jimmy's plane left, I went to the office, still in the drizzling rain. I sat at my desk looking at the papers in the in-box, not caring whether the work got done or not. Several minutes passed and I didn't move. Finally my boss noticed and asked if I was all right. I began to cry. Through my tears I said I wasn't all right, that Jimmy had left for the RAF and that I was going back to Marblehead. I picked up my purse and walked out, leaving my lawyer-boss standing there unable to speak. I knew it wasn't fair. I should have given notice, but I wasn't in a mood for fairness. The rain continued through Thursday and I remained in the apartment, sleeping, reading, and drinking red wine. The phone rang several times, but I didn't answer it. On Friday, the sky cleared and I roused myself enough to drive to Marblehead, where I spent the day sunning myself on the dock. My parents hovered on the veranda sneaking glances in my direction and looking concerned. I was grateful they kept their distance. About midafternoon I must have fallen asleep because a voice awakened me.

"Ummm, excuse me." It was a deep, resonant voice. I opened my eyes and shielded them from the sun with my hand. The voice belonged to a nice-looking man in khaki shorts and a white polo shirt. Most prominent, from my viewpoint, were two knobby knees.

"Uh, you're lying on one of my lines," he said apologetically.

"Oh," I said, sitting up. The line in question was coiled under my right calf. "I'm sorry."

"That's okay." He picked up the line. "I'm sorry to have bothered you."

"Is this your boat?" I asked. I was sitting next to the sailboat named *White Wings*.

"Yes." He began releasing the line from a cleat on the dock.

"Then you're Reverend Harrington."

"Uh-huh. But that's not the way you say it. That makes 'reverend' an adjective meaning I'm especially holy, which I'm not."

"What?" I asked, confused.

He continued releasing the lines for his boat. "If you want to use it as a title, you say, 'the Reverend Taylor N. Harrington' or 'Mr. Harrington' but never 'Reverend Harrington.' How did you know my name, anyway?"

"My folks told me when I asked about the boat." I looked at him as he moved about the dock making his boat ready for sailing. He had brown hair, closely cut and carefully combed. His face was slim, as was his whole body, and his straight, narrow nose gave him a refined appearance. He was a little taller than I and looked to be in his mid-twenties.

"So, what do I call you? 'Hi the Reverend,' or 'hello there Mister?' " I said mockingly.

He stopped and turned toward me. He smiled over my sarcasm. "Call me Taylor."

"Okay. You have a beautiful boat, *Taylor*."

"Thank you," he said as he jumped in and shoved off from the dock. The wind caught the sail and he moved smartly into the channel. Then he leaned back and called, "And what's your name?"

"Becky, Becky Bu . . . DeWolf."

"Nice to meet you, Miss Becky B. DeWolf."

"Call me Becky, Reverend."

He laughed, then turned his attention to *White Wings*. I watched him until he disappeared around the yacht club, then stood, shook my shoulders, and stretched. For the first time in two weeks, I felt something other than anger and loss. I actually felt invigorated.

I spent only four days with Mother DeWolf. Alan and Sarah arrived on Sunday and set out to check the neighboring cottages for friends. I went with them. We found a group of nine couples, some married and some who had brought friends from their hometowns in Connecticut, New York, and Massachusetts. Nine couples and one single person—me. Everyone wanted to know about Jimmy and was very gracious to include me, but I felt like a fifth wheel. The most fun I had was covering for Sarah when she'd sneak out of the bedroom we shared and go down the hall to sleep with Alan.

Jimmy was on my mind. The anger I had first felt, and then the sadness, had been replaced by loneliness, especially when I was around Alan and Sarah and the other couples. Seeing my brother-in-law hand in hand with Sarah and hearing the sounds of love through the bedroom wall at night made me long for my husband.

I knew it was time to leave when the man next door, who had been watching me in my two-piece bathing suit as I crossed his lawn on the way to the swimming dock, invited me in for a drink.

He was about forty-five, handsome and well built. I knew it was time because I was tempted to take him up on it.

On the way home I passed a series of Burma-Shave signs.

> Her sweet love left
> She cried and cried
> Until another
> Love she tried.
>   Burma-Shave

The lease on our apartment in Lynn, which had originally been Jimmy's, had expired two months previously and we had extended it on a month-to-month basis. As soon as I returned from Maine, I gave notice I would be leaving at the end of July. I endured the lonely apartment with all its remembrances of Jimmy for four more weeks while I looked for a place in Marblehead. Mom and Dad cautiously asked about my plans, wanting to know if I planned to work or go back to school. I had no answers.

The second week of July a letter came from Jimmy. He gave me a military address but said he couldn't say exactly where his base was. He was learning how to salute and march, to shoot a rifle and sing "God Save the King." He could hardly wait to start flying. The other boys, he said, were mainly from Canada with a few from Poland. They were a good bunch and he'd found a few friends. English beer was especially good, much better than American. He ended with "I love you, please write, Jimmy."

I wrote immediately, telling him about my trip to Christmas Cove and how Sarah, Alan, and I had deceived his mother. I said I was moving to Marblehead and would send my new address as soon as I had a place. I signed it "Love, Becky."

Every day the *Boston Globe* was filled with bold headlines about the war. With Jimmy over there, I was paying much more attention to the news. Hitler was in Paris, a puppet government had been set up in France, and the Italians had joined the war. There were pictures showing English women and children crawling over the rubble in some coastal villages bombed by the Germans. Churchill was pleading for more American aid, which Roosevelt was promising to send. Maybe Jimmy was right. Someone had to stand up against the Germans.

On Sunday, July 28, I moved to a four-room apartment on State Street in Marblehead. I rented a truck and, with Aggie's help, rallied some of my former classmates to help load and unload. Four of them showed up—Cindy Franklin, now Cindy Gerard, married with an eight-month-old baby boy; Sandy Fellson, who worked in a Marblehead bookstore; Lori Tanner, engaged to a teacher in the Salem school system; and Phyllis Shade, a sophomore at Wellesley who was home on summer vacation. We dressed in work clothes and pretended we were moving men. Sandy had a pack of Camels tucked into her rolled-up sleeve, Cindy mastered an excellent spitting technique, and all of us whistled at men who came in and out of the building while we carried furniture. When we finished moving in, I passed around bottles of Schlitz and we guzzled beer while cooling off.

"Hell," Aggie said, "I think I'll get a job as a mover. It's easier than lobstering. Have a look at this." She pulled up her sleeve and raised her right arm, making a muscle.

"Wow!" Phyllis exclaimed. "Have you got the biceps."

"Yeah," Aggie said proudly. "Comes from pulling a couple a hundred pots a day."

"I envy you," Sandy said. "You're outdoors while I'm stuck in the bookstore."

"And I'm changing diapers," Cindy added.

I got out more beer. Everybody took one.

"This has been fun," Lori said. "I've missed you guys."

"Me too," Cindy agreed.

"I haven't had so much fun in months," I told them, "and that includes about half the time when Jimmy was still here."

"Hmmm," Phyllis said.

"I mean, it all got so serious when we left school: getting married, getting jobs, going to college, having babies. I've missed just horsing around like we did today. It's like we're all growing up too quick."

"Tell you what," Lori said. "Let's get together again, have a picnic or something. I'd like you to meet Stewart and I'd like to meet your husband, Cindy."

"And I'll bring a picture of Jimmy," I said sarcastically.

"No, it doesn't have to be like that," Lori said. "I'm not talking about a couple thing. Just good friends."

"I like the idea," Sandy said. "But Becky, would you mind if I asked a date to come along?"

"No. Hell, I might ask somebody too." Everyone laughed.

Cindy said, "We could have a picnic out on Lighthouse Point."

"I'll do you one better than that," Aggie said. "If Becky'll help, we can get *Bright Star* cleaned up and have a party on board—take a cruise of the islands."

All agreed and we made plans for the following Sunday afternoon.

As they were leaving, Phyllis said, "The person I want to ask—I don't know if he'll come."

"Who's that?" Lori asked. "Do we know him?"

"Maybe," she said slyly. "He's the new curate at our church."

"The Reverend Taylor N. Harrington?" I asked.

"You know him?" Phyllis said, surprised.

"Of course," I said, raising an eyebrow and cocking my head, "but I haven't seen him since he woke me up to get my leg off his coil."

23

My second letter from Jimmy, dated July 22, arrived on Thursday, August first. I took it upstairs to my apartment, made a glass of iced tea, and sat on the sofa.

Dear Becky,

Today I had my first flight in a fighter. Fantastic. It's a Hurricane, not a Spitfire, but it's a great airplane. I've never felt such power and speed. Since there's only one seat, there was no way I could have an instructor with me. I just got in and flew it. Of course I did a lot of practice in a simulator before I took off. It was great. The controls are much more sensitive than the Waco and need only the slightest touch.

I'm moving ahead fast. I'd like to think that's because I'm so talented, but they're pushing all of us into fighters as soon as possible. So far I haven't seen any Germans but I read in the papers they are attacking ships in the Channel and a few towns on the coast. Now that they've got France under their thumb, it's only a matter of time before they really hit England. I haven't been off post since that first night just after I arrived. Fortunately we have an officers club where we can get a pint (as they say) before turning in. We're all working day and night to get ready for the German offensive when it comes.

Being in England is like being in a different world. There's hardly a person who hasn't already lost a buddy or relative in the war. There's food and gas rationing and all kinds of restrictions. But morale is high.

I'm sorry for all the problems my coming here has made for you, but the truth is, I'm glad I came. I know I'm doing the right thing.

Time to turn in. Weather permitting, I'll be up in the Hurricane tomorrow morning. I can't wait.

I love you Becky and I miss you.

Jimmy

I read the letter a second time, then let it drop to my lap. The windows were open and I could feel a cool breeze off the harbor. The room was quiet. Outside a gull was squawking as it flew overhead. The idea that people in Europe were fighting and bombing each other seemed unreal. Yet Jimmy had written about an impending attack by the Germans. I drank some tea and thought about past nights when I, in my loneliness, was sure Jimmy was curling up with some English girl. Instead, he was hard at work learning to be a fighter pilot. Now I felt guilty for not trusting him. But the thought lingered—of course he couldn't chase girls, he was confined to base. Or had the war changed him?

Setting my doubts aside, I wrote him a letter saying I was proud of him for enlisting in the RAF and excited about his flying Hurricanes. "Maybe they'll put you in Spitfires soon, because I know how much you want to fly one." I even said I was glad he was so busy he couldn't go off post. "I would be jealous of those pretty English girls you'd meet in the pubs." I ended by telling him to be careful because I loved him very much and wanted him to come home safely. Then I signed it "With all my love, Becky." Sealing the envelope and writing his military address, I realized I meant every word I'd written.

Sunday I awoke to a warm, beautiful morning. After breakfast at her house, Aggie and I headed for the commercial pier to get the boat ready for our outing. We rowed her dinghy halfway across the harbor to *Bright Star*'s mooring, boarded, and motored back to the pier. In spite of Mr. Sparr's hosing down of the decks after yesterday's lobstering, there was still a scent of fish bait and lobster. While Aggie cleaned up the litter-strewn cabin and scrubbed out the head, I scoured the deck with a coarse brush and soapy water. Down on my hands and knees, I was so absorbed in my work I didn't notice another lobster boat pulling up beside us. Then I heard a familiar voice.

"Taking up lobstering?" Karl Kramer asked.

I closed my eyes and froze in place. I hadn't seen Karl to talk to since graduation last year. His voice filled me with dread. It had been my date with Karl that spoiled Aggie's plans for my seventeenth birthday and almost broke up our friendship. It was my fault, though. I was starry-eyed in love with Karl.

Our romance had started like a rocket: very hot and very fast. For the first time in my life, someone wanted me as much as I wanted him. I was sure it was true love. We started out going to parties and double dating, but soon it was just the two of us heading out alone as fast as we could to a country road in his dad's Chevy. Each night we discovered some new thrill in kissing or touching or fondling. Before long, as soon as we parked, he shifted to the passenger seat, I straddled him, and we began stripping off each other's clothes.

As the thought of it flashed across my mind, much as I tried to resist it, I felt a tingle of arousal.

"Oh, hi, Karl," I said with little enthusiasm. "How was the catch today?"

"Not bad. You signed on with the Sparrs?" God, I thought, that tone of voice, so belittling. How did I ever love this guy?

"Hardly," I laughed. "Just helping Aggie get her boat cleaned up." I was afraid if I said we were having a party, he'd want to come.

He walked onto the stern of *Bright Star* and sauntered over to sit on the gunwale next to where I was kneeling. He walked with a rolling gait due to injuries to his knees during the last big high school football game.

More memories returned—Karl in the hospital recovering from torn ligaments and damaged cartilage in both knees. I had tried to continue as the loyal girlfriend, seeing him in the hospital and helping him keep his homework up to date, but it wasn't working.

He began to resent my help and I began resenting him for not appreciating the sacrifice I was making.

"How's Harriet?" I asked. He'd gotten married a few months ago.

"She's okay. Gonna have a baby come Christmas."

"No kidding," I said, not appreciating the way he was looming over me. "You don't waste time, do you?"

"Well, you know, it just happens." His laugh had a smutty tone to it. "Hear your husband's gone to England to fight the Germans."

I poured some soapy water from a bucket onto the deck near his boots and began scrubbing again. "That's right. Left the end of June."

"You must be gettin' pretty lonely?" Here it comes, I thought.

"Nope. Keeping busy."

"Scrubbin' lobster boats, huh?"

"Whatever."

"Just thought you might like to go out for a spin on our boat sometime. I could pick up some beer and we could, I don't know, recall old times or something."

Old times, I thought. Yeah. Like the time at his house after he got out of the hospital but before he could go back to school. I wanted to break up with him, but like a dope I continued to help him with his school work. One day when we were alone in his house, he asked me to sit beside him to help with a math problem. Suddenly he started grabbing at my breasts and putting his hand up my dress. I tried to get up but he pulled me down on the sofa and threw himself on top of me. His knees were injured but his arms and shoulders were as strong as ever. "Who you givin' it to now, Becky?" His voice sounded crazy. My God I thought, he's raping me. When he let go with one arm to get his pants down, I rolled out from under him and ran from the house.

I looked up at him now as he stood over me. The sneer on his face and the leer in his eye said he'd try it again given half a chance. Smiling, I sat back on my haunches and said, "Go out on your boat? Sounds like a great idea." His eyes brightened. "I'll give Harriet a call and see what would be a good time for her." Then, leaning forward, I returned to my floor scrubbing.

He got up abruptly and put his foot on my brush, pinching my fingers against the deck. Glaring down, he said, "Damn you, Becky. You never quit, do you?" He stomped off the boat and began helping his dad unload boxes of lobsters.

"You fucking bastard," I said under my breath.

"Ahoy down there!" Lori called from the top of the quay. It was one o'clock, the time we'd agreed to meet. She and her fiancé were carrying a grocery bag and a picnic basket.

I waved. "Come on down."

As they started down the ramp another car pulled up, so they waited. It was Cindy, who with her husband began unloading a portable crib and a satchel filled with baby things. Pretty soon the four of them were coming down the ramp, arms filled with boxes, bags, cribs, satchel, and baby.

"What a beautiful day," Cindy said. "Did you order this, Aggie?"

"Sure."

"Hi," Cindy's husband said, "I'm Jerry."

"And this," Cindy said, cradling the baby in the crook of her arm, "is Michael Gerard." Two big eyes studied us. He was dressed in overalls over a cotton sweater and had on blue bootees.

"I better get the crib set up so we can put Mikey down," Jerry said. Aggie suggested he put it in the wheelhouse out of the wind.

Lori introduced Stewart Mann, her fiancé, and told us he was a math teacher at Salem High School. Down the ramp came Sandy Fellson with a date. Before they reached the bottom Sandy was saying, "Hi, everybody. This is Frank Coleman. You know, Coleman's Grocery Store."

"We all know Frank," Aggie said. "You can't live in Marblehead and not go to Coleman's Grocery Store." Everybody greeted Frank and Lori introduced him to Stewart. Then Aggie spoke. "Okay, folks. I'm captain of this boat, and I say we stow this food in the wheelhouse and make ready to get under way."

The men set to work stowing the picnic supplies, and Aggie started the engine.

"Hey! Wait for us." It was Phyllis calling through cupped hands from the top of the ramp. She turned to shout back toward the car.

"Taylor, you bring the record player and records and I'll carry the wine." In a moment they were cautiously climbing down the steep ramp.

"How about this," Lori said. "We'll have music."

"Yeah," said Phyllis, "I thought you might like that. Brought wine, too."

"Great," Jerry said. "Wine, women, and song."

"And this is Taylor Harrington," Phyllis announced as if introducing a celebrity. Taylor looked embarrassed.

While the men shook his hand and the other women made their hellos, Aggie called from the wheelhouse, "Two of you let go the stern lines." I released one, Jerry the other, and we were under way.

Soon we were out of the harbor and feeling the long, gentle roll of the swells. I stood next to Aggie by the wheel and observed the people forming two groups. Jerry was holding his son, Mikey, and talking with Frank Coleman and Stewart Mann. They were asking Jerry about his job as a policeman in Marblehead. "Except for teenagers getting drunk and driving too fast and a few break-ins, it's quiet most of the time."

Phyllis, her arm tucked through Taylor's, was describing his work with the young people at St. Paul's Church while Cindy, Sandy, and Lori looked on admiringly. For an instant Taylor's eyes met mine, and I could swear he rolled them skyward in what might have been a prayer for divine release. It worked, and a few minutes later he strolled into the wheelhouse. "I like your boat, Aggie. It looks like it's weathered a few storms."

"Oh, it's been around. Dad had it built twenty years ago and he's been lobstering with it all these years."

Taylor turned to me. "Hello, Mrs. Becky B. DeWolf."

"Hi, the Reverend Taylor Harrington." I smiled.

"Phyllis says you're married. I didn't realize that the other day."

"Would it have made a difference?"

"I probably wouldn't have swept you into my arms if I'd known."

Aggie gave us both a puzzled look. "What have you two been doing?"

We laughed and instantly Phyllis was upon us. "Taylor,"

she said in a high voice, "don't you just love this boat?" She took his arm.

The other three men joined us in the wheelhouse. Stewart asked where we were headed.

"Cat Island," Aggie said, pointing to a long island with a few low hills not far beyond Lighthouse Point. "It's got a dock where we can tie up." Soon we were there and unloading supplies. We laid out blankets for the picnic and set the bags and baskets on them for later. Frank and Jerry brought up a bucket filled with ice and beer.

"Beer?" Jerry offered. Aggie and I accepted in the same breath.

"I'm going swimming," Phyllis said. "Where can we change, Aggie?"

"There's a shed up there, or you can use the cabin in the boat."

"Boys in the shed, girls in the boat," Phyllis ruled. "Go on, Taylor, get your suit on."

I whispered to Aggie, "You're captain on the boat. She's captain on the island."

"Yeah," Aggie agreed.

The day was warm but the water cold, so we swam for only a short time, hurrying to stretch out on the blankets and dry ourselves in the sun. Cindy set little Mikey on the blanket between herself and her stocky husband, Jerry. She was heavier now in the hips and legs than before her pregnancy and was hiding it with a bathing suit that had a skirt. Phyllis, lying next to Taylor, had a trim little figure that looked sexy in a two-piece suit. Lori, confident of her well-formed figure, wore a one-piece suit with a low-cut back that showed her off to the fullest. Her fiancé, Stewart, adoringly rubbed suntan lotion on her back and beneath her shoulder straps. In his mid-twenties, bespectacled and skinny, he'd won Lori's heart, I was sure, by his gentleness and caring. Sandy sat holding her knees while her date, Frank Coleman, lay stretched out on the blanket beside her. Frank was at least fifteen years older than she and divorced, but a hard-working, well-respected man. I always thought Sandy had become a cheerleader in an effort to overcome her shyness. She'd excelled as a cheerleader but she was still shy.

"How about some music?" Phyllis suggested.

"What have you got?" Cindy asked.

"Well," she said, sorting through some records, "how about 'Falling in Love With Love,' or 'This Can't Be Love,' or 'Moon Love'?"

"Sounds like you're promoting love, Phyllis," Lori joked.

"Oh, be quiet. I'll play this one," Phyllis declared, putting a record on the machine. It was "Over the Rainbow." As the clear voice of Judy Garland longed for a world where troubles melt like lemon drops, the men began talking.

"Roosevelt's pushing the draft again," Stewart said, worried. "If it passes, I'm in the right age group."

"Yeah," Jerry laughed. "You and Lori better get married quick and have a baby."

"A lotta good that'd do," Frank said. "The way Roosevelt's going, we'll be in this war before you know it. Then we'll all have to go. We oughta listen to Lindbergh and stay out. It's none of our business."

"I don't believe in war," Taylor said, "but it's still our business. There's thousands of people over there without food or clothing."

"Maybe," Frank continued, "but as soon as one of our supply ships gets torpedoed, everybody's going to be calling for war." He sat up to gain a more commanding position and added, "That's exactly what Roosevelt wants, to get us into the war. You know why? Then all his Jew friends connected with the munitions manufacturers can make money."

"That's not true," Taylor rebutted. "The big companies are owned by Christians."

"I didn't say 'owned.' I said connected. Everybody knows the Jews own the banks and those Christian-owned companies get their money from the banks. Don't get me wrong. Hitler's a bad individual. But he's got the right idea when he takes away the Jews' power—kicks 'em out of the banks and takes away their businesses."

"Yeah. Then tortures and kills them by the thousands," Taylor said sarcastically. "You call that the right idea?"

"More Roosevelt propaganda. Anyway, you're a minister. You're supposed to say things like that. Me, I gotta deal with these people every day when I buy produce. They're some of the goddamnedest—excuse me, Reverend—pushiest people you'll ever meet."

"Hey! Hey! Time out," I shouted. "This is a picnic. We're supposed to be having fun." The men looked at me surprised, the women relieved. I stood up with the intention of setting out food for lunch, but then my anger boiled over. "Frank!" I said too loud, "it doesn't matter what you say. Hitler's going to attack England any day now. And my husband's going to be up there in an airplane fighting for you so you can sit on your sunburned ass and have a picnic." Red-faced and on the verge of tears, I ran from the group to the other side of the small island. Now I've done it, I thought, spoiled everybody's fun.

I heard footsteps behind me and turned to see Aggie. She put her arm around my shoulder and said, "Good for you. No wonder the bastard's divorced. Who could stand him?"

"Poor Sandy. I've ruined her date."

"Yeah, and maybe saved her life."

In a few minutes we returned to find everyone engaged in a softball game as if nothing had happened. Frank and I kept our distance for the rest of the afternoon. From time to time the girls made trips to the boat and the boys to the other side of the hill to relieve themselves. When Taylor approached me, I glanced around to see Phyllis disappearing into the cabin on *Bright Star.*

"Hi," he said.

"Hi."

"I only wish I'd said it myself."

"Thanks."

"Tomorrow's my day off and I'm taking the sailboat out. Would you like to come?" Then he added hurriedly, "I know you're married and I'm not trying to . . ."

"I know. I'll be there. When?"

"Ten o'clock." I nodded and we drifted apart.

After lunch we finished Phyllis's wine and sang along with the records she'd brought, from the "Beer Barrel Polka" to "Three Little Fishes." We were all laughing and the earlier tension was gone. On the way home, Frank took me aside and apologized.

"Becky, I'm sorry for going on like I did out there. Sure didn't mean anything against your husband. He's a brave guy to enlist like he did."

"Thanks, Frank. I'm sorry I blew up, too."

It doesn't pay to hold a grudge in a small town where you have to do business every day with the same people.

24

Taylor squinted at the club flag flying on the mast next to the OYC, and said, "Winds out of the south, about ten knots. How much time do you have?" We were standing on our dock next to *White Wings*, both of us dressed in shorts and polo shirts. Taylor wore a long-brimmed yachting cap and I a bandanna.

"As much time as we need."

"Good. I've got all day. If we head out beyond Lighthouse Point and tack south into open water, it'll take a while, but the sail back will be like flying. Okay with you?"

"Sounds great."

We pulled *White Wings* around to the head of the dock and tied her with her bow facing the south wind.

I couldn't believe I was doing this. Here I was, a married woman, about to spend whole hours alone on a boat with a man not my husband. I was embarrassed at how excited I felt. Nice man, too. I watched him out of the corner of my eye as he knelt to cleat the line. His thigh muscles were firm and his arms strong. He moved with smooth agility, like a dancer. Removing the canvas sail cover, he was all business and didn't seem to notice me in the way I had just looked at him. That was probably a good thing, I tried to tell myself. Unless, of course, he didn't find me attractive. I was still a little self-conscious about how my body had changed over the last year. My breasts were larger, the soft muscles in my arms and legs had firmed and the hollows around my shoulder bones filled in and smoothed out. At nineteen, almost twenty, my body had matured.

"While we're still tied up," Taylor said, "I'll hoist the mainsail, then you hoist the jib."

Soon the sails were up and luffing in the wind. I stepped back onto the dock and, at Taylor's command, released the forward line. Jumping aboard again, I gave a good push to the dock, swinging the bow into the channel. As the boat came around, Taylor released the stern line, we hauled in on the sheets, and we were under way. The sails billowed, sending us northeastward out of the harbor on a broad starboard reach. We flew past the boats moored in the harbor, coming too close to an inbound boat on a port tack.

"Let out the jib sheet, Becky. Spill some of the wind. We're too fast for these close quarters."

As I let go the jib sheet, he eased out the main. At a slower pace we moved out of the harbor beyond the last of the mooring buoys, then headed toward Lighthouse Point on a beam reach. We trimmed the sheets, securing them in jam cleats.

"We're in good shape. Sit back and relax."

I sat on the starboard bench and stretched out my legs over the centerboard well.

"Like it?" Taylor called, holding the long tiller in his left hand.

"I love it."

"Just wait till we round the point. The Neck's been blocking the full force of that south wind. We'll have ourselves some fun."

As the lighthouse, really a light-tower, passed off our starboard beam, I could feel big ocean swells rise beneath us and the wind increase dramatically. "We'll stay on this tack, but we'll be close-hauled to the wind, so bring in the jib sheet."

I'd done enough sailing to know what he wanted. I hauled in the jib sheet until he nodded, then secured it in the jam cleat. He brought in the mainsheet until the sail was close-hauled. With the wind and the waves approaching our starboard bow, we seemed to be moving very fast. The smaller waves, riding atop the swells, slid beneath our overhung bow as we tobogganed into the troughs. Then up the following swell we'd climb, gliding over its crest.

"Wow! Wonderful." The tip of a wave caught the bow, sending a fine spray across the deck. I wiped the salt water from my face and turned to Taylor. His eyes, deep set under thick eyebrows, were intent on the interaction of boat, wind, and ocean as he shifted his gaze from main and jib to the waters ahead. There was a touch of mastery in his expression that was made even more convincing by the slight aquiline curve of his nose. His head was turned upward, his jaw lifted, and his hair damp with spray. Lips slightly parted, he was the picture of excitement and profound satisfaction. I had not realized how full and sensuous his lips were.

"Something wrong? You were staring."

"No. Nothing," I said, embarrassed, and turned toward the bow.

"Wind's picking up. I'm afraid we're getting more sea than *White Wings* can handle."

"I love it, but you're captain."

"We'll come about on a reverse course and start falling off the wind. You let out the jib after we've come around. Okay?"

"I'm ready."

"Coming about," he called, pushing the tiller to the port side. Immediately, the bow swung to starboard and the boom passed over our heads. When the jib luffed, I let go the port sheet and pulled in the starboard. Holding the mainsheet, Taylor did a rolling turn with his body to the port side of the cockpit. I jam cleated the jib sheet and started to move aft, but Taylor told me to wait.

"Stay there. As we're falling off, I'll pay out the mainsheet and you do the same with the jib." Soon we were on a broad reach. At first it appeared we were moving slower than we had on the close reach, but as I watched us pass Marblehead Rock I could see we were flying. Like a bird in flight, *White Wings* lifted out of the water and began surfing down the swells.

"*White Wings.* The name's perfect. We're really flying." Taylor smiled proudly. Excitedly I called, "First mate requests permission to stand by the mast."

Taylor laughed. "Permission granted."

Carefully I climbed out of the cockpit and, holding the mast to steady myself, I stood. With my right hand on the mast, my left on the shroud, and my feet wide apart, I raised my face in challenge to the waters ahead. "I feel like a figurehead," I called, turning to look back at Taylor.

"And a beautiful one at that."

So, he had been looking at me. Facing forward again, I smiled.

We sailed before the wind all the way into Salem Sound, where we hauled in the mainsail and jib and made toward Juniper Point on a beam reach.

"What say we tie up and get a bite to eat in that amusement park?"

"Fine by me," I said. "It's called Salem Willows."

Soon we were walking under the gently swaying willows and tall maple trees to a concession stand, where we bought two hot dogs each and beers. Returning to the quay, we sat side by side on the rock wall.

Watching the sailboat bobbing next to the dock, I asked, "Where'd you get the name *White Wings?*"

"I didn't. My mother named the boat. It was hers before she married Dad."

"She picked a good name."

"It comes from a song she liked when she was a young girl. 'White wings, they never grow weary.' I'll play it for you on the piano sometime."

"I'd like that. Where do your parents live?"

"In California. They moved there last year. Dad used to work for Grumman Aircraft Company on Long Island, but went to California to work with Douglas. He's an aeronautical engineer. That's when Mom gave me the boat, when they moved."

"I'll bet your mom misses *White Wings.*"

"Probably. Her parents used to summer in Glen Cove on Long Island Sound. They gave her the boat when she was fourteen and she raced it every year until she married Dad. It's a Buzzards Bay 15. There were eight or nine in Glen Cove. Mom could beat 'em all. When she was nineteen she won a Long Island regional meet."

"Does she still sail?"

"No. Not for the last five years. They put the boat in the water each year and I used it when I was home on college vacation, but Mom had lost interest."

"Where'd you go to college?"

"I got my B.A. from Williams College, and then I went to ETS, that's the Episcopal Theological Seminary, in Cambridge. How about you? Where did you go?"

"You're kidding, aren't you? It was only last year I graduated from high school."

"Huh!" He took a drink of beer. "You seem older than nineteen."

"I'll be twenty in October." I wadded up my paper napkin and the cardboard holders from my hot dogs and stuffed them into the paper bag from the concession stand. "It does seem years ago that I graduated. So much has happened. I got married, went to night school, started a business with my husband, Jimmy, saw him through a long period of recuperation after a plane crash, and said good-bye to him when he left for the RAF."

"You miss him a lot?"

I thought for a moment, then said, "Yeah. I do."

Taylor added his napkin and hot dog holders to the bag. "What did you think about that business with Coleman yesterday at the picnic?"

I leaned back, braced my arms, and lifted my head to the sun. The light shone through my closed eyelids. "Frank's a bigot and a loudmouth," I said, "but he runs a good grocery store. He apologized to me on the way home." I opened my eyes and looked at Taylor. "Said he didn't mean anything against Jimmy."

"Well," he said, shaking his head disgustedly, "I was upset that anyone could be so oblivious of Hitler's torture and killing of innocent people."

"You mean the Jews? You think that's true?"

"I know it's true. I've talked to people who've escaped from Germany. There was a fund raiser in Boston last year for Jewish refugees. I heard what they said. It's appalling."

I sighed. "People in Marblehead don't care that much about what's happening in Europe."

"Except your husband."

"Jimmy?" I laughed. "All Jimmy wants to do is fly Spitfires. I don't think he gives a damn who he's fighting." I realized I'd said "damn" to a minister, but he didn't seem to notice. "What about you? You said we shouldn't get into this war."

"What I meant was, war doesn't solve anything."

"Oh," I said, more serious than I intended. "And what does solve things?"

He regarded me defensively, then the hardness in his jaw subsided and he smiled. "I wish I knew." He gazed longingly out to sea as if the answer was just beyond the horizon. "I wish I knew . . ."

"Changing the subject, I'm really glad you asked me to go sailing, but why me instead of Phyllis?"

"Ha!" He lifted his bottle and finished his beer. "Let me tell you what it's like to be a young unmarried minister in a new parish. Every week I'm invited to a house for dinner where there's a young unmarried daughter who happens to be home from college. That's how I met Phyllis. 'Mr. Harrington,' Phyllis's mother said, 'have dinner with us and come early so you can play tennis on our court with Phyllis. She's going to Wellesley, you know.' "

"Oh."

"Yeah. Right. And on Sunday morning I look out from the lectern and see five or six beaming faces just waiting for some indication I'd like to get to know them better. It sounds conceited, but it's true."

"Hmm." I looked at him through narrowed eyes. "And I'm safe because I'm married."

"In a way, yes. You're safe with me and I'm safe with you."

"And why are you so safe?" I joked.

"Why?" he asked with mock surprise. "Because I'm a deacon, soon to be a priest, and you're a married woman."

"Whew," I said, drawing my hand dramatically across my brow. "That's a relief. I guess we can be friends, then."

He laughed and, taking my hand in his, said, "Let's shake on it." I laughed too, but the ease with which my hand fitted into his warm, moist palm sent a shiver of excitement through my body. Part of me did not want to let go, and part of me said I'd better.

"Let's go sailing," he said, bringing me back to earth.

The way home was one tack after another, each close-hauled and driving into the wind. We made a good team, I on the jib and Taylor on the mainsheet and tiller. As we rounded Coney Rock and headed toward Marblehead, he said, "Want to take the tiller?"

"Love to." I slid past him and he moved forward. With the tiller in my left hand, I could feel the pull of the rudder. I watched the sail to keep it as close to the edge of the wind as possible without luffing. Taylor looked on approvingly. We exchanged smiles. Pretty soon he lay down on the floor of the cockpit in the shade of the sail and closed his eyes. I could reach the jib sheets, so when it came time to come about I did it myself. As the boom swung over and the sun fell on Taylor, he opened his eyes. Putting his arm across his forehead to shield them, he turned toward me.

"Not bad," he said.

"Thanks. Want to take over?"

"No, you're doing fine." He closed his eyes again. I executed several more tacks and he didn't move. As we neared the mouth of the harbor, I touched his foot.

"Taylor! Better take over."

He sat up quickly, rubbing his eyes. "Huh, I'd fallen asleep." He remained sitting for a few moments, then came aft to take the tiller. "Gosh, we're practically home. You did okay."

"Anytime, captain." I moved forward on the bench. Our close-hauled port tack took us most of the way to the hotel with only one starboard tack through the moored boats and a final port tack to bring us smartly in to the dock. After we'd tied up and furled the sails, I asked Taylor if he'd join me in a beer. He seemed uncertain at first, and I wondered if he was concerned about being seen too long in the company of a married woman. He puttered with the lines already secured to the dock cleats and finally said he'd like that. I told him to take a seat at the lawn table near the dock while I went to the hotel bar for the beer. When I returned we toasted our marvelous day of sailing.

"I can't tell you how much I've enjoyed myself today, Becky," he said with his arm on my shoulder in a comradely fashion. At his touch I caught my breath. Did he notice? But then he dropped his hand and continued. "I felt totally relaxed. Even went to sleep. You know, that's the first time ever I've slept while someone else was sailing *White Wings*. You're comfortable to be around."

I wanted to say he was too, and I'd sail to the ends of the earth if he'd ask. But I said nothing. Then he shattered my fantasy by saying, "You're so much like my sister, I can't believe it."

"That's a line if I've ever heard one." I forced a laugh.

He waited a minute, then said, "She died six years ago."

"Oh God, Taylor, I'm so sorry."

"That's okay. How could you have known? Her name was Virginia. We called her Jenny. She was five years younger than I. About the same as you."

"How did she die?"

"It was a car accident. Mom was driving. They'd gone into the city for a matinee and were on their way home to Glen Cove. Mom survived with a broken arm but Jenny was killed instantly."

"How terrible for your mother."

"Yes. She can't get over it. Blames herself even though the other driver was drunk and ran a red light. She had a nervous breakdown a few months later and spent two months in a hospital. She's never come back to her old self."

"How about you? How's it been for you?"

"We were very close. I was her big brother. The one who could do no wrong." He took a drink of beer.

"Dad was home when the call came. He ran down to the dock and hailed me. I'd been sailing *White Wings*." His shoulders slumped and he fell silent. "It's so strange," he said. "I never saw Jenny again. It was a closed casket funeral." He turned to look at me. "I wouldn't be surprised if, right now, Jenny were to come running down from the hotel across the lawn asking where I'd been and saying she'd been looking for me."

I covered his hand with mine gently.

"I might as well tell you the whole story now that I've started. Do you mind?"

"No. Please go on."

"I said Mom never got over it, and she hasn't. Mom's an artist, or, at least, was an artist. She studied in New York and Paris before Dad met her and was quite good. I've got a painting she did of *White Wings* in my apartment. It's beautiful. Soon after Mom and Dad were married, they moved into my grandparents' summer place in Glen Cove because it was an easy drive to Grumman. Also it was the perfect place for Mom to live, because Sea Cliff is right next door. It's an artist colony, so she found a group of people with whom to further her career. Unfortunately, it also furthered her problem with alcohol. When Jenny was killed, she went off the deep end. It was more than a nervous breakdown. It was a severe case of the DTs. She recovered, more or less, and she and Dad struggled for three years to get her back on her feet. Finally, when the offer came from Douglas, he took it, thinking a change of location away from all the things that reminded her of Jenny and away from her friends in Sea Cliff would help."

"And?"

"Actually, it has helped. Dad is working hard in his new job and isn't home much, but Mom's doing better, teaching art in a local high school."

"And what about you?"

"Me? I guess I'm still searching—trying to make sense out of all that's happened."

"I thought ministers had all the answers."

"I'm supposed to. I guess I know what they are. Now I've got to make them my own."

"While you're working on it," I said, pushing thoughts of Jimmy from my mind, "let me know if you need a good first mate to sail with again."

"You're on, Becky. How about next Monday?"

"I'll be here," I promised.

On the last Monday of August I waited on the dock for Taylor to arrive. For the entire month, his Mondays off had become our days for sailing. Today I'd gone to the boat half an hour before Taylor was due so I could surprise him by having everything ready: the cockpit covering removed and the deck scrubbed of bird droppings. As I'd done on our two previous trips, I'd prepared a picnic and stowed the basket under the foredeck. I told myself I wanted to impress Taylor, but I knew it was more than that. Mrs. James DeWolf was losing control of her feelings and, what's worse, was relishing it. This bothered me, not so much because I was married, but because I might scare Taylor off. To hide my joy at seeing him, I pretended a growing craze for sailing. This wasn't hard because we were having so much fun with *White Wings*, exploring the islands and rocks around Marblehead and testing the boat against all kinds of sea and weather.

And there was always something to talk about. We compared Marblehead with Glen Cove and my high school with St. Mark's, the boarding school he'd attended in Southborough. He wanted to know about the flying service Jimmy and I had, and I asked him about his work at St. Paul's Church. We talked about his love for music and my experiences growing up in a hotel. Each time we raised *White Wings*'s sails and ventured out into the ocean we drew closer to one another in an increasingly comfortable relationship.

The attractive force between us was becoming palpable, so we were careful not to sit too close or look at each other for too long. Instead, we satisfied our urge to touch with quick handshakes or pats on the back for jobs well done. But even this escalated. Last week, on our third trip, we picnicked on one of the islands. After a relaxed luncheon of wine, cold chicken, and potato salad, I rested my head on his stomach as we stretched out in the afternoon sun. It seemed so natural I did it without thinking. When it was time to wade back to the boat anchored just offshore at keel depth, we casually entwined our fingers.

At ten sharp, Taylor walked onto the dock.

"Look at this," he raved. "All ready to go." He patted me on the shoulder. I beamed.

"Hop in, skipper, and we'll shove off."

"Do you want to take her out?"

"Yes!" Today the wind was northwest but shifting almost ninety points on the compass as it found its way between the houses and hills of Marblehead. I was constantly adjusting the sheet between a close-haul and beam reach while dodging moored boats. Taylor sat in the front of the cockpit watching me with amusement. I saw him mimicking me by snaking his tongue out the edges of his mouth. Glaring, I clamped my lips shut. Finally we reached the harbor mouth.

"Where are you taking me today?" he asked.

"We haven't been to Manchester. It's a ways, but we've got all day. Ought to be a straight shot on a broad reach."

"Let's do it."

As Eagle Island passed on our port beam, I spotted *Bright Star*, Aggie's boat. Her father was at the wheel and she was winching up pots, removing the lobsters, and rebaiting the pots. She was so intent on her work that she didn't see us until we were nearly on them.

"Hi, Aggie," I called. "How's the catch today?"

"Mine's fine," she called back. "How's yours?"

"Only one, but a lot better looking than yours."

Taylor shook his head disgustedly.

"Can I come over when you cook him?"

"Sure," I yelled back to her as we sped away. "It'll take two of us to get him in the pot."

Out of earshot of *Bright Star*, Taylor said, "Good grief, Becky, I'm glad no parishioners heard that."

"Do 'em good, Reverend. They'd know you're not a stuffed shirt."

He sulked for a minute, then said, "Do you think I am?"

Keeping my eyes on the sail, I answered, "A little. But that's okay 'cause I love to tease you."

"I know you do, and I don't mind out here. But in town it's a different story. People have a certain image of what a minister is and I've got to respect that."

"I'm glad I don't have to," I said.

"Have to what?" he asked uneasily.

"Have to respect your image." I could feel myself getting annoyed. "I've seen you around town in your round collar. Frankly, you look pompous as hell. I don't think I want to know you when you're being the Reverend Taylor Harrington."

For the next five minutes we said nothing. Finally he spoke. "But I am the Reverend Taylor Harrington whether I'm out here or in town at St. Paul's Church. I'm not two people, Becky."

"Huh! Well, I didn't see Reverend Harrington complaining when I put my head on his bare stomach last Monday. Maybe that's because it was *Taylor* Harrington's stomach."

He gritted his teeth and sighed. "That's another thing. We're getting too familiar."

"Come on, Taylor," I said harshly. "You enjoyed it as much as I did."

He was quiet again, looking away from me and working his jaw.

"You know what I think?" I added. "I think Reverend Harrington uses Taylor Harrington whenever he wants to have some fun."

We sailed on for another five minutes in silence, avoiding each other's eyes. Eventually the gentle roll of the sea and the soft ocean breeze began to soothe my anger. As my blood cooled, my pleasure in having kicked Taylor squarely in the middle of his pomposity gave way to regret. I'm going to lose what I've got if I'm not careful, I thought.

"I'm sorry, Taylor." I turned to him. "That was a nasty thing to say."

"I'm sorry, too." He smiled, and I smiled back.

Between occasional glances at the sail, I continued staring at him. With a quizzical expression he asked, "What?"

"What?" I said. "Oh, my looking at you?"

"Yeah."

"I just like to look at you," I said in a dreamy voice.

He exhaled a long, deep breath. "I know what you mean. I like to look at you, too."

"It's scary, isn't it?" I said. "I'm married and you're a single minister in a small town."

He nodded. "I remind you of your sister."

Sadness crossed his brow. He nodded again.

"I'm lonely. My husband's in England. And I have more fun with you than I've ever had with anyone in my whole life, Jimmy included."

"I know." He glanced at me quickly and sighed. "I struggle through the week just waiting for Monday."

"What are we going to do?"

Taylor clenched his jaw. "Whatever we do, we can't go beyond just being friends. I'm a deacon in the Episcopal Church; soon I'll be a priest. It's not just a matter of scandal. Hell, I could cope with that. Move or something. It's a matter of vows. It's a matter of being called to the ministry." His eyes met mine with a look of sadness and deep sincerity. "I believe in what I'm doing, Becky, and I want it more than anything. It's my life."

My first thought was to make light of his words, to say he was kidding himself if he thought I'd ever get involved with him, but I knew he was right. I wanted to let go the tiller and crawl to him, throw my arms around him and tell him I loved him—tell him somehow we could work it out. But I also knew those were the very words I couldn't say. So we sailed on in silence, to an uncertain destination through an uncharted sea.

We returned in late afternoon, secured the boat, and said goodbye. Taylor trudged up the hill toward his apartment. I sat at the picnic table near the hotel dock. After several minutes I heard footsteps behind me. I turned to see Dad approaching with two bottles in his hand.

"Hi. Thought you might like to join me in a beer."

He sat down. We sipped our beer and watched the boats in the harbor.

"How's your minister friend getting on in Marblehead?"

"Okay, I guess. We don't talk much about it. Too busy sailing."

"Where'd he get the boat? It's a beaut."

"His mother gave it to him. It's been in their family for, let's see, over thirty years."

"Still in good shape, isn't it?"

"Yeah." I wondered where this small talk was leading. Dad hadn't said this much to me in years. Maybe he was concerned about the amount of time I was spending with Taylor. Or was I the one concerned?

"Becky, I've got a request." Here it comes, I thought. "How would you like to work for the hotel?"

"Waitressing?"

"No. Not waitressing. That was okay when you were growing up." He paused, took a deep breath, and continued. "Felix has been our bookkeeper and accountant for I don't know how many years. He's retiring—going to Florida. We've got to find a replacement. What do you think? It'd be good experience."

I didn't know what to say. I was pleased he'd thought of me, but combining one's parents with one's boss was pretty intimidating. As a waitress I'd reported to the chef, and Mom and Dad stayed out of it. Now I'd be reporting to them directly. Taking criticism or correction was not one of my strong points, especially from my parents.

Dad continued. "I'm sure you could handle the job. It's not full time, about twenty hours a week, but it'd give you a chance to learn more about the business. We'd pay you the same we paid Felix."

"It's not the money. I'm in good shape financially, though I like it that you'd pay me the same. Frankly, I'm not sure I could work for you and Mom."

Dad laughed. "Mother and I weren't sure we wanted you as an employee. We've gone back and forth about this a hundred times. Sometimes you can be a pain in the butt."

"Nooo. Really?"

"Yeah, really."

"Let me think about it overnight and I'll tell you tomorrow. And thanks."

He put his arm around my shoulder. "Truth is, Becky, Mother and I would be proud to have you working with us. In time, if you're comfortable with it, we'd like to share the management responsibilities as well."

I was surprised that I wasn't surprised when Dad mentioned management. In the back of my head I guess I'd always known they would like me to help run the hotel and eventually take it over. It would be either that or sell it. In the next ten years they would want to retire. Leaving the hotel to me would solve their problem and give me a guaranteed income and job. But I was married now. If I stayed married to Jimmy, and if he returned from the war alive and uninjured, who knew what the future held?

"I appreciate your confidence, Dad, but I can't see beyond the next couple of months, much less the next ten years. I'll think about the bookkeeping and let you know tomorrow."

I decided not to have dinner at the hotel with Mom and Dad as I usually did, to avoid any further talk until I'd had a chance to figure everything out. Instead I went to my apartment and called Aggie.

"Hi. You busy?"

"No. Just fixing dinner."

"How about coming over for hamburgers and then a movie? *My Favorite Wife*'s showing."

"Who's in it?"

"Irene Dunne and Cary Grant."

"Okay. Got to get Dad's dinner first, then I'll be over."

Aggie arrived twenty minutes later. I had laid out the buns, relish, and slices of onion. The hamburger patties were made and ready to fry.

"How about a Coke or a beer before we eat?"

"Beer, thanks."

We took our drinks down the steps to a patio behind the building. An enormous beech tree spread its branches over the yard, shading an iron table that was forever wobbling on the irregular bricks of the patio. We sat and balanced the beer bottles on the wrought iron flowers of its top.

"Thanks for asking me over. I needed to get out."

"And I needed somebody to talk to."

"Bet I know what about." Just as I started to speak, Aggie interrupted. "But let me go first."

I gave her a nod. Immediately she cut loose.

"I'm so damned tired of lobstering I could scream. I'm tired of spending all day with Dad, coming home, feeding him, and sitting around the house. What kind of future is that? And I'm lonely. You've got Taylor, even if you can't have him. At least it's somebody to talk with. If I didn't have you, Becky, I'd have nobody. And you and I are just like Taylor and you. I've got you but I can't have you."

"God! Aren't we a pair? So what're you going to do?"

"I don't know, but I'm sure as hell not going to go on lobstering all my life." She paused to take a drink of beer. "Saw an ad in the paper this week. GE in Lynn is hiring. They're gearing up for war work. Had a list of job openings a mile long."

"Women included?"

"It didn't say."

"And what about experience? Don't they use drills or lathes and things like that?"

"Hell, Becky. Don't rub it in. What I don't know I could learn."

"I can see some guy teaching you. Every time you made a mistake he'd shake his head like you're a dumb female."

"Probably, but I've got to find something. Dad's driving me nuts." She leaned over, picked up a stone, and threw it squarely against the trunk of the beech. Looking down at the ground for another stone, she said plaintively, "I thought maybe if I got a job I could make some friends—meet somebody. You know." I knew. "Well, I'm glad I said it. Now, what's with you and the Reverend? He's one good-looking guy."

"I know. We've had a lot of fun sailing on his day off."

"Yeah. That's what Karl said."

"Kramer?"

"Uh-huh. Now, you're not going to like this, but he claims he saw the two of you out on Ram Island and you were lying all over Taylor. Said he watched with his binoculars."

"That son of a bitch. Anything else?"

"He said he didn't think a minister would last long in Marblehead making out with married women."

"Oh, for God's sake. Wait till I see that bastard. I suppose he's told it all over town."

"Maybe. Maybe not. He said to tell you you better shape up and act like a married woman or he'd get word to Jimmy."

"God. I don't believe it. What business is it of his?"

"None. But you know Karl. He's still mad at you for leaving him. If he can't have you, nobody's going to."

"Shit, shit, shit." Aggie was right. I didn't like it. I sat there, jaws and teeth clenched. Finally I said, "Come on, let's go up and cook the hamburgers."

Sitting at my kitchen table eating dinner, Aggie gave me a penetrating look. "Is it really a story he's telling or did he see something he shouldn't have?"

I thought for a few moments, then said, "Taylor and I had finished our picnic lunch and were lying on the grassy top of the island. We were kind of dozing off and I rested my head on his stomach."

"That's all?"

"Honest. That's all we did." I paused. "But the truth is, I would've liked to have done more. Aggie, I'm falling in love with this guy."

"I can see. And Jimmy?"

"Jimmy? I don't know. I owe him a lot. I drive his car, I collect his trust fund income plus an allotment from his pay. If it weren't for him I'd still be living in the hotel instead of an apartment, working for nickels and dimes as a waitress. And he's off risking his life as a fighter pilot while I'm safe at home falling in love with a local minister."

"What makes you think he won't fall for someone over there?"

"He might. Or he might just sleep with her. Probably will, in fact. I could get a divorce, but, God, can you imagine how bad that would sound. LOCAL GIRL DIVORCES WAR HERO TO MARRY LOCAL MINISTER."

"See what you mean."

"Taylor and I talked about this today." Aggie looked at me sharply and I nodded. "He feels about me like I do about him.

We've decided to take it easy for a while and see if we can't get things back into balance, whatever that means. Anyway, next Monday's Labor Day and they're having a church picnic, so we won't be going sailing. Also, Dad's asked me to work for the hotel as bookkeeper and accountant. It'd keep me busy twenty hours a week and give me something to do."

"You going to take it?"

"Maybe I'd better. Get this juvenile delinquent off the streets."

"More'n that," Aggie said reprovingly. "Might make an honest woman out of you."

Two days later I ran into Karl Kramer in front of Coleman's. Carrying two large bags of groceries, he leaned against a light pole to ease the burden on his unsteady legs.

"Hello, Karl." I approached him with a wry smile.

He regarded me suspiciously. "Hello, Becky."

"Got a load there."

"Harriet's gettin' the car. Be here in a minute."

I stood on the curb about six inches from his face. His breath smelled.

"Aggie tells me you've been spying on people with your binoculars."

He sneered. "Hah. Right. You worried?"

"Not really. What have I got to worry about?"

"You oughta know."

"You see, Karl, I've done nothing wrong. It's only wrong in your dirty mind. And if I ever hear that you've told your stories to anyone besides Aggie, I'll tell Harriet you got the hots for me— that you're dying to get into my pants like the time you tried to rape me in your living room. I'll tell her I'm afraid of you and ask her to please try to keep you under control."

The familiar old Chevy coupe pulled up to the curb.

"Oh, here she is now," I said. "Why wait? I'll tell her now."

"You wouldn't dare."

I turned to Harriet and waved. "Hi, Harriet. Got a minute?"

"Sure," she called to me innocently as she got out of the car. "What's up?"

"Becky. Don't," Karl stammered.

I turned back to him, still inches from his face. "What have I got to worry about, Karl?"

"Nothing, Becky. Nothing."

"You're right. Make sure you keep it that way." Then, turning to Harriet, I said, "I hear they're starting a group to roll bandages for Britain over at St. Paul's Church. I've been thinking about going over there and thought you might like to join me."

Harriet came up to us. "That's very thoughtful of you, Becky. Let me know when they've set a time, and I'll see what I can do."

"I hope you can. We've lost touch with each other lately and it'd be nice to get back together. There's so much we could talk about." I looked at Karl and smiled. "Well, see you later."

Karl's face looked like he had something to worry about.

W e sailed only one more time after our trip to Manchester and that was the third Monday in September. Dressed in a rain slicker under which I wore only my bathing suit, I came down to the boat at six a.m. carrying a picnic basket. Only the service people at the yacht club were around, sweeping the deck after a Sunday night party. They noticed nothing beyond the end of their brooms. The lobster boats on their way to their pots had long since passed our dock. Taylor had stretched a rain canvas over *White Wings*'s boom, creating what looked like a tent covering the cockpit. I slipped beneath this cover and curled up under the cramped forward deck, resting my head on some life preservers, waiting.

I listened to the sounds around me, the sloshing of water in the centerboard well, the gentle bumping of the hull against the dock, the distant sound of a foghorn, and the tapping of a pulley block against the mast. I felt protected in the arms of *White Wings*, secure from the prying eyes of town gossips and sheltered from the drops of rain that spattered from time to time on the deck above. The boat I had first seen as a phantom sailing out of the fog had become my companion and source of joy.

I was not aware I had fallen asleep until I was awakened by the sound of familiar footsteps. Taylor was moving around on the deck above, washing off the bird droppings and unhooking the canvas cover. When he stuffed it into my hiding place, he saw me and gasped with surprise.

Recovering quickly, he whispered into the darkness of my cubbyhole, "I must tell Captain Bligh. We have a stowaway aboard."

"Oh, good Christian, don't tell the captain."

"Then you'd better behave and do what I tell you."

"Try me."

He smiled knowingly. "We'll start by you staying there until we're out of the harbor."

I remained hidden until I felt the rise and fall of swells beneath me, then slithered aft to where Taylor, in a yellow slicker, sat with his hand on the tiller. I stayed well below the gunwale, crawling until my head was next to his feet. Slowly I removed his shoes and began giving him a foot massage, first with my hands and then with my mouth and tongue. After several minutes his eyelids drifted shut and his breathing came in short gasps. Dreamlike, I felt as if the boat and I were one, making love to Taylor. With my rain slicker open in front, the cool, varnished ribs of *White Wings* melded against my ribs and the motion of the boat became the motion of my hips against the floorboards. *White Wings* had become my accomplice at love. The brazenness of my mouth and tongue fed my desires. Caressing his foot, I eased it into the top of my bathing suit, brushing his toes against my nipples and burying them between my breasts.

Suddenly he jerked back his foot, his eyes popped open, and he groaned, "Ready to come about—coming about." I collapsed onto my back where I lay for a long time until my breathing returned to normal. Then I crawled to the front of the cockpit, still remaining below the gunwales, and leaned against the life preservers.

"Close call," I said, breathing heavily.

"Too close." He sighed.

Then, with faltering voice, I said, "I lov—"

"Don't say it, Becky."

I looked at him for a while. "Well, you know."

* * *

Each time we parted, I was afraid I might not hear from him again. Sometimes I waited a day, sometimes a week, but he always called.

Early in October he telephoned. "Want to go for a ride out to Williams College?"

"Sure," I replied without a moment's hesitation. "What's happening?"

"I'm giving a talk on the Jewish refugee problem in Germany. Doesn't that sound exciting?"

"No, but being with you does."

Ignoring that, he said, "The fall colors should be great. Why not ask Aggie to join us?"

"Aha. A chaperone."

"In a way, yes."

The three of us left early for the long drive out Route 2 to Williamstown in the Berkshires. While Taylor attended a luncheon and gave his talk, Aggie and I roamed the town, visited the shops off campus, and had lunch. Then the three of us set off for Mount Greylock near North Adams, the highest point in the Commonwealth. We parked partway to the top and hiked the rest of the way by trail beneath tall pines, great oaks, and maples. The sunlight filtering through the fall leaves turned everything to hues of gold and red.

It was growing dark when we left for home. Aggie slept in the backseat.

"Mind if I take a nap?" I asked.

"Help yourself."

I lay down across the front seat.

"Put your head in my lap," he offered. "I'll be your pillow."

I did. We drove for many miles, his hands glued to the steering wheel and mine tucked in front of me. I dozed off. At a stoplight in Fitchburg, the change in motion of the car awakened me, but I didn't move. When we started again and he finished shifting, I felt his hand come down to my head and stroke my hair. How long had he been doing that? I wondered. Now fully awake, I relished this first cautious advance Taylor was making, hoping against hope his hand would move to my neck and ease itself beneath my blouse. But it didn't.

* * *

On the way to Williamstown, Aggie had offered her basement to Taylor for storing his boat during the winter, provided her father agreed. Mr. Sparr said if Taylor was willing to clear a space through twenty years of accumulated junk, he was welcome to use it. Toward the end of October we sailed *White Wings* down the harbor to a boatyard near Aggie's house, unstepped the mast, and lifted the boat onto the trailer using a stiff-leg derrick. Then Taylor towed the boat to the Sparrs' and, with Aggie and me making turning and stopping directions, after fifteen tries backed it into the garage under their house.

"Think your dad would mind if I worked on the boat some this winter?" Taylor asked.

"Help yourself. I'll give you a key and you can come and go as you please."

I gave him a pleading look. "Can I help?"

"I'm counting on it."

I ran into Taylor, dressed as usual in his black suit and round collar, in front of Coleman's Grocery on Wednesday, November 6. He had just picked up a copy of the *Globe* and was reading it as he walked along.

"Aren't you going to say hello?" I said.

"Oh, hi, Becky. Great news, isn't it? Roosevelt winning."

"Not great news in Marblehead. I take it you voted for him."

"Well, didn't you?"

"Taylor, damn it. You know I'm not old enough to vote."

"Oh, yeah. Sorry." But he didn't look sorry. He was jubilant. "I would have voted for Eleanor if I could, but I had to settle for Franklin." This astounded me, because Eleanor's buck teeth and travels were the butt of many jokes. "Of the two, she's the one with compassion. Franklin goes along with social programs if it's politically expedient."

I thought I'd never understand Taylor. My parents, staunch Republicans, had voted for Wendell Wilkie, saying Roosevelt was hell-bent on getting us into the war regardless of his promises to the contrary. To my surprise, the DeWolfs, also lifelong Republicans, had voted Democratic for the first time, because of

Roosevelt's stand on lend-lease to Britain. Jimmy could use all the help he could get, they said. Now Taylor went on to say that Eleanor was the only one who understood what Hitler was doing to the Jews in Germany.

On November 14 I received another letter from Jimmy. He'd been writing me about once a week and I didn't expect anything out of the ordinary from him, though I was puzzled by a new military address on the envelope. I opened it and the first words struck me between the eyes.

Dear Becky,
I've been in the hospital for a week. I was shot down during one of the raids on London.

Immediately my eyes misted, my vision became blurred. I felt weak and sat down. Wiping my eyes with the back of my hand, I read on.

I'm okay now. It really wasn't so bad. My right tibia was shattered by a bullet and my hands were burned from a fire in the cockpit. I bailed out of the Hurricane and injured my leg some more by snapping the fibula when I hit the ground. They got me to a hospital right away and doctors repaired the damaged bones and treated the burns on my hands. You can see by the fine handwriting that I'm not writing this. I'm dictating it to one of the volunteers who helps out here. It's a nice hospital. Actually, it's an old manor house and has beautiful lawns and gardens although there's nobody to really keep them up now. I'll be here for a while so I'll write again soon and let you know how things are. Please read this to Mom and Dad and give them my love. Be sure to tell Mom I'm okay. And Becky, I miss you and love you very much.

Jimmy

That night I went to the DeWolfs' for dinner and took the letter. I wanted George and Florence together when I read it. The minute I entered the house, Florence knew something was wrong.

"What is it, Becky? What's happened?"

"Jimmy's had some trouble, Mom, but he's okay now. He's been wounded."

Instantly she burst into tears.

I got her seated and George came to her side. Embracing her, he said, "Becky, read us the whole letter."

We'd grown accustomed to Jimmy's self-censorship in his letters. He skipped over details of the fighting, never mentioning where he was or when certain events took place. But by comparing his letters to newspaper accounts we were able to piece together the picture of the air battle between the RAF and the German Luftwaffe. In his letters from last August, he told us how he was flying every day from dawn to dark and was so tired he often fell asleep at the dinner table. He praised the courage of his buddies, some of whom he said he would never see again. In a September letter he mentioned that his second Hurricane flew just as well as his first, and we wondered if he'd been shot down and had to bail out. At about that time the *Boston Globe* was describing the waves of Messerschmitt fighters and Dornier bombers, sometimes seven to twelve hundred in a wave, that were crossing the Channel and attacking airfields and aircraft in the hopes of wiping out the RAF prior to an invasion attempt. When the bombing of London and other cities began that month, the paper was full of stories about the valiant defense the RAF was putting up against the Germans. We didn't dare talk about it, but we were sure Jimmy was involved. This last letter confirmed it.

Searching for a way to accept the latest news, Florence said, "Maybe it's a blessing. Maybe he'll come home now and leave the fighting to someone else."

But that wasn't to be. After two months recovering, he was flying again.

It was the letter from Jimmy about his being wounded that provided the final push to get me to join the Bandages for Britain group at Marblehead's St. Paul's Church, the same church where Taylor was curate. Every Saturday morning beginning in December, I met for two hours with about twenty other women in the parish hall. We sat around long tables laying out and cutting sheets of gauze and rolling them into neat square bandages. The work was rewarding because of Jimmy, but I had little in common with the other women. The young mothers talked about their babies, the middle-aged about their teenagers, and the older ladies about their rheumatism and bunions. I was in a separate category, treated with sympathy and respect as the only person in Marblehead whose husband had actually been wounded in what was being called the Battle of Britain, a hero who might have been a recipient of the very bandages we rolled.

It was strange, sitting there in the church rolling bandages for Jimmy and knowing that Taylor was close by. My love for Jimmy was real, and yet one look at Taylor could send my heart spinning. Since the episode last September in *White Wings*, I had become the very picture of a respectable married woman minding the home front while her husband was in the service overseas. My job at the hotel had quickly expanded from twenty to thirty-five or forty hours a week as I took on more management responsibilities. I was aware of no whispers about a relationship with a certain young minister in town or rumors about mice that play while the cat's away. According to Aggie, people in the town considered me a dutiful wife and spoke well of my courage when Jimmy was wounded.

The day I joined Bandages for Britain, I was terrified of meeting Taylor in some hallway. It wasn't until the second week that I ran into him when I was looking for the ladies' room and wandered into the nave of the church. There he was, looking like a Catholic priest in his long black cassock and round collar. This was the Taylor I didn't want to know. A flock of preschoolers and first and second graders were scattered around the sanctuary. Taylor was standing in front of the altar talking to Phyllis's mother, Mrs. Shade, who was dressed in a tweed suit with a red and green scarf tossed rakishly over her left shoulder. I evaporated into the shadows under the balcony and sat down.

"But it's so simple, Mrs. Shade, and so much more fun for the kids."

"That's not how we do a Christmas pageant at St. Paul's, Taylor. We have a tradition that goes back as far as I can remember. Last year's angel is this year's Mary and last year's Joseph is this year's narrator and so on down the line to the wise men, the shepherds, the little angels, and even the sheep."

"But they all know the story. We can have them do it *ad lib*. They already know what they're supposed to say."

"Fine. Fine," Mrs. Shade said, her voice raspy. "But if you think my name is going to be in the program as chairman of a Christmas pageant debacle, you're wrong. You want it that way, you run it." She turned and stomped out of the church.

Taylor watched her leave as the children sank onto the carpet. Then he walked to the center of the sanctuary and sat down on the top step. Without speaking, he gestured for them to gather around him. Cautiously at first, they crept up to him until they were on the steps by his side and around his feet.

"Today," he said, "I want you to tell me the Christmas story, and in a couple of weeks you can tell the whole congregation."

What a guy, I thought. He loves those kids and they love him. I watched for a while, then quietly returned to my bandages.

Christmas came and Aggie and her father invited Taylor and me to her house for dinner. On his days off Taylor had been working on *White Wings* in the Sparrs' basement, so it was possible for him to sneak upstairs and for me to arrive by the back door without causing comments from the neighbors. It was a beautiful night with fresh snow that was continuing to fall.

After dinner, hidden by the darkness of the night, Taylor walked me home in a roundabout way that took us to the hill behind the ball field. Several children were trying out new sleds on the hill, so he and I tramped through the snow into the woods above the hill. There, under the boughs of a large pine tree heavy with the new snow, we exchanged presents. I gave Taylor a brass compass so he could always find his way home, and he gave me a bottle of Chanel No. 5 so I'd never be able to sneak up on him again like I did in the boat last September.

Suddenly a breeze moved the pine tree and the bough above released its burden of snow on us. Laughing, we shook our heads, then Taylor took off his mitten and brushed the snow from my face. As it melted, he drew his fingers through the droplets, massaging the soft flesh in the hollows of my cheeks and tracing the crest of my lips around and around until my body tingled. I lifted my face and pressed my body against his. Tilting his face to mine, he said, "You are the most beautiful person I've ever known." Then he placed his lips on mine and kissed me. "Becky, I love you. I've tried so hard not to, but I can't help it." He kissed me again on my lips and my nose and my eyes.

"I love you, too," I said, frantically returning his kisses. It was as if a dam had burst and the passions we had so long contained enveloped us.

Then I felt his hands on my arms, moving me back, pulling my lips from his. "Becky, Becky," he moaned, and he began to cry until his crying wracked his whole body. I held him, burying my head in his shoulder, my eyes filling with tears. The wall that separated us, restrained us, returned—he, the deacon about to become a priest, on one side of the barrier, and I on the other, a married woman duty-bound to love her overseas husband.

I saw little of Taylor during the next two months. Both of us were trying to sort out the confused emotions that had erupted Christmas night. I knew I owed Jimmy my support while he was overseas, and in some ways I still loved him, but I knew that if Taylor asked me to leave Jimmy and marry him, I would do so in a minute.

Why didn't he ask?

The answer came, indirectly, one night when we were working on *White Wings* in Aggie's basement garage. He was carefully sanding away the varnish from the mahogany brightwork and replacing it with linseed oil which he applied with endless rubbing.

I said to him, "I hear Sandy and Frank are getting married in June in the Congregational Church."

"That's what I hear." Rub, rub, rub.

"Didn't they ask you to marry them?"

"Yup." Rub, rub, rub.

"Why aren't you going to?"

"Can't." Rub, rub, rub.

" 'Cause you're only a deacon and not a priest?"

"Nope." Rub, rub, rub.

"Will you stop rubbing for a minute and answer me in more than one word?"

He put his oily rag down and sat up. "They're getting married in June. I'll be ordained to the priesthood by then. That's not it." He wiped his hands on a dry rag. "Frank was married before."

"Well, he got a divorce, didn't he?"

"That's right, but that's not how it works in the Episcopal Church. Marriage is a sacrament, which means it's a bond made between the two people and God. Divorce dissolves the legal contract of marriage, but there's still the sacramental bond."

"But Frank wasn't married in the Episcopal Church."

"Doesn't matter what church he was married in."

Suddenly I realized we were talking about ourselves. "Well, that's bullshit. Where does the Episcopal Church get off being so damned cocky?"

"It's always been that way. Marriage is one of the seven sacraments."

"That's as bad as the Catholic Church."

"Bad or good, it's the same."

"And what do you think?"

"I think you don't mess with the sacraments."

I jumped off the workbench I'd been using as a seat. "Well damn you, Taylor, I'm just glad I'm not an Episcopalian." I stormed out.

Walking back to my apartment through an April rainstorm, I cried. The lines were drawn—and had been drawn from the beginning. I just hadn't realized it. Either Taylor remained an Episcopal priest and we didn't marry, or he gave up the priesthood to marry a divorced woman. It was a dead end. There was nowhere to go.

April gave way to May, but showers lingered on and dark clouds blotted out the warming sun. In the church parish hall another session of bandage making was coming to an end.

"Well, that's it for today, ladies," said Mrs. Palmer, the coordinator of our bandage group. "I thank you all very much for coming. We'll meet again next Saturday."

I helped clean up our work area and carry the boxes of

completed bandages to Mrs. Palmer's car for delivery to the Red Cross office in Boston.

As I was picking up my jacket, I heard the organ playing in the church. Only Taylor, who was far more proficient than the regular church organist, could play like that. I walked into the nave and sat in the rear beneath the balcony. "A Mighty Fortress Is Our God" thundered through the church, vibrating the ancient stained glass windows. His head, just visible above the altar rail as he sat at the organ, moved up and down with the same driving intensity as the music.

As I watched, I could feel the hopes and fantasies I had so carefully nurtured over the last year bend and break under the crushing weight of reality. There he was, The Reverend Taylor N. Harrington, black suit and round collar, clergyman, sitting at the organ of St. Paul's Church. Not the Taylor Harrington about whom I fantasized, the Taylor who sat in *White Wings* with his hand on the tiller and the wind blowing his hair, the Taylor who looked into my eyes and kissed my lips, the Taylor who said he loved me.

Without thinking, I began walking toward the chancel until I was standing beside the organ. His jaw, rock hard, beat out the notes, but his half-closed eyes were filled with sadness. Sensing my presence, he looked up and, still playing, beckoned me to sit beside him. I sat down and watched his hands and feet fly over the keys and pedals until he reached the final chords. As the reverberation died in the darkened nave, he put his arm around me and pulled me to his side.

"It's as hard for you as it is for me, isn't it?" he said.

"It's awful."

We sat holding each other for several moments, my head on his shoulder. When he turned toward me, the softness had returned to his face and there was a trace of a smile at the corner of his mouth.

"I want to play something for you. It seems years ago that I promised I would."

He adjusted the stops on the organ so only the sound of a flute was heard and quietly ran through the melody. Then he sang the words.

White wings, they never grow weary,
They carry me cheerily over the sea:
Night comes, I long for my dearie,
I'll spread out my white wings and sail home to thee!

"Becky," he whispered, "let's make *White Wings* our secret place, as far away from the world as we can get, where only we decide what's right or wrong."

27

Thursday, May 16, I clutched a copy of the *Marblehead Messenger* under my arm and stormed into Aggie's basement. Taylor had asked me to help him put the final touches on *White Wings* so we could launch her on Monday. Before I could speak, he said, "I take it you've seen Frank Coleman's letter to the editors?"

"I can't believe it." I spread open my paper on the workbench. "What's it all about?"

"A discussion I led for seniors at Marblehead High School. About why Congress keeps procrastinating over the refugee problem. You know the Wagner-Rogers Bill?"

"No."

"Well, it would have brought in twenty thousand refugee children from the Continent, but Congress argued and argued about it, finally defeating it. Then they passed the Mercy Ships Bill to bring British children here. So, do you know why the one failed and the other passed?" I shook my head. "Because the first one would have brought mainly Jewish children from Germany and France and the second one brought nice little blond kids from England."

"Well, what's Frank got his ass in an uproar about?"

"The truth? I think he's mad at me because I wouldn't marry them."

"Maybe." I looked down at the paper. "Sounds like Sandy had a part in this too. The bigotry's Frank's but the writing's too good to be his." I read aloud:

" 'Just let government cross into the realm of religion and the Church has a fit. But apparently the Rev. Taylor Harrington has no objection to crossing the line the other way into matters that belong to government.

" 'His double standard is bad enough, but contaminating young minds with his simplistic religious liberalism . . .'

"Now that *has* to be Sandy's.

" '. . . is inexcusable. Who isn't shocked by what the Nazis did to the Jews on Kristallnacht—'

"What's that, Taylor?"

"When they broke the windows of Jewish stores and houses, and drove them from their homes."

I read on:

" '. . . the Nazis did to the Jews on Kristallnacht, but you don't solve these complex problems just by opening the doors to more immigration.

" 'What Rev. Harrington seems to overlook is, we're practically in a war with Germany. It's an established fact that the Nazis hide their fifth column spies among the refugees they send into our country. Can you imagine what 20,000 Hitler Youth disguised as Jewish refugees could do to our children?

" 'I ask the teacher of the civics class where Harrington spoke to read this letter to his children so they won't condemn Congress for being realistic when hard choices have to be made.' "

Taylor shook his head in disgust. "I think I'll write a letter answering this back."

"Forget it. Leave it be. He's probably stirred up enough trouble already." I closed the paper. "How did he find out you were there?"

"I told him."

"You told him?"

"Yeah. I was buying a quart of milk and he asked what I'd been up to lately."

"And you told him all this stuff about Jewish refugees?"

"No. Just that I'd spoken to the civics class."

"Well, he must have talked to some of the kids or the parents, Taylor." I took his shoulders and turned him toward me. "Drop it. They'll run you out of town on a rail. What's the big deal, anyway?"

He sighed. "Becky, if I lived in Germany, I'd be in a concentration camp. My grandmother, my mother's mother, was a Jew. That'd make me Jewish."

"But you're a Christian minister. How can you be Jewish?"

"As far as the Nazis are concerned, it's a race, not a religion."

"Yeah, and here too. In Marblehead, I mean. Drop it."

When the boat was finished and it was time to put it back in the water, a sixth sense told me not to be seen alone in the boat with Taylor. Aggie joined us and the three of us sailed it back to our hotel dock. The day was rainy with increased winds expected for the afternoon—not a good day for sailing. During the short ride from the boatyard, Aggie said she had some big news to tell us after we'd docked. I suggested we go up to the hotel for coffee.

In the dining room I asked, "What's the big news?"

"I've got a job at GE in Lynn."

"Congratulations, Aggie," Taylor and I said in unison.

"And it pays almost twice what Dad and I can make in a week lobstering, but don't tell him."

"What's he going to do without you in the boat?" I asked.

"He may have to cut back on the number of pots, but he'll be all right. Took him a while to accept the fact I'd be leaving, but, hell, I've got a life of my own to lead."

"Are you moving to Lynn?" Taylor asked.

"Not at first. Give Dad some time to get used to me being away during the day. I can take the train. It's easy."

Mom and Dad stopped by the table to say hello and to add their congratulations when they heard about the job.

"Oh, by the way," said Taylor, "my parents are coming to my ordination to the priesthood and asked me to make reservations for them here."

"We'll be pleased to have them," Mom said. "When are they coming?"

"They're making a little vacation out of it, arriving on Saturday, May twenty-fourth and leaving on Monday, June second. The ordination's on Sunday the first at the eleven o'clock service. You're welcome to come."

"We might just do that."

Taylor turned to me. "I hope you and Aggie will come, too."

Aggie laughed. "Taylor, I haven't been in a church since baccalaureate."

"I know." He laughed, too. "Why do you think I'm getting ordained?"

"Well, maybe." Aggie frowned.

"I'll be there," I said quietly, but I was thinking that his parents being in Marblehead meant ten days without seeing him.

I went alone to the ordination, both my parents and Aggie declining. Mom and Dad felt that one of them had to remain at the hotel and the other didn't want to go alone. Aggie, of course, never did plan to go. The church was crowded. An usher led me all the way down the aisle to the second row from the front. Were all these people here for Taylor, I wondered, or was it the visit of the Rt. Rev. John Kline, Bishop of Massachusetts?

Taylor's mother and father, Vivian and Clifford Harrington, were across the aisle in the front row. I'd seen her in the hotel during the past week but hadn't spoken to her. Why should I? Who was I to her? And Taylor hadn't bothered to introduce us. I imagined myself walking up to her and saying, "Hi, Vivian. I'm your future daughter-in-law, as soon as I can unload my current husband." Instead I watched her from a distance. Attractive in a regal sort of way, she was tall and slim with severe features. On Monday she and Taylor had gone sailing in *White Wings*, and I'd watched, burning with jealousy as they left the dock. *White Wings* belonged to Taylor and me—it was our secret place not to be shared.

The service began with the ordination and the bishop asking Taylor if he thought he was truly called to the priesthood. Taylor said yes. Several more questions were asked to which Taylor gave answers written in the prayer book. It seemed so mechanical—stand, kneel, say what's written, don't think for yourself. "Darling," I wanted to shout, "don't let them hook you. Come away with me before it's too late."

The words of the bishop again penetrated my consciousness.

"Will you fashion yourself a wholesome example and pattern to the flock of Christ?"

To which Taylor read, "I will apply myself thereto."

That's it, I thought, there goes our chance ever to be together again. I began looking around at the aisle and the doors, searching for a way to escape.

When the ordination part of the service ended, Bishop Kline climbed into the pulpit before I had a chance to leave. As he preached, I heard him speak of injustice, prejudice, and greed, but it meant nothing to me. My mind was beset by one overpowering question. Taylor, why are you doing this? Why are you throwing away our love, our chance to be together?

When the sermon ended, they moved directly into Holy Communion. Again there was no way I could make a discreet exit. After several prayers at the altar, Taylor and the bishop turned to the congregation, each holding up a wafer above a Communion cup. At this signal Mrs. Harrington went to the altar rail with tears streaming down her cheeks to be the first to receive Communion from her son.

I could stand no more. I slid out of the pew and into the aisle, pushing myself past the people coming forward for Communion. Running out the door and down the walk, I started crying. I had lost him forever. Lost him to the priesthood and lost him to his mother.

Taylor's parents left the next day. I was so angry with Taylor that I wouldn't answer the phone for more than two weeks in case it was he calling. Three times he telephoned the hotel but the desk clerk, at my instruction, told him I was busy. I felt miserable, my stomach hurt, I was hardly eating, and I was bitchy to everyone.

By Saturday the twentieth, I decided to hell with it. I wasn't going to let Taylor ruin my life and I certainly wasn't going to let his mother get in my way. That night the phone rang and I picked it up.

"Hello," I said defiantly.

It wasn't Taylor. It was Jimmy.

28

I was thunderstruck. "Jimmy. My God! Where are you?"

"In Washington. Oh, Becky, it's so good to hear your voice."

"Yours too," and I think I meant it. "Are you coming home?"

"Just for two days, then I fly back to England."

"You okay? You're not sick or anything?"

"I'm fine. Homesick. I've missed you."

I mumbled something about missing him, too. Then I asked, "How come you're here, in the States?"

"I'll explain when I get home. I'm at the airport. I leave in a few minutes on Northeastern flight 258 and get in at ten. Can you pick me up?"

"Of course I can. See you then, darling."

I hung up and remained seated by the telephone table in the hall of my apartment. I couldn't believe it. In three hours I'd be seeing Jimmy. And I was excited. Did I say darling? Guess I did miss him. What would it be like being with Jimmy, I wondered, putting my arms around him, kissing him? And Taylor? How did I feel about him? In the meantime I called the DeWolfs, got Florence, and gave her the news.

"You've got to stop by the house, Becky. I don't care how late it is."

"We'll stop by for a while, but then we'll go on to my apartment. I'm sure you understand."

"Of course, but plan to come back here tomorrow afternoon and stay for dinner. When does he go back?"

"He didn't say the hour, but sometime day after tomorrow."

"Such a short time. Please let us have as much time with him as possible, Becky."

"Don't worry, Mom."

I went to the gate next to the ramp when the DC-3 taxied up. The door swung open and the stairs lowered. At least ten people deplaned before I saw Jimmy. He stopped for a moment, looked over the crowd of greeters until he saw me, then waved. I jumped up and down, waving my arm in the air. Slowly he came down the steps, holding the rail with his right hand. In his left was a cane. He crossed the tarmac with a quick but halting stride, leaning on his cane with each step. I eased myself past the crowd at the gate and ran to him. We kissed and, arm in arm, headed for the gate. I noticed he wore a pair of kidskin gloves.

"Lieutenant!" a stewardess called from the door of the plane. "Your bag." She held up a small overnight case and, seeing Jimmy's cane, brought it to us. "You might need this."

"Thanks." He smiled, and said to me, "That wouldn't have happened in England. There're so many with canes and crutches."

"Let me carry that."

"I've got it. I'm really all right. It's just nice to get the attention."

"You've lost weight."

"Yeah. About twenty pounds." The boyish fullness in his face was gone, causing his jaw and cheekbones to stand out sharply. He looked even handsomer in a gaunt, rugged sort of way. With strands of his blond hair falling from beneath the hat cocked on the side of his head, and his uniform rumpled from the long flight, he was as striking a war hero as any girl could hope for. I felt proud walking beside him with my arm around his waist.

"The car looks great, Becky. You've been taking good care of it."

"Thanks. Hop in. I'll drive." We left the lot and started for Lynn. I could see his head beginning to nod before we'd left East Boston. "Has it been a long flight?"

"Well, let's see. Five hours to Reykjavik, Iceland, seven to Gander, Newfoundland, and five to D.C. Then three more to here. That's what?"

"Twenty hours. You must be exhausted."

He didn't answer. He was asleep.

When we pulled into his parents' driveway, the house was ablaze with lights. His mother and father burst from the front door as I turned off the ignition. With hugs and kisses from his mother and slaps on his back from his dad, they greeted him. Then his mother saw the cane and cried. "You *are* hurt."

"No, Mom. It just keeps me steady when I walk. The leg's all healed."

"Well, come in and sit down. I've fixed some apple pie and ice cream for you."

"If you don't mind, I'll take a rain check. I haven't slept in two days and I'm exhausted."

We assured them we'd return as soon as he got up the next day, and headed for Marblehead. He nodded off again on the fifteen-minute trip along the shore. I parked behind the building and roused him enough to climb the steps to my apartment.

"Nice place, Becky." He wandered through the rooms, barely glancing at them until he found the bedroom. "How about a nightcap? I've got some Irish whisky in my case. Would you mind getting it while I undress?"

"Coming up." I went to the kitchen for ice.

By the time I'd brought two glasses to the bedroom, he was in bed sound asleep. I undressed, brushed my teeth, and crawled in beside him. It felt so good to have a warm body pressed against mine and so natural that it was Jimmy's. Gone was the uncertainty of how I would react to him. It was as if he'd never left. I spooned up next to his back, reaching over his side to hold his hand. I couldn't see them, but I felt the hard blisters that covered his hand like the scales of a fish. No wonder he wore the gloves.

He was still asleep at noon the next day when I gently shook his shoulder.

"Hey, Flying Officer DeWolf, you'd better get up. There're people waiting to see you." He jerked up looking confused, then relaxed onto his back. That old bewitching smile lit up his face. He reached for me and we kissed, but I quickly got up from the bed.

"Let's save it for later. Get your shower and shave. Mom called and invited us for lunch."

While he'd been sleeping that morning, I'd ironed his uniform and shined his shoes. He looked striking as we entered the DeWolfs' house. Florence's eyes grew moist as he removed his gloves and she saw his scarred hands.

"Why don't they send you home?" She was on the point of tears. "You need a cane and your hands—can you use them?"

"'There, you see?" He flexed his fingers and thumbs but had difficulty clenching his fist. "I'm too valuable to send home, Mom. They need pilots, and besides, there're guys flying who are in much worse shape."

His father put his arm around Jimmy's shoulder and led him into the dining room. "What brings you here?" George asked. "You on leave?"

"No, they arranged it so I could come home for a couple of days. Nice of 'em, huh? We flew some senior officers to Washington to handle the replacement of British troops in Iceland by American soldiers. The Brits have been there since the Nazis took Denmark. This'll free 'em up to fight in Africa. They said they needed a navigator familiar with U.S. airports, but I think it was just an excuse to give me a couple of days off."

Mom had prepared steak and eggs with toast and homemade strawberry jam. Jimmy put cream and sugar into his coffee, smelling its aroma as he stirred it.

"We don't get food like this. Meat, eggs, sugar, and coffee are all rationed. We do better at the airfield than the people in town, though."

"Can I get you some more?" Florence was up and on her way to the kitchen before Jimmy could say he was full.

"I'll just have more coffee, thanks." He sat quietly, no longer the exuberant Jimmy always anxious to get moving. When the conversation lapsed, he withdrew into himself and sipped his coffee or looked out the window. He smiled when spoken to and perked up to answer questions, but let others take the lead, again unlike the old Jimmy. I found myself drawn to him in a different way. In the past I was cautious, on my guard, ready to parry hurtful remarks. Now I felt comfortable, without fear of reprisal.

Florence poured him some more coffee, then returned to her chair. Hesitantly she asked, "What time do you have to go back tomorrow?"

"I have to catch the seven a.m. flight to Washington, so I'll need to leave Marblehead at six. I think I'd better just go straight there."

She dabbed at her eyes with her napkin and began carrying dishes to the kitchen.

"Let's make the most of today, then," his dad interceded. "Alan and Sarah are coming up from New Haven about three o'clock and we've invited Becky's parents along with your Uncle Howard and Aunt Regina for dinner."

"Sounds like a busy day," Jimmy said wanly.

"There's a lot more people who'd like to say hello, but we thought we ought to keep it small."

"Thanks."

Dad continued. "We've been following what's happening over there in the newspapers, trying to match it up with your letters. We figure you're somewhere near London."

"Right. I'm with the Eighty-fifth Hurricane Squadron out of Debden, which is a few miles northeast of London. But I'm being transferred when I go back."

"Do you know where? It helps if we know so we can follow it in the paper."

"North African theater. Malta, maybe Alexandria."

"Alexandria I know. Where's Malta?"

"It's an island in the Med south of Sicily. Controls access to North Africa. When I go back I'll be checked out in Spitfires, finally, then off to Africa."

The minutes drifted by. George talked hopefully about British advances in Syria and Ethiopia.

"I expect you'll be in the thick of it," he said.

"Probably," Jimmy replied.

After a while Jimmy's mother came in from the kitchen drying her hands on a dish towel and said she'd heard enough war talk.

She invited Jimmy into the garden. He followed obediently. It was a warm, sunny day with billowy cumulus clouds over the water. I sat on the back porch and watched mother and son stroll about the garden, her arm through his. He admired her sweet peas, already ripe on the vine, and the tomatoes climbing up their stakes. Her eyes left Jimmy's face only long enough to point out her prize roses or azaleas. From time to time she touched the corners of her eyes with her handkerchief.

A car tooting in the driveway brought George and me to the front of the house. Alan and Sarah were sitting in a brand-new Ford convertible coupe, a present from his father upon graduation from Yale two weeks earlier.

Jimmy and his mother came onto the porch.

"Ahh! There he is. The conquering hero," Alan exclaimed as he and Sarah walked to the porch. "Get a load of the cane. Very distinguished."

"Like your car."

"Great, isn't it? Want to go for a ride?" Jimmy looked at his mother, who nodded yes, so the four of us got in the car, women in back, men in front. We drove through Lynn at a respectable speed. When we reached Route 1, Alan floored the accelerator and the car leaped forward. He turned to his brother, grinning. "Not bad, huh?"

"Great, and thanks for the reprieve. It was like a morgue back there."

"Yeah?" He edged it up to eighty-five, one eye on the road and the other on the rearview mirror.

"Hey!" Sarah shouted into the wind. "Slow down. We can't talk back here."

"What's to talk about?"

"You know," Sarah said. "Let's tell them."

"Oh yeah." He slowed down to sixty. "Can we trust 'em?"

"I'm dying to tell somebody."

"What's the big secret?" I asked.

"Well, Alan and I are married. We got married last week in New Haven."

"Congratulations." I threw my arms around her and kissed her cheek.

"That calls for a toast," Jimmy said, taking a flask out of his coat pocket. This is new, I thought. He offered it to the backseat but we declined. Alan took a quick swallow out of courtesy, and Jimmy three good swigs.

"Why the secrecy?" I asked.

"It wasn't so much to keep it a secret as to get it done in a hurry. We figured with Alan graduating and losing his student exemption, we just didn't know what could happen. A big wedding would have taken forever to get planned."

"Have you told your folks?"

"No. Mom'll have a fit." She looked at me, her conspiratorial smile saying there was more to tell. "And . . . and I'm going to have a baby."

"Sarah, that's wonderful."

Alan turned to Jimmy, his broad grin saying it all.

"Another toast!" Jimmy pronounced, retrieving the flask from his pocket. "On purpose?" he asked.

"Jimmy," I interrupted. "That's none of your business."

He looked over his shoulder at me and laughed for the first time. "He's my kid brother. I can ask him what I want."

"More or less." Alan gave a quick, taunting look at his brother. "Ever tried it yourself?"

"Maybe I should." He turned to the backseat. "Want a little Jimmy to keep you company?"

"One thing for sure," Sarah said, "this'll keep Alan out of the draft. Now he's both married and a father, or at least a father-to-be."

"Are you going to tell Florence and George?" I asked.

"Not now. This is Jimmy's day."

On the way home, Jimmy celebrated his day with a few more nips at the flask. My folks and Howard and Regina were there when we got back. George hustled us to the back porch where he'd set up a bar. Florence had prepared cold shrimp with sauce and crackers with cheese. The house shaded the porch from the late afternoon sun, making it pleasantly cool. I joined the women seated in a circle while the men stood around the bar. One round. Two rounds, and I could see Jimmy becoming more voluble as the liquor drew him out of his shell. Alan watched with concern, but George and Howard, also on their second drinks, egged him on. He was showing them how the Hurricane fought the Messerschmitt, using his hands.

"They try to come at you out of the sun and get on your tail. They're fast, faster than the Hurricanes, but we've got an advantage. We can make tighter turns." His right hand was a Messerschmitt diving down on his left hand. "The rule is, never try to outrun 'em or you're a goner."

Howard listened mesmerized. "Ever shot one down?"

"Four times confirmed, maybe a couple more."

"Wow!"

"See," he showed them using hand gestures, "he comes at you from behind and above. You pull a tight turn. As he sails past, you turn again and let him have it from his engine to his cockpit."

"And if you don't see him coming?"

Jimmy took his cane which he'd hung on his arm and leaned on it heavily. "Then you're in trouble."

His mother kept up a steady stream of talk so she couldn't hear him. I watched with sadness. The drinks and conversation had let him return to his new life, a life we couldn't comprehend. A life filled with new comrades and friends, people who dared what he dared and suffered as he suffered. I decided the alcohol was his way of escaping not from the horrors of war but from us, aliens to his experience. Or maybe he *was* drinking too much. I had no way of knowing, nor did I care. It was his life to endure as best he could. I was proud of him and pleased to be with him, but he'd become a stranger whom I no longer knew. I loved George and Florence and would do nothing to hurt them, but I knew my future was not with Jimmy. What did he think? My hunch was, he saw his future in terms of days.

After a dinner with champagne followed by brandy, we had our tearful good-byes and I helped my husband into the Buick for the drive to Marblehead. The climb up the back steps to my apartment might as well have been Mount Everest. Between his bum leg and his drunkenness, we stumbled back one step for each two we advanced until we reached my door.

Inside, we lurched our way to the bedroom, where he got lovey-dovey, hugging me and trying to kiss my cheek. I sat him on the edge of the bed and undressed him while his hands wandered over my face and breasts. It'd been so long I was looking forward to some lovemaking. At least I wouldn't have to feel guilty. I quickly got undressed and crawled into bed. The package of Trojans was in a drawer beside the bed, a little treasure I had hoped I would use one day with Taylor. There was no hurry to get them out because Jimmy's eagerness was so befuddled with drunkenness I wasn't sure he could muster an erection. God, his body felt good next to mine. I began moving against him, my legs wrapping around him, my pelvis pushing on his limp penis. He would arouse himself for a momentary sally into sex, then flounder and drift back into unconsciousness. Finally he fell limp on top of me. I lay there for a few moments until my frustration subsided, then rolled him off me. He was dead to the world.

A shower was what I needed. The cool water dissolved my sweat and returned my body heat to normal. As I was drying I noticed his toilet kit sitting beside the sink, still open from that morning. It was new, the leather finely tooled and sewn with an almost invisible stitch. The kit was rectangular with a clasp to keep it closed. Inside were sleeves for a stainless steel soap container, comb and brush, toothpaste and toothbrush. On the inside of the lid was a slot holding a small mirror. What a nice set, I thought. Not cheap. As I was setting it down, the corner of a piece of paper stuck out from behind the mirror. I dried my hands again, caught hold of it with my fingers, and pulled it out. It was a picture of an attractive young woman in uniform, seated sideways. She looked at the camera over her left shoulder with a confident smile. Her hair, cut short, curled around the edges of her cap. I turned it over, knowing there would be a message on the back. There was. "To Jimmy. Take this wherever you go and I'll always be with you. Love, Jennifer."

I stood there, dripping on the bathroom rug, holding the picture in my hand. Very pretty, I thought, and she's part of Jimmy's world. I searched my emotions for feelings of jealousy and found none. Instead, I was pleased for Jimmy and wished the two of them well. I knew it was over for us and I feared that the odds were getting short for him. If he could find some moments of solace with her in the weeks ahead, then more power to him. I returned the picture to its place behind the mirror, wondering if Jimmy had left his kit open on purpose.

Suddenly from the bedroom came screams of terror. I rushed in to find Jimmy caught in the sheet and flailing about on the bed. I put my arms around him and eased him down onto his pillow.

"There, there, darling. It's all right. You're safe here. You're okay." He continued rolling his head from side to side mumbling incoherently. I ran to the bathroom and wet a washcloth in cold water. Returning to the bed, I cradled his head in my arm and wiped the sweat from his brow. "There, there, my baby. I'll take care of you." What battle was he fighting? What terror was he experiencing again? "My poor baby." Eventually his thrashing stopped and he opened his eyes just for a moment.

"I love you," he said and then dropped off to sleep with a smile. Whom did he see in that darkened bedroom, me or Jennifer? Did it matter?

I awoke with a start, knowing I'd turned off the alarm and fallen back to sleep. I looked at the clock. Thank God I'd slept only twenty minutes and we still had forty minutes before we needed to leave. I shook Jimmy until he groaned.

"Come on, big boy. Gotta get going. I overslept." A groan but no movement. More shaking and a kiss on the cheek. "Come on, we're late. You'll miss your flight." That did it. He sat up holding his head.

"Ohhh," he moaned, squeezing his eyes shut. "Got any aspirin?"

"In the bathroom. Hop in there and get your shower."

We were up and moving, no time for farewell sex. I wasn't in the mood anyway and Jimmy was barely coping. At five after six I told him I'd get the car warmed up, and started down the back stairs carrying his overnight case.

"Hurry up. We're late," I called.

Halfway down the steps I froze. Coming around the corner of the building was Taylor dressed in sandals, shorts, and a sport shirt. He looked up, startled.

"I didn't think you'd be up," he called. "I wanted to leave you a note."

"Hi," I stammered. "I'm really busy right now."

"I've been trying to reach you for weeks. I've got to talk with you."

The door to my apartment slammed closed and Jimmy started

down the steps. On the third step he saw Taylor and stopped. For a moment the two looked at each other. Instantly Taylor recognized the British officer. Folding the envelope containing the note, he put it in his pants pocket. Slowly Jimmy began his descent, his eyes fixed suspiciously on Taylor, who looked like he'd been caught with his hand in the cookie jar. I felt like I'd swallowed rocks. Had Jimmy heard Taylor say he'd been trying to reach me?

"Uh, Jimmy, this is Taylor Harrington. Taylor, my husband, Jimmy DeWolf." Terrified, I looked from one to the other, trying to discern their thoughts.

"How are ya?" Jimmy muttered through the strain of climbing down the stairs.

"Taylor's an assistant minister at St. Paul's Church," I said lamely, as if that excused his presence on my doorstep at six in the morning.

Looking up at Jimmy, he smiled weakly. "It's good to meet you. Becky's spoken of you often."

"Often?" His expression was opaque.

I broke in. "What's gotten you up so early, Taylor?"

"My usual morning walk," he answered awkwardly. "Looks like you're in a hurry."

"Right," Jimmy said. "Going to the airport. Heading back to England." Reaching the bottom of the stairs, he turned to me. "We'd better hit the road." As he passed Taylor, he stopped and put out his gloved hand. "Glad I met you."

Taylor, regaining some composure, took the injured hand. "Yeah. Same here."

Jimmy gripped the hand longer than custom allowed and again locked eyes with Taylor, the intensity of his stare a warning. It seemed like minutes, Jimmy clenching his jaw and Taylor playing dumb. My eyes flicked from one to the other. Gradually Taylor's bland expression modulated to annoyance. I better stop this quickly, I decided.

"Come on, Jimmy. We gotta go."

He dropped Taylor's hand and got in the car. We'd gone about a block when he said, "Damned good-looking guy for a minister." I didn't answer. "What's he to you?"

"A good friend." I kept my eyes on the road. Another two blocks passed.

"You sleeping together?" The words were brittle with anger.

"No. Anyway, it's none of your business." I shot back.

"It sure as hell is my business if my wife's sleeping with some guy."

"How about me? Is it my business who you sleep with?" I glared at him. He glared back. "Who is Jennifer, anyway?"

"So, you went through my toilet kit?"

"You left it open with the edge of the picture sticking out. What'd you expect?" He said nothing, but I noticed he'd let his shoulders sag. "Did you want me to see it?"

A couple of minutes passed. "I don't know. Maybe I did."

"Now we both know."

We drove in silence for about a mile. "What're we going to do, Becky?" His voice had lost its anger.

"I don't know. What do you want to do? Marry her?"

He answered quicker than I thought he would. "No. Not that I haven't thought about it. She's a sweet kid." His honesty amazed me. "And she's part of the war, like me. When it ends, though, it'll be over. I'll come home."

"Why not resign now and stay here? Why go back?"

"No. I'm going back. I'm going to stick it out." He paused for a moment, thinking. "As long as the war's going on, I want to be there. For the first time in my life I feel needed. It's a good feeling."

"And us? What about us?"

"I don't want to lose you. You're my anchor." Thanks for the compliment, I thought. Better than being an albatross. "Take the money I send home and my trust money. Bank as much as you can. We did okay with the DeWolf Flying Service. Maybe we can do it again."

"In the meantime?"

"In the meantime, let's hang on to life as best we can." I knew what that meant for Jimmy and I wondered what it could mean for me.

Nothing further was said. An accommodation seemed to have been reached.

*   *   *

Our kiss good-bye at the gate was quick, Jimmy's lips tight and hard against mine. Then he was gone. As the plane taxied away, I waved at the dark windows not knowing if Jimmy was even watching.

When I got back to my apartment, Taylor's envelope was wedged between the door and the jamb.

Dear Becky,
    What's wrong? Why won't you return my calls? Please let's talk. My feelings for you haven't changed. I need to talk with you about what's happening at St. Paul's, if you haven't heard already. I'm sure rumors have leaked out. Please see me, but don't call the church. I'll walk by your place tonight at ten-thirty. Watch for me and come down.

Love, Taylor

And scrawled on the back of the envelope, apparently written after the encounter with Jimmy, was "I had no idea your husband was here. I hope I didn't upset things by coming by."

I was at my desk in the hotel office by ten staring at the figures in the accounts ledger. Mom and Dad stopped in to tell me how much they appreciated seeing Jimmy and having dinner at the DeWolfs'. Seeing my vacant expression, Mom became concerned and suggested I take the day off.

"It's sad. Only two days and he's gone again," she said, consoling me.

Was I sad? I didn't know. I wanted to get mad, but I didn't know at what or at whom. I felt like crying because I couldn't have what I wanted, and at the same time I didn't know what it was I wanted. I felt blocked, out of control. My eyes were moist when I looked up at Mom standing beside me.

"I'm sorry. I wish I could make it right."

I put my arms around her waist and leaned my head against her soft stomach as she stroked my hair. We said nothing for several moments, just held each other. Finally I looked up, dried my eyes on the back of my hand, and said, "I'll stay here, Mom. Better to keep busy."

At the end of the day I ate dinner in the hotel kitchen with the chef and staff and went back to my apartment. It was seven, three and a half hours to wait for Taylor. I tried reading but couldn't keep my attention on my book. Tossing it aside, I slid down in my chair, stretching my legs and holding my head in my hands. The air was heavy. Outside, the wind picked up and I could hear the rumble of distant thunder. The lamp over my chair carved a circle of light around me, forming an island in a sea of darkness. But the blackness beyond, like a rising tide, crept into my soul, engulfing me in loneliness. Apart from Aggie and Taylor, I thought, I have no friends, no one I can call on the spur of the moment or drop by to see for no reason. My life is work during the day and sitting here in the evening. The movies change only once a week, and I can't keep calling Aggie.

I thought again about Jimmy's visit and the unspoken accord we'd reached. He can have Jennifer and I can have Taylor. Just don't get serious, and when the war's over, we'll get back together. Pretty neat. In a way it's perfect for Taylor and me. I can't have him, not openly as my husband. If I get divorced he can't marry me anyway. Unless, of course, Jimmy gets killed. That would solve everything. I shuddered at the thought—even that I was thinking it. No, my relationship with Taylor, if he was willing and I could put up with it, would be a series of furtive moments snatched from our otherwise respectable lives, secret trips to a tourist cabin on Highway 1. But that's not what I want. I want him as my husband. But it's so goddamned hopeless.

The strain of the last three days and the lack of sleep from the night before must have caught up with me. Suddenly I was awakened by rain pelting the windows like pieces of gravel. I jumped up and closed them, then sat by the front window and watched the streetlights on State Street glisten on the wet pavement. Two couples were running for the shelter of a bar down by the town dock. When they disappeared, the street was empty.

I glanced at the clock. Almost ten-thirty. Looking the other way up State Street, I could see a solitary figure crossing the street heading toward my building. He wore a rain slicker. It was Taylor. I could tell by his walk. The sight of him sent a surge of life rushing through me. Dashing to my apartment door, I grabbed my slicker, and raced down the front steps into the deserted street. We met in the middle, clutching each other stiffly through our heavy rain gear.

"I love you. I love you. I love you," I repeated over and over again, kissing his wet lips and cheeks. He closed me in his arms and returned my kisses. "This is what I want," I cried. "I don't care how it has to be or where it'll go. I want to be with you."

"I know. I want that, too."

"Then come inside with me. Right now. Come with me now." I tugged him toward my door.

"I can't, Becky. Not yet, anyway." He pulled me into his arms again. "Especially now. I've got to tell you what's happening. We can walk in the rain. Nobody'll recognize us." With his arm around my shoulder, we headed down State Street. I finished buttoning my slicker and flipped the hood over my wet hair. At the town dock we turned left onto Front Street, passing the bar in which a few late-night people were finding shelter from the rain.

"Well? Tell me what's going on."

His arm pulled me even closer. "I'm getting fired."

"What?"

"Maybe not fired actually, but told to resign. It comes to the same thing."

"But why? You've done a great job here."

"Hendricks, the rector, is taking it up with the vestry when they meet next week. He wants to get rid of me and wants their blessing."

"What's his trouble?"

"The real reason? I'm his first curate and he's a lousy manager. He doesn't know how to give an order or how to correct me, so he sits in his office and gets mad when I don't do what he wants. And instead of backing me up when people in the parish get upset, he agrees with them."

"What an ass. I had no idea you were having so much trouble."

"He called me in last week and listed his grievances. First, I'm insensitive to people's feelings."

"Bullshit."

"Specifically, Mrs. Shade's feelings. That's Phyllis's mother. Remember the Christmas pageant?"

"Yeah."

"Well, when I didn't do it the traditional way, she got in a huff and turned the mothers against me. When they went to Hendricks, he got scared and gave in."

"Coward." We reached Love's Cove where the storm was sending waves breaking over the rocks. I put my arm around Taylor's waist and hugged him.

"Next," Taylor went on, "I'm putting politics before religion and I'm stirring up trouble in the community."

"Frank's letter to the editor, right?"

"Yeah."

"That son of a bitch. I was afraid he'd cause trouble."

"Hendricks said my interest in helping Jewish refugees showed a lack of patriotism. Can you believe it? And he added this was a Jewish problem and had nothing to do with America, much less Marblehead."

We reached Fort Sewall and walked to the outer rampart. Across the harbor the green light in the lighthouse on the end of the Neck shimmered through the blowing rain. Somewhere in the blackness a foghorn harrumped. We stopped, and I moved in front of Taylor, unbuttoning his slicker and mine so I could feel my body next to his. Slipping my hands beneath his shirt onto his bare back, I pulled him close. He wrapped his slicker around me, enclosing me inside, and we kissed. For several minutes we stood like that, locked in each other's arms, sheltering one another from the wind and rain. I pressed my ear against his warm, damp shirt and could hear his heart beating. After several minutes, we buttoned our slickers and continued our walk.

"Is that all?" I asked.

"No. And here's the corker. The head of the altar guild saw me making out with a young woman on the organ bench."

"That was me, I hope."

"It was."

I shook my head. "That's sick. We were just sitting there."

"To hear Hendricks describe it, we were having sex. And you a married woman."

"So he knows it was me."

"And probably everybody else in the church, too."

I exploded. "Damn!"

We walked heads down for several blocks through the empty streets and lanes of Marblehead's oldest section until we reached Old Burial Hill. Climbing to the top of its steep slope, we found a bench and sat down to rest among the tall tombstone slabs from the early eighteenth century. Rising like gray ghosts out of the wet ground, they marched up the hillside from the woods below, harbingers of death. I cuddled up to Taylor, then swung my legs over his, and he pulled me onto his lap. Together we looked out over the rooftops of the town to the harbor below and the sea beyond.

"What happens now?" My lips brushed his as I spoke.

Taylor lifted his head and sighed. "I wait for a week until the vestry rubber-stamps what Hendricks wants, then I write a letter of resignation."

"Why did he wait until after you were ordained? Sounds like he doesn't think you're fit to be a priest."

"I wondered, too. I think the visit of the bishop had been planned for so long he was embarrassed to cancel the ordination, and it might have raised questions about his ability to manage."

"So he was willing to present you as qualified to be a priest, knowing he considered you an adulterer, rabble-rouser, and political troublemaker. What a creep. I think you *should* resign."

"I've got no choice, but I'm amazed it's come to this. I had no idea he was keeping a list, just waiting for it to get long enough to fire me."

"Screw him."

"Yes, but . . . it means I'll have to leave Marblehead. I'll have to leave you."

I hadn't thought about that. Now I felt anxious. "Where would you go?" I asked haltingly.

"Some other part of the diocese. Some other part of the country. I don't know. I'll go see the bishop after I resign, and see what's available."

"Well," I said as if it were a foregone conclusion, "I'm coming with you wherever you go. I'm not going to lose you."

"You make it sound so easy." He hunched me off his lap and we stood. Holding my shoulders at arms' length, he looked in my eyes. "Becky, that's not going to work."

"I could live in the next town. Get a job. You could come over every other night." My tears mixed with the rain on my cheeks. "I love you. I'm not going to let you go."

He pulled me into his arms and kissed me.

We inched our way down the slippery side of the hill to the road below which led toward the water. At a bend in the road was an historical marker. "Come here. I want you to see this." I caught hold of his hand and pulled him to the sign.

"It's too dark. I can't read it."

"I'll tell you. Over there was the Fountain Inn," I said, pointing. "It was before the Revolution. That's where Agnes Surriage worked scrubbing floors. This rich guy from England named Frankland saw her—she was only fifteen—and he took her to Boston and set her up as his mistress." Taylor was looking at me askance. "She followed him everywhere and finally, after a few years, married him, and moved to his estate in England. See?" I said, beginning to sob. "They've been doing it in Marblehead for hundreds of years."

Taylor braced me in his arms as I cried on his shoulder.

"Becky, darling." He tilted my face up to his. Rain and tears filled my eyes. "We'll find a way. Somehow."

We walked for three or four blocks without speaking, then Taylor said, "I don't have to work after tomorrow. I'll be done here at St. Paul's. I've got a month's vacation coming to find a new job, but I can't do anything until I see the bishop next week. A good time for sailing. What do you think?"

"You mean *White Wings*, our secret place?"

"Yes, *White Wings*. She'll tell us what to do."

"When?"

"Day after tomorrow? Seven?"

"I'll be there."

30

I lay in her womb again, curled into a ball, enclosed within her ribs and tucked beneath the skin of her deck. I felt the rise and fall of her breathing as the outgoing tide gently lifted and settled her graceful body. I heard her sigh as the morning breeze moved through her rigging. She spoke to me with words, soft and comforting, as the rudder swayed from side to side and the centerboard touched the walls of its well. I was her unborn child, the child of *White Wings*.

Waiting for Taylor to arrive, I drifted in and out of sleep. Gradually, like the petals of a flower opening to the dawn, it came to me. It was not I who was the unborn child, but the child soon to be conceived within me.

There was no decision, no resolve. *White Wings* had spoken, and I had listened. She had given her blessing and I had accepted. Suddenly I was fully awake, expectant with joy. I would have Taylor's baby.

Snuggled beneath the foredeck of *White Wings*, hiding from whatever prying eyes might add to Taylor's problems, I lay on a lounge pad from the hotel. From my apartment I'd brought two pillows and a blanket on which I lay wrapped. I'd stopped by the hotel kitchen, where Raymond LeBlanc, our French-Canadian chef, had prepared bacon and eggs and toast. When I asked for enough for two, he winked at me.

"Going sailing again, Becky?"

"Yes, and don't you breathe a word to anyone."

He laid his hand over his heart. "I will never tell a soul."

"Good. I'll take a large thermos of coffee, too." I went to the restroom for a last visit, and when I returned, he had a picnic basket ready to go.

"This is my gift to you." His eyes twinkled as he opened the cover. In addition to breakfast, he'd enclosed two bottles of wine, a loaf of freshly baked bread, and a wedge of Brie cheese.

From inside my snug compartment, I could hear rain beginning to fall on the deck. At five-thirty when I awoke it had been drizzling, but now it was getting heavier. I reattached the cockpit cover and lay back to wait. Certainly a little rain won't deter him, I thought. Anyway, the wind is picking up and a sailor can't resist that. Then I heard his footsteps on the dock.

"Becky? You there?"

"Yes."

"It's terrible weather. Do you still want to go?"

"Yes. Quit talking and get the sails up."

"Okay. You asked for it. A fair wind, isn't it? About ten knots."

It took forever to get to open water. The northeast breeze was pushing into the mouth of the harbor, forcing us to tack back and forth. At least we had the outgoing tide to help us. I watched Taylor from my cozy, dry compartment. Beneath the hood of his slicker, his serious eyes studied the wind and chose a path through the moored sailboats. Sitting on the bench, his hand on the tiller, he stretched his long legs in my direction.

"I love you," I called.

His earnest expression melted into a smile. "I love you too."

"Can I come out now?"

"Not yet. About five more minutes. This last tack will take us beyond the lighthouse."

"How's the weather?"

"Perfect. We'll have a great sail. The storm last night's made great swells. Not choppy."

"Can you see anybody at Lighthouse Point?"

"No. Nobody's that dumb, to be out on a morning like this."

"Then I'm coming out." I slipped on my slicker and duckwalked aft, sitting on the bench beside Taylor. The slicker hung below the shorts I was wearing, exposing my bare legs to rain.

"Nice slicker. That all you're wearing?"

"Yeah. Wanna peek?" I laughed. "No, I've got on a blouse and shorts, but I can change that in a hurry."

"Becky, you're wanton."

"Wanting, is more like it." Hugging him, I planted a big kiss on his cheek. "I brought us breakfast. Eggs, bacon, toast, and hot coffee. Why not make the shelter of Cat Island and we'll have something to eat?"

"Good. I'm starved."

The lee side of Cat Island was somewhat calmer. We anchored near shore and dropped the sails. As we huddled together at the front of the cockpit, I pulled the food container to the opening of my cubbyhole and unscrewed the thermos.

"Coffee smells delicious."

"Wait till you smell the bacon and eggs." I undid the lid. "Ah, still hot."

The chilly salt air and rocking of the boat made me ravenous. Our breakfast was gone almost as soon as we started.

Taylor had grown quiet while we were eating. At first I thought it was hunger but then I noticed the sadness in his eyes. Holding his coffee to his lips, savoring the aroma, he looked into the mist. "I feel like I'm at the end of the world."

"You mean cut off from everybody."

"That too, but I meant the end of my world." He was silent for a moment, thinking. "I knew where I was going. From deacon to priest. Curate to rector. I'd have a church of my own somewhere. I'd work in the community. Maybe I'd get an advanced degree. Probably get married and have kids. Then I fall in love with you and Hendricks fires me. Wham. Like the earth shifted on its axis."

"You shouldn't have asked me to go sailing with you that first time."

"You're right. *White Wings* brought us together, didn't she? At first I told myself we'd just be good friends. Have fun together but not get serious. I had this crazy idea I could toy with the possibility of a love affair like a cat plays with a mouse, move closer and closer but stop just in time. Now I don't care. I want you no matter what."

"I feel the same way." Leaning my back so I could look into his eyes, I said, "It's going to be all right. *White Wings* knew what she was doing."

He smiled halfheartedly. "We could have worked it out, somehow, hiding in the sailboat, sneaking into each other's apartments at night. I get scared when I think about it, though. Sooner or later it would have exploded into the open. No worry now, at least as far as Marblehead's concerned. Hendricks took care of that."

"Wherever you go, I'm coming with you."

"I know. We've got to figure out a way to make it work—a mission church in a big city, a college chaplaincy, a remote mission in Alaska—some kind of work that'll let my private life be my own. There might even be a bishop who'd permit a marriage if you were divorced. We're going to work it out, Becky, somehow."

"Will you know where you're going after you see the bishop next week?"

"No. It'll take a while to find a place."

"I can hear it now," I said, and added in a deep voice, " 'What I want, bishop, is a place where I can keep a mistress.' "

He smiled, but his mood was still too serious for a laugh. The sky remained as dark as Taylor's face, the drizzle continuing. I poured us each half a cup of coffee, draining the thermos.

Out of the clear he asked, "Why wouldn't you talk to me after the ordination?"

"I was mad."

"What for? I hadn't even spoken to you."

"For being a priest. For *wanting* to be a priest." I could feel the anger returning. "You and those damned vows. When you agreed to that stuff it was as if you were saying, 'Bye-bye, Becky, it's all over between us.' It just seemed so final, like I was losing you forever."

He took my face in his hands. "That's the last thing you have to worry about."

"Good," I said, "because I'm hanging on to you like a leech." I sat up and stretched my back. "Let's go sailing?" I said.

"You're not mad anymore?"

"For your body, yes."

Instantly, the worried expression returned. "What are we going to do for protection?"

"Don't worry. It's the safe time of the month for me."

"You sure?"

"Positive." My wonderful naive friend.

By the time we had stowed the breakfast dishes and put the sails up, the rain had diminished to a light drizzle. The foghorn continued its steady, deep blasts, closer now than last night, warning us against the patches of mist and fog we could see floating over the water.

"Got your handy compass?" It was the one I'd given him for Christmas.

"Never go sailing without it."

"We might need it today."

Taylor scanned the horizon. "See that island out there? It'd take us a while to reach it and we'd have a rough trip, but I'd like to try."

"Let's do it."

Once we'd rounded Cat Island we found that the wind had shifted slightly to the north, making it possible for us to head almost directly toward the island on a close reach. We sat together on the port side with the wind on our port bow. Beyond Cat we got the full effect of the ocean, its long swells rolling toward us like phalanxes of an advancing army. In the trough of the swells the world ahead disappeared behind a wall of water. Then when we reached the crests, it was like being on top of a hill. We passed only one lobster boat, which I didn't recognize, thank goodness. The skipper shook his head like we were nuts. We were. Either the island was closer than we'd thought or we were going faster than it appeared. Soon the island was slightly behind our port beam. We came about and made a direct shot at its lee side. I crawled to the bow with anchor in hand. Once in the calm waters Taylor headed into the wind and the sails slackened. "Drop anchor."

Ten feet of line went out before it hit bottom. I let out another fifty feet as we drifted away from the island, then cleated the anchor. Taylor dropped the mainsail and I the jib.

Again, the mist and drizzle were turning to rain.

"Got an idea," I said. "Let's put on the cockpit cover like a tent."

"Perfect." With the sail lashed to the boom, he stretched the canvas cover over it and attached it to the rings on the outside of the cockpit coaming. We crawled under it at the forward end and he attached the last two remaining connections. Inside, the floor and sides were wet, but it was shielded from the rain.

"Now for my big surprise." I slipped off my slicker and reached into my cubbyhole, returning with the lounge pad, which I spread out between the rudder post and the centerboard well. "How's that for planning ahead?"

He smiled but said nothing.

"I'm not done. Get your wet slicker and shoes off. I'll be right back." I returned from under the deck with the blanket, two pillows, and the picnic basket. "Have a look at this." I opened the lid.

"Wow!" Taylor beamed like a kid on Christmas morning.

"Now if only there's a corkscrew." There was and I opened one of the bottles. Taylor dug out wine glasses and I poured. We had about four feet from floor to boom in the center of the boat, so we had to sit slightly slumped over, but it was wonderful. Outside the rain was falling harder, drumming on the roof of our tent.

Taylor lifted his glass. "Here's to our own secret world, *White Wings*."

"Where the only thing that matters is our love."

"Hear, hear," we said together and drank. Then I brought my glass to Taylor's lips and he brought his to mine. We toasted again.

Looking around our snug enclosure, he said, "Do you know, you've created exactly what I've fantasized. Maybe I forgot the lounge pad and blanket, but the covering and the wine, yes."

"What else did you fantasize?" I brought my face close to his. He took a drink, then kissed me. I could taste the wine on his lips. "I like that fantasy," I said in a low voice. Then I too took a drink and kissed him, letting some of my wine pass into his mouth. Then I touched the tip of my tongue to his. He sighed.

"Next I imagined finishing my wine." He did, and I followed.

"Anything else?" I asked softly.

"Don't you know?"

"I can guess but I'd rather hear it."

"I fantasized I began unbuttoning your blouse, slowly, taking my time, enjoying the moment." His fingers started at the top button. Eyelids half closed as if in a dream, lips slightly parted, he became entranced with each button. When he came to the last one, he pulled the tail of my blouse out of my shorts so the front hung open. I wore no bra, which he acknowledged with a long resonant "ummm."

"And?" I begged for more.

He eased my blouse off my shoulders and placed his hands beneath my breasts, lifting them. As he kissed them, I shivered. I unbuttoned his shirt, undid his belt and the buttons on his shorts. With his hands on my shoulders he guided me down onto the pad so I was lying in front of him. He finished undressing me.

Looking down, he murmured, "I've dreamed about this, Becky, seeing you like this, waiting for me, longing for me." He began caressing my face and neck, then ran his fingers around my breasts and over my nipples, down across my stomach, tangling them in the hair between my legs and moving them down my thighs. Back and forth his hands played over my body as if I were the keys of an organ. I was ready to explode and tugged his pants down until I could pull them off his ankles.

"You'd better get this fantasy moving or I'm going to burst."

He leaned down and with his lips traced the same course his fingers had followed, kissing my neck, breasts, stomach, and mons. I shuddered and pulled him to me. The joy of touching him, wrapping my legs around him, feeling him slide inside me, hugging his broad chest against my breast, moving beneath him and having him counter each move by thrusting harder and harder, was ecstasy. Finally, with groans as deep as a foghorn, we climaxed.

In spite of the chill air, our bodies were wet with sweat. I continued to hold him fast against me, not wanting the moment to end. Closing my eyes, I pictured a million sperm swimming deep into me, racing, leaping, pushing ahead, trying to be first, and finally one of them finding my egg and burrowing inside just like Taylor had burrowed into me. I giggled.

"What's so funny?"

I rolled over so I was on top of Taylor. "I love you so much I can't stand it." I washed his face with kisses.

Soon the cool air touched our bodies and we wrapped ourselves in the blanket. Taylor poured more wine while I opened the Brie and broke off pieces of bread. With the blanket wrapped around us, we huddled so close together sitting Indian fashion that my knees were over the top of his thighs. Our hands, when not holding a glass or a piece of bread, roamed over the other's legs and shoulders. *White Wings* heightened the mood, settling into a gentle rocking motion that swayed our bodies against each other as we ate and drank. We finished the bottle and half the cheese and bread, putting the remains in the basket. Taylor stretched out and put his head in my lap. We pulled the blanket over my head and around Taylor, making a tent within a tent. With my fingers I combed his hair and let my hand wander over his chest and stomach.

"Becky, let's spend this next week together. I could sail *White Wings* up to Gloucester and you could meet me there, rent a room for the week. No one knows us there and I could dock *White Wings* at one of the commercial piers away from the yachts. I've got six days before I see the bishop and we could be together day and night."

"Like we were married."

"Sure. We could sail during the day and eat at out-of-the-way places where the local fishermen eat."

"And at night?"

"Yes. At night and in the morning."

I cradled his head in my arms and held him to me like the baby I would soon be nursing.

"Tell me. What will we be doing day and night?"

"We'll be . . ." As he spoke my nipples grazed his lips. "We'll be . . ." He pulled me toward him, burying his head in my breasts. Gradually I set him down on the pad and climbed atop his body. We made love again, only slightly more frantic than the first time.

31

During the night the cold front came through, pushing the muggy air and rain out to sea and providing a crisp, clear morning. At nine Taylor and I touched fingertips inconspicuously and said good-bye on the hotel dock.

"Day's perfect." He studied the weather vane and anemometer on top of the Odyssey Yacht Club. "Northwest wind, nice and steady, about twelve knots. On a northeast course it's just under fifteen miles to Gloucester. Five hours at the most."

"It'll take me an hour by car. Soon as I get things straight with Mom and Dad, I'll leave. With luck I'll have us a room by the time you get there. Where'll we meet?"

"Remember the fish packing plant on the north side of town?"

I thought for a moment. "All I can picture is the commercial fish pier. Where's the packing plant?"

"I'm not positive myself. To be safe, let's meet at the post office. There's only one of them and we can ask where it is."

"See you in a little while," I said, squeezing his hand. "I love you."

He got in the boat and I pushed him off the dock. Beside him was a thermos of coffee and a bag of Danish. I watched until he passed in front of the yacht club, then walked to the hotel.

Putting on a sad face, I told Mom I wanted some time off, maybe drive up the coast and visit the DeWolfs in Maine. I was halfway honest—Gloucester was up the coast. It took me fifteen minutes to throw some things into a suitcase and lock up my apartment. I brought my Kodak because I wanted pictures of Taylor in case we had to be apart for a while. Then I was on the road in the Buick, with the top down. I drove through Salem and Beverly and then along the shore through Manchester. At one point the road passed a park overlooking the water and I stopped to see if I could see *White Wings*. In the distance were three boats, but I couldn't tell which one, if any, was Taylor.

On the road again to Gloucester, I passed tree-lined fields with occasional glimpses of the ocean. I was ecstatic—the day was beautiful, the world aglow with freshness, and the wind in my hair. Five glorious days awaited Taylor and me.

When I reached Gloucester, I drove to the north side of town where the commercial fishing docks were and looked for a furnished room a block or two from the harbor. As I started up the hill behind the docks, I saw some FOR RENT signs stuck in front windows, but the buildings, mainly triple-deckers, looked run-down. I imagined dirty hallways and roach-infested rooms. The farther I drove up the hill away from the docks, the better the buildings but the fewer the FOR RENT signs. Triple-deckers gave way to private homes. At the top of the hill was an attractive older house with a turret and wide porch. The small lawn behind a picket fence was nicely kept and lace curtains hung in the windows. Peeking out from the edge of the large center window was a sign FOR RENT. I drove past the house and parked up the street, thinking the expensive Buick might not match the story I would tell. Apart from a lie, I'd nothing in mind.

The lady who answered my knock appeared to be in her fifties, and wore a housedress and a hair net over small metal curlers. I said I was looking for a furnished room for my husband and me.

"Where's your husband?" she asked curtly.

"He's coming by boat. I drove."

"Fishing boat?"

That sounded good to me, especially in Gloucester. "Yeah."

"You can look at the apartment, but I'll tell you right now, I want rent in advance and I want it every week. If he comes in with no fish and no rent money, I'm not covering you."

"I understand." You can have it back in a week anyway, I thought.

"Can I see it?"

"Round back."

I followed her along the driveway and down some steps to a rear door. It was a basement apartment with a concrete floor and small windows opened to ventilate the confined space. Pipes networked the ceiling. A large center room had a table covered with a red and white checkered oilcloth, two kitchen chairs, and two uphol-stered chairs. At one end was a kitchen sink, stove, refrigerator, and counter. At the other end, doors to a bathroom and a bedroom. I glanced into the bathroom and saw a clawfoot tub, sink, and toilet, then walked into the bedroom. An iron bed dominated the room, leaving just enough space for a chest of drawers and one chair. Hooks on the wall were for hanging clothes. The bed's bare mattress sagged atop wire mesh springs that, under the weight of Taylor and me, would tumble us together in the middle. Not a bad thought. I sat on the edge of the bed and bounced the mattress. The springs squealed and scraped and a loose fitting in the iron headboard clanged. Good thing it was a basement apartment.

"There's cooking utensils in the kitchen and plates and silver-ware. I've made a count of everything and I expect to have it all in good condition when you leave. Bed linens not furnished."

She told me the rent plus a deposit and I paid her without com-plaint. As I counted out the bills, she looked at my ring, probably the biggest diamond she'd ever seen. "When's your husband coming?" she snapped suspiciously.

"Soon. The boat'll be in in an hour or two."

"Umph. Fishermen," she said derisively. At the door she stopped and turned. "There's a broom and dustpan in the corner. Keep it clean. And no parties. Oh. Here's the key."

When she left, I pirouetted across the room, took another look at the bed, and set off, walking, to find the post office.

Five and a half hours from the time he'd left, I spotted Taylor a block away ambling up the street toward the post office. His unbuttoned shirt hung loosely over his tanned chest. A shock of brown hair fell into his face. He wore shorts and sneakers but no

socks. In his hand was the thermos and over his shoulder a knapsack. I walked quickly toward him, waving.

"You don't look like you got off a fishing boat."

He looked perplexed. "I didn't."

"When I told our new landlady you were coming by boat, she
assumed it was a fishing boat. Sounded like a good story so I stayed
with it."

"You got us a place, then?"

"It's a basement apartment, not as bad as it sounds." I took his
arm. "Let's eat first. I'm starved and you must be too." We found a
sandwich shop and ate while Taylor told me about his uneventful
trip to Gloucester and finding a place to tie up *White Wings.* Then
we walked to our new home. As we started up the drive, the curtain lifted in the front window. I waved at the face I knew was
there and pointed proudly at Taylor, mouthing the words, "He's
here." The curtain dropped.

We descended the five steps to our door, which I unlocked and
swung open. Taylor stepped in and looked around. "One thing.
Nobody from Marblehead'll find us here."

He dropped his knapsack and kissed me.

Pulling him toward the bedroom, I said, "Here's the best part. It
comes with a trampoline." We sat on the edge of the bed, making a
V between the head and footboards.

"Will it hold us?" He hunched himself up and bounced to the
center, stretching out. I followed. The springs were stronger than
I'd expected but we did lie in a valley.

"See? Even the bed wants us to stay together." We were face to
face, our bodies sandwiched by the mattress. I kissed his nose. He
caught my lower lip between his lips. I moved to his eyes, first one
and then the other. He found the hollow on my neck beneath my
chin. My head tilted back and his tongue explored my right ear,
discovering a pleasure zone I didn't know I had. Our pace quick-
ened as both of us began unbuttoning my blouse. Taylor reached
behind me and unhooked my brassiere, then pressed his warm
chest against my bare breasts. We kissed, open mouthed, tonguing,
our fingers working to free belt buckles and buttons, our feet
pushing off shoes. I pushed down my panties, which he caught in
his big toe and finished the job. Our mouths never separated.

Laughing joyfully, we celebrated our nakedness and freedom by rolling from side to side, first I on top of him, then he on me.

"It's a rough sea, matey," his voice like an old salt.

"Then you'd better come inside, cap'n." I wrapped my legs around him. He entered, and the storm began in earnest. We moaned and the bedsprings groaned. We growled, deeply, lasciviously, and the iron bed clanged like a broken spar against a metal mast. Our bodies hammered the mattress—the springs bounced back. Noise and motion reached hurricane pitch until waves of passion drowned us in climax. We fell back on our sides. The bed tottered to a stop. We were two feet closer to the chest of drawers.

"Still your safe time?"

"It's a little late to ask, isn't it?"

"Well, I thought that since yesterday was. . . ."

"Just kidding. I'm safe all week."

We dressed and went into the other room. Taylor saw the kitchen. "Hey, we can eat in."

"Sorry, buddy. I'm not much of a cook."

"I am. I love to cook. I just don't like cooking for myself."

"It's all yours."

Taylor checked the stove, found it in working order, and we set out to shop for food and linens.

Three blocks away we found a meat market next to a grocery store. I stood beside him as his eyes roved over the meats, chickens, and fresh fish laid out on ice inside the glass case.

"Do you like sole?"

"Love it."

The clerk walked over to us behind the counter. "What'll it be, folks?"

"Two fillets of sole and a pound of butter."

"I can give you the sole but you get the butter next door." We paid and went to the grocery store. Walking up and down the aisles, Taylor examined melons, potatoes, squash, and peas, rejecting some and choosing others for reasons not apparent to me. I carried a basket into which he carefully placed his selections. At the tall red coffee grinder, he poured in a pound of Chase and Sanborn coffee beans. When he flipped a switch, it hummed to life, emptying finely ground coffee into a bag. I put my nose next to the bag and breathed deeply.

"That smells so good."

"Does, doesn't it?" He plopped it into my basket, which was getting heavy.

Here we are, I pretended, husband and wife, out shopping. From here we're going home to our little apartment where we live and play and make love. I squeezed his arm.

He looked at me. "What?"

"Nothing. I just love you."

At the counter a woman in a white smock totaled our purchases and Taylor peeled off some dollar bills, then asked where we could find a bakery and a department store to buy linens. She pointed the way and asked if we wanted to leave our bags there while we shopped. We agreed and thanked her.

"Isn't she nice?" Taylor said.

"Yes. There're nice people in our neighborhood."

He smiled. "You're funny."

"I know. I never played house when I was little. I'm playing house now."

At the bakery we bought bread and a German chocolate cake for dessert. Then sheets and pillowcases at the department store and two bottles of wine at a beer and wine shop. When we picked up the groceries and headed for the apartment, each of us carried two bags. On the way I stopped at a drugstore and bought a *Collier's*.

While I made the bed, Taylor put food away, then we walked down to the harbor so he could show me *White Wings*'s berth. Several trawlers, at least seventy-five feet long, flaking paint, were tied up or maneuvering to the docks. Huge drums on the stern were wound with gray cord nets and black rings cut from old tires to protect the nets as they scraped the bottom. Some had long booms that swung out from their sides to hold the nets when they swept for fish. Winches whirred and men shouted as buckets of fish were lifted from the holds. On the docks, men and seagulls competed for cod, halibut, flounder, and sole. With long iron hooks and wide shovels they pushed and pulled the catches into boxes and barrels. Seagulls squawked at seagulls, charging menacingly at the lucky ones who'd found bits of scraps. The air was heavy with the smell of fish. Being a Marbleheader, I loved it. Taylor didn't seem to mind either.

Beyond these docks another dock reached out into the harbor. At its end was a restaurant. A promenade deck, between the restaurant and the end of the dock, had umbrella-covered tables for outside dining, empty and awaiting the dinner crowd. On the side of the restaurant where the kitchen was, I saw the mast of *White Wings* sticking up above the edge of the dock.

"They said I could tie up here. I figured it'd be safer than the commercial docks and not as conspicuous as the public docks. Can I buy you a beer?"

We sat at one of the tables. A waitress took our order and brought us two bottles of Schlitz.

"In case anybody asks, husband dear, what's our last name?"

"Hmmm. Never thought of that. Pick something."

"How about Hemingway? He's good at making things up."

"Hemingway it is." He was quiet for a while, looking out beyond the harbor. "I love this, sitting here with you, having you by my side, shopping together, making that barren apartment into a home."

"Our landlady saw the ring. Took it for granted we were married." I looked into his eyes, feeling a tear at the edge of mine and a catch in my throat. "Are we, darling? Are we married . . . for this week at least?"

He touched the edge of my eye with his finger and wiped away the tear. In a whisper he said, "We are, Becky, for a week and forever."

Back at the apartment, I sat at the kitchen table reading *Collier's* while Taylor prepared dinner. Humming to himself, he shucked peas and scrubbed potatoes at the sink. Then he sprinkled flour on waxed paper adding a dash of sage and basil, and flopped the sole from side to side. He produced two candles which I hadn't seen him buy, melted the wax on their base so they'd stand on saucers, and lit them.

"Would the lady care for some wine?" With a flourish he uncorked the bottle and poured. I turned off the lights and we sat by candlelight at the kitchen table.

I sighed. "I want it to be forever."

"So do I."

The meal was delicious, climaxed with freshly brewed coffee and chocolate cake. I'd never been treated so lovingly.

After we'd cleaned up, we went for a walk through the darkened streets, choosing the house we wanted. "It's got to have room for at least three kids," I said. "I was an only child and always wished for a brother and sister."

"You're right about three—in case something happens to one." I knew he was thinking about Jenny and I squeezed his arm against me.

Back in our apartment, once we'd shed our clothes and our naked bodies touched, we couldn't stop until we'd made love again. This time the bed moved only three inches. Taylor dropped off to sleep almost immediately. I lay in the darkness by his side, feeling his arm under my head, his hip against mine and his left leg under my right. Knowing we'd spend the whole night together and wake by each other's side in the morning filled me with an excitement that kept me awake. If only it could be forever. The thought rose as a discord beneath my joy and again tears came to my eyes. When I fell asleep, my dreams were of something precious I'd lost and couldn't find, of wandering through rooms and hallways I didn't know among people who turned away from my appeals for help.

I awoke lying on my back looking into Taylor's eyes. Propped up on his left elbow, he was using his finger to make ski jumps off my nose first onto my left nipple and then onto my right. A whoosh sound accompanied his finger as it left my nose and a plop as it landed on my breast. I giggled and slid my hand to his crotch. Uh-huh, just as I suspected. Ready to go again.

Forty-five minutes later I was in the tub watching Taylor standing naked at the sink, shaving. I realized that in the two years I'd been married to Jimmy, I'd never been in the bathroom with him. What an art shaving is. Taylor applied the thick lather to his face with a sensual pleasure that made me jealous. He looked at me and smiled, then walked to the tub and dabbed some on my nose. I caught a glob on my finger and put it on the end of his penis. He looked at me askance.

"Here, let me take care of that." I scooped hot water from the tub and lovingly washed the lather off as his penis stiffened in my hand.

"No more. We'll wear it out." He went back to the sink and drew the safety razor across his face, rinsing the blade in the water.

After breakfast we went sailing. *White Wings* was glad to see us and wanted to know all about our night together. As Taylor brought us out of the inner harbor, I told her, silently, what a wonderful time we'd had. Pleased with our happiness, she caught a sudden zephyr and sailed smartly to the open water. The day was a carbon copy of the day before, only warmer owing to a southwest wind. I had two rolls of film, and took eight pictures of Taylor and had him take eight of me.

"I'm not telling you when I'm going to take one, because I don't want you to pose. You do the same." Looking through a peephole in the back of the box camera, I waited until the tiny image expressed just the attitude and expression I wanted, then pushed down the shutter lever. When it was Taylor's turn with the camera, he had me stand at the mast and clicked my pictures while guiding the tiller under his left knee. I couldn't wait to get them developed.

That night we went to the movies and saw Walt Disney's *Fantasia*. Taylor loved the music; I loved the dancing hippos in tutus.

By the third day the novelty of our married life wore off, replaced by a natural, comfortable rhythm of rising together, bathing, shopping, cooking, eating, sailing, going to movies, sweeping up the apartment, and making love once or twice a day at various times and in various places, including once in the bathtub.

The days drifted by as if in a dream. At night my sleep became more and more troubled with dreams of wandering aimlessly, unable to reach some undetermined destination. By the fifth night, these dreams of futility and frustration took on more reality than my daytime pretense of being married. The morning we were to leave I awoke with a feeling of emptiness, as if my life were draining out a hole in my stomach. Without making love we arose and bathed silently. We planned the cleanup of the apartment and our departure as we ate breakfast. Setting down my coffee cup, I hit the edge of the saucer and spilled it over the table.

"Oh shit," I cried, bringing my fist down on the table, jarring what remained of the candles from their make-believe candle-sticks. Taylor held out his arms to me and I went to his lap where he cuddled me. I bawled like a baby, sobbing until my shoulders shook and my breathing rattled in my throat. I stayed there for several minutes, my face wet with tears, my cheek pressed against his. Then I got up, washed my face, and began packing our things, Taylor helping.

I drove him to the dock and we walked to *White Wings*. With few words he made ready the sails, and we kissed good-bye. The wind had returned to the northwest, assuring a good sail home.

We waved to each other until he was well out of the harbor, then his attention turned to wind and sails. Until I could no longer hold up my arm, I continued waving good-bye to my dream.

That afternoon, back in Marblehead, I saw the boat at the hotel dock. I hoped he'd come by my apartment that night and waited for a gentle tapping at my door, but none came. Finally I fell asleep in a living room chair. His appointment with the bishop was at eleven the next morning. I stayed at home waiting for a call I was sure would come about noon. It did.

"Come to Boston and we'll have lunch."

"Good news or bad?"

"Good, I think. It may be just what we want. Meet me in the lobby of the Statler. I love you."

I drove too fast and walked into the lobby just after one-twenty. He was seated on the circular couch in the center of the lobby under the glass chandelier. He took my hand and led me into the coffee shop.

"Well?"

"I think it's perfect. There'll be no connection between my work and my private life."

"What is it? Where're you going?"

"I had a good meeting with Bishop Kline. He's arranged for me to enter the chaplain corps of the army. I leave for Fort Sheridan near Chicago in two days—just made the class—for three months of training. Then I'm commissioned a second lieutenant and assigned to an army camp somewhere. With all the guys being drafted, there're camps springing up everywhere and they need chaplains."

I looked at him and he saw the fear and uncertainty in my eyes.

"Becky, do you see what it means?" His voice struggled to reassure me. "You can live off base and I can be with you every night I don't have duty."

It sounded like it might work. God, I wanted it to work, to be with Taylor. But what I really wanted was for the dream we'd had in Gloucester to last forever.

32

That night a lone figure sauntered casually down State Street, then cut abruptly behind my apartment building and climbed the stairs to my back door. It was ajar. My bathrobe fell open as I ran to him across the dark kitchen. I pressed against him. His fingers touching my cheeks, he guided my lips to his. Slowly, his hands moved down my neck to my shoulders, where he felt my bare skin beneath the robe. Pushing it from my shoulders, he carried me naked to the bedroom. We made love until long after midnight, when he left.

The next night, the last before he left for Chicago, I met him at the door with tears in my eyes. When he tried to kiss me, I shook my head and buried my face in his neck. Holding me, he stroked my hair.

"What is it?"

"I don't know," I mumbled into his shoulder, wet with my tears.

"It's okay. We'll make it. We'll figure something out."

I leaned back, his face a blur through my tears. "I don't think so. I don't think I can live like this." I pulled away and sat down on one of the kitchen chairs. "Meeting in the middle of the night. Running to bed to make love. Hours and, now, days of waiting until we can see each other again. Damn it, Taylor," my voice too loud for the stillness of the night, "that's not what I want."

He sat beside me, taking my hands in his. "I know. I don't either. But it won't be forever."

"It's too much. Too much strain. I can't stand it." I got up and walked to the window, staring blankly at the night. He followed and put his arms around me from behind.

"It's not what I want either, Becky. I want it like it was in Gloucester, except that we're married for real. I'll be away for a while, but then I'll work it out with a bishop somewhere so you can get a divorce and we'll marry."

"Work it out, work it out. I'm tired of working it out. Taylor, please understand me? I'm at the end of my rope." I turned around and fell into his arms, crying hysterically. After a few moments he lifted me like a baby and carried me to the bed where we lay together, my head on his chest, his arms around me.

We said nothing for several minutes. He massaged my back and neck. Gradually my sobbing subsided.

"It's hard for both of us, Becky. We've turned our lives against the tide. We've got nothing to help us but our love for each other. We've got to believe in it."

"I know. I don't know if I can."

"Please try, Becky. Please try. I don't think I can live without your love. I wouldn't want to."

"I know. But understand, I'm not sure I've got the energy to go through it."

"Keep *White Wings* here," he whispered in my ear. "She'll take care of you. And keep my compass, the one you gave me. I'll write as soon as I know the lay of the land. At least we're not treated like recruits. We'll get time off. I want you to come to Chicago as soon as I get a weekend. I'll get a hotel. By then, maybe I'll know more about where I'll be stationed."

I looked at him, my eyes pleading for him to make things right. Then suddenly the strain of the last few days overwhelmed me with fatigue and I collapsed limp against him. He rolled me onto my stomach, his strong fingers working the tense muscles in my shoulders and the tightness at the small of my back. Softly he murmured, "I love you Becky, I love you Becky," the words like a lullaby.

I awoke with a start a little after three, frantically dashing my hand to the other side of the bed looking for Taylor. He was gone. I wrapped my arms and legs around his pillow and wept. Sometime before dawn I fell back asleep and didn't wake until nine.

* * *

Mid-July and still no period. Ten days overdue. Damn. How could I be so stupid? What did I think I was doing? Was getting pregnant going to keep him here, make everything all right? So I've got a part of Taylor in me, growing. It sure as hell is not the same as having him here. And it's only going to get more difficult. What am I going to say to people when it shows? What the hell was I thinking?

Then morning sickness hit with a vengeance. I awoke with a ton of lead in my stomach, feeling that if I made the slightest movement I'd throw up. The next instant I was running to the toilet, hoping I would. Nothing's lonelier than slumping on cold linoleum with your head hanging limp over a toilet you wished you'd scrubbed out the day before. Finally I made it back to bed where I lay alone and exhausted. No shoulder to lean on. No one to rub the soreness out of my lower back. No one who knew the misery I was going through. I cried myself to sleep, stealing another couple of hours out of my work day. What the hell. Nobody cared anyway.

About one-thirty I walked into my office at the hotel and opened the books. Mom was sitting at the front desk and could see me through the open door. Every time I glanced up, I caught her staring at me. Finally she came to my door.

"You all right? You look miserable." Mother could spot trouble, always.

"I've just got a touch of something—a summer cold, I don't know."

"Did you get some lunch in the kitchen?"

The thought of it turned my stomach. "I ate at home, Mom."

"You sure? I don't think you're eating right. Not the right kind of things."

"Mom, I'm okay. Just tired and a little under the weather." She stood looking at me for several moments, then returned to the front desk. She knows, I thought. Mothers can tell.

Two days later, on a Sunday morning, I called Aggie's house and Mr. Sparr answered.

"Aggie's not here, Becky. I mean she's moved to Lynn, taken an apartment there. I've got her number, though." He gave it to me. I asked him how loberstering was going without his helper. "Oh, I manage okay, but I've cut back on the number of pots. What I miss is seeing Aggie every evening. But don't tell her. She's doing what she wants. Can't expect her to sit around here and take care of an old man all her life."

I wished him well, assured him I wouldn't say anything to her, and rang off. Poor guy, I thought. Guess I'm not the only person who's lonely.

I dialed Aggie's number in Lynn. "Hello," a strange voice answered.

Puzzled, I said, "Aggie?"

"No. Hang on, I'll get her."

After a pause, her voice came on the line. "Hello, this is Aggie."

"Hi, Aggie. Becky. Your dad said you'd moved. Sounds like you've got a roommate."

"Becky, it's been so long. Yeah, I found a friend with a place here in Lynn and she invited me to move in with her. Her name's Casey. Works in the same section at GE." And then in a whisper, "Wait till you meet her. She's a dream."

"I'd love to. In fact, I was hoping we might get together today, but I don't want to interfere."

"Hang on." She cupped her hand over the mouthpiece. Voices mumbled in the background. "Tell you what. Why don't you come over this afternoon. You can meet Casey and see this place. It's really nice. Then have dinner with us."

"I'm afraid I'd be in the way."

Casey came on the line. "Becky, I'd love to meet you. Aggie's told me so much about you. Please come." I agreed and that afternoon drove to Lynn.

The apartment was on the second level of a triple-decker. I rang the middle of three doorbell buzzers and heard Aggie shout from the balcony above to come on up. I climbed the steps to the second landing and knocked on their door.

"It's open." I went in. Aggie ran to me, almost knocking me over, and threw her arms around me, kissing my cheek. "I've missed you." She was dressed in a blue work shirt and dungarees rolled up to her knees. She might have just walked off her lobster boat except there was a new sparkle in her eyes and an effervescence that surprised me.

"I've missed you, too." Over her shoulder I could see a tall, slender woman in her mid-twenties.

"This is Casey," Aggie said, catching hold of her hand and pulling her toward me.

"Hi, Casey." I extended my hand.

"Hi, Becky." She shook it with a firmness that belied her soft, feminine appearance. Immediately I was struck by her long, thin face, as finely carved as a porcelain figurine and almost as pale. Too many hours inside a factory, I thought. Her dark brunette hair, long and straight, was pulled over her right shoulder and fell across her chest. She was wearing shorts and a loose-fitting blouse with the tail out and tied at her waist. Standing beside us and looking from one to the other, she seemed unsure of her place among such old friends as Aggie and me. Aggie, sensing this, put her arm around her and walked to the center of the living room.

"What a wonderful apartment." My eyes did a quick circle of the room. Yards and yards of colorful gauze material, hung from the windows as draperies and, at one corner of the room, flowed downward from the ceiling like the opening of a desert tent. Scrolls of brown paper (I think it was butcher paper) stretched diagonally across a wall, printed with Egyptian characters and stylized figures of dancers and chariots. Beneath the hanging gauze were mounds of huge pillows with colorful geometric patterns. In the center of the room a low table crouched on heavy wooden legs with claw feet rolled inward. In another corner a chaise longue, protruding obliquely into the room, was upholstered in brilliant purple, its legs and frame painted gold.

"Isn't Casey a genius?" Aggie said, hugging her slightly.

"I'm impressed. It's joyful. I love it."

On one side of the living room was the balcony and on the other the dining room. Its furnishings were more conventional: buffet, china cabinet, and table all sheathed in three shades of veneer, an inexpensive version of art deco. Beyond this was the kitchen on the left and a hallway on the right leading to two bedrooms. One had a bed with a quilt comforter as a spread, a chest of drawers, and a chair. On the wall was a picture of Aggie's *Bright Star*. The other bedroom followed a French Impressionist motif with Renoir and Van Gogh prints on the walls and a multicolored bedspread of floral design.

Aggie laughed. "Guess which is mine."

They led me back to the living room. Following them down the hall and through the dining room, I thought they were a most unlikely pair, Casey floating gracefully along and Aggie moving with the plodding solidness of a mariner on land.

We settled in the living room, sprawled on the many pillows. "You should be an interior decorator," I said to Casey. "Your apartment is beautiful."

"Thanks. Actually, we did it together after Aggie moved in."

"Right." Aggie laughed. "You did all the design and I helped tack it up."

"How long have you been here?" I asked Aggie.

"It's been, let's see, four weeks now."

Casey got up. "You two catch up on your lives and I'll make us some wine coolers. Unless you'd like something else, Becky?"

"No. That's perfect for a hot July afternoon." She went to the kitchen.

Aggie was beaming. "I am so happy. We hit it off the day we met. She'd started at GE two weeks before me and knew the ropes, so she helped me find my way around. Then, one night after work, she invited me for dinner here—it was just orange crates and boxes then—and our lives meshed."

"I'm so happy for you." I took her hand and sighed. "A little jealous, too. I've gotten used to having you all to myself. Whenever I'd call, you were there."

"Don't worry. I'm here. And I still love you. But now I'm *in* love and that's all the difference in the world."

"It is, isn't it?"

Aggie heard the sadness in my voice. "Okay, what's wrong?"

Just then, Casey returned with a tray and three tall glasses sparkling with wine and soda. I asked her where she was from. She said she'd grown up in Newton, gone to college at Wellesley, and then gotten married. After three years it ended in disaster.

"What happened?"

"I walked out. Here I was with a college degree in art and all he wanted was someone to stay home, cook his meals, and screw. I can't even say 'make love' because there sure as hell was no love there. I put up with it because my parents thought he was such a great up-and-coming lawyer and because they wanted grand-children. 'Why aren't you happy?' they'd say. 'You've got what every girl longs for.' So, I thought something must be wrong with me. Then a couple of months ago, I saw this ad for women workers at GE, got the job, and walked out on Mr. Right."

"Good for you, Casey!" I toasted. We all raised our glasses and drank.

They told me about their jobs at GE's River Works plant in West Lynn. "They call us Specialists," Aggie said, "not regular workers like the men. Guess they're afraid we'll steal their jobs."

"What do you do?"

"We operate surface grinding machines."

"Whatever that is," I said.

"Yeah. Well, they're big and noisy. Day in and day out, the same process over and over again. Whatever it is we're grinding smooth ultimately becomes a part of the supercharger for a P40."

"And you should see us," Casey said. "My hair is rolled into a bun and tied under a bandanna and we wear these work suits that button up the front. Can't have any loose-fitting clothes to get caught in machines."

"It sounds like you love it, though."

Aggie nodded. "Between the job and my newfound friend, I've never been happier." Her smile faded as she again saw my mixed reaction to her good fortune. "Okay, let's have it. What's going on in your life? I hear Jimmy was back for a quick visit."

I grimaced, then took a drink while I decided if it was safe to tell the whole story.

Aggie said, "Whatever you can say to me, you can say to Casey. When it comes to keeping secrets, we're pros."

I looked at the two of them for a moment, then dropped my eyes and said, "I'm pregnant."

Casey glanced uncertainly at Aggie, hoping for a clue on how to respond. Aggie said, "Hey. That's great." (Casey smiled.) ". . . or is it?" (Casey scowled.) "So, he pops in, dips his dick, and takes off again for Europe."

"It wasn't Jimmy."

Silence. Aggie's mouth dropped open. "Not the preacher?"

"Uh-huh. Taylor."

"Well I'll be damned." She thought for a moment. "Are you sure?"

"Sure Taylor, or sure pregnant?"

"Well, both."

"I'm sure. I even planned it. Told him it was my safe time and, hell, he didn't know any better."

"Does he know?"

"No. He's gone. They kicked him out—not for this . . . well, partly for this. Someone said he was playing around with me when, at the time, we hadn't done anything. So we figured, what the hell? No, that's not true either. When I knew he was going away, I decided I wanted his baby."

"You did it on purpose?"

"Uh-huh. I know. It's crazy. I love him so much I wanted to have a part of him. Now I'm not so sure."

"Where is he?"

"Fort Sheridan, north of Chicago."

"My God!" Aggie exclaimed. "You mean he's in the army?"

Casey, eyes as big and blue as robin's eggs, looked first at Aggie, then at me, then back to Aggie.

"Yeah, but it's a good thing. He'll get sent to some army camp and I can live near him. No church people to bother us. We can see each other every night." The more I explained, the more far-fetched and ridiculous it sounded. "Then he'll find a bishop who'll . . ." My words were getting drowned in sobs. ". . . who'll let us get married."

"Oh Becky, my poor Becky." She eased over beside me, Casey moving to my other side, and they both hugged me. "There, there," they murmured, rocking me gently. The floodgates opened and I cried with abandon for several minutes. The relief of having someone to talk with, someone who loved and understood me, dissolved the fortitude behind which I'd hidden for the last three weeks. Finally, like an old car that keeps sputtering after you turn it off, my crying ended with a series of quick gasps and a hiccup.

They continued to hold me until the hot July afternoon lay a sheen of perspiration where our bodies touched.

I sat up, turning around to look at them. "And I'd do it all over again."

They frowned, shook their heads, then broke into smiles.

"God, but I love him. Not only is he the nicest guy in all the world, he's the sexiest." I told them about our first time on *White Wings*, in the rain under the awning, and then about the trip to Gloucester—the shopping, the cooking, the sailing, the lovemaking day and night—the whole story. I brought out the pictures we'd taken on the boat, and Casey agreed he was very good-looking.

"What happens next?" Aggie asked.

"If I can lick this morning sickness, I'm going to Chicago in a couple of weeks. He's getting us a hotel room."

"You going to tell him?" Casey said cautiously.

"I don't think so. I want him to do what he thinks is right because he loves me, not because he's gotten me pregnant."

"Well, baby, you got a hell of a lot more confidence in men than I do," Casey declared.

"I know this guy, Casey," Aggie said. "He really is okay. It's just . . . you can't hide it forever."

I told my parents that Aggie, her roommate, and I were driving to Vermont for the weekend, but instead I boarded a train for Chicago to see Taylor. The trip was miserable. Twenty-four hours on a rocking, jolting train, an upper berth to climb in and out of, two days in the Chicago Hilton passing off morning sickness as a touch of the flu, eating out in nice restaurants where the very smell of rich food caused my stomach to revolt, and finally, twenty-four more hours on the train back to Marblehead.

It wasn't all bad, though. Saturday and Sunday afternoons we stayed in the hotel making love. I told Taylor I'd had my period just before I came, and he bought my lie again. He was handsome in his uniform, and proud to be in the service, yet it symbolized the power that controlled our lives. Relating stories about his new life in the army, including sleeping with thirty other men in a barrack, I could see an enthusiasm that surprised me. He still had no idea

where he'd be sent when he graduated and became a second lieutenant. When Sunday night came, the agony of parting was as hard,
if not harder, than the first time.

Back in Marblehead, life went on. Either I was getting used to
being pregnant or the little creature in my womb had made peace
with my body. In any case, my morning sickness ended. In fact, I
felt good. I was eating more, my color was good even before
morning makeup, and my breasts were filling out my bathing suit
in a way that drew whistles from sailors on passing yachts. I worked
during the day and went sailing alone in the evening. I could tell
White Wings missed Taylor too, because she left the dock reluctantly, as if waiting for one more passenger. On weekends I spent
the time with Aggie and Casey. Sometimes they'd come sailing
with me on *White Wings*, and sometimes we'd lie around their apartment drinking wine coolers, listening to records or reading. Saturday nights we'd go to a bar in Lynn where other GE workers
congregated: drink beer, dance to the jukebox, flirt, and generally
kid around. Rather than resent the increasing number of women
workers, the men seemed to enjoy having them around, especially
after hours at the bar. Some were intent on finding partners to take
to bed, both men and women, but for the most part it was a community of people letting off steam after a week of hard work in a
place where there was too much noise to talk. Aggie and Casey
made sure I was brought into the group, and before long I'd made
several friends.

Mom continued to eye me suspiciously, even to the point of
suggesting I might feel more comfortable in a slightly larger
bathing suit. "Especially around the chest." At least once a week
I'd have dinner with the DeWolfs. It wasn't until the first week of
August that I got a letter from Jimmy. I'd been writing Taylor
every day and getting three or four letters a week in return, so the
arrival of Jimmy's letter seemed out of place, connected with a life
I'd put behind me. I faked excitement when I read it to his mom
and dad. Cryptically, he said he was in the place he'd said he was
going to—either Malta or Egypt—and was flying the plane he'd
been so anxious to fly, the Spitfire. He talked about the heat and
dust so we decided it probably was Egypt. One sentence in the
letter was directed to me. "Several of the people I'd known at my

last base are here too, including some of my closest friends." So Jennifer was in Egypt too. Mrs. DeWolf said, "Isn't that nice he's among friends." I was quick to agree.

Taylor finished chaplaincy school the end of September, was commissioned a second lieutenant, and was given a few days' leave before traveling to his new post. In our letters we had agreed to meet in New York for two or three days, depending on the amount of time he had. I'd told him I couldn't face another forty-eight hours on trains to and from Chicago. New York, only five hours away, was a breeze. Wearing a new navy blue dress and jacket and a wide-brimmed hat, I felt refreshed when Taylor met me in Grand Central Station, one single gold bar glittering on each shoulder.

After a long kiss, he held me at arm's length. "You look absolutely beautiful, Becky." I told him he looked nice in gold bars and asked where he was being sent. "Let's sit in the bar over there and I'll tell you."

We pushed our way into the crowd, finding a stand-up table near a window facing out on the main concourse of the station.

"Well?"

"It's perfect. I'm going to the Philippines. I'll be the chaplain at Clark Field."

My face dropped. "Perfect? Isn't that all the way on the other side of the Pacific Ocean? How can I ever see you?"

"I checked around. Officers can have their own homes off the army facility. It's so cheap you can have maids and houseboys and gardeners and live like a colonial governor. What I do when I'm not working is my own business. They say there're officers with wives in the States who have live-in mistresses, so nobody's going to squeal on somebody else."

"But the Philippines." I scowled, disillusioned. "How do I get there? What do I tell my folks?"

"Well, how about the truth?"

"The truth—that I'm going to the Philippines to be somebody's live-in mistress? You've got to be kidding."

"We'll have to face it sooner or later. We can't keep everybody happy all the time."

A waitress brought us two draft beers. As I raised mine to drink, someone behind me jostled my arm, spilling part of it on my new dress.

"Sorry," he said over his shoulder and continued talking to his friend.

"Oh shit. Look at my dress."

"Becky. It's okay," Taylor pleaded. "I'll buy you a new one. We should be celebrating, not getting mad."

I closed my eyes for a minute, trying to calm down. When I spoke, it was slow and decisive. "Taylor, I love you and I want to work this out. But I'm not going to live as your mistress for the rest of my life with no certainty of getting married." He looked hurt and disappointed. "I've got to know there's a bishop who'll annul my marriage. Then I'll divorce Jimmy and we can be married. As much as I love you, I'm not willing to abandon everything and rush to the other side of the world."

"But I thought that's what we wanted."

"It's what *you* wanted," I said, so loud the klutz who'd spilled my beer turned to listen. I glared at him, then, again in a whisper, continued. "Do you realize we'd have no problem at all, if you'd just give up being an Episcopal priest? I could get divorced, which I'd do in a minute, and we could get married. But that's more than you're willing to do. I haven't pushed you on it. But I think it's high time you started seeing that I have a life too, and things that I want."

He looked down at the table, sliding his glass around on a smear of moisture. "I'm sorry, Becky. I want you so much I wasn't thinking about what you want."

I put my hand on his. "Why aren't you a son of a bitch, so I could get mad at you and walk away?"

"Don't ever do that, please."

"I won't, but we're going to have to figure something out fast." Because, I thought, I'll be getting bigger and bigger and won't be able to travel at all. "Don't wait, Taylor."

"I'll start right away to find a bishop. I promise."'

I lifted his chin and kissed him. "Right now, we're wasting good time talking. Where's the hotel?"

In minutes we were in our room at the Park Regency hurriedly undressing each other. Taylor went wild over my enlarging breasts.

He lifted them in his hands, as if weighing them, then kissed the nipples and buried his face between them. When he dropped his hands to my bottom and pulled me up and toward him, he exclaimed, "Wow."

"Really, Father!"

I pulled him onto the bed and we made up for five weeks of celibacy.

Later, as I lay on the wrinkled sheets, he got up and went to his overnight case. I stared at his lanky frame, wanting to burn it into my memory, so I'd never forget the broad shoulders, the tight buttocks, the long muscles in his thighs. Returning, he sat cross-legged on the bed beside me and handed me a long, narrow box.

I looked at him and he smiled, nodding for me to open it. Inside was a bracelet composed of several gold pieces the size of nickels, each ornamented with filigree, connected by gold links. I stared, speechless.

"Put it on."

Removing it carefully from the box, I laid it across the back of my wrist.

"Wait. Before you attach it, look behind this one." He turned over one of the gold pieces. Inscribed there, were the words "To Becky, love, Taylor."

"It's beautiful." Looking into his eyes I began to cry. A going-away present, I thought. He's really leaving.

My first letter from Taylor arrived the end of October. The Philippines were all he said they'd be. He'd taken a house near the field and not far from Manila. It was not large but had a lawn, garden, and hanging flowers everywhere. He'd hired a houseboy, cook, and gardener who treated him like a general. The pace at Clark Field was slow and regimented, with enough work and training to keep the men busy, but not so strenuous that there wasn't time for swimming, sailing, polo, and entertaining at the officers' club. He'd written his classmates from the seminary, inquiring about their bishops' views on annulment, but hadn't heard back from any of them. He said he missed me and loved me. At the end he asked if I'd haul *White Wings* and find a place for her during the winter.

I asked Mr. Sparr, Aggie's dad, if I could keep *White Wings* in his basement again, and he said of course.

"We'll hook up Taylor's trailer to my truck," he offered. "I'll help you get it into the basement." I thanked him, grateful for his kindness; with Aggie working, I had nowhere else to turn.

We used the derrick at the boatyard near his house, hoisted the boat from the water, and positioned it over the trailer. As we began lowering it, the hull swung against one of the derrick's legs, wedging itself so that we couldn't move it up or down without scraping it. The two of us tried pushing it free but couldn't budge it.

"Got a problem?" came a voice from behind. Without turning around I recognized the tone of ridicule that could belong only to Karl Kramer. He'd come up quietly and was sitting on the stone wall at the edge of the quay. "Come on, Becky, you know how. Just push hard, baby." Detestable bastard, I thought.

"How about a hand, Karl?" Mr. Sparr was asking before I could stop him.

"Sure," he said smugly. "Always ready to help a lady in distress."

I drew back out of his way as he approached, not trusting him within arm's length.

"This is the preacher's boat, isn't it?" he said suggestively. "You two kinda hit it off before he left. Did he give you the boat?"

"No. Just helping him out while he's away."

"Uh-huh. Yeah. Well, come on, let's get at it." He spoke as if we were a couple of slackers. "Mr. Sparr, you on the bow pushing that way, and Becky, you back here with me pushing the other."

I narrowed my eyes threateningly to let him know I wasn't going to take any shit, and walked to the stern. We put our hands to the hull and he whispered, "Never seen you lookin' better, Becky." I said nothing. Then he raised his head and called out, "Okay, push." *White Wings* didn't budge. "Again." And to me, "Come on, Becky, I know you can push harder than that." I ignored him.

"We gotta try somethin' else, this isn't workin'." He stepped back and, grasping the large electric drill that provided the power to the winch, said, "Push when I tell you. Okay, both of you, push hard."

He pressed the "on" button, the winch whined, and *White Wings* went scraping up the side of the fixed leg of the derrick.

"Stop! Stop, you idiot," I yelled, not caring what I said. He stopped the winch. "Look at that. You've scraped the side." I touched it with my fingers. "You've even gouged the wood."

"Sorry. Didn't mean to hurt the preacher's prize possession," he said sarcastically. "You shoulda pushed hard, Becky, like I said. It wouldna happened."

"Just get the hell out of here," I said, glaring at him. Mr. Sparr listened, stunned at the level of my anger. Karl turned, gave me the dumb-broad laugh, and walked away.

Mr. Sparr and I finished the job.

The following week I was sitting on the DeWolfs' back porch overlooking their garden, having drinks before dinner. George was worried about the news from North Africa.

"That Rommel's a tough individual. His panzer divisions have got our boys on the run. Now it looks like they're getting ready for another big offensive."

Florence, who shied away from war talk, headed for the garden and invited me to come along. "Come help me pick the last of the tomatoes. We could get a frost any night now." When we reached the garden, she asked, "How's work going, Becky?"

"Just fine. It's pretty easy when your bosses are your mother and father."

"You look good. I don't think I've ever seen you with more sparkle." We set the basket in the midst of the vines and started picking big red tomatoes. When it was full, Florence asked, "Mind carrying the basket? My back's a little out of whack the last few days."

"Be happy to." Hoisting it, I leaned backward to straighten my back and saw Florence eyeing my waistline.

"Becky," she said, half curious. "You're not pregnant, are you? Come here. Let me look at you." Well, I thought, it had to happen sometime. Her hand roved over my belly, then she looked at me with a sly smile. "You little devil. You are pregnant and you haven't told us."

"Yeah. You're right. I am." What do I do now, I wondered.

"This is wonderful news." She called up to the porch. "George, guess what? We're going to be grandparents." So, I thought, Alan and Sarah still hadn't told them Sarah was pregnant.

"What? What do you mean?"

"Come on," she said to me. "Let's go up to the porch. Here. I'll carry that basket. You've got enough to carry."

33

Bubbling with excitement, Florence hustled across the lawn. "Does Jimmy know?" she asked over her shoulder. "You've got to write him right away and tell him. Imagine, our boy being a father." We started up the steps to the porch. "George. Becky's having a baby. Isn't this wonderful news?"

"Well, I'll be," George said, folding his paper under his arm and coming to the head of the stairs. "What a nice surprise."

I felt like I was climbing the steps of a gallows. At the top I would die. What the hell was I going to say? The loose blouses were supposed to do the trick until Taylor could guarantee an annulment. Too late for that now. Eventually my foot reached the top step and I raised my eyes to the beaming faces of Mom and Dad DeWolf.

George put his arms around me, then stepped back and, holding me by my shoulders, said, "How about this, Florence, we're gonna be grandparents."

I smiled sickly.

His joy changed to concern. "Are you okay? Here, sit down."

"I'm all right." But I did sit down.

"I was going to offer you a drink, but maybe I'd better not."

"It's okay, believe me. I'd love a martini."

He nodded, a bit uncertain, and went to fix the drinks. Mom sat at my elbow. "How are you, really? Is it going along all right?"

"I feel fine now. It was a little hard at first."

"And what does your doctor say?"

"I haven't been to one yet."

"Becky, you need to make an appointment tomorrow. Let's see, it's been the last week of June, all of July, August, September and three weeks of October. That's three, no, four months. You need to see a doctor right away."

"I promise. I'll call tomorrow."

Florence, counting on her fingers, continued her deductions. "March. That makes it the third week of March. A springtime baby. How perfect. We'll have to plan a shower . . ."

I wasn't listening. By default, my decision had been made. I would lie, at least for a while.

That night, going along with the lie, I told my mom and dad. It was the easiest thing to do. The next day Mom called Florence and together they shared the happiness of first-time grandmothers. When the nurse in our doctor's office heard I was four months pregnant, she got me in to see her boss the next day. I was pronounced healthy as a horse.

I decided I'd better tell Jimmy the "news." Thought he should hear it from me before he got a letter from his mother. Lying was like building a brick wall. One solitary lie on the bottom row supported two lies above it and three lies above that until the whole wall became a lie. Once I'd started, it was easy. I didn't elaborate to Jimmy. Just said I'd been to a doctor and discovered his two-day visit in June had produced a baby which should arrive in March. I managed the lie but could not generate any enthusiasm to go with it. Whether he believed it or not, or whether he even cared, would be up to him.

Mom and Florence, Dad and George spread the news, drawing solicitous grins from their friends and limp handshakes for me. I smiled weakly, feeling rotten inside, not from the pregnancy, from the lie. Aggie and Casey became my mother confessors. Our Sunday afternoons in their apartment started with me wringing my hands as I described the growing tentacles of the lie. But as we lowered the level in the jug of wine, the lie got funnier and the reaction of people to it more and more hilarious until the whole thing became a big joke. I went home feeling great until Monday morning when I'd look at myself in the full-length mirror. My belly, like Pinocchio's nose, grew larger as the lie spread.

On Tuesday, November 11, Armistice Day, I joined other Marbleheaders at the town square across from the railroad station where the high school band played military marches and some men dressed like Revolutionary War soldiers fired their muskets in honor of our boys who made the supreme sacrifice in the Great World War. I read their names carved on a bronze plaque attached to a boulder at one side of the square. No Butlers, I noted. Then I found myself looking for the name DeWolf. Instantly I began to shiver and turned toward home, a premonition of what was to come quickening my pace.

I arrived at the hotel as a Western Union man walked through the front door. Standing in the middle of the lobby I watched him go to the desk behind which Mom and Dad stood. I watched him show them the telegram and heard them mumble my name and point toward me. He approached slowly, sorrowfully, and handed me the envelope. Quickly I tore it open, knowing the news it contained. Through watery eyes I read

IT IS WITH DEEPEST REGRET THAT WE INFORM YOU OF THE DEATH OF YOUR HUSBAND FLYING OFFICER JAMES DEWOLF, WHO DIED IN THE SERVICE OF HIS MAJESTY ON 9 NOVEMBER 1941.

I stood there in the center of the room, tears running down my cheeks, staring at the words I could no longer see. It had finally happened. Jimmy was gone. The love that I thought had died suddenly returned and I cried for him. Mom and Dad came to my side, she putting her arms around me and he taking the telegram to read. My sobbing continued, but what they didn't know, couldn't know, was that I cried not only for Jimmy but also from relief that it wasn't Taylor.

That evening, when we were sure George was home from work, Mom and Dad came with me to the DeWolfs'. Florence, hearing our car in the driveway, came to the door. The surprise at seeing the three of us, with me supported on Dad's arm, was immediately replaced with horror. She called George to her side.

"Is it . . . ?"

Dad said we should go into the living room and sit down. Florence sat stiffly on the edge of a chair with George's hand on her shoulder. Her terrified eyes flicked from me to George and back. As I took the telegram out of my purse, she gasped. "No . . . no!" George read it first and began to cry. He knelt beside his wife and put his arms around her. Holding each other, they wept. After several minutes, she took the yellow piece of paper from his hand and read it. Tears came to my eyes not for Jimmy, who had died the hero he had longed to be, but for the DeWolfs. And strangely, I cried for Jennifer, the English girl somewhere in Egypt who was weeping for her lover.

A sealed casket, which they said contained his remains, arrived at the Lynn funeral home I had specified on Friday, November 21. The funeral was the following Tuesday. Jimmy was the first war death on the North Shore, and the Lynn Congregational Church was filled not only with family and friends but with people who came to acknowledge the young hero who had given his life to stop the Nazis. I sat next to Florence, with my parents on my left and George and Alan and Sarah on her right. A military honor guard from nearby Fort Devens followed the casket carried by Jimmy's friends. The British consul general from Boston read a message from His Majesty's minister of war and presented me with a posthumous medal for Jimmy's outstanding heroism. A letter from his squadron commander described Jimmy as a man among men, a loyal fellow soldier who always went above and beyond the call of duty, who had given his life fighting off three enemy aircraft attempting to strafe a fellow pilot parachuting from his disabled plane.

I held Florence's hand in which she had wadded a lace handkerchief. From time to time she wiggled it free to dab at her eyes beneath her dark veil. My eyes were red but I sat erect, proud of Jimmy for having found the role that allowed him to demonstrate his best qualities. I loved him for his daring, and grieved that only by dying was he able to gain the appreciation he long deserved from his father. At the interment, while a cold November wind scattered leaves across the cemetery and shook the awning under which we huddled on metal chairs, the honor guard fired a salute, then removed and folded the American flag, snapping it tight at each triangular fold, and presented it to me.

We returned to the DeWolfs', where friends and relatives brought food, and aunts and uncles organized the flow of traffic so that Florence and George and I could receive condolences.

When the last of the friends left and only a few family members remained to clean up, George asked me to come with him to his study. He said he had kept up a life insurance policy, unbeknownst to Jimmy, ever since he'd taken up flying, and had made me the beneficiary when we were married. Also, the trust fund was written in such a way that it passed to Jimmy's heirs upon his death, which meant that the child soon to be born would receive the benefits. While in its minority, the money would come to me for the child's support, then when he or she reached majority or married, it would go directly to him or her.

My lie guaranteed me and the child in my womb financial independence. Was it worth it? With Jimmy buried, I let my mind consider the opportunities my new freedom presented and the consequences of telling the truth. No longer did Taylor have to search for a bishop willing to grant me an annulment. No longer did he or I have to worry our consciences about a clandestine love affair. Both he and I were free to marry. It would be up to him to decide whether or not to admit the baby's paternity, and if he chose to tell the truth, I would gladly forsake the fiction of Jimmy being the father. The DeWolfs would be devastated by the loss of their grandchild as well as their son, and undoubtably would take me to court to recover the trust fund and the insurance money. Even my own parents might disown me. But I would be with Taylor and our little family would be complete.

On Sunday night, November 30, I wrote him.

My Dearest Darling,

I don't know how to say this without sounding cruel and heartless, so I'll just say it. Jimmy is dead. He was killed Nov. 9th in an air fight over N. Africa. They shipped his casket home and we had the funeral Nov. 25th. He was a good guy in his own way and he died doing what he wanted to do. The DeWolfs are heart-broken and they, as well as my folks, think I'm being very brave accepting it so well. But the truth is, inwardly I am so excited I can hardly contain myself. Taylor, my love, this means we can be married without worrying about annulments and divorces. Do you still love me? Do you still want to marry me and live with me the rest of our lives? Please tell me you weren't procrastinating about finding a bishop to grant an annulment because you were losing interest in me. I'm ashamed I even think such a thing, but being so far away from you and loving you as much as I do, I sometimes get frightened. I'm willing to give up everything to be with you, and I must know as soon as possible that you feel the same way.

And there's more. We're going to have a baby. Please forgive me, but I didn't tell the truth when I said it was my safe time. My reason, however dumb at the time, was to have a part of you with me after you left. I haven't told you about the baby before now because I didn't want you to think I was forcing you to marry me. If Jimmy hadn't died, I don't know what I would have done. Each day it was getting more and more noticeable. Then, the end of October, Mrs. DeWolf saw I was pregnant and the news was out. Because we started the baby right after Jimmy was here, everybody assumed it was his. But Jimmy and I never had sex. You've got to believe me because it's true and when you see your baby, you'll know for sure.

As I read what I have written, I sound like such a liar. I lied to you about my safe time and now I'm lying to everybody here by letting them believe the baby's Jimmy's. Taylor, it's awful. I want to get out of this mess. I want to be with you. I don't care how many people I hurt by coming over there and finally telling everybody the whole truth about us and the baby. Being with you will make everything all right. My appointment with my doctor is next week, and I'll ask him if it's safe for me to travel. If he says no, I think I'll come anyway and just be careful. I'm five months along so I've got to take it easy. The baby's due in March.

Taylor, I love you so much. I know you love me, but I've got to hear it again. . . . I just went back and reread some of your let-ters. Yes, I'm sure. You do love me. Is your house big enough for the two of us and is there room for a nursery? You know I'm not religious like you, but THANK GOD this has all worked out so we can marry and be together. I'm getting big as a house but soon I'll have the baby and be slim and pretty for you. We'll lie side by side and feel our bodies touching. We'll wake in the morning and be together. At night we'll have dinner together and then go for a walk with our baby carriage. All that we've waited for and hoped for will happen.

With all my love, Becky

The following week I had dinner with the DeWolfs on Wednesday night and endured the pain of lying to them yet another time. When Florence talked about the baby, she'd break down in tears, knowing that Jimmy would never see the little one. They took some consolation in the fact that Alan and Sarah would have a baby in February, but even this seemed to remind them of the loss of their son. They urged me to come live with them when it was born, saying they would take care of me and the baby. I fended off their offers by saying I planned to live at the hotel with my parents so I could keep working and be close to the baby. With promises that I would bring the baby to their house several times a week, I escaped both from them and from the sticky web my lies created.

It was a relief to go to Aggie's and Casey's the next Sunday afternoon. I told them about my letter to Taylor and how I sounded like an inveterate liar.

"How can he still love me?" I moaned.

"Don't worry, sweetie," Aggie said. "He was willing to live a lie himself when he climbed into that pulpit on Sunday while he was climbing into your bed on Saturday night. He's not lily white himself."

"But I'm afraid he'll think I tried to trick him into marrying me by getting pregnant."

"Ha!" Casey laughed. "No man is so dumb he'd keep thinking you were safe every time he wanted to make love. Whether he admits it or not, he knew what was going on."

"Oh, I hope so."

"I know so. Now, how about a hot toddy? Just the thing to relieve anxiety on a cold December day." We seconded the motion and Casey got up to go to the kitchen. "Oh. Look at the time. The New York Philharmonic's on. They're doing my favorite, the Brahms Second Piano Concerto. You don't mind if I turn on the radio?"

While she was in the kitchen, Aggie said their life together was going well, some disputes like any couple has, but they resolved them in short order. Casey returned and passed out the hot toddies.

Suddenly, like a sword piercing the air, a voice cut short the music.

"We interrupt this broadcast to bring you a special report. The Japanese have attacked Pearl Harbor. I repeat, the Japanese have attacked Pearl Harbor."

We looked at one another, puzzled. What did he say? What does it mean? I thought we were negotiating with their peace envoys in Washington.

"My God," Aggie said. "We're at war."

"No, it can't be," Casey said. "It's an Orson Welles thing. They'd never attack us."

I said nothing for several minutes, listening to the radio. Then I asked, "What about the Philippines? Do you think they'll attack there?"

The next day the newspapers confirmed that the Japanese were bombing Manila and Fort William McKinley and Nicholas Airfield in the Philippines. Nothing as yet about Clark Field. A day later, on Tuesday, there were reports of Japanese attacks on Singapore, Hong Kong, and the Burma Road, but nothing new about Manila.

On Wednesday I went to the doctor for my monthly checkup amidst news of attacks on Cavite Naval Base near Manila and Japanese landings on northern Luzon. The doctor was concerned about my level of stress, but simply attributed it to the beginning of the war. I asked him if it was all right for me to travel. He wanted to know how far and by what means. I said by train and ship to the Far East.

"You might be able to make it, but nobody's going to be traveling across the Pacific except soldiers for a long time to come."

With each day the news about the Philippines became more grim. The Japanese were landing at several points and pushing toward Manila. The American and Filipino armies were consolidating on the Bataan Peninsula, from which they intended to make counterattacks.

I wrote Taylor after my doctor's appointment and said that even though I was strong enough to travel, it was unlikely I would be able to get transportation. "But just as soon as this war thing gets clarified, I'll be on my way."

Each day I watched for the mailman, desperately longing to hear Taylor's response to my letter about Jimmy's death and our baby. Now, more than ever, I wanted him to know he was to be a father and we were free to marry. For myself, I wanted to know he was safe and that he loved me as much as I loved him.

Monday, December 22, I was pacing back and forth across the lobby waiting for the mailman. If I mailed it on November 30, I thought, it's just possible he could have gotten it by now and sent a letter in return. As the mailman came up the walk, he waved an envelope in my direction. I flung open the door and raced down the drive toward him, my arm outstretched.

"Take it easy. Take it easy," he said, handing me the envelope.

I looked at it perplexed. "Why does this have my handwriting on it?" I asked him. "Why is it addressed to APO San Francisco?"

And then I saw the government stamp.

RETURN TO SENDER—UNABLE TO DELIVER

PART THREE

Taylor Hayakawa

DECEMBER 1994

34

"There're no secrets now," Aunt Aggie said as she handed me an envelope, yellow with age, across the front of which was the stamp return to sender—unable to deliver.

It was Sunday, one week before Christmas, and Rebecca, Matthew, and I were in Aggie's living room seated on the floor amid scraps of newspaper articles, old pictures and letters that had belonged to my mother, Becky DeWolf.

The room was decorated for the season with a Christmas tree in one corner, pine boughs around the windows, and a crèche on the dining room table. Even the quiche Aunt Aggie had prepared for the brunch we'd eaten earlier had been adorned with the colors of Christmas, red pepper slices and green basil leaves. My concession to the season was the miniature sleigh bells I'd pinned on my blouse. Rebecca was wearing a silk brocade jacket flecked with subtle reds and greens, and Aggie a bright red blouse with a sprig of holly. Matthew wore his usual heavy knit Irish sweater.

But uncovering the startling events of Becky's life had shattered the mood of Christmas

After brunch, the four of us had gone to the basement to get the boxes Aggie had stored for Becky more than twenty years ago. That's when Matthew found the bullet lodged in *White Wings*'s hull. Stunned by this discovery, we wondered what it could mean. Was it fired at the boat on the day it was wrecked? Could it possibly be connected with the death of my mother?

With these questions unanswered, we'd carried the boxes to the living room and started exhuming my mother's life from the disorganized scraps and records of her existence that took us back fifty-five years. The task was both emotionally wrenching and physically draining.

Among the last items in the box was the letter, sealed and still in its envelope, addressed by Becky to 2nd Lt. Taylor Harrington, APO, San Francisco, California, and postmarked Marblehead P.O. November 30, 1941.

With compassion in her heavily lined face, Aggie said, "You might as well open it and read it."

I did. The yellowish brown envelope was brittle with age. Carefully I removed four handwritten pages. I read the first couple of lines aloud.

My Dearest Darling,
  I don't know how to say this without sounding cruel and heartless, so I'll just say it. Jimmy is dead.

I looked up at the others and stopped, my face tight, my lips trembling. "I'm sorry. I can't read it aloud. I'll give it to you in a minute." I continued silently, reading about Jimmy's death, and my mother's confession that she had lied to Taylor about her "safe time" and then to the DeWolfs about who my father was. I could feel the anguish of her guilt, as well as her fear that Taylor would not believe her and that their love might be extinguished. When I finished, I handed the letter to Rebecca, who read it and passed it to Matthew.

"And he never got the letter," I stated more than asked.

"Apparently not." Aggie sighed. "Becky must have tossed it in her box of keepsakes still sealed."

Outside, a wintry wind rattled Aggie's storm windows, and I shivered as I reached for a picture of this handsome young man sitting in *White Wings* on a summer day with his hand on the tiller and his face to the wind. "And this is my father, Taylor Harrington?"

Aggie nodded.

I studied it for several seconds, searching his facial features for contours that resembled mine. The nose, I thought, maybe the nose, but the picture was too small to tell for sure. How strange, I thought. All these years I've looked at the framed photograph on my bookcase shelf of James DeWolf in the uniform of an English flying officer and taken it for granted he was my father. "Whew," I said, shaking my head to realign conflicting thoughts.

"What happened after that?" I asked Aggie.

"You mean after the letter was returned?"

I nodded.

"The bottom line is, she never did hear from him. The Japanese took more and more of the Philippines until they'd squeezed the Americans and Filipinos onto the Bataan Peninsula and into Corregidor." Aggie stopped for a minute to straighten her back and stretch. "Worrying about Taylor wasn't her only problem. She had to pretend her distress was due to Jimmy's death. The DeWolfs were constantly telling her how much Jimmy had loved her and how he'd want her to come live with them. Poor thing. She was worn to a frazzle by the time you were born in March."

"Here," said Matthew, picking up the birth announcement Becky had saved from the *Marblehead Messenger*. He was sprawled across the floor, half on and half off the photos and clippings. Aggie had put a Band-Aid on the finger he'd scratched when he found the bullet hole. He read the announcement.

Born to Rebecca Butler DeWolf, a baby girl, 8 pounds 3 ounces, at 4:30 PM on March 20, 1942, in Salem Hospital. Flying Officer James DeWolf, the baby's father, was killed in action while serving with the RAF in North Africa on November 9, 1941.

Matthew squinted at the paper, then looked up at me. "That's funny. Doesn't mention your name."

Aggie grunted. "Wasn't funny at the time. Becky fought for a week with the DeWolfs for the name Taylor. 'It's not a family name,' they said. 'Sounds like a boy's name.' But she didn't give in and you were named Taylor Butler DeWolf. Your grandmother Butler never said anything, even to the day she died, but I think she suspected the truth about your father. It was a victory for Becky and renewed her strength for a while, but the strain of worrying about her lover and the constant pretending took its toll. You got colic and then her milk dried up and she became more and more withdrawn. Finally, the Americans surrendered at Corregidor. She didn't know if Taylor was dead or taken prisoner.

"The middle of May, Martha, that's Becky's mother, called me—said Becky was in her room with the door locked and the baby was crying her head off. Becky'd moved back to the hotel by then and was in her old room next to her parents on the top floor. I went over and begged her to open the door. Nothing—just you screaming. I didn't know if she was alive or dead. We got a passkey and I went in. Becky lay with her face to the wall curled up like a baby."

Aggie looked at our faces creased with pain and said, "Well, enough said about that. We took her to the hospital and they treated her for postpartum depression. She was there three weeks. I was the only one she'd see. Toward the end of her stay, she claimed she'd faked the hysterics just to get away from the pressure of lying to the DeWolfs. Just like Becky, huh? But I doubt she was faking. She was one sick kid."

"She was lucky to have you, Aggie," Rebecca said, almost at the point of tears.

Aggie shrugged and went on. "The first week of June I said I needed help getting *White Wings* ready for launching. This got her up and moving. We scrubbed and scraped and painted for most of June and then put the boat in the water."

"What was happening to me all that time?" Taylor looked slightly aggrieved.

Aggie laughed. "There was no problem getting you taken care of. Your grandmothers fought for the chance. Becky took full advantage of their offers and sailed *White Wings* every day. It was good to see her get back her color and some of her old spirit.

"The last weekend of June 1942—I remember because it was after the twenty-fifth—Becky took me and Casey out for the day. I may have trouble remembering what happened yesterday, but I can tell you word for word what happened that day, fifty-some years ago."

Aunt Aggie began her story, drawing us into it as if we were there.

White Wings's sails were full and we were moving smartly away from the mouth of the harbor toward Cat Island. I sat on the starboard

seat, Casey on the port. Becky had the tiller in one hand and the sheet in the other. I could see *White Wings* pulling energy from the wind and the sea and injecting it into Becky's body. Casey winked at me, then nodded toward Becky. We both smiled surreptitiously.

Becky saw us. "So? What's the secret?"

"You're smiling," I called back to her. "Haven't seen you do that in a while."

"Hmmm. Didn't realize I was."

"What's up?" Casey asked.

Becky thought about this for a moment as if wondering if she should tell us, then said, "Do you know what the twenty-fifth of June was?"

"Yeah," I said. "Thursday."

"Nooo. I mean, what anniversary?"

I thought for a minute, "Oh. Yeah. It's got something to do with your baby, hasn't it?"

"Uh-huh. I told you about it. The day on the boat under the awning. Remember?"

"Yeah," I said. "Pretty hot stuff."

"Well, *White Wings* and I celebrated it with a wine and cheese picnic anchored at the same island where Taylor and I were. It was like he was there, with us." Her lip trembled slightly. "No, I'm not going nuts again. I may have drunk a little too much wine and I might have drifted off to sleep once or twice, but his presence was so real I could almost reach out and touch him. I could smell the sweat on his chest. Sometimes I'd feel his hands on my body." Her voice began to falter. She was trying not to cry, but tears started anyway. I went aft and took the tiller. Casey slid over and held her in her arms. After a few minutes she sat up and dried her eyes with the back of her hands.

After a moment, she continued, "I cried then, too, lying on the pillows here in the cockpit. Then *White Wings* began rocking, ever so gently, comforting me. I may have fallen asleep, I don't know, and I know this sounds crazy, but *White Wings* spoke to me." She dropped her head, embarrassed, and looked up at us out of the corner of her eyes. "*White Wings* told me Taylor's alive. He's not dead and someday I'll see him again."

"I believe you," I said. Casey nodded too.

*   *   *

As daylight faded from the gray December sky, shadows crept from the corners of the living room and settled themselves on the papers strewn across the floor. We had been there all afternoon.

"Matthew, hop up and turn on that lamp, if you don't mind," Aunt Aggie said.

The light drove the shadows back to their corners.

"Well, Taylor, what do you want to do?" Aggie asked me. "Take this stuff home or talk some more?"

Before I could answer, Rebecca said, "I've got to go back to Boston early tomorrow, and I can't be out here again until next weekend. I'd just as soon talk a little more."

"Fine by me," I agreed.

Matthew joined in. "I can stay too if you want to go on."

"Good." Turning to him, I said, "I'll pay for pizza, if you'll run down and get it?"

"Glad to," he said.

I got up from the floor, stretched, and called Marblehead House of Pizza for a large with mushrooms and anchovies.

"By the way," I said to Matthew, "do you still have that bullet?"

He looked straight at me. "Right here in my pocket."

"What are you going to do with it?"

"Thought I'd take it to a gun shop I know up in Maine and see what they can tell me about it."

"Shouldn't you go to the police?" Rebecca asked.

"It's up to you, Taylor. What do you want to do?"

"Let's let it ride for a while. Like you said, the bullet's been in the boat for twenty-one years or maybe long before that. Who knows? Ask the gun shop. See what they say. But don't lose it."

Thirty minutes later we were again in the living room sitting on the floor, eating pizza sections and licking the cheese from our fingers. Aggie had made a tossed salad and produced four beers from the refrigerator.

"I remember hearing stories about the Bataan Death March," Matthew said, looking with dismay into the pizza box and finding it empty. "Hmmm," he said, "I should've bought two." Then, coming back to his subject. "It must have torn Becky apart, reading about it in the papers."

"We never knew about that until MacArthur returned to the Philippines. Censorship, I guess. Instead, we read about Americans and Filipinos holding out in the mountains. She figured Taylor was with the guerrilla fighters. See, she always believed he had survived.

"It all came to a head in June of forty-three, right after we'd put *White Wings* in the water. Taylor's parents showed up from Los Angeles. They'd come to get Taylor's boat. Becky'd gotten a mooring on the West Shore while she waited for one here in the harbor, so it wasn't tied up at the hotel. Vivian Harrington was in a bad way—pale, eyes red, nervous—back on the booze, I think. Becky and I were picking you up, Taylor, to take you to the DeWolfs' for the afternoon so we could go sailing. We were crossing the lobby with Becky carrying you just as the Harringtons were checking in. I thought Becky was going to die on the spot."

Again we were drawn back some fifty years, transfixed as Aunt Aggie spoke:

"Christ," Becky whispered in my ear. "It's Taylor's parents. What're they doing here?" She turned quickly into the dining room where she could watch them.

"Oh my God," she cried, a sudden realization of what their visit must mean. "Taylor's dead. They've come for his boat." She began to shake uncontrollably. "And I can't even ask them if he's alive or dead. They don't know me. Don't know I exist." I put my arms around her, and she sagged against me. Clifford Harrington looked our way, then he and his wife crossed the lobby in our direction.

"He's coming this way, Becky," I said. "Can you handle it?"

"I'll try," she answered wiping her eyes with the edge of the baby's blanket.

"Hello," Harrington said, looking at Becky. "My name's Clifford Harrington and this is my wife, Vivian. Your father told us you've been taking care of our son's boat since he left for the army." His smile matched the softness of his voice. Mrs. Harrington, however, looked at her with cold disregard.

"We've come for the boat—*White Wings*," she said in a voice that was all business.

Becky stood, hoisting the baby to her shoulder and clutching her in both arms as if they were planning to take her as well as the boat.

"The boat?" she stalled, looking for a way out.

"Yes," he said. "It was tied to the dock when we were here two years ago for the ordination. Your father said you were taking care of it for our son, the Reverend Taylor Harrington. Certainly, you remember. He was curate at St. Paul's Church here in Marblehead."

"Yes, I know," she stammered.

"Were you friends," Vivian asked, "or was he paying you to look after it?"

"Friends. We were friends. Have . . . have you heard from him?"

"No!" Vivian shot the word at her. "I would have thought someone here in Marblehead—from the church—would have told you. He's dead."

Becky collapsed. I managed to reach her before she hit the floor and Vivian Harrington, with amazing swiftness, caught the baby and held her in her arms. Graham and Martha Butler rushed into the dining room, he kneeling beside Becky and she stroking her head. Vivian had placed the baby on her own shoulder and was gently patting her back.

Vivian spoke. "I'm sorry. I didn't know it would hit her this way. I thought they were just acquaintances. Someone should have told her. We'd written Father Hendricks."

"She's been under tremendous strain, Mrs. Harrington," I said. "Her husband was lost in North Africa and she's had the baby to take care of."

"I'm terribly sorry," she repeated. "I do know what she's going through. I was too abrupt."

"Can you tell me, please, something about Taylor?" Becky was looking up at Mrs. Harrington. "When . . . what . . . happened?"

Vivian, finding comfort for herself in holding a baby, related to Becky the only facts she knew. "It was last month. The International Red Cross notified the army and they told us. He died in a Japanese prison in the Philippines."

"Is there any chance they've made a mistake?" Becky asked.

"No, there's no chance," Vivian said. Then, "You were good friends, weren't you?"

"Yes," Becky said as if speaking from a dream. "We were good friends."

Vivian Harrington said nothing for a moment, then, smiling, said, "You have a beautiful baby, Becky. At least you have that much." Watching her, I thought, if only you knew the baby you're holding is your granddaughter.

Mrs. Harrington handed Becky her baby and asked, "Can you tell us something about the boat?"

"Not now, dear," Mr. Harrington interceded. "We can take care of the boat in the morning."

Becky sat up straight and took little Taylor in her arms. "That's all right, Mr. Harrington. The boat's gone," she said. Martha and Graham Butler looked at her surprised, but said nothing.

"Gone?" Mrs. Harrington said with disbelief. "How can it be gone?"

"You must know," Becky began speaking quickly. "Last year. October. Two men pulled it. They said you'd sent them. Taking it to Long Island, they said." With each sentence Vivian's eyes narrowed.

"What are you talking about?" Her voice was now hard, accusing. "I never sent any men."

"Vivian," her husband said firmly. "We'll handle it in the morning."

"We certainly will," her voice angry. "We're going to the police and get this straightened out first thing in the morning." She marched toward the elevator, her husband following. Becky's parents looked on, nonplussed.

"If you've ever backed me up on anything," Becky said to her mother and father, "back me up on this. I'm sorry she's upset, but Taylor gave me that boat to keep for him and I'm going to until he returns."

"But, baby," Graham pleaded. "They said he's gone. He was . . ."

"Well, he's not. He's coming back, and until he does, I'm keeping *White Wings* like he wanted me to."

Becky lifted her baby onto her shoulder and with blazing determination headed for the stairs.

Martha Butler whispered, "I'm afraid she's getting sick again."

Graham tried to calm her. "It'll be all right, Martha." And then to me, "Aggie, help her if you can. The shock was too much."

I went to her room. She'd left the door open, knowing that I'd follow her.

Whirling toward me as I entered, Becky declared, "She's not getting *White Wings*."

"Of course she's not, but we'd better think fast. The boat's in the West Shore harbor, so, we've got to hide it." I thought for a minute. "Think we can get it back in my basement tonight?"

"We'll need help."

"Yeah. We'll have to tow *White Wings*. We'll need somebody with a boat, and I'd rather not get my dad involved."

"There's always Karl Kramer," Becky said uneasily. "But I hate to think what he'd want in return."

"Hell, Becky, he's a harbor policeman now. You want him to help steal a boat?"

Karl had tried to enlist in the service, but because of his injured knees was turned down. The harbormaster, however, was glad to get him.

"Actually, that's perfect," Becky said with a sly smile. "We get him to help hide the boat tonight, and then tomorrow morning Officer Kramer pretends to help the Harringtons find it."

"And when he comes to collect for his favor, what are you going to do?"

"I'll think of something," she said.

She telephoned Karl and I could tell from her expression he was agreeing but was being his usual obnoxious self.

That night, the three of us met at the commercial pier. Karl was dressed in a dark blue sweater and wore knee-high boots over his dungarees. He was a good-looking guy in a rugged sort of way and I could see how Becky could have fallen for him in high school. But admiration vanished as soon as he opened his mouth.

"Hi, Becky," he said as we walked up. "Knew you'd come beggin' for me one of these days."

"Let's get this straight, Karl," she said firmly. "What we're talking about here is a favor to an old high school friend. Nothing more."

"D'you want my help or doncha?" he snarled.

"Karl, get your goddamned boat started," Becky ordered. "Quit acting like a royal turd."

He growled and climbed aboard his father's lobster boat, the two of us following. We towed *White Wings* back to the boatyard, put it on Taylor's trailer, which was parked at the yard, and drove to my house. Becky opened the basement double doors and Karl backed *White Wings* into her place of refuge.

"See ya later, Becky." His tone was suggestive.

"Right," Becky answered curtly. "Tomorrow morning. And be in uniform." Karl slunk away into the darkness.

I was working the next day, but Becky called me later and told me what happened. Karl came to the hotel, looking official in his Harbor Police uniform and together they went to the dining room table where the Harringtons were having breakfast. He wrote down the report of their stolen boat and even offered to give them a tour of the harbor in the police boat to see if they could find *White Wings*.

Later that morning, with the harbor tour producing no results, the Harringtons left. Vivian still suspected some kind of shenanigans. But at least they were gone.

Becky said Karl came by the hotel that afternoon, explaining to her that he could lose his job for what he'd done, even go to jail. Becky said she thanked him and really appreciated what he'd done. When he tried to make a date to go out on his lobster boat some night, she said forget it.

I asked her, "Do you think he'll settle for that?"

"Ha! You know Karl," she said, resigned. "He'll never give up till he gets what he wants."

The four of us had grown tired of sitting on the floor and had moved to chairs as we listened to Aggie relate the story of hiding the boat. When she finished we sat quietly, absorbing what she'd said.

Rebecca broke the silence. "So Captain Kramer was telling the truth. You and he really did help Becky steal the boat."

"Afraid so."

Still caught up in the emotion of Aunt Aggie's story, I said, "I'm glad you did what you did. Until she died, *White Wings* meant everything to my mother. And now I understand those trips she made in the boat every June twenty-fifth." I looked again at my father's picture. "But why didn't she tell me about him? Why keep it secret?"

"Becky had gotten herself into a lie," her old friend explained, "and didn't know how to get out of it. She'd talk to me—I guess I was her safety valve—but she'd built such intricate webs of deceit around you and your father there was no way of unraveling them without hurting a host of people."

"I know, but still I'm sorry she didn't tell me." I picked up several more pictures of Taylor Harrington sailing *White Wings*, each view from a different angle. "Aggie, do you have a magnifying glass?"

"Sure. Right here where I read the paper. Darned fine print," she said, handing me the glass.

I examined the pictures more closely, studying his eyes, the line of his nose, his jaw.

"Except for the pictures of my father, I'd just as soon leave everything here until we get together next weekend."

"Fine. Let's box it up," Aggie said.

For at least a full minute I continued to stare at the pictures of the man sailing *White Wings*. Was it because I saw myself in this man that made him look familiar?

35

I awoke as always, alone in my queen-sized bed in my large
Pleasant Street house which my mother had turned into the Fair
Winds Inn thirty-six years before. It was six-fifty-eight on Wednesday, December 21, with a sky still black from winter's longest
night. In the kitchen to the rear of the house I could hear the cook
preparing breakfast for the guests who had come to Marblehead for
the Christmas season. My day would begin, as every day before it,
with breakfast in the kitchen followed by a second cup of coffee in
my apartment while I read each page of the *Boston Globe*. The bell
in Abbot Hall tower rang the hour. I counted each ring, from one to
seven, intending, as was my custom, to throw back the covers on
number seven, put on my robe and slippers, and hurry across the
cold bedroom to my bathroom for a hot shower. Number seven
rang and I didn't move. For three days I had successfully encapsu-
lated my reactions to last Sunday's revelations about my mother,
but now the burden of confining them exceeded the fear of facing
them. Taking courage from the security of my big bed, and
wrapped in the warmth of my comforter, I let my mind wander
where it would.

Gradually the full implications of what we had learned last
Sunday began to sink in. I had a new name. No longer Taylor De-
Wolf Hayakawa, I was now Taylor Harrington Hayakawa. Does
that make me a new person? I wondered. I considered this possibility for a while and decided I didn't feel like a new person.

Instead, I felt bereft of my past and uncertain about my future. The DeWolfs, who had been my grandparents all the years I was growing up, who had loved me, taken me on trips, doted on me, and given me whatever I asked for, were no longer my grandparents. In their place were an alcoholic grandmother and an overworked businessman grandfather whose names were Harrington.

But what difference did it make? They were all dead, the DeWolfs, the Harringtons, and my mother's parents, the Butlers, whom I loved dearly until they perished in the hotel fire on my fifteenth birthday. Jimmy DeWolf, who I grew up thinking was my father, and Taylor Harrington, my real father whose name I'd never even heard, were both dead. As was my mother. So what difference did it make? I was still a fifty-three-year-old divorcee who lived alone whether my maiden name was DeWolf or Harrington.

Suddenly I was angry, furious at my mother. I clenched my fists and pounded the mattress. Deceiving me all these years—my whole life. Depriving me of my real father. Secretly hating the one whose picture stood on the shelf. Weaving me into her falsehoods so she could keep the insurance money and the trust fund. Me, the pawn to retain the DeWolfs' good favors. Me, the seed of her lust so a little bit of Taylor would always be with her. I rolled over and buried my head in the pillow to muffle my crying. "You had no right, no right to use me."

Eventually my sobs turned to mournful sighs. In the suffocating darkness beneath my pillow another level of realization presented itself. Growing up with Mother in the hotel and, later, in this house, I knew something was wrong. Gram and Gramp Butler never mentioned Jimmy, my supposed father. When pressed by a question from me like "How did he die?" they would tense and brush it off with an abrupt answer such as "In the war." I could see I was trespassing even to ask the question.

As for Mother, there was nothing I could do to ease her dark moods. I tried to be the perfect daughter, never making a mistake or doing bad things, and still she'd look at me as if I were the cause of her suffering. I tried to cheer her up with stories or songs we'd learned in school and she'd ask me please to be quiet. I felt I'd placed her in some dark prison, locked the door and, through my own negligence, lost the key. Her long walks alone, her trancelike gazing into the harbor, and especially her trips by herself on *White Wings* every June twenty-fifth, I was certain were escapes from the dreariness of motherhood that I had inflicted on her. As a child and even as an adult, I didn't know what I was doing or not doing that caused the people I loved to be sad or tense, but I knew it was my fault.

So, to avoid hurting people, and to keep what was left of my mother's love, I withdrew into myself, carefully picking my way across the stepping-stones of adolescence and young womanhood.

Now I knew the truth. Last Sunday it had lain bare on Aggie's living room floor. I wasn't the problem. It was my mother. Her lies. Her deceit. Her self-centeredness. Again a surge of anger swelled in my throat, setting my teeth edge to edge. Into my pillow I yelled, "God damn you, Mother. All this and you die on me so I can't get back at you. I hate you for my loneliness, for my . . . my fear of . . . liv-liv-living." Sputtering and gasping, I cried for all my years of isolation.

An hour later, limp and exhausted, I knew what I had to do. Showering, dressing, and catching a cup of coffee, I called Aggie and said I was coming over.

As soon as she opened the door, I struck at her with the words, "How dare you not tell me what was in that box?"

I went to the kitchen, stood by the sink, and waited for her to follow me there. Slowly she made her way in, but kept her distance from me. I began to calm down a little. In a softer voice I said, "I can understand you keeping quiet while my mother was still alive. Hell, if you'd said anything, she'd have killed you. But after she died. I was here. I'd come back from Japan to live here. Why didn't you tell me then? It was my life you were toying with.

"It was twenty-one years ago Mom died. I was thirty-one then, a young woman. I would have known I wasn't the cause of her sadness, that it wasn't my fault everyone walked on eggs around me. After I got married and my husband played around with other women, the first thing I did was blame myself. When Mother died, I felt my deserting her and living in Japan had killed her. No wonder I never remarried. No wonder I live alone. I'm afraid I'll ruin someone else's life. If you'd told me the truth back then, I could have changed. I'd have been a different person."

"And what else?" Aggie asked, her voice calm in the face of my tirade.

"Rebecca. That's what else. We hardly speak. I don't think we've ever had a heart-to-heart. She hates me and why shouldn't she? How the hell do I know how to be a mother with Becky as my role model?"

Aggie got two mugs from the cabinet and filled them with coffee. "Here. Have a seat." She waited until I sat down. "You're right. I probably should have told you after Becky died. She carted all that stuff over here about a month before the accident, as if she'd had some premonition. She said in case anything happened to her she didn't want the letters and pictures lying around for just anybody to go through. She said to let you have them when you asked for them. You never asked until now."

"But how could I? I didn't know they existed."

"Maybe so, but you were never even curious. You knew how close I was to your mother. You knew that if there were any secrets I'd have known them. Like, where did the name Taylor come from? Why, supposedly, did Jimmy own *White Wings* when all he was interested in was flying? Who was sailing the boat in the picture when your mother stood at the mast? You didn't want to know." Aggie sighed. "But now, I don't know, maybe you're right. I should have told you anyway. I never fully realized how much trouble you had growing up." She touched my hand. "I'm sorry."

"I know." A long sigh escaped me. "I only wish you'd told me earlier."

"Would it have made a difference?"

"God, I hope so. I could have blamed all my problems on Mother," I said wistfully.

"Well, that's what mothers are for."

We laughed a that's-not-funny laugh.

"Now you're free. From here on there's nobody to blame but yourself."

"Thanks a lot, Aunt Aggie. But do we have to blame somebody?"

"No, but we do it anyway."

The next Sunday was Christmas. We got together at my house to share a Christmas dinner which we spent the afternoon together preparing in the inn's kitchen. Rebecca made an hors d'oeuvre tray built around pâté she'd brought from Paris. I did the turkey and stuffing, Aggie onions and sweet potatoes, and Matthew a flaming plum pudding. We had as much fun preparing as we did eating.

Before dinner we gathered around the fireplace to exchange gifts. Mine had been purchased in local antique shops and Rebecca's in Japan. Aggie gave us each a Marblehead collectible she'd bought at some past festival and Matthew painted each of us a small water-color of a Marblehead scene. After a round of Merry Christmas toasts, we ate dinner.

"I feel like I'm part of your family," Matthew said over dessert.

"So do I." Aggie laughed. "Don't forget I'm not related, even if you do call me aunt."

I gazed around the table at each of my guests. "It's strange, isn't it, how we've been drawn together over the last three months?"

"It's *White Wings*," Matthew reminded us. "It all started when I came to your yard sale last October."

"And that got us to Grandmother's stuff in your basement," Rebecca said to Aggie.

"The good thing is, we're here together," I said, then turned to my daughter. "What I really mean to say is, I'm glad you're here, Rebecca."

She looked at me and smiled cautiously.

"I feel I can say this in front of all of you because we are family." I paused. An uneasy silence fell across the table. Matthew wiped his mouth with his napkin, Rebecca sipped coffee, and Aggie looked straight ahead at the opposite wall. "This has been a very difficult week for me. I discovered my mother lied to me and to everybody else except you, Aggie, about my father. I grew up in a world of falsehood—pieces didn't fit, things were askew. There was always an undercurrent of fear and guilt. I thought it was my fault."

Rebecca looked at me critically. "Come on now, Mom, that's putting an awful lot on yourself."

Her words were cutting, but I was determined to plunge ahead. "And especially you, Rebecca. I feel I've let you down as a mother, that I've put you off, that I haven't been here for you when you needed me."

"Mom, you've done just fine." The words were right but her voice disparaging. "I don't understand what you're going on about."

For an instant I was ready to strike back, to join again the battle that had gone on for years. Instead I said, "Whether you know it or not, I've shut you out. I've been afraid to be open, to show you how much I love you and how much I need you. I've been afraid because I was sure if I did, I'd drive you away."

I was on the edge of crying. Matthew looked down at the table awkwardly and Rebecca seemed embarrassed. Aggie sought to lessen the tension.

"As they say, confession's good for the soul. Enough maudlin talk for Christmas Day. I think we ought to take a walk down to Washington Street, work off some of this dinner and look at the Christmas lights."

Had I done it again? Had I ruined our dinner? I was a fraction of a second from jumping up and running to my bedroom. Gripping the edge of the table to calm myself and taking a deep breath, I forced out the words, "Good idea."

Already it was dark but not too cold for a winter's night. A few inches of clean white snow still covered the lawns from a snowfall the previous day. There were piles along the curbs left by the snowplows and mounds by the sidewalks where people had shoveled. Huge wreaths hung on the large doors of the eighteenth-century homes and Christmas tree lights could be seen in the living rooms. In each window on each floor of several homes a candle (now electric) glowed.

Matthew and Aggie walked ahead of Rebeccca and me, Matthew taking her elbow at each patch of slippery sidewalk. Aggie was telling us about the snowfall of '36 that brought Marble-head to a stop with thirty inches of snow. Taking a chance, I put my arm around Rebecca as we walked. I felt her body stiffen, so I dropped my arm. At least she didn't move away. For the rest of the walk we stayed close together and even bumped shoulders a few times. Small victories, I thought, but I'll take them nonetheless. I remembered past Christmases walking by myself, watching families celebrating in the warm glow of Christmas lights, and returning home alone. When you're by yourself, Christmas is the loneliest time of the year. Now I was with friends and with my daughter, even if she wouldn't let me put my arm around her. We were walking home together.

As we parted that night, Aggie said she had a few letters Becky had written her that weren't in the box. She thought we might like to see them and invited us to her house the following day. Rebecca announced she was taking off the week between Christmas and New Year's (news to me) and, except for a short trip to New York, would like to spend time in Marblehead. Matthew, of course, was on holiday from school, so we all agreed to meet Monday afternoon.

When I arrived the next day, Rebecca and Matthew were already there, working on *White Wings* in Aggie's basement. "Come on down and see our progress," Rebecca called up the stairs.

Aggie and I went to the workshop. Rebecca was dressed in jeans and a gray sweatshirt with her hair tied up in a bandanna. Several strands of hair had escaped and hung loosely around her face. A smear of dirt was on her right cheek where she'd pushed hair out of her eyes with dirty hands. For an instant I saw her as my little girl who had come in from playing outside in the dirt. I wanted to rush up and hug her but I didn't dare. Smiling proudly, she leaned against the hull of the boat.

Matthew was dressed much the same minus the bandanna and in a dark blue sweatshirt. He had the look of a satisfied carpenter, but there was more. I wondered if it had something to do with his having spent the morning with Rebecca.

"Look." Rebecca pointed at a gaping hole in the side. "We cut away the broken pieces of wood back to a frame so we can connect the new pieces." She leaned over to Matthew and patted him on the back. "This guy really knows what he's doing."

I thought, what a change of attitude. I asked Matthew, "What comes next?"

"About a hundred things," he said. "We've got to drop the keel and see how much damage there is, strip away all the broken planking, and figure exactly what wood we need to buy."

"Then," Rebecca chimed in, "we're going to a place in Maine Matthew knows about and buy lumber."

Matthew stood grinning at the enthusiasm she was showing for the job.

"But we're taking a couple of days off. I told you I was going to New York. Well, Matthew agreed to drive me down. I'm visiting a friend I met on our London trip who lives in New York, and Matthew has an old girlfriend he's looking up."

Hmm. I'd thought something might be developing between them, but I must have been wrong.

Aggie said it was time for all of us to go upstairs and have lunch. She'd prepared tuna fish sandwiches. We sat around the kitchen table eating and listening to Matthew describe the lumber he would select for the boat. Oak went here and cedar went there and it all had to be planed and cut and bent to shape. It was more than I understood. After lunch we took our coffee cups into the living room and sat in a circle around the same boxes we'd faced the week before. Aggie went to her bedroom and returned with two envelopes.

"I guess right now," Aggie started, looking me in the eye, "you don't think much of your mother. But really, Taylor, there's more to her character than you might think."

"What about the letters?" I asked.

"I'm getting to that. When the war was over, Becky was still convinced Taylor Harrington was alive. She tried to reach his parents in California, but they had moved and left no forwarding address. She called the War Department in Washington. They wouldn't even talk to her because she wasn't next of kin. So she took the train to Washington and went to the Pentagon to find out in person. After two days of searching she spoke to a WAC corporal her own age. Becky told her the truth about Taylor, that he was the father of her child, that she loved him and was convinced he was still alive. The corporal said she'd go through the records and for Becky to come back the next day. Becky was there bright and early, and the WAC told her the bad news. Taylor had died on board a prison ship transferring POWs from the Philippines to Japan in May of 1943. It was confirmed by the International Red Cross on the basis of dog tags taken from the Americans who had died.

Becky told the woman she still didn't believe it, and began to cry. Then she pleaded with her for the names of other men in his regiment or POWs who were in the same camp. Again the young soldier said she'd do her best and for Becky to come back yet another day. This she did, and was given the names and home addresses of twenty-five soldiers and three army nurses. Then the corporal wrote a note to a friend of hers in Veterans Administration asking her to assist Becky in obtaining current addresses for the people on the list."

Aggie stopped to take a drink of coffee. "At the VA the friend of the corporal looked at the list and said up-to-date master lists of veterans were, unfortunately, not available in Washington. What current addresses there were, were kept in regional offices, and these were only for those veterans who had made use of veteran services. Becky asked where the regional offices were, and the clerk looked at the list of names and old home addresses. Most of the people on the list were either from California or Wisconsin, so the regional offices would be either in Los Angeles or Chicago."

"How discouraging," Rebecca said.

"You'd think so, but not for Becky. She went first to Los Angeles and then to Chicago."

"Did she find anybody that knew Taylor?" I asked.

"She did. These are the letters she sent me from L.A. and Racine, Wisconsin, after she'd talked to them."

I opened the first letter and began reading aloud.

Wednesday, March 6, 1946

Dear Aggie,

I'm really doing it. Crossing the country on a train. It goes on and on. Especially Iowa and Nebraska. Fields as far as you can see. Sleeping on a train is great: like being rocked in a cradle. I have an upper berth. We left Chicago this morning. Last night a guy invited me for a drink in the club car. I went. It was something to do. When I told him I was going to California, he said his brother-in-law had a friend who was a director and he could help me get in the movies. Can you believe it? The drink was nice anyway. Three more nights on the train. I'll add to this later.

Friday, March 8

Hi again,

We went over some mountains and they added two engines to the train. The Rockies make our mountains look like hills. In one of the passes snow was piled so high on each side of the train we couldn't see out. I met a girl my age who's on her way to meet her husband coming home from overseas. Lucky girl. His ship is due on Monday so she and I are planning to do some sightseeing this weekend. The VA offices will be closed tomorrow, so I'll have to wait until Monday anyway.

Wednesday, March 13

Hello again,

I went to the VA office on Monday, showed them my list and explained I was trying to find people that had known my fiance (well, he almost was). Apparently there are a lot of people trying to track down friends of husbands, sons and lovers and the clerk was very understanding. She gave me eight names in the Bay area. I found a room on Ventura Blvd., which is on a bus line. I share the bath with two other roomers. It's not much but it's cheap. I got a bunch of nickels and started making phone calls from the drugstore on the corner. Out of the eight names, four didn't answer the phone and one had died. The wife of another said he'd reenlisted and was gone. One guy said his brother was in prison for shooting somebody in a bar. The last name is a nurse who works in Letterman Hospital and I'm calling her tonight.

Friday, March 15

Me Again,

I met Lt. Betty Minor last night. Just when I was getting discouraged about finding someone who knew Taylor, Betty said, "Sure, I knew him." They called him Chap, for chaplain I guess. She was surprised that I was his fiance because he never spoke about me. Not that he played around. Never. She said he was as straight laced as they come. She knew him at the officers club at Clark Field before the Japs attacked. A real nice guy, she said. After the surrender she heard he was in Cabanatuan Prison but didn't know what happened to him after that. She'd been interned in Manila with officers' wives and civilians. Then she remembered a sergeant named Kelly who was at Cabanatuan. He's in Letterman where she works. She's going to check on his condition on Monday and see if it's okay for me to see him. God, how this drags on.

Tuesday, March 19

Dear Aggie,

I found out something today that just might be good news. I met Sgt. Kelly in the psychiatric ward. He's in his late twenties but looks about forty. We sat in the day room among several other patients, some pretty far gone mentally and others who just looked bored. Kelly talked and talked. I think he was glad to have the company. He didn't look like a mental patient to me, but the more he talked the more I could see his problem. He's married but his wife left him. He said he'd fly into these rages for no reason at all and smash things. Every night he wakes up screaming and it's always the Japs beating him.

When I asked about Taylor, he said, "Oh you mean Chap." Then he told me an unbelievable story. There was a guard in his barracks they called Slant and he beat prisoners for no reason at all, like maybe he thought they stared at him too much. One day he beat this guy with a club and fractured his skull. When Chap heard about it, Kelly said, he went to the Camp Commander and complained. Because he complained about a guard, they took him to a special building that had little cubicles not big enough to stand up in or stretch out. He had a bad case of dysentery and they let them out to use the latrine only once a day. You can imagine what it was like in his cell. He was pretty weak from the dysentery and when he was walking to the latrine he tripped and fell. The guard came over and hit him in the middle of the back with the butt of his rifle and kept hitting him until he went unconscious. Then they got some corpsmen and took him to the hospital. It was weeks before they saw him again, he said. At least the Camp Commander removed the guard that had caused the trouble in the first place.

He said he was with Chap's group that got shipped to Japan. The Japs crammed them into the hold of an old freighter, a thousand men. They had only one small hole in the hatch through which they passed down food and water and lifted up honey buckets (you know what that was) and dead bodies. He said men were dying all over the place. They'd been so weak from disease and starvation when they were captured and then with months in the prison being beaten and overworked, they were like the walking dead. He said they were kept in the hold of the ship for a week before they left Manila harbor waiting for a convoy to form. It was about 125 degrees in there and guys were going crazy. They were lying on top of each other because there wasn't room, they were fighting for water and they were ankle deep in their own shit. A guy could get killed, he said, just for sitting on somebody's legs or taking his canteen. There was other stuff he wouldn't even tell me about. Just when it was time to leave, the ship's captain said a body had been sent up through the hatch without a dog tag. He got mad because he had to account for the thousand men on board either with a live person or a dog tag for the dead ones. If they didn't find the missing dog tag, he was going to cover the hole. Chap sent his dog tag up through the hole and the captain was satisfied. When they got to Japan, Chap was beaten for not having a dog tag.

I asked him if he thought that was why the Red Cross said he was dead. He said yes—if the Japs had the dog tags, the person had to be dead. I asked if he knew where he went in Japan. He said he thought he went to Kawasaki near Yokohama, but he didn't know for sure. Told me to check with some of the men in the Wisconsin National Guard because some were sent there.

So that's it. Taylor didn't die in the Philippines. I knew it. I'll find him yet.

When I left the hospital, Kelly asked me to come back and see him again. He asked me to sneak in a bottle of Wild Turkey.

It's a long letter and time I sent it off to you.

Love, Becky.

Monday, March 25, 1946

Dear Aggie,

You must think I've left home for good. I'm in Chicago at the Conrad Hilton, remember, where Taylor and I spent a weekend. I called Mom and asked her to keep Taylor a little longer and she agreed. She didn't question my reason for being in Chicago, which is to see a high school friend who moved here, because I think she knows I'm trying to find out about Taylor. I got in here last night and today went to the mid-west office of the VA. They gave me six addresses of people who'd served with Taylor, people who were part of the Wisconsin National Guard stationed in the Philippines when the war broke out. I got hold of five of the six and actually found one, a Michael O'Malley, who was in the same prison camp as Taylor in Japan. He lives in Racine. Tomorrow I'm taking the train there to meet him in a bar called The Rose of Sharon. He suggested I might like to buy him a drink. Sounds weird but if he was really with Taylor, it'll be worth it. I'll add more later.

Wednesday, March 27

Hi Aggie,

I'm on a train back to Chicago. The news is not good.

I met Michael O'Malley in the bar. The place was dark even at one in the afternoon and smelled of stale beer and cigarettes. There were four or five men sitting at the bar and I felt uneasy until one of them asked if I was Becky. He said he was Mike. We sat at a table and I had a beer. He drank boiler makers, whiskey by the shot with beer chasers. I lost count but kept buying so he'd keep talking.

He said they were in Subcamp No. 3 in the town of Kawasaki between Toyko and Yokohama. The Japs had them working at the port rebuilding bombed out warehouses. Sometimes they'd unload ships. When Taylor arrived at the camp he was so weak he couldn't work. Had dysentery pretty bad. After a week or so he got a little better and they put him to work. Mike said he was so thin he looked like a stick figure. When he'd bend over to pick something up, he could hardly get back up again. I almost cried to hear how he suffered. A town doctor came into the camp once a week and did what he could for the sick prisoners, but he had practically no medicine. They called him Doctor Sicko because his name was something like that. In any case, he befriended Taylor and was probably responsible for keeping him alive.

Mike kept drinking. I've never seen a man drink so much and appear so sober. He told me they started seeing B29s toward the end of November 1944. They were so much bigger than the B17s. They'd bomb Tokyo and Yokohama when they could but the weather was usually cloudy. Then in March of 1945 the weather cleared and the B29s started coming in low and dropping incendiary bombs. He said they'd sit outside and watch Tokyo and Yokohama burn. The flames would whip upward like huge tornadoes. They could even hear people screaming. When day came it was still as dark as night from the smoke. The guards would take out their anger on them after the raids, beating them unmercifully.

During the summer the raids took place every night with some of the bombs hitting the camp. He said, by then, Taylor was back in the little dispensary with a recurrence of the malaria he'd picked up in the Philippines. There were two other prisoners in there with him. At night when the raids came, they'd put them on stretchers and carry them to a big concrete culvert. One night, a concrete bunker took a direct hit and most of the camp's guards were killed. Mike said discipline got pretty lax after that because the replacement guards were mainly civilian volunteers. They'd march them into town to help dig out people buried in the rubble. They didn't give them a lot of trouble but every once in a while one of the guards would go nuts and start slamming them with the butt of his rifle or slashing them with his bayonet. The end of July they really started getting clobbered by B29s and Navy dive bombers. There was hardly anything to eat, but they were no worse off than the Japs. Everybody was starving.

One night just before the planes came, he said he and some of his buddies went to the dispensary to get Chap and the other guy—the third one had died—to carry them to the concrete culvert, but they weren't there. A Jap guard said they'd both died and the doctor buried them. Mike said he was sorry to have to tell me, but that's what happened. How he lasted as long as he did, Mike didn't know. So Aggie, I've come to the end of the road. I guess I'm crazy but I still think he's alive somewhere in the world, but I have no idea where to look.

I'm going to spend a couple of days here trying to see if the VA can give me any other leads and then I'm coming home. I miss little Taylor. Thank God I've got her.

Love, Becky

When I finished reading aloud the last letter, we sat in silence for a time. The war had been so long ago and the horror of it so quickly forgotten. For Rebecca and Matthew, and even for me, it was a couple of chapters in a history book.

"What happened when she came home, Aggie?"

"Well," she said mournfully, "she never gave up believing he was alive, and her insistence became a kind of mania. Once I tried to talk her out of it and she practically bit my head off. I never tried

again. She read every book written about the war in the Philippines and the prisoners interned in Japan and she wrote every
group or association of ex-POWs she could discover, but she never
found another lead."

"I was four years old. I can remember she went on a trip and
Gram took care of me, but that's all. And after the fire, Aggie, when
I was fifteen, we came to live with you for a few months. By the
way, what ever happened to Casey?"

"When the war ended, so did our jobs with GE. We tried to stay
on together in Lynn but there was no work. Dad wanted me to
come home and pretty much take over the lobstering—he was getting too old to pull the pots—and Casey wanted to get into interior
decorating. She finally got a job in New York and we each went our
ways. We saw each other as much as we could on weekends, but
we drifted apart after a few months."

"How sad," Rebecca said. "She sounded like such a nice
person."

"She was. She died of lung cancer in 1979." Again silence while
we soaked up the sadness in the room. "I need to get up and move
around a little," Aggie said. "Anybody want anything from the
kitchen?"

We all stood and followed Aggie into the kitchen. "I'd like a cup
of tea," Rebecca announced. "If you'll show me where the tea is,
Aunt Aggie, I'll fix some for everybody." We stood around the
kitchen, propped on various counters, while Rebecca worked.
When the tea was ready, we sat at the kitchen table.

"You were talking about coming to live with me after the fire,
Taylor. Dad had died three years before, so I was glad for the company. You lived upstairs in the apartment Matthew has now. You
remember?"

I nodded.

"I guess you all know Becky was special to me and having her
here in the same house was a joy. She needed a lot of care and support after her mom and dad died in the fire, and I loved giving it to
her. The two of you were here for a whole year before she bought
the place on Pleasant Street and made it into an inn."

"I loved it," I said. "You let me help on your boat. At least you
said I was helping. And Mom took us sailing on *White Wings* when

she wasn't getting the inn ready. We did have fun together, didn't we? I'd forgotten that time." We were all quiet for a while. "Then I went to college and met Tad Hayakawa. After reading these letters, I can see why Mom was livid that I was dating a Japanese. When I told her about him she said, 'Don't you ever bring that Jap in my house.' I couldn't believe she was so bigoted."

"Too bad she couldn't tell you the reason," Matthew said.

I pondered that. "Maybe, maybe not. The DeWolfs were practically sending me to college. If she'd told me the truth, I'd have had to choose between being a part of her lie or going to college. God, I don't know. I'm just glad it's over."

"Did she ever come around as far as Tad was concerned?" Matthew asked.

"Never. Wouldn't come to the wedding and wouldn't see me off when I left for Japan. It really hurt. We didn't write for two or three years. After I got there, I realized I'd made a mistake. Tad was no company and I had no friends. Finally I wrote Mom a letter, and she answered it. Just superficial stuff, but we started writing. Then, when you were two, Rebecca, we came home for a visit. Mom was uneasy at first, but she fell in love with you."

"What you don't know," Aggie said to me, "is how hard it was for Becky. She was crushed you'd left home to live in Japan of all places, and with a Japanese. It was as if you'd gone over to the enemy."

"I can understand that now. As it turned out, he was the enemy, the bastard."

Rebecca shifted uncomfortably in her chair. "I don't want to go into it now, Mom, but for the record I don't agree with that. He's my dad and not the monster you've painted him to be."

"And how would you know?"

"Well, he *is* my dad."

I should have known. She'd seen her grandparents until they died four years ago, but I never thought about her father.

"So you've seen him?"

"Of course. The last time about two weeks ago."

The words were a slap in the face. Traitor, I wanted to yell. Instead I pursed my lips and tightened my fists. "And how is he?" I asked coldly.

She saw how it hurt me and went on casually. "He's fine. In good health. Married with a teenage boy and girl. My half brother and sister. They live in Yokohama in his parents' house. You remember it."

I looked down at the table shaking my head. "I figured he was dead. Hoped he was dead." I started to get up. "Sorry. I've got to go. With the letters and now this, it's too much."

"It was going to come out sooner or later, Mom. I'm glad you know and I'm sorry it's upsetting, but that's just the way it is."

"Take it easy, Rebecca," Matthew said.

"Don't talk to me that way," she snapped at Matthew. "This is none of your business. I don't care how close you are to my mother." She jumped up, pushing her chair back, tipping it over. "I'm going home. I'll walk." She went to the basement, got her coat, and left.

"I've done it again, haven't I? Sorry, Aggie, to have botched up your day."

"We'll get over it." Aggie shrugged. "It's been a tough couple of days, full of surprises. It's hit us all pretty hard."

I said my good-byes and started for my car. Matthew came down the walk with me. "Are you all right?"

"Yeah." I sighed. "In time. It's just a lot all at once."

"If there's anything I can do, let me know."

I got in the car and turned on the engine. He was standing by the door. I rolled down the window. "There is something you can do. It's about my father, my real father. I'd like to be able to really see him, but the pictures are so small. Do you think you could come by and pick up the photos of him and draw an enlarged sketch?"

"Sure. That'd be no problem."

"Draw him looking at us, full face, you know?"

"I can do that."

"And then I want you to add about thirty years to his age. Possible?"

"Police artists do it all the time. It'll take some research on the technique. Why do you want me to do it?"

"Just an idea I have."

37

Fight or no fight, I had to feed Rebecca. The cupboard was bare, to say nothing of the refrigerator. Leaving Aggie's house, I turned left on Atlantic and headed for Swampscott and the Stop & Shop in Vinnin Square. Slate gray clouds hung low over a darkening sky and it was only three-thirty. Passing Tedesco Golf Course, still covered with patches of mushy snow despite the mid-thirties temperature, drops of rain blurred my vision. I turned on the windshield wipers. Flop flop, flop flop. I could see again, but what a dismal view. Why aren't I in Florida or the Caribbean, I wondered, like most of the other innkeepers in Marblehead?

I found a parking place about fifty car slots from the door and dashed through what was now a torrent. Passing a man holding a golf umbrella and casually strolling toward the entrance, I heard him say, "Here. Under here."

I ducked under. "Thanks."

"Taylor! I didn't recognize you at first."

I looked at the face next to mine. It was familiar but . . . "Sam? Is that you?"

"In the flesh—and, in the new beard. Like it?"

"No, I don't. Makes you look twenty years older."

Sam Russell was another Marblehead innkeeper and, apparently, one of the few who hadn't gone south after Christmas. Years past he'd made a name for himself in advertising, becoming a partner in Russell, Hartage and Quick. Then six years ago he resigned, sold his share of the company, and bought an inn in Marblehead. We'd gotten to know each other through the meetings of our local innkeepers' association. Then, soon after he was settled into his new life, his wife, Gwen, got a kidney disease and died two months later.

After the funeral he went into a deep depression and had to spend a few weeks with his daughter in Rochester, New York. He returned much thinner and quite subdued. At our winter association meeting he said he planned to remain closed and, in the spring, put his inn on the market. Despite our overtures of assistance and words of encouragement, he remained adamant.

As it turned out, what we couldn't do by persuasion, the economy did by a drastic downturn in real estate values. Only one prospect made an offer and it wasn't sufficient to cover the balance due on the mortgage. Sam had no choice but to stay in business. It was a good thing he did, because he gradually regained his emotional stability. Now in his mid-fifties, with glasses and rounded shoulders, he'd become the picture of a man willing to amble into old age, taking what life had to offer.

We entered the supermarket, pulled off our gloves, unzipped our winter jackets, and each tugged free a cart from the rows jammed together near the door.

"Why the beard?"

"I always wondered what I'd look like with a beard, so I quit shaving last month." He turned his face from side to side, for me to get a good look at his new creation. "It grows on you," he said, laughing.

This is Sam, the solemn innkeeper? What's come over him?

We pushed our carts side by side into the produce section. I selected a package containing three tomatoes, the cheapest ones there, while Sam chose two organically grown giants.

"Ever tried one of these? They're the only ones you can get in the middle of winter that don't taste like plastic." There was a slight gesture of his head toward the ones I'd bought.

"But look at the price. Twice what I'm paying."

"So?" We moved to the green produce counter. As I dumped a tightly wrapped head of iceberg lettuce into my cart, Sam was inspecting the bottoms of the Boston lettuce. Finding just the right one, he placed it carefully in his cart.

At the seafood counter I was pleased to see swordfish half the price it had been the week before. I asked for two small steaks, which the clerk weighed and wrapped. Sam was ordering a pound of medium shrimp when I mentioned the good deal I'd gotten on swordfish.

"I saw that too, but I try to stay away from fish that's previously frozen."

"Okay, Sam, what's going on? I've known you for six years and you've always been a hamburger, pizza, and frozen-dinner man."

"That's true, and I've got the belly to prove it." He patted his stomach. "I've also got a higher cholesterol level than's good for me. A month ago I bought a low cholesterol cookbook and started making my own dinners. I love it. Didn't know it could be so much fun. Then yesterday, for Christmas, my daughter gave me a wok and a Chinese cookbook. So now I'm into Chinese. Very low on calories and cholesterol. Tonight it's stir fry shrimp and snow peas."

"Is your daughter still here?"

"No. Left this morning. I'll be eating all by myself."

We moved down the line of counters to the meat section where I found two small steaks, thick and well marbleized.

"I see you're cooking for two." He pointed at the swordfish and steaks in my cart. "Houseguest?"

"My daughter, Rebecca. You've met her."

"I certainly have. A beautiful woman."

"And most annoying at times."

"Daughters can be, can't they? Sons too, I expect, though I don't have any."

"Just when I thought we were getting closer, we had a fight this afternoon. It's going to be a long week."

"Christmas is a hard time," he said. "Lots of tension."

"Maybe that's it."

"Well, I'd better move along. It's been nice seeing you, Taylor. Take care of yourself. I'm off to the ethnic food section to stock up on Chinese oils and sauces."

We'd said good-bye and were turning into separate aisles when I called, "Sam. Wait a minute." I caught up to him. "Do you know about the Chinese Supermarket in Boston?"

"Didn't know there was one."

"I used to go there when I got back from Japan. It's been years but I expect it's still there."

"Where?"

"Near Franklin just over the Mass Pike. As I remember, the prices are only a third of what you'll pay here and the selection's endless."

"Sounds like a good place to stock up. I'll have to try it sometime." Then, almost as an afterthought, he said, "Taylor, why don't you and Rebecca have dinner with me tonight? Might ease some of the tension."

"Thanks, Sam, but I think we need to work this out alone."

Half an hour later I carried the groceries into the inn's kitchen and put them in the sections of the refrigerator and cupboard reserved for my use. Entering my quarters, I called to Rebecca, saying I was home. Silence. I could feel the emptiness. There on the table was a note.

> Mom—this isn't my picture of a week's vacation. I need rest, not arguments. I'll be at my place in Boston or in New York visiting my friend. Rebecca.

"Well, that's a relief," I said aloud to the silent room. I waited for the guilt to kick in, but it didn't. Instead I went to the phone.

"Hello, Sam? This is Taylor. Is that invitation for dinner still open?"

"Sure is."

"Good. I'm on my way."

"Will Rebecca be with you?"

"No. Just me."

I'd forgotten how much fun it is to play. No family. No unresolved issues insinuating themselves into conversations. No anger lurking beneath the surface waiting to erupt. Just fun.

Sam was a breath of fresh air. He looked good: face and waist slimmer and he seemed to stand taller. When I arrived he led me to the kitchen, handing me an apron. Then he took a small pitcher of hot sake from a pan of warm water on the stove and poured me a small cupful. As he started to pour his, I put my hand on his arm.

"No. Bad luck. You never pour your own, at least not in Japan." I took the pitcher and filled his cup.

"Here's to a daughter-free dinner—yours and mine."

"Hear, hear."

Sam sat me at the kitchen counter with a bowl, scissors, and the bag of peas. As I snipped off their ends, he blanched the shrimp and shucked off their shells. My next job was slicing scallions into long ovals while he prepared the wok. During this time we continued to fill and refill each other's sake cup.

"This is supposed to serve four," he said. "I'm not much good at cutting recipes in half, especially after this much sake."

We toasted his inability to cut recipes and sat down at the kitchen table to eat. An hour later we'd finished the entire dinner for four. Over cups of green tea, he told me he'd started flying lessons at Hanscom Field. Said he'd always wanted to fly, so why wait? And the end of January he was taking a three-week vacation to the Antarctic to see penguins. I was impressed and a little envious.

As I was leaving, I asked Sam if he would like me to show him the Chinese Supermarket in Boston. He was thrilled with the idea and suggested we go on Thursday and take in a matinee at the Schubert Theatre.

At the door he took my hands in his. "Taylor, I love to cook but I hate to eat alone. Let's do this again."

"I hate to eat alone too. Let's do that."

The excursion to Boston was a success. Sam bought hoisin sauce, teriyaki sauce, soya sauce, peanut oil, sesame oil, bags of sesame seeds, raw peanuts, and four packages of frozen Beijing raviolis. I bought a bag of candied ginger which we nibbled in the show. Sam hadn't been able to get tickets to the matinee, so we went to the movies and laughed our heads off at *Mixed Nuts*. After the show we were having so much fun we decided to extend it to dinner at the Cactus Club on Boylston Street. The crowd was young and raucous, which fit our mood perfectly. It was after ten when he dropped me off at home.

Late the next afternoon, Friday, Rebecca called and asked if she could come home for a couple of nights. Automatically I switched to maternal mode.

"What's wrong, darling?"

Her voice quivered. "New York was awful. I just want to come home."

"Of course you can come home," I said. At the same time, I was feeling the visit an intrusion. I was tired of our incessant bickering, and frankly uninterested in the crises of her love life.

An hour and a half later her sleek little Ford Probe pulled into the driveway. She came through the kitchen door and down the hall to my apartment and dropped her overnight bag in the middle of the living room floor. Sloughing off her trench coat, which fell beside her bag, she shrugged her shoulders and let out a sigh of despair.

"He has no intention of leaving his wife," she announced.

"Who, darling?"

"Reggie. Reginald Davis." As if I should know.

"And he's married?"

"That's what I said. We met in London at the travel show. He's from the Markham Hotel in New York, so we were in the same booth. We just hit it off. He said he was starved for affection, and he thinks his wife is fooling around when he's away. He couldn't do enough for me. Took me to dinner the first two nights and then I moved into his room. He said he loved me, that he'd been looking for someone like me all his life. Then he came with me to Tokyo for the World Travel Fair."

"And he said he was going to get a divorce."

"Right." She was surprised at my wisdom. "So I told him I'd come to New York after Christmas and we'd make plans. He got me a room in—to be honest—a cheap hotel off Broadway—but I didn't care. All I wanted was to be with him. It was the middle of the afternoon when Matthew dropped me off—"

"Matthew? Did you and Matthew go together?"

"Well, yeah. Why not?"

"I thought you just told him to stay out of your life."

"Oh, that was Monday. He called the next morning and apologized for butting in. Anyway, I needed a ride to New York."

"So?"

"So Reggie and I were in bed five minutes after we got in the hotel room. Then, after we made love, he says he's sorry but he can't leave his wife because of the kids."

"The kids?"

"That what I said. He's got two kids, little ones. 'But darling,' he says, 'I love you. We can still be together.' I told him I wasn't going to be his fucking friend, and left."

Rebecca came to the sofa where I was sitting, flopped down beside me, and put her head on my shoulder. It felt good and I was truly sorry for her.

Instantly she popped back up. "You know what I think?"

"No."

"Besides sleeping with me, I think the bastard was stealing my leads. Especially in Japan. We'd make calls together on clients I've gotten to know over the past three years and he'd carefully collect all these business cards. I'll bet he's written every one of them by now and invited them to the New York Markham. How could I be so stupid? I let him have whatever he wanted."

I nodded equivocally, not daring to let her know I agreed. "Where'd you go when you left him?"

"I called Matthew. He was staying with his friend Miranda. Has he told you about her?"

"In passing, yes."

"I took a cab to her place and, guess what? She's got Matthew in the guest bedroom because she's got a new friend. Matthew's really pissed, but doesn't want to spend the money for a hotel. Doesn't bother Miranda, though, to have him in the room next to hers. In fact, when I arrive she says why don't the two of us, Matthew and I, share the guest room? Well, not Matthew. He gives me the room and spends the night on the sofa in the living room. But before that, the four of us—Marvin is Miranda's friend—go out for dinner at a Mexican place and dance and sing and drink tequila till two in the morning. That was this morning. God, I can't believe it."

"And Matthew drove home after that?"

"We slept until ten, so it wasn't so bad. He's home now taking a nap, I think."

"You've had a time, haven't you?"

"Tell me about it." She leaned her head back against my shoulder. "Let's not argue, okay?"

"Truce?"

"Truce."

"Hungry?"

"Yeah."

"I've got two beautiful thick steaks in the refrig. Sound good?"

"Well, actually, no. I'm off meat now."

"Oh. You're in luck then. I've also got two swordfish steaks. They're in the freezer, but I can defrost them."

"Previously frozen? They're not fresh?"

When I told Rebecca I had a date for New Year's Eve, I thought she was going to go catatonic. Like clicking a VCR on pause, she froze, attempting to compute the astounding information that her mother had a date. When she spoke, there was a tone of disapproval in her voice.

"A date? With whom?"

"Sam Russell. You've met him. He has the inn on Franklin Street."

"Oh. Yeah. When did all this get started?"

I looked at her and smiled. "Surprises you, huh?"

"A little. I just hadn't thought about you dating."

"You're invited too, if you'd like to come along."

"On a date with my mother?"

"It's not like a date-date. We're getting together at his place for dinner and bringing in the New Year. I'd like you to come. Maybe Matthew'd come too. Sam's an excellent cook. It'll be fun. Come on!"

"I'll think about it. Maybe I'll call Matthew."

Drinking more champagne than we should, the four of us, under Sam's direction, prepared a four-course Chinese dinner in his kitchen. Matthew told his version of the trip to New York, including his surprise when he opened Miranda's door and was greeted by Marvin. The lapse of three days combined with the champagne made the story hilarious.

At midnight, after demolishing the dinner, we turned on the TV to catch the festivities at Times Square. Sam and I were sitting on the sofa and Rebecca was on Matthew's lap in a nearby chair. When the ball dropped, I saw Rebecca turn her face toward Matthew and they kissed. Why not? I thought. I turned to Sam and kissed him on the cheek. At first he was surprised. Then he put his arms around me and kissed me on the lips like I haven't been kissed in thirty years.

38

I don't make New Year's resolutions. Too many "shoulds" in my life already. However, this morning, New Year's Day, my body overruled my mind and made a resolution of its own. The remembered warmth of Sam's arms, the taste of his lips, the smell of ginger on his breath, and the sparkle in his eyes titillated desires I hadn't felt in years. My body resolved to have more of Sam Russell.

When Rebecca plodded heavy-eyed into the bathroom, I'd finished my shower and was humming as I dried my hair. She regarded my mood with disgust and stepped into the shower. Later in the kitchen as I floated from table to refrigerator to sink preparing her favorite breakfast of dry cereal, fruit, and yogurt, her gaze followed me suspiciously. I set two bowls of cereal on the table and was getting napkins from the drawer when the antics of two chickadees on the bush outside the window caught my attention. I watched, transfixed, as the little birds flitted from branch to branch, clinging upside down and sideways, occasionally brushing wings and singing their morning song.

"Mother! You've been standing there for five minutes. Will you please sit down. You're making me nervous."

"Oh. Sorry." I sat. "The chickadees."

"The chickadees what?"

"They're in the bush outside the window."

"And?"

"I don't know. They look so happy." I smiled. "It's such a nice morning."

"Eat your breakfast."

Rebecca left soon after we ate, returning to her apartment in Boston. What a relief. The house was mine except for three guests still on the second floor, and the day was mine. To relish the moment, I poured a second cup of coffee, turned on the radio to a string quartet and piano playing Schubert's *Trout Quintet*, and sat by the front window in a large upholstered chair. Sipping my coffee, I watched the passing scene—a squirrel descending one of the oaks and hopping across the matted brown grass, a blue jay in the other oak scolding him for some earlier infraction, my neighbor, Mr. Simmons, trudging up the sidewalk from the White Hen carrying his Sunday paper. I'd forgotten how beautiful the everyday world could be. Smiling contentedly, I snuggled into the chair.

A cloud crossed the sun and my view returned to winter. What if I'm imagining this? What if it was just the champagne? Sam's going through a change. Maybe he's experimenting. I'm fifty-two years old. Why would he fall for me? "Fall for me?" I said aloud. "I sound like a teenager." Or don't they say things like that now?

The phone rang. I unwound myself from the chair and sprang to answer it.

"Hello."

"Hi, Taylor. It's Sam."

"I know. I thought it would be. I mean I hoped it would be."

"Rebecca still there?"

"No, thank goodness, she's gone back to Boston."

"What are you doing?"

"Oh, just sitting here looking out the window and drinking coffee."

"Last night was fun."

"Yes."

"Taylor ... I ... When I kissed you ... I ... I hope I didn't offend you."

"Offend me?"

"Well, you didn't think I was being fast?"

"Fast? I don't think they use that word anymore."

"You know what I mean."

"No, I didn't think you were being fast." Pause. "How about me? I had something to do with that kiss too."

"I know. You curled my toes."

I laughed. "Curled your toes? Where do you get these expressions?"

"I'm not very good at this, am I?"

"You're fine. How's this? You made the palms of my hands tingle."

"Not bad. So you don't think it was just the champagne?"

"Partly. But not all of it."

"Want to go for a walk? It's a beautiful morning."

"I'd love to."

We walked to Fort Sewall, looking for a place to get coffee along the way, but everything was closed for New Year's Day. Standing on the walk around the embankment of the fort, Sam took my hand, casually, as if he'd always held my hand. I wished our gloves were off so I could feel his warmth. We stood without speaking, looking out across the harbor and hundreds of empty mooring buoys rocking on the incoming tide. A cloud, racing on a north-westerly wind, passed over the sun, stealing what little warmth it had provided. I shuddered and Sam put his arm around me.

"That better? I mean, does it help keep you warm?"

"Both." I smiled. He did, too.

Without looking at me, he said, "I don't know what I'm doing, Taylor. I've got feelings I thought I'd never have again."

"I know what you mean."

"You too?"

"Me too."

"This last week has been wonderful. The first time in a long time I've played. Had fun."

"Right."

His arm tightened around me. "What's going to happen?"

"I know what I want to happen, but I'm afraid even to think it."

He nodded. "I'm scared to death. I never thought I'd be close to anyone again or asking someone for a date or inviting her over. I don't know how to go about it."

"You're doing great. Let's not worry about it. If it's the thing for us to do, to be together, it'll happen. And it'll feel natural. There's no need to hurry and no need to hold back."

"A day at a time, huh?"

"Yeah, a day at a time," I said. "But let's make it every day. Or most every day."

"That's what I'd like. When I'm not with you, I'm thinking about being with you."

"Mmm. You know what else was fun? Watching the frown on Rebecca's face when you kissed me last night. I thought she was going to die on the spot. I loved it."

At the end of January, Matthew told me he'd completed the sketches I'd asked him to make. I don't know when he'd had time to do it, because he'd been working on *White Wings* almost every night. Weekends Rebecca had come home to help him with the boat, and on the long weekend that included Martin Luther King Day the two of them went to Bristol, Maine, to the Elwell lumber yard. They came home with several pieces of lumber tied to a rack on Matthew's Jeep. They'd spent the night in Bristol because Matthew needed time to choose the lumber piece by piece and to visit the gun shop with the bullet he'd found in the boat's frame. I don't know how chummy he and my daughter were, but it was clear they enjoyed each other's company and were having fun working on the boat. Rebecca, much to my joy and relief, was less of a twit when around me. Whether this was due to her new relationship with Matthew or her acceptance of Sam, she sounded less like a dorm mother.

Sam left on his Antarctic cruise with the promise he'd bring me a penguin. When it came time to go, he said he didn't want to leave me and begged me to come with him. I actually considered it, but finally decided not to. For three months I'd had a floor man lined up to refinish the living room and dining room floors plus the upstairs hallway, and I needed to get it completed during low season. The previous three weeks we'd seen each other every day: shopping, cooking, eating, going to shows and the theater, choosing new draperies for his inn, going out for dinner. When he'd leave me off at night he'd pull me to his side of the front seat and we'd kiss. Each night it took longer to make our good-byes, but he was as scared as I was to move our relationship into the bedroom.

To celebrate the viewing of the sketches, I invited Aggie to join Rebecca and Matthew and me for dinner on the last Saturday of the month. Over cocktails for me and Aggie, wine for Rebecca, and beer for Matthew, he lined up the sketches beside the original photographs.

"I asked Matthew to make some sketches of Taylor Harrington based on the pictures Becky took, but to add about thirty years to his appearance."

"How strange," Rebecca said, looking at me as if I'd lost my senses. "What for?"

"I've got an idea I want to . . . Well, you'll see if it works out."

"I made extra copies of these two," Matthew said, setting them to the front. "They're the best ones. We can make changes on the copies if you want to."

The four of us studied the sketches. Aggie said if it was supposed to be a picture of a man in his fifties, Matthew hadn't added enough fullness to his cheeks. Rebecca thought he'd made him too handsome and didn't show the wear and tear of age.

"I still don't understand why you're doing this," Rebecca repeated.

"Just curious." I stepped back, cocking my head to one side and then to the other. "Matthew, take one of the copies and make the cheeks thinner."

He thought for a minute and, taking a gum eraser and soft pencil, began altering the picture.

"How's that?"

"Not quite. You're too kind. Be more harsh. The cheekbones need to stand out more and the hair's too thick." He set to work again. Both Aggie and Rebecca looked at me questioningly.

"Now, what do you think?" He stepped back.

"Almost. Can you make the eyes gaunt but still keep them gentle?"

"Hmmm." He began shading the hollow under the brows and adding crow's-feet at the side of the eyes. When he lowered the eyelids slightly and put the hint of a smile on the lips, I stopped him.

"There. I think you've got it."

"Got what, Mom?" Rebecca asked, exasperated.

I gazed at the picture for several moments, my mind going back to the stone church on the bluff in Yokohama. I had sat across from this man twenty-two years ago, crying as I unloaded the sadness and loneliness of my marriage to Tad Hayakawa.

"Listen to me and don't laugh, please. That's he, the priest in Yokohama at Christ Church. The one I went to for counseling. And Rebecca, I'm sure that was your grandfather. My father. I knew him. Spoke to him. He touched my hand."

Aggie shook her head slowly. "Taylor, I think you're reaching for a dream. Maybe the sketch does look like the priest in Yokohama, but it doesn't look like the photographs of Taylor Harrington anymore. If he had lived, Becky would have found him. Lord knows she searched long enough."

"Damn it, Aggie, I'm not crazy. I saw this man three or four times during the week he was filling in for the regular vicar. You saw him too, Rebecca. We went to church on the Sunday he took the service."

"Mom, I have no memory of this at all. I don't even remember the church."

"Well, I do and I'm sure I'm right. I was at the end of my rope and he helped me."

"Mom, I'm not doubting that. I'm sure he did. I just don't think he could be my grandfather. The man from Racine told Becky he died in the prison dispensary."

"And Mom didn't believe it. She still thought he was alive somewhere."

Matthew shuffled through his working drawings until he found a large photograph. "I had a negative made of one of the pictures and enlarged to the size of the sketch. It's very grainy but you can still see the basic features of the face." He set it next to the altered picture. "The bone structure in the face in both of these is the same. See the eyebrows and the cheekbones. The jaw is the same. All we did was change the fleshy part of the face and the hair. It could be the same person."

"Oh hell, Matthew," Rebecca said, "you'd say anything to make Mom happy."

He shrugged but didn't answer.

"I don't know," Aggie said, examining the enlargement, "there is a strong similarity. But it couldn't be Taylor Harrington. I knew the two of them, Taylor and Becky. If he'd been alive he would have contacted Becky. He knew where she was and would have written. He loved her. He would have come back."

"Maybe he couldn't. Maybe something stood in the way." I stopped. I could see myself sitting in the church study on the day I poured out my soul. "When we talked there in the church, he spoke to me like I imagine a father speaks to his daughter."

"For God's sake, Mom," Rebecca said, "that's why they call priests Father."

I snapped, "I don't see why you keep putting this down."

"Because I'm concerned about you. This whole business has been upsetting for you and I'm worried."

"You think I'm making it up, imagining it?"

"I think you want to believe it, so you're remembering things from twenty years ago that may never have happened."

I closed my eyes and forced myself to relax. God, I wish Sam were here, I thought. He'd believe me.

"So," I said, looking first at Rebecca, "you think I'm nuts. And you, Aggie, think I making it up, and," to Matthew, "you're keeping your mouth shut." I squared my shoulders and announced, "I know I'm not making it up and I'm going to prove it."

That night, I heard the bell in Abbot Hall tower ring twice and couldn't go back to sleep. I was positive I was right, but how could I find out more? I had two leads: Christ Church and the doctor the man in Racine had called Dr. Sicko when he told Becky about the Kawasaki prison camp. The second one was a long shot, but the first had possibilities.

What the hell, I thought, I'll telephone the church. What have I got to lose? I knew it was futile to try to use my Japanese. It'd been more than twenty years since I'd spoken it. But they probably understood English.

It was either three or four on Sunday afternoon in Yokohama, depending on how daylight saving time affected the calculation— another thing I couldn't remember. I called the international operator, who said she'd stay on the line until the information operator in Yokohama gave me the telephone number of the church. I needed someone willing to be helpful and thanked her. The Japanese operator spoke English and gave me the phone number as easily as if I were calling St. Paul's Church in Marblehead. The American operator asked if I wanted her to ring the number, and I said yes.

Listening to the different cadence of the telephone ring, I was taken back to my years in Japan. How strange to be calling a number in the town where I had lived for nine unhappy years. It continued ringing. My mind and body vibrated with anticipation.

Someone lifted and then fumbled with the receiver. *"Mushi, mushi."*

"Hello. Is this Christ Church?"

An elderly voice said something in Japanese I couldn't understand.

"Christ Church? Is this Christ Church?"

"Ah sodesuka. Hi, hi. Christ Church."

"Is there someone there who speaks English?"

More Japanese I couldn't understand.

"May I speak with the vicar?"

More Japanese. Just as I was about to hang up, I felt Rebecca's hand on my shoulder. "May I help?"

I handed her the phone with a sigh of relief. "I think I've got Christ Church but that's as far as I've gotten."

"Anone?" Rebecca began and continued talking for a minute or two. When she hung up she said, "That was the vicar's mother. He's out for the afternoon and will be back at eight o'clock their time. That'll make it six a.m. here."

"Thanks, darling. I wasn't getting anywhere."

"You're really doing it, aren't you?"

"I am. I surprise myself. If it doesn't go anywhere, at least I'll know I've tried."

She gave me a hug and said, "I'll try again at six. Let's go back to bed."

If I slept, I wasn't aware of it. I counted each hour the tower bell tolled. At five-thirty I got up and made coffee and, at five to six, woke up Rebecca. She dialed the number and this time talked for five minutes. When she hung up, she was as excited and wide awake as I.

"I got him, the vicar. His name is Father Ohari. He understands what we're trying to find out and will help."

"Wonderful. Did he give you any indication if he thought he could trace Taylor?"

"The name Harrington wasn't familiar to him, but he said he'd look at the Record of Services Book for March and April 1973 and write you. He'd also ask some of the older members of the parish. I told him we thought Father Harrington might be your father and my grandfather who had stayed on in Japan after the war. This got his interest and I think he'll do what he can."

Two weeks later I got a letter from Father Ohari. He said a priest named Harrington had taken services in March of 1973 while the then vicar was on retreat and had filled in for him on four or five other occasions. Also, two members of the parish remembered him. As they were elderly, he didn't think they could speak English and suggested I find someone in Japan who could meet with them in person.

I was elated and called Rebecca immediately. She said she was going to Tokyo and Osaka in April on a sales mission and would take some extra time to go to Yokohama.

"I want to come with you. Would you mind?"

"Mom, I'd love it."

39

Sam called from JFK. He was changing planes and would be back in Marblehead about seven-thirty.

"May I take you to dinner?" he asked eagerly.

"Aren't you exhausted?"

"Not too bad. I started this morning from Rio de Janeiro, but I slept some on the plane."

We agreed on eight o'clock. After I hung up I sat for some time by the phone pondering Sam's return. He'd been gone for three weeks and I *had* missed him—especially when everybody thought I was crazy. But I noticed how easily I'd slipped back into my old unattached life, not needing a man to lean on, nor a man's feelings to worry about. Our romance of only one month had stirred up passions that surprised and excited me, yet during his three weeks' absence the desires had subsided, as if tucked away again at the bottom of my dresser drawer. Now, in less than three hours, he'd be knocking on my door. I could tell by his voice he was ready to take up where we'd left off, seeing each other daily, sharing chores and pleasures. Inevitably our lives would become more and more entwined. Did I want this? In time he'd begin to expect things of me and I of him, and rightly so. My independence would be limited. When I wanted to do something, I'd have to take his desires into consideration. Didn't I have enough as it was with Rebecca, to say nothing of a few hundred guests a year in my inn?

Now, my total focus was on finding my father. Sam's return was an interruption.

Three hours. I still had time to dust and replace some of the end tables, lamps, books, and odds and ends that had been shifted around to accommodate the floor refinishers. The job had taken days and seemed endless. Redoing floors, I decided, is like redoing the foundation upon which your life sits. The once cherished furniture and knickknacks that had fit so well with the old, lackluster floor now looked shabby against the restored natural beauty of the wide pine boards. The heavier pieces had been returned to their original positions a week ago by a team of husky moving men, and each day I had carried back lighter items.

Holding a lamp rescued from the hotel fire some forty years ago, I looked at the old furniture. What a pile of junk, I thought. It should have been put in a fire sale when we lost the hotel. I walked around the room touching the tired, stiff leather of the couches and overstuffed chairs, then into the dining room with its dark walnut furniture, chipped and scratched with age. It all seemed out of place against the bright beauty of the shiny polyurethaned floor. Why, I wondered, have I been taking care of this old furniture all these years? And for whom? Certainly not for me. I've never liked it. For whom then? My question hung in the air as an answer formulated in my mind. "Of course," I said aloud, "like everything else in my life. For my mother." Well, no longer, I resolved. From now on I'm living for Taylor *Harrington* Hayakawa.

Setting the lamp on the dining room table, I went to the telephone and called an antique dealer I knew at Pickering Wharf in Salem. Catching her as she was closing, I told her I wanted to sell all the furniture in the common areas of the inn and asked her to come as soon as possible to make a bid. She was delighted and agreed to come the next day.

Smiling, I hung up the phone. "Aren't I something?" I said aloud. "I can't believe I did that." Still smiling, I went to my bedroom and began undressing for a shower. This will be fun, I thought, buying new furniture. Maybe I'll even get new wallpaper. And draperies, too. And how about getting the outside painted this summer? As I pictured myself walking through furniture stores and selecting wallpaper and draperies, I saw Sam by my side. "This would be nice," he would say. "This bright floral pattern is like you, Taylor. It'd make beautiful drapes." Hmmm. That's just what he'd say. Strange how he sees me as beautiful. On the way to the shower I passed my full-length mirror and stopped. Each morning before venturing forth to face the world, I reviewed my outfit in front of this mirror, but never, never did I look at myself unclothed. I noticed I didn't use the word nude. "What a prude," I said to the image in the mirror. "You know what you are? You're a prude nude." I laughed. Putting my hands on my hips, I turned to the right, then to the left. I cocked my shoulders this way and that, then turned around and regarded my backside from over my shoulder. "Not great, but not bad. No extra fat. Just a little fullness in the waist and a little sagging in the butt." I turned forward again and cupped my breasts, putting my shoulders back and taking a deep breath. When I exhaled my breasts stood firm. "Can't complain about that." Humming, I headed for the shower.

The warm water cascading over my head and down my body washed away the aches and pains that moving furniture had caused. I doused my hair with shampoo, scrubbing it in and building a mound of lather which I used to massage my shoulders, breasts, stomach, and hips. The motion of my hands was comforting and relaxing, so I repeated the process, stepping back under the warm water and applying more shampoo. Dreamlike I let my mind wander over the day that had been and the night to come. I'm actually getting rid of all that old furniture. I'm starting over. My mind turned again to shopping and to Sam standing by my side, no longer an interruption but a companion.

At eight sharp he knocked. I opened the door to a blast of winter cold as a foot-long box torpedoed in my direction from a man encased in a parka so rotund he looked like the Michelin Man.

"Hi," he said, beaming. "This is for you."

"Sam, a present?" I took the beautifully wrapped box tied with a bow and bearing a sticker from a Rio de Janeiro department store.

"Like the jacket?" he asked as he came through the door. The words "Antarctic Expedition, 1995" were stitched on the left side of the chest. "They gave them to us on the ship."

"It looks warm. Come on in. I want to open my present."

Sam dropped his parka on a chair and we went to the living room. He caught me by my arm and turned me toward him. "I've missed you," he said, bringing his face to mine.

Whatever misgivings I'd had about Sam melted away as we put our arms around each other and kissed.

"I missed you, too. So much has happened." I sat in a chair and placed the present in my lap. Sam sat on the floor in front of me.

"Well, open it."

I removed the bow and slipped my finger under the fold, carefully sliding it along so as not to rip the paper.

"Forget the paper. Just open it."

"But it's so elegantly wrapped."

Sam sighed, despairing. Setting the wrapping aside, I removed the lid and folded back the tissue paper. There was a penguin, soft and fuzzy, wearing a plaid scarf around its neck.

"You remembered." I lifted it from the box. Then I saw it. Around the neck of the penguin, tucked beneath the scarf, was an opal necklace set in gold. I gasped. "It's beautiful." Removing it from the penguin, I caught the chain through my fingers and held it up against my palm. I began to cry. "This is the most beautiful gift I've ever received."

He sat up on his knees and embraced me. "I'm glad you like it."

I couldn't speak. I laid my head against his cheek and wept into his shoulder. No one had ever given me such a gift, not my mother or the DeWolfs and certainly not my ex-husband. Finally I spoke through my tears. "It's lovely, Sam. Thank you." He helped me hook the necklace and I walked to the mirror. With Sam by my side, the two of us looked at the necklace in the mirror. "It's so tasteful."

"It's as lovely on you as I'd hoped."

"It's much too much, Sam, and I'm going to keep it anyway."

"Good."

"Let's have a drink before we go and you can tell me about your trip." I brought two scotches from the kitchen and we settled on the couch. He told me about the cruise to the Antarctic, the small boats that took them ashore, the miles and miles of barren rolling hills covered with patches of flowers clinging to bits of dirt between the rocks, and the flocks of penguins wobbling from side to side and belly flopping into the surf. He showed me picture after picture until I said I'd had enough. "Okay," he said reluctantly. "Your turn."

"Two things. First, a couple of hours ago I decided to sell all the furniture in the common room and the dining room. It's old and shabby and looks dead against the beautiful new floors. I'm buying all new stuff."

"Good for you. Can I help?"

"I hope so, and new wallpaper and drapes too."

"I should go away more often. You unfold."

"Ha. I guess I have, but it's not from your going away. I'm tired of the old junk Mom saved from the fire and I'm tired of scrimping and saving. And Sam, there's something else I haven't told you."

"Is this the second thing?"

"No. Well, maybe it is. I hadn't even intended to tell you, at least not yet, but I want to get it off my chest." Sam looked at me with a trace of fear as if I were going to say I was secretly married or dying of cancer. "I'm not who I've told you I am. I'm not Taylor DeWolf Hayakawa. I'm Taylor Harrington Hayakawa."

He squinted, dumbfounded. "Oh? And that means . . . ?"

"Mother said my father was James DeWolf, and we lived our lives as if he were my father, the pilot killed in North Africa in World War Two. It was a lie. My real father was an Episcopal priest named Taylor Harrington who lived in Marblehead before the war. He was my mother's lover. I found it out just before Christmas from records Aggie had saved in her basement."

"Hence the name Taylor."

"Yeah."

"But why didn't she tell you?"

"It was something she started and couldn't stop—or, at least, chose not to stop."

And then I told Sam everything I knew about my father.

"Is Harrington, your real father, still alive?"

"He'd be close to eighty if he were, so I guess it's possible. But here's the strange part. I think . . . I know, I met him. Actually talked with him when I lived in Japan. He was a substitute priest at this little church in Yokohama and I went to him for counseling."

"Now that is weird. How did you discover this?"

I told Sam about the sketches, and the frustration I felt when the others thought I was nuts, and finally about making contact with the current vicar of the church who confirmed that a Taylor Harrington had indeed filled in at the church some twenty years ago.

"Rebecca and I are going to Japan to meet some older people from the congregation and see if they can give us leads on where to find him, or at least find out about him."

We decided to continue the conversation over dinner and walked to Michael's House, a restaurant a few blocks down the street. Sam had a hundred questions and I did my best to fill in the blanks. Finally, it was a relief to change the subject and talk about buying furniture, wallpaper, and draperies. After dinner we returned home and I invited Sam in for a nightcap.

"I'm glad you're back," I told him as we sat together on the sofa sipping brandy. "You fill a gap in my life I didn't know I had."

He smiled, then turned serious. "Gaps I know about. When Gwen died it was like losing a part of me. And it happened so quickly I hadn't time to get ready for the possibility of losing her. Suddenly she was gone and I was half a person. It was months, years, before I could stand up without the fear of falling into the gap she left. Then last fall, I don't know why, I began to feel whole again. I guess, in time, our mind and emotions heal like our body heals. Then I saw you that rainy day in the Stop and Shop." He set his glass on the coffee table and, picking up my hand that rested on his knee, kissed it. "Taylor, you've come to mean so much to me, and it's more than filling the gap left by Gwen. It seems as if a doorway is opening to a new life and we're stepping through it together."

"It does, doesn't it?" I set my brandy down and stood up, still holding his hand. For several moments, I looked down at him and he looked up at me. "Sam, come with me. I need someone to unhook my beautiful new necklace."

Sam spent the night. I awoke to the unaccustomed downhill slant of the mattress and the warmth of a body next to mine. He was still asleep. Hesitantly I propped myself up on my right elbow and looked at him. Lying on his back, his head was turned toward me and he was snoring gently. His breath smelled of the garlic in last night's dinner. The sheets and blankets, caught around his right leg, revealed a bare calf and foot. He was on the right side of the bed where I usually sleep because it's closest to the bathroom and has a night stand for my morning coffee and reading material. Already I'm having to make adjustments, I thought, smiling.

Carefully, so as not to wake him, I laid my head on his bare chest where the blankets had been pulled down and listened to his insides. Air came into his lungs in long steady pulls and was exhaled with quick puffs. His heart ba-bumped, ba-bumped slowly and steadily. Something gurgled from one part of his digestive tract into another. A lyric popped into my mind: *Getting to know you, getting to know all about you.* I laughed to myself.

The meshing of two approaches to lovemaking, one tried and tested over years of married intimacy and the other, mine, a quick tumble that had released Tad's urges and left me hanging, began awkwardly but ended gloriously. After Sam had removed my necklace, I preferred to undress myself; he wanted to help. Then he wanted the light on and I, self-conscious about my middle-aged body, wanted it off. We compromised by leaving the light on in the bathroom and closing the door to a crack. He was enthralled with my breasts and wanted to nuzzle them and kiss my nipples. At first I was repelled because of the brutal treatment they had received from Tad, but Sam's gentleness gradually changed my mind and I found myself enjoying the sensation. When he found my left hand under the blanket and brought it to his erect penis, I pumped it energetically until he placed his hand over mine, slowing my motion to a gentle massaging. Unhurried, his hands and lips roamed my body until I thought I would explode, and still he continued. Tad would have finished his business and been asleep by then, but Sam was loving it, loving my body and loving me. He moved his head to my stomach and kissed my navel while his hand found its way between my legs and his fingers found my clitoris. That was my first orgasm and two more followed—one as he moved inside me and the second during our cool-down. I had had no idea lovemaking could feel so good and be so loving.

Now, with my ear pressed against his chest and my side against his side, I absorbed the warmth of his body and listened to the pulsing of his heart. My left leg climbed over his, inching upward until it lay across his waist. My stomach, pressing against his hip bone, enticed me to move my hips slightly. I could feel him growing hard beneath my thigh. His eyes opened, barely, and he smiled sleepily. Half snuggling, half climbing, I rolled on top of him. Taking him inside me, I let my body move forward and back over his, like the gentle lapping of waves on a beach. And with each wave the intensity grew, releasing within me a primal urge that set my mind aside and took command of my muscles. I could hear myself, as if another person, moaning uncontrollably until an orgasm wrenched itself free and shot like steam from every pore in my body. Collapsing into his arms, I caught my breath

As my body relaxed, I began to cry. The excess of feelings, so strange to me, stirred up a mixture of grief and joy: grief for the passion I had denied myself over the years, and joy for the loving care I now experienced in the arms of Sam. After several moments the sobbing ended and I began kissing him and laughing at the same time.

"I did that? I can't believe I did that."

"Uhh. You did it all right."

"But I don't do things like that."

"You do now."

I laughed and laid my head back on his chest. "I'm going to say it. Are you ready?"

"If it's what I think you're going to say, I've been ready for a long time."

"Okay," I said, "here goes. I love you."

"I love you, too."

40

Racing the sun toward Japan, I felt my memories of the abuse and humiliation I'd received from my ex-husband grow stronger. Rebecca and I had taken United to Dulles and boarded All Nippon Airways Flight 1 which departed on Monday, April 10, at 11:50 A.M. Rebecca had used her connections with All Nippon Airways to get us upgraded to first class, so we were riding in the lap of luxury. But in spite of attractive attendants in colorful kimonos, champagne at takeoff and before meals, a seven-course dinner, and two feature movies, the dread gripping my throat tightened with each passing mile. Twenty-some years earlier, when I'd returned to Japan after a visit to Marblehead, Tad's black Mercedes and driver were there to meet me and whisk me off to our home in Yokohama. Three or four days later he'd casually walked into my bedroom with a smug expression of satisfied lust, and I knew he had been with his mistress. When I turned away revolted, he stomped from the room, confirmed in his opinion of my unworthiness as a wife.

Why, after all these years, should the horror of those times still have such a hold? Sipping an after-dinner brandy, I looked out the window at some peaks of the Canadian Rockies penetrating the cloud carpet that stretched from horizon to horizon. I told myself there would be no black limousine to meet me and no Tad to degrade me. Rebecca's hand, gently touching mine, startled me.

"You seem so sad, Mom. Missing Sam already?"

"No. I wish it were that." I wondered if I should tell her. The last time I was honest about my feelings toward her father, we had a fight. "Isn't it strange?" I said, instead. "Here we are, both traveling to the land of our fathers. You've already found yours, plus your half brother and sister." I raised the brandy to my lips, thinking. "Do you love him, Rebecca?"

She tensed momentarily, then relaxed. "I'm not sure. What does it mean to love a father who is seven thousand miles away whom you see once or twice a year? When we meet, he seems pleased to see me. He gives me gifts and invites me to stay in his home as long as I want." She turned toward me with a look of sudden realization. "It just occurred to me. He's never touched me and certainly never kissed me. The closest he comes to me is the other end of a present when I arrive. His own children—funny I should put it that way, I mean his pure Japanese children—used to kiss him when they were younger. They don't now because they're growing up, but they still seem close. Sometimes I get the feeling he looks at me as a kind of trophy, like I represent his conquest of America." There was hurt in her eyes. "When he takes me to his club for lunch, I feel like I'm on display."

"That must be hard."

"Not really," she said, rallying her spirits. "I kind of like it, all these old guys drooling in their shark fin soup as they look at me. I'm much taller than most Japanese women and I'm not bad looking." She laughed. "Maybe it's my victory over my half siblings." Then, more thoughtfully, "Maybe it's what I'm willing to settle for as his love."

"Why are these guys, fathers, so important to us?" I asked, more like a friend than a mother. "Here I am chasing halfway round the world to find out if my father is still alive or at least what he was like." Then I had a revelation. "What I really want to know is why he abandoned my mother and me. He knew where she was. Why didn't he come back to Marblehead or write her? She devoted her life to looking for him and was true to him the whole time, even though I didn't know what was going on. Did he just stop loving her . . . and me?"

"At least I know who my father is."

"And you see him and talk to him. I envy you."

"What will you ask him if you find him?"

I thought about that for so long that Rebecca returned to the magazine she'd been reading. When I spoke, my voice caught in my throat. "I'd ask him if he loves me."

Through the haze beneath us the outline of Hokkaido took shape and soon we were crossing into northern Honshu. As the giant 747 began its descent I could make out villages along the shore and farms inland. The midday sun reflected off hundreds of earth mirrors which at first I thought were ponds and lakes but, as we came lower, I saw were greenhouses. Inside the plane people were beginning to stir, making last-minute trips to the lavatory to comb hair and check makeup. Flight attendants were folding up video screens and gathering cups and glasses. We were reminded to fill out our entry forms and have them ready with our passports for immigration. With a change in engine pitch and a noticeable slowing of speed, the landing flaps were extended, followed by the wrenching sound of the landing gear locking into place. Out the window, dots on the roads became cars and trucks, shadows and blotches of dark green became farmhouses with tiled roofs and, almost too quickly, the land beneath us became runway. The wheels screeched, and we landed in Japan.

"Welcome to Narita International Airport," the flight attendant announced. "The time is 2:25 p.m."

The sun had won the race by two and a half hours.

We sailed through immigration without so much as a nod from the inspector of passports and, being first class, had to wait only minutes for our bags to tumble out on the carousel. Rebecca assured me the shuttle bus service to Tokyo was almost as fast as a taxi and a fraction of the cost, so we wheeled our bags to a line of people standing by the curb and boarded the bus to the Ginza Tobu Hotel. Inching our way through jams of cars and trucks, we arrived at the hotel an hour and fifteen minutes later, tired and grimy. The Ginza Tobu is moderately priced but very pleasant and well appointed. Our double room was large and the bathtub deep. After a twenty-minute soak for each of us, we felt refreshed enough for a short walk down the Ginza and dinner in the hotel. We were asleep by eight.

At 1:24 A.M. by the glowing digital numbers next to the bed, I was awake again, my confused body clock thinking it was time to get up. Instead I lay there feeling surprisingly serene. Here I was in the center of Japan and no bogeyman had me yet. My conversation with Rebecca had gone well and each of us, surprisingly, had heard what the other was saying. Tomorrow—actually, today—we planned to spend in Tokyo seeing the sights and resting up, then the next day we'd go to Yokohama for our meeting at Christ Church.

A sudden specter arose in my mind. What if I were to run in to Tad on a Yokohama street? I laughed at myself. Not likely, I thought. He doesn't walk, he's driven. Nor would he go to the New Otani Hotel where we'd be staying. It was nice but not one he'd use for business meetings or assignations, if he was still into that.

And would it be so bad if I *did* run in to him? I think I'd say, "Hello there, Tad. It's been a long time, hasn't it?" Then I'd kick him in the balls.

After breakfast we walked through Hibya Park, exploding with cherry blossoms and flowering plum trees. Children in school uniforms sat in clusters near the edges of ponds, giggling with one another and skillfully painting the scenes in watercolors. Swans moved smoothly over dark waters through which huge white and orange carp materialized and disappeared beneath lily pads. This was the grace and beauty of Japan I'd forgotten, squeezed from my memory by the bad thoughts I'd let take hold of me. It was good to be back, good to see it again, good to have the evil expunged.

We took the train from Tokyo's Central Station to Yokohama the next day. I continued to feel balmy from jet lag and would occasionally drift into unconsciousness with my eyes still open. As I remembered, it took me three full days before I returned to normal. During our cab ride from the Yokohama station to our hotel, I craned my neck to look up at the many new buildings erected in the last twenty years. Our hotel, the New Otani, was one of them. Once settled in our room, Rebecca called Father Ohari and confirmed our appointment the next morning at eleven. More time to wait, but I didn't mind. I wanted to be well recovered from jet lag when I met the two parishioners from Christ Church.

That afternoon, on a whim, I arranged with the hotel for a car and driver familiar with the surrounding region to drive me and Rebecca to Kawasaki, just north of Yokohama.

"There is nothing pretty there," the concierge said. "Only factories and a port. Wouldn't you rather see Mount Fuji?"

"No. Kawasaki."

Our driver, about forty years old, tried his best to find points of interest along the way but gave up and concentrated on the traffic.

"Is there some place in Kawasaki you want to see?" he asked.

"Yes. The waterfront—the harbor area." I saw his eyes look questioningly at me in the rearview mirror before he turned off the expressway, down a ramp, and onto a broad commercial street filled with trucks carrying ocean-going containers. Soon I saw lines of gantries and cranes hovering over ships like giant mechanical birds tending their nests. Modern warehouses lining the piers had names like Kawasaki, Sony, Toyota.

"There used to be a prison camp along here somewhere during World War Two. Do you know where it was located?"

"Mother." Rebecca sighed with embarrassment. "I can't believe you're doing this." I ignored her.

"Prison camp? Here?" He shook his head repeatedly. "I know nothing about prison camps."

So much for history. We returned to the hotel.

I wanted to arrive at Christ Church on the Bluff early so I could walk around the grounds and settle past memories, whatever they might be, before our appointment. The Bluff, as the area was called, looked down on the harbor to the east and a sprawling industrial area to the west. As it was before the war, it had once again become an exclusive residential area for wealthy Japanese and foreigners with business in Yokohama. Somewhere—the exact location I had put from my mind—was the home of Tad Hayakawa, inherited from his parents when they died. I had visited his parents there many times and Rebecca had stayed there as recently as last

December, when she came to see her father. Probably out of deference to me, she didn't mention the location.

The church was the same as ever. Large oaks still shaded the yard. The red door, open, beckoned you to enter. The gray stone walls still held the bronze plaque. "Destroyed by earthquake, 1923—Destroyed by firebombs 1945." We stepped into the cool interior and sat in a pew near the back. Afternoon sun shone through stained glass windows to my right, and in the shadows of the sanctuary I could see the altar draped in purple. The crosses and statues were covered in black gauze. I'd forgotten. It was Holy Week, Good Friday—the day of the crucifixion. Here, twenty-two years ago, I knelt and wept, praying for deliverance from a marriage that never should have been. Here, I think it was this very pew, my father had come to sit beside me and ask if I wanted to talk. That was the first of three counseling sessions during the week he was filling in at the church.

I was startled from my reverie by Father Ohari walking down the aisle. Dressed in a black cassock, he was of medium height and in his mid-thirties. A shock of unruly black hair stood upright despite his continued efforts to push it down. He wore black horned-rimmed glasses and a welcoming smile.

"Mrs. Hayakawa?" he said, not bowing but extending his hand. "I'm Father Ohari."

"How do you do. And this is my daughter, Rebecca Hayakawa." They shook hands also.

"You're right on time. Shall we go into the church parlor?" We followed him through a door to the left of the chancel and into a room where he'd arranged some comfortable chairs in a circle around a small table. Seated there were two older people, a man in his late sixties and a woman who must have been well into her seventies. The man stood as we entered.

"Mrs. Hayakawa and Miss Hayakawa, I'd like to introduce Mr. Sato and Mrs. Tamura. Sato-san and Tamura-san have been members of this parish all their lives. They were baptized here as children." We bowed and bowed again. "Please sit down. My wife will bring us tea." As if on command, the door to a kitchen opened and Mrs. Ohari entered with a tray. Like her husband, she was mid-thirties, attractively dressed in subdued colors appropriate for

Good Friday. She set down the cups of green tea and was introduced by her husband. We bowed and thanked her for the tea, and she departed.

Ohari spoke first. "I've explained to Sato-san and Tamura-san that you lived in Yokohama some time ago and were married to a Japanese man named Hayakawa. I did not mean to be personal, but they thought you were Nisei." They recognized the word "nisei" and nodded, smiling. I said it was right for him to have explained my name. "I've also told them that you are looking for information about Father Harrington, whom you believe to be your father." He then spoke to them in Japanese, gesturing to Rebecca.

Sitting properly on the edge of her seat, her hands folded in her lap, she addressed them. After exchanging two or three sentences in Japanese she said, "I asked them if they remember him, and they said yes."

Sato-san then began speaking and talked for some time. He was a short man of spare build, well dressed in a dark gray suit, and rather distinguished looking. He spoke with energy and authority, and I imagined him to be a senior executive of some company. From time to time I heard the name Harrington and occasionally recognized some Japanese words.

"He says he remembers Father Harrington very well because he spoke Japanese fluently, and his sermons were always interesting." Sato-san nodded his head as Rebecca spoke and I assumed he understood some English. "He thinks he was connected with St. Paul's University in Tokyo, because he looked like a professor. But he's not sure."

She turned to Tamura-san, beginning with the opening words that custom dictated and then asked about Father Harrington.

Tamura-san, her voice weak and scratchy, spoke only three or four sentences. Rebecca translated. "Yes, she too remembers his visits to Christ Church." Hiding a laugh politely behind her hand, she added, "Because he was so tall." Tamura-san spoke again, and again Rebecca translated. "He was a good friend of Dr. Seiko, who was Senior Warden here for several years." Her eyes brightened as she said Dr. Seiko. "Mrs. Tamura says the doctor lives in Zushi."

"So he's still alive?" I said.

Rebecca put my question to Tamura-san, who laughed and replied.

"She says very much alive. He comes to church here every Sunday."

"Ask her if she knows his address and if it would be all right for us to visit him."

Father Ohari interrupted. "I'm sure he would be happy to see you and I'd be pleased to ask him. It never occurred to me that Dr. Seiko might have known Father Harrington, but I can see now that he most probably did. He's always had his finger on the pulse of this parish." He smiled at his medical allusion.

"And would you ask if we could visit him soon?"

"Of course. I'll call right now if you'll excuse me." He spoke to Sato-san and Tamura-san, stood, bowed several times, and left the room. Rebecca picked up the conversation in Japanese and the three of them exchanged pleasantries for several minutes. Ohari returned and sat down.

"I have good news. I talked with Dr. Seiko, and he would like to meet with you tomorrow at eleven o'clock at his home."

"That's wonderful," I said.

"I should tell you something about him." First he filled in Sato-san and Tamura-san on what was happening. Then he continued, "Dr. Seiko's father, also a doctor and a member of this parish, had his practice in Zushi, not far from here. After the war, his son went into practice with him and eventually moved into his father's house after he died. The home was located on a large piece of land, and following the war the father and son set up an orphanage and school on this property for children who'd lost parents in the bombings. I think the school is still there. Dr. Seiko lives in the original house."

"He must be getting on in years?"

"Yes. I would guess he's in his mid-eighties, but he looks and acts much younger."

"Rebecca, would you ask Tamura-san if there is anything else she remembers about Father Harrington?" Rebecca nodded and addressed the elderly lady.

"Only that Dr. Seiko was his friend and spoke well of him."

I realized we had exhausted their information, so I thanked

them for their help and complimented them on their beautiful church. Ohari-san gave me his card on the back of which he'd written in Japanese directions to Dr. Seiko's home in Zushi. We thanked all three of them again, called for a taxi, and said our good-byes.

In the cab on the way back to the hotel I was exuberant. "We're making progress. Dr. Seiko has got to be the same Dr. Sicko the man in Racine talked to Becky about."

"He'd be the right age, too."

"Let's go to Zushi today. I'm too excited to spend another night here in Yokohama."

As I packed our bags, Rebecca got on the phone and found us an inn overlooking the beach in Zushi, and we were on our way. After a twenty-minute wait in the Yokohama train station, the train pulled in. Thirty minutes later the loudspeaker droned, *"Zushi, Zushi, Zushi gozaimasu."*

We were swept from the train and through the station by the crowd of weekend visitors to the town. How different from Yokohama! The tallest buildings were six or seven stories, and there were only a handful of those. Like spokes on a wheel, narrow streets lined with small shops reached out from the circle in front of the station. We found a cab on the circle and Rebecca told him the name of our inn. Five minutes later we were there.

The inn was Japanese-style with tatami floors, shoji screens, low tables, pillows, and a balcony that looked out on a wide expanse of dark gray volcanic sand that made up the beach.

"Now you're really in Japan," Rebecca said, putting on a pair of tabi, the slipper socks with a divider for the big toe so it would fit into the flip-flops called zori.

"It's lovely." I had slid back the shoji screen and was standing on the narrow balcony. "So peaceful." But I didn't feel at peace. "Rebecca, it's the middle of the afternoon and I'm too excited. Let's go for a walk. Follow the directions Ohari-san gave us and see where the good doctor lives. Then we'll know how to get there tomorrow."

"If we're going walking, I'm switching back to shoes. I *am* only half Japanese," she said with a laugh.

Following directions in Japanese is never easy. We asked several people for help and each pointed a different way. In time, we were wandering down quiet residential streets lined with high walls above which we could see sloping tile roofs. The road we were following began winding up a hill, and after a few blocks we were able to look down on Zushi: the ocean to the left, the train station to the right, and the residential area in between hidden in trees. There was no one on the road from whom to ask directions, so we trudged on. Instead of walls, now there were gates beyond which driveways disappeared into beautifully landscaped lawns and gardens. These were more than homes—they were estates.

Suddenly Rebecca stopped. Attached to one of the stone gateways was a small bronze plaque.

"My God! Oh my God!"

"What is it?"

Rebecca walked to the gate and, following the words on the sign with her finger, read, *"Shiro i Mane Kirisuto Kyoto no Gakkou."*

"Well? What is it?"

She looked at me, stunned. "White Wings Christian School."

41

"I did not know Father Harrington had a daughter, Mrs. Hayakawa." Rebecca and I were sitting in Dr. Seiko's office, at a coffee table across the room from his desk. The room, more like a study than an office, combined Western furniture and sliding glass doors with shoji blinds that opened to a Japanese garden. It blended the best of both styles to create a comfortable and tranquil setting. I could see why Father Ohari said Dr. Seiko looked much younger than his eighty-some years. His face was devoid of age wrinkles and the flesh around his jaw firm. His most salient feature was an abundance of pure white hair combed back in waves hiding the tops of his ears. Handsome, cultured, he seemed at peace with himself.

"Nor did I, Dr. Seiko, until last Christmas when I discovered letters written by my mother that described her relationship with Taylor Harrington before the war."

"Then your maiden name is Harrington?"

Drat it, I thought, another long explanation. "No, they weren't married. My mother was married to a man named DeWolf who was serving overseas in the Royal Air Force when she met Taylor Harrington. He was a curate in Marblehead, Massachusetts, and they fell in love."

"I see," he said. "And you didn't know he was your father until you read your mother's letters?"

"I didn't even know he existed. Mother kept it from me all her life."

The door to the interior of his house opened a crack and I could see a maid peeking in holding a tray. He nodded to her and she entered, bowing, and served each of us a cup of tea.

"Or would you rather have coffee?" he asked.

"Tea is fine."

When she departed, closing the door silently, he continued. "Then you learned from your mother's letters he was in Japan?"

"She didn't know where he was. In World War Two he was listed as having died on a prison ship somewhere between the Philippines and Japan. But after the war she talked with a man who had been with him in a Kawasaki camp right up to the end of the war."

The old man nodded his head. "And what did that man tell her?"

"He said that during the summer of 1945, Taylor was sick with malaria and dysentery and finally died in the prison dispensary."

"Hmmm." His face was expressionless. "May I ask how you connected Father Harrington, whom you believe to be your father, with Christ Church in Yokohama?"

Rebecca gave me an encouraging smile. I said, "I met him when I lived in Yokohama."

A modicum of surprise showed itself on the doctor's face.

"I was having personal problems and went to him for counseling while he was filling in for the regular vicar."

"But if you knew nothing about this Harrington, what made you think he was your father? Please understand, I don't mean to make this sound like an interrogation. I'm just trying to understand."

"That's all right. I know it sounds farfetched. At the time I was simply thankful to be able to talk with a priest who understood my problems. It wasn't until I saw pictures my mother had taken of Taylor Harrington that I noticed the resemblance. That's when I called Father Ohari and found out a Father Harrington had indeed substituted from time to time at the church. So I came to Japan and Father Ohari arranged for me to talk with an older lady in the parish named Tamura-san who remembered my father."

"But there must be more than one Taylor Harrington in the world. How can you be sure this one is your father?"

"I can't be absolutely sure, but Mother tracked him as far as the Kawasaki prison camp where the man said he died in the dispensary. That man said the doctor at the camp was called Dr. Sicko, which I thought might be a corruption of Seiko. Then, Tamura-san said you were a good friend of Taylor Harrington." The old man raised his head and our eyes met. "If you are that doctor, then you hold the key to resolving this matter."

He sat quietly for several moments as if his mind was reaching far into the past. Then he spoke. "I am he, the one they called Sicko."

Rebecca put her hand on mine and squeezed.

"Then . . . can you tell us? Is Father Harrington my father?"

"What I can tell you is this. The Taylor Harrington who was in that prison camp is one and the same with the Father Harrington who filled in at Christ Church."

"Then he is my fath—"

"But what I can't say is that Father Harrington is your father." He saw my face fall and added, "I know this may sound cruel, but if you are his daughter, then questions of inheritance arise. There may be property and money, I don't know, and someone might claim to be his daughter in order to gain this inheritance."

Hurt that he should think such a thing, and feeling anger boiling up inside me, I said, "I can assure you I have no interest in claiming inheritance. I am simply looking for my father or information about him."

"Please don't be upset. I'm just setting out the limits of my information. I can tell you about the Father Harrington I knew, but I can't confirm that he's your father."

I looked down at my cup of tea, trying to calm myself. Rebecca spoke.

"We appreciate your willingness to share this information and we understand it does not prove my mother is Taylor Harrington's daughter. Please believe that our interest is truly to seek information and not an inheritance. But from what you are saying, are we to conclude that Taylor Harrington is dead?"

"I think he is, but I cannot say for sure. He left here in June of

1973, saying he had an emergency trip to the States and would return as soon as he could. He never came back and we never heard another word from him."

We sat quietly for several moments, each sipping tea, then it occurred to me. "That was right after I met him in March."

"And," Rebecca added, "the same month Grandmother died."

"Did you try to find him—trace him?" I asked.

"We knew that he bought a round-trip ticket on JAL and flew to Los Angeles, but then he transferred to another airline and we were unable to track him further."

"Mother, when you talked with Father Harrington at Christ Church, did you tell him who you were or where you were from?"

"I may have. But it would have been small talk, the kind of thing you say to get acquainted. I don't remember."

"It is coincidental," said Dr. Seiko, "that he left soon after seeing you and in the month your mother died. How did she die, if I might ask?"

"She was lost in a boating accident. And, Dr. Seiko, the boat was named *White Wings*, the same as the school. Do you see, now, why I feel sure your Harrington is my father?"

"It's compelling, isn't it?"

The maid appeared again at the door and, after a nod from the doctor, entered and refilled our cups.

"Dr. Seiko, please tell us how you came to know Taylor Harrington."

"Yes. That is why you have come, isn't it?" He looked out into his garden and, leaning back in his chair, began. "Fifty years ago—it seems ages ago, doesn't it—I was an army doctor. I had finished my residency at Mass General in Boston and returned to Japan just as the war was starting. Immediately I was shipped off to Southeast Asia where I was promptly wounded and returned home. I was assigned to the three prison camps in Kawasaki, tending to the medical needs of the prisoners as well as the camp guards. It was a good assignment for me because it allowed me to be near my church, Christ Church, and not far from my home here in Zushi. When we received prisoners, they were usually in miserable condition: starved, sick, and terribly weak. The prisoners from the Philippines were especially bad off because they had fought so long without food and medical care. They were almost dead by the time they were captured. They were brought to Japan because laborers were needed in the mines and factories and ports. Some of them were so sick they couldn't work or, when forced to, would collapse. Taylor Harrington was such a one. He had not only recurring malaria but a severe case of dysentery. He was skin and bones. Must have weighed no more than a hundred twenty pounds. He became a familiar sight in the dispensary.

"I asked him one day, when we were alone in the dispensary, why they called him Chap or Chappy. He said he was a chaplain and an Episcopal priest. I told him I too was Nippon Seiko Kai, which is the Episcopal Church in Japan. He asked about my fluency in English and I told him I had interned at Mass General in Boston. Then he said he'd gone to ETS, the Episcopal Theological Seminary in Cambridge, right across the river. Our friendship developed, but we were careful not to let it be known.

"No sooner did Harrington get well enough to return to work than he would collapse on the job and receive another beating. I spoke to the commandant of the Kawasaki prisons about these beatings, not specifically Harrington's but all of them, saying it was unproductive—that it was putting laborers in the hospital and taking them away from their jobs. His answer was to refuse permission for men who had been beaten to go to the hospital or dispensary. One day when I was walking through the barracks, I found Harrington unconscious on his bunk with a high fever. I ordered him brought to the dispensary and convinced the camp commander he was very sick—and he was.

"This happened once more and by then it was the summer of 1945. Tokyo, Yokohama, Kawasaki—the whole area was being bombed heavily. Starting in May the incendiary bombs had turned the area into a firestorm. Thousands of people were killed and almost every dwelling destroyed. As more and more waves of B29s arrived it became clear to many of us that Japan was on its last legs. Most of the army guards at the prisons in Kawasaki were replaced by civilians who came to work outraged over the bombings and looking for revenge. Discipline was cracking and it was impossible for me or anyone else to stop the beatings and murders in the prison camps. There was little food and no medical supplies, not only in the camps but in the surrounding cities and towns as well. Japanese were starving along with the prisoners.

"One night at the beginning of August, just before the atomic bomb was dropped on Hiroshima, Harrington was back in the dispensary with such a high fever he was delirious. There was another patient there also who was just as sick. I called my father here in Zushi to see if he could arrange for an ambulance to come to Kawasaki to pick up four patients who were very ill and needed to be transferred to a more secure area. I also had two Japanese patients, severely burned, whom I was tending in my apartment. The ambulance arrived and I put the two Japanese in racks in the back and drove to the prison. There was so little discipline left in the camp that no one stopped me. When I got to the dispensary, the other prisoner had died, but I put both him and Harrington in the ambulance, telling the guard they were dead. I said I was disposing of the bodies because they had died of an infectious disease.

"The bombers were overhead again as we drove down the coast, dodging craters in the road and flying debris, but there were no police nor fire wardens around to confiscate the ambulance. Once in Zushi, we put Harrington and the two Japanese in my father's dispensary and buried the dead prisoner. Ten days later we surrendered and the war was over.

"It was a month before any American official arrived in Zushi, but Harrington was far too sick to be moved. I tried several times to report his presence in my father's dispensary but was ignored until well into October. By then he was able to sit up but could not walk without support. Finally, an American ambulance arrived and took him away. I learned later he was flown to a hospital in St. Louis where he spent six months recovering.

"While he was in the hospital he wrote me saying he wanted to return and set up an orphanage for children whose parents were lost in the bombings. He said he was willing to invest money inherited from his parents, who had been killed in an automobile accident during the war, and his back pay accumulated over the last four years."

If he could write Dr. Seiko, I thought, why couldn't he write my mother?

Dr. Seiko continued with his story. "My father and I said we would donate a section of this property. When he was released from the hospital and discharged, Harrington returned, designated as a missionary by the Nippon Seiko Kai.

"Because he was an American and an ex-POW, he was able to make friends at Yokosuka Naval Base and Camp Zama, and secure building materials by midnight requisition, as they say. Japanese parishioners from Christ Church as well as U.S. Navy and Army personnel helped build the dormitories and classrooms. The project became an example of what Americans and Japanese could do when they worked together.

"How well I remember seeing Father Harrington with the children. He would sit out there on the lawn and tell them stories. I think that was how he began to learn Japanese. When he made mistakes, they'd giggle and he'd ask them to tell him the right words. They loved him and he loved them. The numbers grew rapidly until we had over a hundred fifty children. More dormitories were needed and, thanks to Father Harrington, they were provided. Two or three years into the occupation we discovered another group of children needing help—unwanted babies whose fathers were American service personnel. Again Father Harrington mobilized help from the surrounding bases and camps to expand the school.

"It was only at nights that the horrors of his imprisonment seized his mind. More than once I rushed to his quarters to find him screaming from some nightmare. And there were recurrences of the malaria. Gradually over the years he regained strength both in his body and in his mind. It was the school, however, that kept him alive and moving ahead."

"Did he ever marry?" I asked.

"Never. I thought perhaps he'd taken a vow of celibacy, but I was never sure. His personal life was very much his own. He did buy a sailboat which he kept here in the river just off the bay. He named it for the school, *White Wings*. At least that is what I always thought until you told me there was also a *White Wings* back in Marblehead. The boat was his chance for escape. Over the years I noticed he always took it out by himself on June twenty-sixth. It was a ritual. I asked him what significance this date had. He answered enigmatically, 'Because our twenty-sixth is the twenty-fifth in Massachusetts.' "

"Dr. Seiko, my mother followed the same ritual. It was only after I read her letters that I realized what it meant. My birthday is March twentieth, approximately nine months later."

"Mrs. Hayakawa, you present a very convincing case that he is your father. Before you go I'd like you to meet Mr. Nakamura, headmaster of White Wings Christian School. I've asked him to give you a tour of the school."

He led us out through his garden and across a lawn to a series of buildings that appeared to house administration, dining hall, classrooms, and dormitories. It was lunchtime and I could hear the chatter and laughter of children in the dining hall. Mr. Nakamura met us on the steps of the administration building. In his mid-forties, he was tall and, except for his eyes and cheekbones, could have passed for an Occidental.

"Welcome to White Wings School," he said in perfect English.

"Thank you," I responded as we approached. "It's taken us a long time to get here."

"I've arranged for you to join our staff and the children for lunch."

"Thank you," I said.

We followed him to the dining hall, and as we entered, a hundred fifty boys and girls rose from their seats and said in unison, "Welcome to White Wings School." It was clear we weren't their first American visitors. The children, who looked to be between five and eleven, sneaked glances at us throughout lunch and gathered their heads in little huddles to giggle and point. The boys wore short, dark blue pants and the girls dark blue skirts. All wore white shirts. They were adorable. Mr. Nakamura, lowering his voice, explained they were chosen on the basis of academic promise and financial need. No longer was admission limited to orphans.

After lunch, on our way to the classrooms and dormitories, Rebecca said to him, "I think we have something in common."

He nodded. "I think you're right. You're half Japanese and I'm half American."

Rebecca smiled. "All in the way you look at it, I guess. How long have you been at White Wings?"

"Since I was two years old. I was one of Father Harrington's first mixed-nationality orphans."

"I spent my first six years here in Japan," Rebecca said, "and found it very difficult, especially when I started school."

"I'm not surprised. Japanese are still insular when it comes to race. You should have tried it as an orphan. Without Father Harrington, I might not even be here. I owe him my life."

As we toured the facilities, I saw some of the children leaving the school grounds and others returning to the dormitories. I asked Nakamura-san about it.

"We have a half day on Saturday. As you can see, some of the children are boarders and some live nearby. Those are on their way home now. The ones who remain will have some planned activities and some free time. Tonight we're showing the film *The Lion King*." The tour ended at the athletic field and gymnasium/auditorium which was already set up with chairs for the evening movie. Beyond this building was a grove of trees and a small Japanese-style cottage.

"What's that building?" I asked.

"Father Harrington's home."

"Would it be possible for us to see it? Perhaps Dr. Seiko has told you I believe Father Harrington was my father. It would mean a lot to me."

Nakamura-san hesitated. "I'm afraid we don't allow visitors in his cottage. It's locked and just as he left it twenty-two years ago. We have always thought, and hoped, that one day he'd return, so we're preserving it as his private residence. You see, for us, especially those who considered him our father by adoption, it's practically a shrine."

"I understand," I said, "but I consider him my father also."

Dr. Seiko spoke up. "She has a very good case, Nakamura-san. There are many things that support her."

"I'm afraid Dr. Seiko and I don't agree on all things, Mrs. Hayakawa. I would have to be convinced by some visible proof that you were his natural daughter before I could let you enter. If you could offer such proof, then you would have the right not only to enter but to take possession of his personal effects, as well as property and investments, if there are any. You can see that your claim is very disconcerting for us, so I hope you'll understand my asking for conclusive proof."

I don't believe this, I thought. First I find my father, and then a rival sibling.

I tried to be understanding when I spoke, but I knew there was an edge to my voice. "I have letters and pictures, Nakamura-san, that are proof enough for me. I hope you will accept them and allow us to settle this matter amicably."

On the way back to our inn, Rebecca said it was a good thing Nakamura-san was half American and had studied in the States, because what I said would have been fighting words to a Japanese.

"Well, I was pissed off. Here we travel halfway around the world and actually find the place where my father lived, and he won't let us in."

"All he wants is more proof—something he can see."

"But what is proof for us may not be proof for him. All we've got is that letter Mom wrote that was returned and the pictures of him in the boat."

"Maybe the sketches would help. Let's call Matthew tonight and ask him to FedEx them. We'll get them on Monday and you can show them to Nakamura-san. I've got to go to Tokyo tomorrow and meet up with the sales mission. Can you handle it without me?"

"Oh, I'll be all right. I promise I won't blow my stack."

We reached Matthew that night, which was Saturday morning for him, and told him what we wanted.

"You'll get more than that," he said from seven thousand miles away. "I was working on the decking last night, removing the separated section from the deck beams, when I found two letters, wrapped in plastic and jammed up behind the clamp beam in a frame bay at the underside of the deck. Listen to this. They're from Taylor Harrington, Zushi, Japan, and postmarked in April 1973."

42

Monday morning the FedEx envelope arrived at the inn. I tore it open and read the two letters Becky had received from Taylor. "Hot dog!" I said aloud and called Dr. Seiko, telling him what I had and asking him to intercede for me with Nakamura-san.

"I'm sure these letters will convince you and Nakamura-san that Harrington is my father. And if his cottage has been untouched since left, I'll bet we find the letters my mother sent in return."

"Please read me a part of the letter that you feel proves he's your father. It will help when I talk to Nakamura-san."

"Okay." I let my eyes scan the first page of the second letter until I found the sentence I was looking for. " 'Now you say Taylor is our daughter. I'm deeply moved. We joked about our names being the same, but I wouldn't even let myself dream she might be mine. I wasn't as naive as you may have thought, though. I knew we were taking a chance and I didn't care.' How's that, Dr. Seiko?"

"It sounds convincing to me."

"What I want is access to the cottage to see if we can find my mother's letters to him. She must have written, and it would help both of us discover what happened to my father and maybe even my mother."

"If need be, I'll pull rank on Nakamura-san. After all, I am Chairman of the Board of Directors of the school."

Seiko-san called me back half an hour later. "Everything is set.

Come to my house at one-thirty and we'll go down to the school together. Nakamura-san is meeting us at the cottage."

I tried to call Rebecca at her hotel in Tokyo but she was out. I left word for her to call me that evening at six.

I took a cab to the doctor's home through a steady drizzle, just heavy enough to require the windshield wipers. Then, under umbrellas, we walked together to the cottage. Nakamura-san stood under his umbrella, waiting for us by the door.

"Good afternoon," I said amiably, starting off on the right foot.

"Hello." He said without a tone of defensiveness. "Dr. Seiko says you have letters from Father Harrington that were sent to your mother just before he left. I would like very much to see them unless you feel they are too personal."

"They are personal as far as my mother and Harrington-san are concerned, but it was a long time ago and he is so important to the three of us, I don't think he would mind if we shared them."

"Shall we go in out of the rain?" He produced a ring of keys and unlocked the cottage. We closed our umbrellas and entered the small house. Removing our shoes in the vestibule, we stepped up onto the tatami floor where slippers were lined up for the use of visitors. The room was about fifteen feet square with a low black enameled table in the center. Beneath it was the pit for the hibachi that would have been laid with charcoal in the winter months to keep my father's feet and legs warm as he sat at the table. A tall cabinet, like an armoire, was against one wall with a chest of drawers next to it. Against another wall was a low desk-table with a drawer, lamp, telephone, and tray for pens and pencils. All the furnishings were matched, black enamel. Pillows were placed in front of the desk and around the center table with extras stacked in a corner. A prie-dieu stood in another corner facing a wall on which a crucifix was hung. The two remaining walls were shoji blinds that I assumed opened to the narrow catwalk surrounding the house. Daylight, such as it was, coming through the shoji screens cast a pale tint of pearl on all the contents. Rain drummed steadily on the roof.

"I'm sorry if I sounded overly protective of Father Harrington's cottage on Saturday. This has all come about suddenly and it's taken me time to adjust to the prospects of him having a relative.

He was so much a part of this community it's hard to picture him as having a life beyond Japan."

"It's been sudden for me too, discovering who my father really was. Then, having tracked him all the way to Zushi, I let my feelings get the best of me when you wouldn't let me into the cottage. I apologize for being impetuous."

We nodded slightly to one another; the apologies were accepted.

"Shall we sit at the table and read the letters?" Dr. Seiko suggested.

"Nakamura-san," I said, "would you mind first looking for any letters my mother might have sent back to Taylor, perhaps in his desk?" Again he hesitated, but a glance from Seiko-san sent him reluctantly to the desk. And there they were, neatly stacked in one corner of the drawer, two letters postmarked Marblehead, Massachusetts. He handed them to me and we sat down.

"If it's too cool," Nakamura-san said, "there's an electric heater in the closet, or I could have the charcoal lit in the hibachi."

"I'll just keep my coat on," I said, "but the hibachi would be nice."

He went to the phone, said something in Japanese, and returned.

I arranged the four letters by date and laid them on the table. "Shall I read them aloud?"

"Please," said the doctor.

With trembling fingers I removed the first letter from its envelope, knowing that both my father and my mother had touched it and held it in their hands.

April 23, 1973

Dear Becky:

I've debated now for a month whether or not I should write you. I don't want to stir up the past but the most extraordinary thing has happened and I must share it with you.

Last month I met your daughter, Taylor Hayakawa. What a lovely person. I was substituting at Christ Church in Yokohama for a week and she introduced herself to me. I also met your granddaughter, Rebecca. You're fortunate to have such a beautiful family.

Since the war I've been director of an orphanage and school

here in Zushi, Japan. I've never married, but you might say these children are my family.

Actually, I knew you had a daughter. After the war I spent some time in a veterans' hospital in St. Louis recovering from malaria and getting my head straightened out. I called you one evening at the hotel and a desk clerk said you and your daughter were having dinner with your in-laws, the DeWolfs. So that's how I knew.

I'm glad things worked out well for you and I hope, after all these years, that you and your family are happy.

I'll send this to the hotel, hoping they'll forward it to your home.

Please write. I'd love to hear from you. Do you still have "White Wings"?

Sincerely,
Taylor Harrington

I set the letter down as carefully as if it were a piece of Dresden china. So he did try to reach my mother, I thought. How different their lives might have been if she'd been home that evening. I tried to imagine mother reading this letter, sitting by the front window as she always did with the day's mail in her lap. My eyes moistened. It was too much to conceive. Discarding the thought with a shake of my head, I picked up the second letter, my mother's answer to his.

May 1, 1973

Dear Taylor,

I knew you were alive. I searched for you for years. First the army said you were dead. Then a man who was with you in the Kawasaki prison camp said you had died there, but I've always known you were alive.

After Jimmy died in November, 1941, I wrote you a long letter telling you about his death and that I was pregnant. I told you the whole story, but the letter was returned, undelivered. I wrote other letters after the war started but apparently you received none of them. After the war, I went to San Francisco and met a nurse who knew you before the Japanese attacked, and another man who was on the prison ship with you. They told me how terribly hard it was for all of you during the war.

When I read the part in your letter about your calling me from St. Louis, I cried for an hour. I'm crying again as I write this. If only I had been there. If only I could have talked with you and explained all that had happened, our lives might have been different. Now so much time has passed and we are so far apart— our lives so different. How strange you should be in Japan. I hated the Japanese for what they did to you, and now you're living among them and you call them your family.

You ask about "White Wings." Yes, she's fine. Your parents came for the boat after you were reported killed. I hid her in Aggie's basement and Karl Kramer, who had started working for the Harbormaster, told them it had been picked up by two men from Long Island. We lied. If I couldn't have you, I was going to have your boat. I sail her a lot and always on June 25th to remember our time together. Each time I take her out, she tells me you are alive and one day will return.

I might as well be honest with you. I love you, Taylor. I've never stopped loving you. There's never been anyone else. And you'd better sit down to read this—my daughter, Taylor, is your daughter also. I explained all this in the letter I wrote that wasn't delivered. When Jimmy was killed in North Africa I thought the door had opened for us to be married. I was pregnant with Taylor but let everybody think Jimmy was the father while I waited for you to say we could be married. I was ready to fly to the Philippines and didn't care if they knew I'd lied to them. When the war started and the letter was returned I didn't know what to do. Finally Taylor was born and I let the lie about her father go on and on. I'm so ashamed. I didn't even tell her. She still thinks Jimmy's her father.

Now you know. You may not want to write again, but at least I've finally told the truth. I thank God you're alive. I knew you were. It's a good thing your name, Taylor, worked for either a boy or a girl, because I was determined to name our baby Taylor.

Your letter was addressed to the hotel which burned down in 1957, a fire which also killed my mother and father. I took the insurance and bought an inn on Pleasant Street. A person at the post office must have seen my name and forwarded the letter. The address of the inn is on the envelope.

I'm glad you told me you tried to reach me when you were in the hospital. I was afraid you'd forgotten all about me.

Here I am, fifty-two years old, talking with you as if I were twenty. I guess I'm a foolish old woman obsessed with a love that never could be. Waiting for you has been my life.

Whatever you feel about me, please write. Please let me know. I've waited so long.

You're alive. I've always known it.

I love you, Becky

The three of us sat around the table, not speaking, eyes down as if in prayer. Tears streamed down my face.

We were startled by a voice outside the door. *"Gomen kudasai."*

Nakamura-san got up and opened the door. A man in a dark blue maintenance uniform brought in a brazier of hot coals and we all stood aside so he could put them in the pit beneath the table. When we sat back down, Nakamura-san placed a futon quilt over the tabletop and all of us tucked it around our laps. Soon the heat of the charcoal was warming our bodies.

"Do you want me to go on?"

I could see them struggling with the embarrassment of peering into someone's personal life and the desire to know more about Father Harrington. Heads down, they nodded almost imperceptibly, and I picked up the third letter.

May 9, 1973

Dear Becky,

Your letter arrived this morning. I confess that when I wrote I secretly hoped we might be able to reestablish a friendship, but what you've said in your letter bowls me over. You raise thoughts and feelings in me long laid to rest.

I wish I'd called you back again and again from the hospital until I reached you. Our lives would have been different. I can say that now, but then I was so broken in spirit the slightest hint you were still married to Jimmy was more than I could bear. I backed off, pulled into my shell, and when I was well enough, crept off to this side of the world.

You say you still love me. Your words are more than I can comprehend. Not that I haven't thought about you. Sometimes, when I see couples walking arm in arm, I think of us, but I'm quick to put the thoughts away. The pain of remembering is too much. Except for once a year. Some time ago I bought a boat which I named "White Wings II." I sail it in the bay off Zushi usually with staff members or students. But on June 26th, that's June 25th in Marblehead, I pack a picnic lunch and a year's worth of memories of you, and sail out alone. I drink some wine and think of you standing at the mast with the wind in your hair, and I cry. Then, after a couple of hours I come back to wait for another year. Sick, isn't it?

Now you say Taylor is our daughter. I'm deeply moved. We joked about our names being the same, but I wouldn't even let myself dream she might be mine. I wasn't as naive as you may have thought, though. I knew we were taking a chance, and I didn't care. I don't blame you for saying she was Jimmy's. With him dead and me missing it would have made it impossible for you to do otherwise.

As I reread what I've written, I see I'm skirting the issue. You say you love me. I believe you love the person I once was, but I'm no longer he. I'm fifty-six years old and look sixty-six. I'm skinny, balding and in bad health. I wear glasses. And I've finally managed to extinguish those feelings I only remember as sexual desire. I love my work as a teacher and priest and know that the staff and children here think fondly of me.

And yet there is a part of me that would cast caution to the wind. When I think about you, so gay and free, so determined to get what you want from life, I could get on a plane and fly to you in a minute. But it's all a dream. We're no longer a couple of twenty-year-old kids, with our lives before us, able to grow up together, molding ourselves around each other. We're old fogies, set in our ways, chasing a fantasy.

I don't know. Maybe our fantasy is what is real and the world around us the dream. Or maybe it's all real, our lives today and the love we had.

Becky, if I were to come to Marblehead, we could at least see each other and talk. As I wrote that, the old fear came back that I'm a broken man whom no one would want, those feelings I had when I called you from the hospital. If I were to come I'm afraid I'd fall in love again, and I'm not sure I could take it if you didn't want me. But the truth is, I long to see you, and seeing you again is worth the risk. If you really do want me to come, I would regret it the rest of my life if I didn't.

Maybe we'd just talk over old times, decide what we should say to our daughter about me being her father and then say good-bye. This alone would be a good thing. Let me know what you think. It's been a while since you wrote. Maybe you've had second thoughts.

Love, Taylor

I placed the letter on the table as Nakamura-san looked up. "You *are* his daughter. I apologize again."

"Thank you." I looked at him, my half brother by adoption, and smiled. "I'll read the last letter."

May 18, 1973

Dearest Taylor,

Come. Come now. Get on a plane and come here. I'm glad you're fifty-six because I'm fifty-two. We'll be old together.

I'll save you a room in my inn so you'll have a place to stay. I'm not going to send you away no matter what. I've waited too long and searched too far for you.

Don't be afraid if I say I love you. I can't help it, I just do. But I won't force it on you. Come and we will talk and get to know each other again.

Telephone me and tell me when you will be here. I can't wait for a letter. But please try to be here before June 25th so we can sail together on *White Wings*. Do you remember the song? She's bringing you home to me.

With all my love, Becky

"So he went to Massachusetts," Dr. Seiko said. "Tell me, Mrs. Hayakawa, what do you think happened?"

"I was in Japan at the time, but what I was told is this. My mother went sailing in the boat called *White Wings* on June twenty-fifth. The weather was bad and got worse while she was out. When she didn't return, the Coast Guard was called and boats sent out. Late that night *White Wings* was driven onto the rocks at the mouth

of Marblehead Harbor. There was no one aboard. If Taylor Harrington was in Marblehead, no one knew about it. If he was on the boat, he was never found, nor was my mother."

"Perhaps he was with your mother and they were lost together," Nakamura-san said pensively.

"We may never know for sure," I said.

We sat for a few moments and then Nakamura-san got up. "Our school chorus is giving a concert later this week and they are rehearsing this afternoon. I must go. If you'd like to hear them, Mrs. Hayakawa, come to the auditorium in about an hour. They're very good."

"I'd like that very much. Thank you."

The doctor rose also. "I too must be going. It's been a pleasure meeting you, and if you should find out any more about Father Harrington's visit to Marblehead, please let me know." We shook hands and he headed for the door. "Why don't you stay here until the children are ready? It's a very restful place."

"Thank you. I will."

When they were gone, I slid back the shoji screen and, leaning on a pillow, looked out at the garden and school lawn. The sound of rain on the roof was mesmerizing. Lines of water ran from the eave like a beaded curtain, falling into puddles just beyond the cat-walk. White stones in the garden, raked into a swirling pattern around a black volcanic rock, glistened. Cherry blossoms overhanging the rock danced and bobbed as drops of rain hit them.

This is where he lived, I mused. This was the scene he saw when it rained. I wished I could have known him as my own father and not just as Father Harrington. I put my head down on the pillow, pulled a futon quilt over my shoulders, and was either close to falling asleep or was in the process of being awakened when I heard the voices of the children rehearsing. I got up, straightened my clothes, stopped at the door to put on my shoes, and headed for the auditorium under my umbrella.

I tried to slip in quietly and take a seat in the rear but Nakamura-san saw me and invited me to come forward.

He spoke to the children in Japanese and I heard both my name and that of Father Harrington. Then the children all stood and applauded me.

"They are pleased to meet the daughter of our founder. Won't you please say something to them?" About thirty children, all ages, were standing in tiers on a raised platform, all smiling and watching me eagerly.

"I am pleased to be here with you and to see the school my father founded." Nakamura-san translated, and I continued. "It is very beautiful and I will always remember it." I sat down, he translated, and they applauded again.

Nakamura-san turned to me and said, "There is a song, like a school song, that we always sing at concerts. They will sing it for you now." With beaming faces and voices like crystal bells, they sang in English.

> *White wings, they never grow weary,*
> *They carry me cheerily over the sea;*
> *Night comes, I long for my dearie,*
> *I'll spread out my white wings and sail home to thee!*

PART FOUR

⁓

Rebecca Hayakawa

⁓

43

Slow down, I told myself, maybe you can lose them. Lingering in front of a camera store window, I watched the reflection of my cohorts move ahead of me down the busy street. One day of sales calls and already I was tired of them. Or maybe it was just the sales calls I was tired of. Still a week and a half to go. For three of them, this was their first trip to Tokyo and they couldn't see enough. The other two, like myself, were old hands at Japan. Wandering down one of the streets in the Rapungi section, jam-packed with midscale restaurants and nightclubs, we were part of a river of young Japanese and foreign visitors looking for food, drinks, and a good time. Horns blared as taxis inched their way through the bustling mass of people filling the sidewalks and overflowing onto the street. Entranceways glittered with colorful neon and flashing strobes. The smell of shrimp tempura, beef sukiyaki, spicy Indian cuisine, and even American hamburgers filled the air, enticing passersby to come in and satisfy their hunger. I had seen it all before, many times, and my interest was growing thin.

"God, Rebecca," Reggie called back to me. "Can't you keep up?" Reginald Davis, my two-week lover from our last sales mission, the same Reggie who was desolate when he told me he couldn't leave his wife and two children but would be happy to keep me on as his girlfriend, now walked arm in arm with one of the new people, an attractive young woman who had recently joined the international sales team of the New York Markham

Hotel. She looked at me over her shoulder with a smirk that said, I win, you lose. Good luck, I thought. He's all yours.

I managed to let more and more people squeeze between me and my associates as I stopped to read signs or peer into the darkened interior of old-style Japanese restaurants. At the entrance to an arcade filled with raucous teenagers playing shoot-em-up video games were two mirrors, one a regular mirror and one a wavy mirror like you see in a carnival. If I stood up close to the wavy one, my head and waist were tiny and my chest and legs like balloons. When I backed up I had a huge head and looked very pregnant. I smiled and moved to the regular mirror where I saw a young Japanese-American in a colorful silk blouse and baggy silk slacks who obviously had a flair for exotic clothes. Her wide-set eyes were soft yet tired and her full lips seemed to struggle with the fatigue in her face to produce a smile. Who are you? I asked silently. She didn't answer but we exchanged identical frowns. Then I said, I'll tell you who you are. You're your own person and don't let them lead you around. With that, we both lifted our heads and smiled.

Ambling along, I found myself behind a couple carrying a little girl in a backpack strapped to her father. As her head lolled from side to side, she smiled at me. I smiled back. She giggled. I giggled. Then I opened my eyes into large O's. Her eyebrows rose. I scrunched up my nose and showed my upper teeth. Her nose wiggled slightly. I'd found a friend.

"See ya later." Reggie's voice came back to me, barely audible against a blast of country-and-western music. "You know where we're going." He and the others disappeared into the swirling crowd. Yes, I knew. They would turn right at the next corner, go into a long, narrow bar with seating in the rear. After a few drinks, someone will pick up the karaoke microphone and perform an embarrassing imitation of Elvis Presley singing "You Ain't Nothin' But a Hound Dog." After an hour or two, they'll all leave for another bar that will look just the same. Have fun, I said silently. I've better ways to spend my time. I headed for my hotel, a long, hot bath, and a good P. D. James mystery.

That afternoon when I'd arrived back at my hotel room, the message light on the phone was blinking. I returned Mom's call after six, as she requested, getting the news about the four letters and her meeting with Nakamura-san and Dr. Seiko in Grand-father's cottage. She said she was returning to Tokyo in the morning and flying home on Wednesday.

"I've got some free time tomorrow afternoon," I said. "Let's have lunch."

"Good. There's so much to tell."

"I want to hear it, too. And I've got something for you and someone I want you to meet."

"Rebecca," she said warily, "it'd better not be Tad."

"God, Mother. Give me some credit. I wouldn't do that."

"Who, then? A new boyfriend?"

"Nothing like that. It's a business prospect for you. I'll tell you at lunch."

I picked her up at the Ginza Tobu Hotel and we went around the corner to a small sushi bar. Between dishes of fish, shrimp, octopus, and seaweed wrapped around rice stuffed with spicy roots, Mom handed me the letters one by one and I read them. It was eerie holding a piece of paper my grandfather's hand had touched, seeing how his hand shook as he scratched his pen across the page. When I came to the part in the first letter, written after he'd met Mom and me, where he said we were part of a beautiful family, I stopped.

"What?" Mother asked.

"It's strange. I think I've always felt more Japanese than American. Going to school in Marblehead, the other kids consid-ered me Japanese because I didn't look like them. I knew I was half and half, but the first six years in Japan with Dad, and my Japanese grandparents, and all the pictures on the walls of their parents, seemed so ... solid. Like a strong foundation. I knew Grandmother Becky, but I saw her only three times. That's where my American relatives stopped. Jimmy DeWolf was no more than a picture of a man in a uniform. He never seemed real. Hah." I laughed. "He wasn't. Now I have a real American grandfather."

I read the second letter, where Grandmother said she'd cried about the phone call she never received. I cried with her. Mom looked at me compassionately, knowing the part of the letter I was reading.

"He didn't run out on us after all," she said, and I nodded.

I finished the letters and looked at Mom. "All these years his letters were tucked under the deck of *White Wings* waiting to be found." I reflected for a moment. "It's a good thing Matthew saw *White Wings* in your garage and kept at you until you let him rebuild her."

"It's . . . more than that," Mom said. "I think *White Wings* found Matthew. I think she waited in our garage for twenty years until he came along, then spoke to him. I saw it. It was weird. And you saw it the second time, when he found the bullet hole."

"Yeah. But why Matthew?"

"Who knows? Maybe he's an unusually sensitive person." She paused. "Whatever the reason, Matthew wouldn't be rebuilding *White Wings* if there wasn't some strange connection between the two of them."

"At least we know Taylor Harrington was your father and that he came back to Marblehead."

"I wonder if he really did."

"I've thought that, too. I'm surprised Aggie didn't say anything about it. Either she's holding out on us again or she didn't know."

"But why would Becky have kept it a secret? She told Aggie everything else."

"In the last letter, Grandmother asked him to telephone. Maybe he called and said he wasn't coming after all."

"No, because Dr. Seiko said they found out he flew to L.A."

"We need to talk to Aggie again. Can you wait to see her until the end of next week? I want to be there too."

"I think I'll keep myself busy when I get home." I could tell by the look in her eyes she was thinking of Sam.

"Oh, one more thing," she said. "Would you call Dr. Seiko again and find out the date of Taylor's flight to L.A.? It would give us an idea of when he arrived in Marblehead, if he did."

I said I'd call the next day.

The sushi maker gave us each a dish with two pieces of sliced raw tuna laid over a ridge of rice. I rolled my eyes. "If I eat this, I'll burst. But I can't resist." I added more green mustard to my soy sauce, picked up the tuna and rice with my chopsticks, and dipped it in the sauce. Two bites and it was gone.

Over coffee, Mom said, "What do you want to tell me and who am I going to meet?"

"Yesterday, I was calling on Holiday Tours and the assistant manager asked me if I knew of any New England inns that would like to be in a new travel package they're planning. I told him I could do him one better than that and introduce him to a New England innkeeper."

"Me?"

"Right."

"I'd like to talk with him, but you know we're pretty well booked up in the summertime." She didn't sound enthusiastic.

"How about the shoulder season? Spring and fall?"

"Well, it might be a help in the spring, April and May, or the last of October after the foliage season."

"Talk to him anyway. He'd be interested in your slant on his idea. Who knows, something might come of it."

In the cab on the way to the offices of Holiday Tours, I told her about the assistant manager, Ken Shimizu. "I want you to meet him. He's an old friend—known him since I started coming to Japan four years ago. A really nice guy."

"Hmmm. Do I hear some romantic interest here?"

"No. There was once, that first year. He'd gone to Berkeley for college and missed American women—he looked on me as an American—and I liked the idea of dating a Japanese who wasn't hung up on Japanese customs. We saw each other when he came to the States for field inspections and when I'd come over here for sales calls. Then we drifted apart and he fell in love with a neat woman in his office. He introduced her to me a couple of years ago and she is a dear. They were married last year. I went to the wedding. We're still good friends. You'll like him. He's more American than an American, but he's still nice."

We were ushered into a conference room with interior windows looking out across a sea of desks and several young men and women busy at computers. Green tea arrived a minute before Ken Shimizu, who bounded into the room with a familiarity unlike most Japanese. I introduced them and he said he was honored to meet the mother of one of his best friends. He and Mom then exchanged business cards.

"Please let's not be formal. Call me Ken."

"And my name is Taylor."

We sat down. "Show Mom the pictures of the new baby, Ken. She's so cute." Ken produced three photographs and Mom oohed and aahed like I hoped she would.

He put away the pictures and we settled down to business. He told Mom about his idea for a travel package that would allow individuals, couples, or families to book inns in New England, and asked her about her inn—the number of rooms, facilities, meals, security. As Mom answered his questions, he nodded and made notes. Then he asked if she thought other New England inns would be interested in his idea.

"This would take some checking. I could write the various associations."

I could see Mom's interest didn't match Ken's excitement, especially when he said, "Of course, if we guaranteed bookings for the shoulder season, we'd want to have a commitment from you for rooms in the summer as well."

"That sounds fair, but I doubt many innkeepers would be willing to give up their regular summer visitors for an untested program."

This seemed to bring the discussion to an end and we left with Mom promising, "I will look into it and let you know."

In the taxi on the way back to her hotel I said, "I think you're missing a good opportunity, Mom."

"Do you have any idea how difficult it would be to line up innkeepers for a program like this? We're too independent."

"Stubborn, is more like it. And narrow."

"Whoa there. Don't get mad at me. I'm just telling it like it is."

"I'm sorry. I still think this has some possibilities."

"But the amount of time, Rebecca! I couldn't devote the time— or the energy, for that matter—to setting it up. I've got an inn to run." We drove in silence for a few blocks, then Mom said, "Why don't you do it?"

"Me? I've got a job. Such as it is."

Mom looked at me. "You don't sound very happy with it."

"Just bored . . . and maybe a little unhappy. I can't see where it's going. Maybe, in a few years, I could be director of sales and marketing for one of the Markham hotels. But is that what I want? It would mean a lot of transfers. A couple of years here, a couple there. No chance to settle down. Oh well," I said, squeezing her hand, "don't worry about me. I'll get over it."

I let Mom off at her hotel, reminding her not to tackle Aggie until I got home, and took the cab to meet my sales group for a three o'clock appointment. Before joining them, I called Ken again and said I wanted to talk more about his travel package. In his usual un-Japanese fashion, he suggested I come to his apartment after work for dinner.

That evening Ken met me at the door and brought me into the living room where his wife, Kimiko, aglow with motherhood, was breast-feeding little Akino-chan.

"Hi, Rebecca," Kimiko said. "I'm glad you could come."

"I had to see the baby. Kimiko," I gushed, "she's beautiful."

Akino-chan's round face was pressed against her mother's breast as her little mouth worked frantically at the nipple. Miniature fingers grasped a button on her mother's blouse and hung on for dear life.

"Isn't she big?" Ken said. "She's put on eight pounds since birth."

"You two make a beautiful baby."

"Thank you, Rebecca-san," Kimiko said, blushing.

Soon the baby had stopped sucking and lay fully asleep in her mother's arms. "Would you like to hold her?" Kimiko asked.

"I'd love to, but I'm not good at it."

"It's easy. Here. Just cradle her in your arm and hold her head in your hand. There. You've got it."

I looked down at Akino-chan asleep in my arms. I could feel the heat of her body against mine, the pressure of her head against my breast. She yawned a great big yawn and blinked open her eyes. Oh-oh, I thought, she's going to know I'm not her mother. Instead, she closed her eyes again and began nuzzling me, deciding it was my turn.

"I don't think she's done," I said, embarrassed. "You'd better take her again." They laughed as I handed the baby back to Kimiko.

Kimiko put Akino-chan in her crib and went to the kitchen to finish dinner preparations. The apartment was very small, so a pass-through from the kitchen to the dining area next to the living room allowed us to include Kimiko in our conversation.

"Kimiko has been helping me with the new travel package while she's home on maternity leave," Ken told me. "She's gathered maps and brochures, but we really need someone to call on the innkeepers. I'm sorry your mother wasn't more interested. She would have been perfect."

"It's more a matter of time. Running an inn is a full-time job."

"Do you know anyone who might be able to help us?" Kimiko said from the kitchen.

"That's what I wanted to talk to you about. I still have some vacation time left and could take a week when I go home. I could talk with several innkeepers about your idea and see if there's enough interest to pursue it further." I saw Ken's eyes brighten. "The problem is, innkeeping is usually a family-run business. They're very conservative and independent."

"But you'll try?"

"I'll try, but don't hope for much."

"And what if there is some interest in the idea? Would you stay on as our agent in New England?"

"Me? I've got a job," I said for the second time in five hours.

"But you'd do so well, and we'd make a good team—you in the States and Kimiko and I over here."

"Kimiko?" I appealed to the kitchen. "Your husband's badgering me."

"I don't understand badgering. What is that?"

"He's pushing me. Pushing me to be your agent."

"Will you?" she badgered.

The next evening I pampered myself with dinner in my hotel room and a long hot bath. At eight o'clock I stretched out on the bed and flicked the TV from one channel to another. Nothing. Then, on impulse, I reached for the phone and dialed the States. On the third ring, it was answered. I could hear someone fumbling with the receiver.

"Hello?" a voice said sleepily.

"Hi, Matthew. Did I wake you?"

"Yeah. Who's this?"

"Rebecca."

"Rebecca? Are you home?"

"No. Still in Japan. Sorry I woke you. I thought you got up about six."

"I do. Wait a minute. Let me turn off the alarm before it goes off. There. What time is it there?"

"Eight in the evening."

"Are you okay?"

"I'm all right. Just bored. How's *White Wings* coming along?"

"Great. Well, pretty good. I was working on her last night, dropping the keel off the keelson. A couple of the big keel bolts were sheared and the rest were bent. We'll have to get them specially made in a machine shop."

"Is that hard to do?"

"No, but it'll be a while before they can get at it."

"Oh. That's too bad."

Pause.

"Are you sure you're all right?" he asked.

"Yeah. I guess so."

"You don't sound all right. Is Reggie there?"

"He's here. Got himself a new girlfriend. They're probably out at some bar right now."

"Is that the problem?"

"Absolutely not. She can have him."

"Good for you." I could hear a yawn. "How did it go with finding your grandfather?"

"Great. Mom can tell you all about it. She'll be home this afternoon, your time. But I hope you'll wait. I want to tell you myself."

"Okay. I won't ask her."

"Heard anything from Miranda?"

"Yeah. She called a couple of days ago. Broke up with that guy. She wants me to come down this weekend."

"Are you going?"

"No. Told her I had to work on the boat."

"Really!"

"Yeah." Pause. "When are you coming home?"

"Home?"

"Yeah. Marblehead."

44

The sudden change in speed and engine pitch as the landing flaps were lowered woke me. I was leaning on my right hand with my elbow propped against the window. My hand was asleep at the wrist and my neck so stiff I could hardly lift my head. As the wheels clunked into position I looked out the jet's window and saw the small islands dotting Boston's outer harbor, the old Boston Lighthouse, and the striped water tower on the hill in Winthrop sweep past beneath me. Rapidly the bay rose to meet us as if we were planning a water landing. Then, just in time, the end of the runway appeared, the wheels bumped down, and we were on the ground at Logan International Airport.

Matthew had offered to meet me and drive me home to Marblehead, but that was days ago when we'd talked on the phone. I wondered if he would remember. In a way I hoped he'd forgotten. I was too tired for a joyful homecoming. Also, I looked like hell. Twenty hours of travel without benefit of shower, sleep, or a chance to put on makeup had turned me gray. And I was discouraged. Earlier in the trip, before my brain atrophied and I could still think, I'd done a pro-forma on the potential income as an agent for Holiday Tours. It looked as though I would have to line up at least a hundred inns to get the same income I was currently earning at the Markham. There was no way I could do that. What ever made me think I could? Shit! I wished I'd never thought of the idea.

Head down, toting my heavy carry-on bag, I followed the crowd through the jetway and into the waiting room.

There he was, waving to me. "Rebecca!" he called. "Over here!" Suddenly his smile, like a jolt of caffeine, lifted my spirits.

"Hi, Matthew," I said. "You remembered."

"Sure. Let me take your bag."

I slipped it off my shoulder and let it drop. I thought he was reaching for the strap, but instead he put his arms around me and gave me a hug. Not being much of a touching person, I tried to remain stiff, but I was too exhausted. I slumped into the circle of his arms. It felt good.

With my head against his chest I could smell fresh-cut pine on his denim jacket. He must have been working on *White Wings* before he came to the airport. As I backed away I could see traces of sawdust clinging to his jeans. I glanced up at his face, so boyish-looking in spite of his needing a shave. God, but he's comfortable to be with, I thought. I'd take his gentleness and sincerity any day over the confident sophistication of some of my male coworkers. I hugged him again.

"Thanks for coming," I mumbled against his warm shoulder. Then, leaning my head back, I said, "This is the first time I've returned from a business trip and someone's met me at the airport."

"No kidding. I would think there'd always be someone to meet you—roommates, boyfriends." He picked up my carry-on and we started down the corridor toward baggage.

"You don't know this business. Coming home is one more part of a lonely, boring job."

"Well, I'm glad you're home." He put his right arm around me as we walked, while my heavy bag, hanging from his left shoulder, bounced his hip against mine at each step.

After an interminable wait of twenty minutes, during which I answered his probing questions about the trip with one-word responses—yes, no—we retrieved my suitcase and went to the Central Garage, third level, to his car. By the time we'd fought our way through the traffic leaving the airport, my eyes were closing and my head nodding.

"I'm sorry," I groaned. "Guess I'm not much company."

"Why not lie down and take a nap?" He reached into the

backseat and found a pillow which he put over the divider between the two front seats.

"I'll take you up on that." I loosened my seat belt and lay down.

"Close your eyes and relax. We've got at least a forty-minute drive in this traffic."

I closed my eyes. Somewhere along the way I was awakened as he slammed on the brakes and swore under his breath at another driver. In a minute we started again and I felt his leg move as he stepped on the accelerator. I realized my head was in his lap and he was stroking my forehead and temple. Too tired to move, I let him massage me back to sleep. In a minute, it seemed, I heard him say, "You're home."

The next day, Sunday, we gathered at Aggie's house for an early dinner. Mom and I had gone by to pick up Sam because the two of them were going to a show in Boston later that evening. We all contributed to the meal: Mom a tossed salad, Matthew three loaves of warmed French bread, Sam a half gallon of butter pecan ice cream, I a jug of white wine, and Aggie a large steaming pot of clam chowder.

"You were mean, Rebecca, to make us wait until you got back," Aggie said, actually looking a little hurt as she set the pot in the center of the table. "Your mom told me Taylor Harrington was in Japan after the war, but wouldn't say more. Said I had to wait for you to get home."

Mom nodded, pleased with herself for having resisted the temptation to tell all.

"Good for you, Mom."

"Did the letters I found help?" asked Matthew.

"Couldn't have done it without them," Mom said. "When we found the school he started and the place where he lived, his letters were the proof we needed that I was his daughter. Then they let us go through his private records where we found Becky's letters to him."

"Start from the beginning," Aggie said. "Tell us how you found the school."

Aggie ladled out the soup and I poured the wine as Mom began the story, starting from Christ Church on the Bluff in Yokohama. I chimed in with some details and the others asked questions. When Mom got to the part where Becky asked Taylor to call her about coming to Marblehead in June of 1973, the chowder and salad and bread were gone and Sam was scooping out ice cream for dessert.

"I wish you could have heard those children singing 'White Wings, they never grow weary,' " Mom said. "Becky had taught it to me when I was a little girl, but I had no idea what it meant to her—that it was her assurance Taylor would come back to her. I wept when they sang it."

"I've never heard it," I said. "Do you remember how it goes?"

"I'll never forget it."

"Let's sing it together," Aggie said.

"You know it, too?" Mom asked.

"Sure. Becky and I used to sing it when she'd take me sailing."

The two of them looked at each other shyly and, searching for a common key, began the song.

> *White Wings, they never grow weary,*
> *They carry me cheerily over the sea;*
> *Night comes, I long for my dearie,*
> *I'll spread out my white wings and sail home to thee!*

" 'And sail home to thee,' " Matthew repeated. "Do you think he did?"

Mom cocked her head. "That's what we want to ask you, Aggie. Did he sail home to Becky? If anybody would know, you would. She told you everything."

All our eyes were on Becky's old friend. Finally she spoke. "I don't know. I never saw him if he was here, but that doesn't mean he wasn't."

"Can you tell us anything about that time?" Mom asked. "Was there any clue that she'd found Taylor?"

"What I remember about that time is this. First, you, Taylor—" She stopped abruptly. "Too darned many Taylors around here. You'd reached the end of your rope with your husband and were ready to call it quits. Becky talked a lot about that. She was still convinced you'd married Tad to spite her."

"There's some truth in that. By the time I graduated from high school I hardly knew her. She'd grown so distant and morose. I felt deserted."

Aggie continued. "When your marriage fell apart, she talked a lot about you. She was worried sick and wanted you to come home. She loved you. Don't forget, you were Taylor's baby and that meant everything to her."

"I know that now," Mom said sadly. "Wish I'd known it then." After a moment she asked, "What else do you remember? Any hint that my father was coming?"

"Not directly, but this much I know for sure. All of a sudden Becky seemed to come out of her depression. It had become so much a part of her that it showed in her face. Her skin was pale, her eyes dark, and she let her hair go. Then one day, I think it was the beginning of June, she came here to the house. She looked like a new person. She'd had her hair done and was wearing makeup— and in a dress instead of her old jeans. 'What's come over you?' I asked. She said something like, 'Oh, nothing. It's springtime, and I'm happy.' Well, she took me out to lunch and talked about getting *White Wings* into the water, giving the inn a coat of paint, and starting a garden."

"But if this had to do with Taylor coming," I asked, "why didn't she tell you? Why keep it a secret?"

"Yeah. That's what bothers me. I'm sure she'd have told me."

"I think I might know," Sam said. He adjusted his glasses and leaned back in his chair next to Mom's. His cardigan sweater opened across his round chest as he squared his shoulders. "From what you've told me, Taylor, she'd built up so many lies around her relationship with your father that she wanted to be sure how he felt toward her before she told anybody—even you, Aggie. Don't forget, the money she'd gotten from the DeWolfs for your support, Taylor, was obtained under false pretenses. And there were still people around Marblehead who remembered the Reverend Taylor Harrington and the rumors about his affair with Becky. Maybe she wanted to be sure where she stood with Taylor before she let a soul know he was coming back."

"That makes sense," I said. "I know that if I want something, really want it, I'm afraid if I talk about it, I won't get it. And I try not to think too much about it. You know, get my hopes too high."

"Well, Becky was in a good mood about something," Aggie continued. "In the restaurant she talked with people she hadn't said boo to in years. Walking back here we ran into Karl Kramer and she said hi as nice as you please. 'Bout knocked him over. Then she asked him to help her launch *White Wings* the next weekend. Good old Karl, the bastard, misread her intentions and invited her to take a ride in his new boat after they got *White Wings* in the water. He'd just bought this big expensive cruiser. Becky, like I said, was riding on a cloud and agreed to go out with him. I told her that was stupid, but she said she'd treated him pretty hard over the years and maybe she should give him a chance."

"How did it work out?" Matthew asked.

"He tried to rape her."

"He what?" I was thunderstruck.

"You heard me. And that's the other thing I remember about that time. I've never told a soul. Becky made me promise not to. Said she'd put Kramer in his place and it was over. But now, now that Becky's gone, I think you should all know the kind of man Kramer really is."

"What happened?" Mom asked, a pained expression on her face.

"The three of us got the boat out of our basement and launched it. Then he and Becky took off in his big cruiser. It's the one he still has, *My Turn*. Some name, huh? Becky said they went way out to one of the farthest islands where he dropped anchor and went below. She thought he'd gone to the head, but after a while when he didn't come out, she called down to him. 'Come on down,' he said. 'Got something I want to show you.' She went below to this big cabin where he'd opened a bottle of rum and was sitting at the table in the galley. She said he poured her some rum and told her he was glad she finally decided to be his friend after all he'd done for her. She didn't like the way things were going, but said that she did appreciate his help in getting the boat launched.

" 'Not that,' he said. 'I mean the cover-up job I did for you back in the forties so you could steal *White Wings*.' Now Becky was scared," Aggie said. "She got up and moved toward the hatch but he reached out and took hold of her arm.

" 'Come on, Becky,' he said. 'You owe me.'

" 'I don't owe you a goddamned thing,' Becky said.

" 'You owe me and I'm going to collect.' Well," Aggie continued, "he stood up and grabbed her blouse and ripped off the buttons, but she managed to kick him in the crotch and push him back onto a bunk. Then she looked around the cabin for something to defend herself. She began pulling open drawers in the galley looking for a knife. That's when she found his revolver. She pointed it at him but he just laughed and came toward her. 'You don't know how to shoot a gun, Becky,' he said, and Becky pulled the trigger. She told me the roar of the gun in that cabin sounded like a cannon."

"Did she hit him?" Sam asked.

"No, but she scared him good. He knew she meant business. She made him go up on deck, keeping the gun on him, and told him to take her back into port."

There was a general sigh of relief as we thought Aggie had finished her story.

"But that's not the end of it," she said. "If Becky'd stopped there, things might have cooled down. But not Becky. Having the gun pointed at him, she went a little further. She asked him about the gun, and why he needed it, and about his new boat, where he got the money for it.

"Kramer yelled something like, 'None o' your damn business,' so then Becky confronts him with the rumors about him running dope. Kramer about goes crazy with that.

" 'That's bullshit, all bullshit,' he shouts."

We were all on the edge of our chairs, spellbound by Aggie's story.

"But Becky wasn't done with him. She said something that may or may not have been true.

" 'I saw you out there last year,' she said, 'in your boat meeting up with that yacht. If you ever try to lay a hand on me again, I'll go to the police.' Apparently she hit the nail on the head because Kramer exploded and started yelling, 'If you ever say a word about that, you slut, I swear I'll kill ya.' Becky just laughed in his face.

"When they tied up there were people on the dock, so she felt it was safe to give him back his gun. She told him again he'd better watch himself. When he got the gun, he called her a lyin' whore. Said he'd get her one way or another so she'd better be careful every time she went out in *White Wings*. Then she came up here and told me the whole story."

"No wonder you hate him," Matthew said. "God, I feel stupid. Did he ever try it again?"

"I don't think so. At least, Becky never said. It was only a couple of weeks before she was lost in the storm."

"Did she say what kind of gun it was?" he asked.

"She didn't have to. It was his service revolver he had as harbormaster. A .38 police special. I've seen him with it on his belt."

"The bullet you found in *White Wings*," I said, gripping Matthew's arm. "Was it a .38 caliber?"

"Don't know yet. I left the slug with the gunsmith up in Maine. He was going to check it out and get back to me. I'll give him a call tomorrow."

"Does anyone else know about that bullet besides us?" Sam wondered.

"I haven't told anyone," Matthew said, looking around the table. We all shook our heads.

"Then I suggest we keep it that way."

I yawned. "It's been quite a night and I'd like to talk more, but I'm zonked out with jet lag. Let me help you clean up, Aggie, then I'm going off to bed."

"No. You go ahead. I don't mind."

"Are you sure you don't mind cleaning up?" Sam said. "Taylor and I had better get started if we want to make the curtain. We can drop you off on the way," he said, looking at me.

"No need," Matthew interposed. "I'll help clean up, then drive Rebecca back to the inn."

"Good," I said. "I'm not that far gone. I'll help too."

Mom and Sam left, and Matthew and I had the kitchen cleaned up in ten minutes. He drove me back to the inn and parked in front of the house. I remained in my seat looking out the front window.

"I wish I lived here in Marblehead. Tomorrow I've got to get up early and drive in to the hotel, spend the day writing reports and follow-up letters, and then go to my apartment in Back Bay." I turned to Matthew. "I'm tired of it. I know you think I lead this glamorous life, racing around the world, meeting exciting people, but it's not like that at all. Travel's boring." I put my hand on his. "And lonely. It was nice to have you meet me at the airport yesterday."

"I missed you. I've gotten used to the two of us working on the boat. I'm glad you're back."

"Wasn't this the weekend Miranda wanted you to come down to New York?"

"Actually it was last weekend, but when I said I couldn't go then, she asked for this weekend, too."

"I thought you and she hit it off. How come you didn't go?"

"I don't know. Didn't feel right about it. She's fun but—too young."

We sat quietly for a while. The hand I'd covered with mine moved up and over my hand. Thinking about my future, maybe even with Matthew in it, I said, "I want to quit my job, but I don't know what I'd do. I need to work. I've got some money from a trust fund from my father, but it's not enough. When I was in Japan I came up with this idea of representing a Japanese tour company here in New England and setting up tours to various inns. It might work but I don't think I could make ends meet."

"Would you move back to Marblehead?"

"That's one of the reasons I like the idea. I could get out of Boston and live here."

"Could you live with your mother in the inn?"

"Four months ago I'd have said no, but now I think we could do it."

"That would be great. You could work on your project during the day, and we could work together on the boat every evening."

"That's what you want, is it?" I laughed. "Somebody to help you finish *White Wings*. And I thought you might want me here because you like my company."

"I do. I do. It's just that I know you like *White Wings* and I wasn't sure you liked me."

I leaned over and kissed him on the cheek. "Try me."

His eyes opened wide.

I said, "See you tomorrow evening."

45

Entering by the side door of the Markham Hotel, I eased my way past several smartly dressed men and women in the lobby on their way to the coffee shop for breakfast or checking out, nodded a restrained good-morning to the desk clerks and the concierge and two bellhops, and ascended the stairs to the hotel business offices on the second floor. Partway up I looked back at the swirl of activity below. Four Japanese in Armani suits left the elevator and headed for the coffee shop, an English woman dressed in an outdated Givenchy suit and bedecked in colorful scarves waved to a friend coming in the front door, two Arabs in long white robes stood near the desk while an attendant settled their bill, and a black African in a caftan asked questions of the concierge. The world has come to Boston, I thought, and I had a share in making it happen. Maybe it's a good job after all.

I opened the clear glass door of Sales and Catering as I had done so many times over the last four years. Beyond the reception area against the inside wall were the desks of our sales and catering staff, separated by flowering plants and desk-high file cabinets. Against the opposite wall were the cubicles of the managers of international sales, domestic sales, convention sales, and catering. The international sales cubicle was mine. At the end of the aisle against an outside wall, which means they had windows, were two offices, one for the director of sales and one for the director of catering.

As I walked down the aisle I was surprised to see all the desks empty. Then I saw why. All the secretaries and staff people were in my cubicle arranging a bouquet of flowers. Approaching, I knew I was interrupting some kind of a surprise. It's not my birthday, I thought. What's going on?

"Rebecca. Hi," said Patty, the receptionist, a jonquil in one hand and a sprig of baby's breath in the other.

"Hi," I said expectantly.

"Hope you don't mind us using your desk to arrange the bouquet. Didn't know you'd be back today." Her receptionist voice, charming but impersonal, sent my excitement into a nosedive. Obviously, the bouquet was not for me. "It's Candace's first day as director of sales. She'll be here in a minute and we want to surprise her."

"At least you could have put a newspaper under the vase," I said with undisguised annoyance. "You're getting water all over my desk."

"Don't worry. We'll clean up." She and the others, ignoring me, went about their business of flower arranging as if I weren't there.

I sat on the edge of the desk across the aisle, exiled. What did she say? Candace's first day as director of sales? Candace? What the hell is that about? Has John left? God! I'm away for two weeks and there's a palace revolution.

"Oh, I forgot," Patty was saying, not bothering to look up. "Mr. Steiger said he wants to see you ASAP."

Her words hit me like an ax. "Be sure you clean that up when you're done," I said and headed for the general manager's office.

His secretary, Susan, a tall blonde in her mid-thirties, greeted me warmly, as if she'd been waiting all morning just for me. "Oh, hi, Rebecca. How was the trip?" And not waiting for an answer, "Just go on in. He's expecting you."

The door was ajar, barely, part of his cautious open-door policy, so I walked in. He was sitting at his oversized desk signing papers. Hans Steiger was at least six foot three, two hundred and twenty-five pounds, about fifty years old, with a face like chiseled rock, hair graying at the temples, and a strong German accent. A dueling scar from his days at Heidelberg would have been appropriate, but he didn't have one.

"Good morning, Rebecca," he said, not rising. "I hope you had a successful trip. Lots of new business from Japan, huh?"

"It was a good trip."

"Fine. Fine. Please sit down." He gestured to the sofa against the opposite wall. I sat, looking at him fifteen feet away. It was a safe distance for him, farther than I could reach. "Sooo, Rebecca. I guess you've heard John is gone, transferred to Atlanta?"

"I heard he was gone but I didn't know where."

"Yes. And Candace is the new director of sales and marketing." Without waiting for any comment from me, he hurried on. "Headquarters in Atlanta has ordered us to downsize. I've accomplished this by eliminating the managers and having the sales staff report to the two directors, sales and catering."

"But why Candace?" I said. "I've been here longer than she has, and, frankly, I've done a better job."

"Well, that's a matter of viewpoint. Please understand, I'm not saying you haven't done a good job. But the bulk of our business is domestic and that's where we're putting our emphasis. Anyway, international sales for the East Coast will be conducted out of headquarters in Atlanta."

"So I'm being demoted to a sales staff position?" I could feel my face burning and fought to keep my voice steady.

"Just relax, Rebecca, and let me finish. True, if you stay here you would be in a staff position limited to domestic sales. But there's an opening in San Francisco where they're still doing their own international. And Japan is their biggest market, as you know."

"And that's where you want me to go?"

"Not necessarily. You're a good worker and a pleasant person and we'd love to have you remain here. It's up to you."

I was rigid with anger. Work for Candace? Fat chance! As much as I tried to gain control, tears were starting and my voice was faltering.

"How soon can I go?" I was careful, at this point, not to say what I meant by going.

"Right now if you like."

"Thanks." I got up and walked out, leaving the door open wide, exposing him to the perils of employee confrontation, and passed his secretary without acknowledging her polite smile.

*   *   *

My expense statement and sales report from my trip to Tokyo and Osaka were completed in an hour and a half and I was back in Marblehead by twelve o'clock, sitting in Mom's living room with my head on her shoulder, weeping.

"I never did trust that bastard," I said through my tears. "All that grandfatherly bullshit when he first took over. How interested he was in each one of us. Yeah! Just a chance to put his arm around us, the lecher."

"I'm sorry, darling. He's not a good man."

"After all I've done—all the business I've brought in. I don't understand. Is it me, Mom? Am I missing something?"

"Of course it's not you. And from what you said, he did say you were doing a good job. Maybe his hands were tied."

"But Candace! What a schmuck."

"Well, San Francisco's a nice town. If I couldn't live here, I'd like to live there. And you'd still be able to do international sales."

I sighed and, closing my eyes, let my mind go blank. Gradually the anger subsided as Mom ran her fingers through my hair. After a couple of minutes I said, "I feel ten years old sitting here like this." I looked up at her. "In fact, it's been about twenty years since I've let you hold me." She gave me a squeeze and began rubbing my head again. I sank back down to her shoulder.

"I'm not going to San Francisco and I'm not working for Candace. I'm quitting." She said nothing. "I'm tired of hotel sales and I'm tired of always being on the move. I want to settle down in one place for a while."

"Marblehead's a nice place. Why don't you move back here? I'd love to have you close by."

"Ken Shimizu wants me to be his agent in New England for Holiday Tours. I know I could make it go, but it wouldn't provide much income, especially at first. I could get by with the trust fund, but just barely."

"Dry your eyes," she said gently, lifting me off her shoulder, "and come into the kitchen. I'll make you a cup of tea. I've got something to tell you and I want you to be sitting up and alert when you hear it."

I took a Kleenex from the box on the table, dabbed at my eyes, and blew my nose. After stopping in the john to check my makeup, I walked into the kitchen. Mom was taking two cups of Harvest Spice tea from the microwave. I sat and she joined me at the table.

"Last night, after the show, Sam took me to the lounge at the Four Seasons for a drink. He asked me to marry him." Mom held out her left hand and there on the third finger was a diamond ring. How had I missed it earlier? She must have curled her finger into her hand so that she could listen to my news before telling me hers. "I said yes."

"Oh Mom, that's wonderful!"

Tears came to her eyes. "I was afraid you wouldn't approve."

"Approve? Of course I approve." I took her hand. "Sam's a great guy."

"Thanks, Rebecca. I think so too."

"Have you set a date?"

"We haven't pinned it down, but we want it to be before the tourist season begins."

"That soon?"

"Yeah. We're thinking mid-May at the latest."

"My God, Mom, that's in two weeks."

"I know," she said with a giddy smile.

"Gee, I'd better quit my job just so I can help you get ready for the wedding."

"I knew there was a reason you should quit."

"I'm not kidding. I'm calling Herr Steiger today and telling him."

"Will you come back to Marblehead? You could live here, you know."

"I surely don't want to stay in Boston. Maybe if I could stay here in my old room for a while. I don't want to impose on you and Sam, though."

"You won't be imposing on us. We're going to live at his inn. He's got a whole separate house attached to it. It's very private and has plenty of room. After the wedding you can have this apartment to yourself."

Suddenly I was feeling a lot better. "All right, I will. You'll be here until the wedding?"

"Oh, back and forth."

"I can't say I approve of that—before you're married?"

"Prude," she said, flashing me a grin. "Why not call Matthew after school and ask him to come for dinner? I'll call Aggie and Sam and we'll make an announcement."

"Great. And Mom, I'm very, very happy for you."

Driving back to my Back Bay apartment that afternoon, I felt as if I'd been liberated from prison. I filled three boxes and two suitcases, enough to settle into my room at the inn until Matthew and I could move the rest of the stuff.

While there, I telephoned the Markham, my finger shaking as I punched the numbers. "Executive Offices, please." Pause. "Hi, Susan. This is Rebecca. May I please speak with Mr. Steiger?"

"I'm sorry, Rebecca, he's busy right now. What did you want him for?"

"I'll just leave a message. Tell him I quit."

There was silence for a moment, then, "I think you'd better call Personnel and discuss this with them." Her voice had turned to ice.

"I'm sorry, but I'm busy right now. I'll call them when I have the time. If they want to call me, they can reach me in Marblehead." I gave her the number. "Good-bye, Susan."

God, that felt good. Childish, maybe, but very good.

"As if you haven't already guessed," Mom said that evening, "Sam and I are going to be married." She and Sam stood arm in arm before Aggie, Matthew, and me in the middle of her living room.

Aggie snapped, "Well, it's about time for both of you. I wish I'd found somebody twenty years ago when I was your age. Better'n living alone, I'll tell ya."

I passed a tray with glasses of champagne and Matthew proposed a toast. "To Taylor and Sam!"

"Hear, hear!" Aggie and I responded as Mom and Sam beamed.

"So when's it going to be?" Aggie asked.

"Sunday the twenty-first of May," Mom said. "We decided just before you arrived."

"So soon?"

"Yes. Why wait? The wedding will be right here in the common room. We'll invite Sam's family, and you of course, and some friends and neighbors. It'll be small."

"Where will you live?" Matthew asked.

"In my house," Sam answered.

"Then you'll run this inn from there?"

"I can answer that," I said. "And this is the second announcement of the day. I've quit my job at the Markham and I'm going to live here in Mom's apartment and run the inn. Mom asked me this afternoon."

Aggie raised both eyebrows. "Great!" she hollered.

Matthew beamed. "What a perfect idea."

Mom had set the table in the dining area off the living room and called us over to sit down. From the kitchen she brought a pot roast, carrots, and boiled new potatoes. A tossed salad was on the table. As we passed the food and praised the cook, I felt I was at home with my family. For me this day had been a crossroads. I'd quit my job and started a new venture. I'd left Boston and found a place to live in Marblehead. I felt like a bird released from its cage with the whole sky opening up to me. Mom and Sam were happy, and I had a feeling of contentment I hadn't had in a long, long time. When my eyes met Matthew's, he smiled as if he knew what I was thinking.

Aggie broke my reverie.

"Matthew. What did you find out about the bullet?"

"Not now, Aggie," I said.

"Oh, it's all right," Mom said. "I want to know myself."

"I called the gunsmith today and he said the slug was pretty well beat up, but he's fairly sure it's a .38."

"So, Kramer took a shot at *White Wings*," Aggie snarled as she forked another piece of pot roast onto her plate.

"That's a strong accusation, Aggie," Sam said. "There's no way we can say that for sure."

"Yes there is." She chuckled. "Get his revolver. Fire it into a sandbag and check the marks on the bullet against our bullet. I'll bet you a buck they're the same."

"Good idea," I said. "I'll go ask him for his gun. Tell him I want to see if he murdered my grandmother."

"Humph," Aggie muttered without looking up from her plate.

"Even if we could determine the bullet comes from his gun," Sam pointed out, "it doesn't mean he shot . . . well . . . anybody. It just means his gun put a bullet into *White Wings*. Doesn't even say he fired it."

"Well," Mom said, raising her hands to call a halt to the subject, "I suggest we let it go. It happened a long time ago and there's no way we can prove anything. At least we found where my father was and that he probably came back here to see my mother. *That's* what I'd like to know more about, but it's a dead end, too."

"So, one chapter's closed and another's beginning," Sam said, taking Mom's hand and leaning over to kiss her cheek. I smiled until my gaze fell on Aggie. I could see by the angry look in her half-closed eyes that she was still thinking about the bullet and Karl Kramer.

Wednesday night Matthew and I were working on *White Wings* in Aggie's basement. While I'd been away Matthew had finished repairing the deck and cutting the planks for the damaged siding. I'd missed working on the boat and was impressed with the progress he'd made.

Outside, the weather had taken a turn for the worse, with a wind-driven rain beating against the basement door. But inside we were snug and warm. The lights glowed over the workbench and *White Wings*. There was the smell of cedar shavings in the air and something else I didn't at first detect. It was the warmth of companionship. It was being with Matthew.

"What can I do?"

"A lot. Here's where we are. I need you to help me get the keel in place, then while I'm finishing that and replacing the topside planking, you can do the final shaping of the mast with the drawknife."

"What's a drawknife?"

"It's a blade with a handle at each end and you pull it toward you to shave and shape a board, in this case a mast." He went to one of the drawers in the workbench and removed a drawknife. "Here it is, but let's practice on a piece of scrap before you start on the mast." He put a stick of spruce into the vise and showed me how to pull the drawknife to you following the slope of the wood grain. A fine piece of shaving curled upward above the blade as it came toward him. "Here, give it a try."

I grasped the two handles and pulled the blade, but it skidded across the wood.

"No. Turn the handles down slightly."

"Like this?"

"Yeah. Now pull."

I did, and the blade dug into the wood and stopped.

I sighed. "This isn't as easy as it looks."

"Here. Let me help." He stood beside me, placing his hands over mine, and gently pulled back. A shaving appeared and rolled over the blade. "See? Let's try again." As our interlocked hands pulled the blade toward us, he tipped his head so that his cheek lay next to mine. His hip and leg pressed against me. The blade reached the end of the board and stopped. The stubble of his day-old beard rubbed my cheek and I could smell, almost taste, his warm breath. Slowly he turned toward me, hesitant at first until I bent my head slightly in his direction. Closing my eyes, I let my lips touch his. We kissed long and gently, moving our hands across each other's back and shoulders and neck. When our lips parted we continued to hold each other, relishing the feeling of our bodies pressed together. Then he gently released me.

"So *that's* how a drawknife works?" I said.

"Yeah. Works every time." We laughed.

He took a deep breath and asked, "Back to work?"

"Back to work."

"Right now I need your help with the lead keel. I've got the bolts we had specially made, but I need you to hold the keel in place while I climb inside and put the keel bolts in. It weighs five hundred pounds, so I hope you're feeling strong tonight."

"Are you kidding?"

"No. It really does. It's lead. But look under here." We crouched

down under the hull. "I've got it wedged up there fairly tightly, but I want you to press down on this lever to hold it snug in place."

I tried it once and saw the heavy ballast seat itself against the wood backbone.

"You've got it, but for God's sake be careful. Stay back out of the way. I don't want that falling on your leg."

"Don't worry." I remained at the end of the lever ready to press downward while he climbed into the hull. I could see him through the openings in the side where he'd yet to replace the planks, and hear him moving his tools around as he fitted things together.

"Damn," he exclaimed. "I'm missing the socket that fits these bolts." He got up and looked at me over the side. "Well, there's nothing to do but run down to the hardware store and get the right size. They're open till seven. I've got thirty minutes."

"I'll stay here and practice with the drawknife, but it won't be the same without you."

As he opened the door to leave, a blast of wind and rain struck him. "Great night, huh?" he said, pulling his coat around him. "I won't be long."

"Hurry back." I went to the workbench.

Suddenly, with Matthew gone, the basement seemed cold and dark. There was one light over the bench and two over the boat, but I'd never realized how many dark corners and hidden shadows there were.

Grasp the handles of the drawknife, I instructed myself, and tip it down just enough to cut into the wood. Now pull. A wisp of a shaving curled up. Not bad, I thought. I tried it again and this time a more substantial shaving appeared. Again and again I pulled the blade, each time with more success.

Outside the rain was beating harder against the door. I heard a garbage can lid blow down the street, making a lonely, eerie sound. I wish Matthew would get back, I thought. Shivering, I set the drawknife down and put my sweater on. The door was open a crack, so I started toward it to close it all the way. I stopped, petrified. The door was opening, slowly. It wasn't the wind. Someone was pushing it.

"Matthew? Is that you?"

Suddenly it swung open. A man, a big man, stepped into the basement.

The shade on the overhead light hid all but his feet in shadow. He started toward me, shuffling across the concrete floor. Terrified, I eased myself backward toward the workbench and seized the handle of the drawknife.

Out of the shadows his form took shape, hunched over in a yellow slicker, no hat, long arms dangling out of sleeves too short, rain dripping from his straggly hair. The rim of light from the shaded bulb caught a deeply lined face, stubble of beard, slack mouth, eagle beak nose. It was Captain Kramer. I gasped and the story Aggie had told about him trying to rape Becky flashed through my mind. I slunk backward along the bench, staying well away from him. A few feet into the basement he stopped and let his rummy eyes wander, not fixing on anything in particular. A sneer twisted his bony face. With unsteady steps he began to move again, his knee-high black boots clomping on the concrete floor. When he reached the other end of the workbench I could smell the liquor.

He saw me. His head snapped back in surprise, then he cocked it to one side, trying to bring me into focus.

"Oh, it's the Jap girl. Saw the light through the crack in the door. Thought I'd come in, take a look at the boat."

Holding the drawknife behind me, I backed toward the stairs, ready to bolt if he made the slightest movement in my direction. As he neared the bow of *White Wings*, his attention shifted from me to the boat.

"So this is it." He lurched forward, steadying himself with his left hand on the bow stem.

With escape to the kitchen easily achievable, the shock and initial fear I had felt gave way to anger and I found courage to speak.

"Captain Kramer," I said with a firmness that surprised me, "I want you to leave, now. You're not welcome in this house."

"Now that's not a nice way for a little Jap girl to talk." His eyes didn't leave the boat as he spoke. Instead they moved along the edge of the deck and down the hull. I realized I was not an intended victim, only a distraction from his real purpose.

"Get out!" I commanded.

"Don't get your ass in an uproar. I'm not gonna hurt you." He continued examining the boat, running his hand over the planking. "That young fella, the teacher, that's workin' on the boat said to come by and take a look."

"He'll be back any minute now. He doesn't want you here either."

"It used to be Becky's boat, y'know?" He started down the side of the boat on the opposite side from me. "'Fore that it was the preacher's." Then he stopped when he saw the gaps in the hull where the planking hadn't been replaced. Distracted, he turned back to the bow. "Ol' Becky. She was somethin'." He mumbled as he examined the area around the bow. Then he looked again at me, taking a moment to focus his eyes. "You're pretty, too, like Becky, even if you're part Jap." His attention drifted as he ruminated on some lost reverie. "Becky was somethin', all right," he repeated, his voice faltering. "She and I were in love once, y'know?"

"In love?" The thought repulsed me. "My grandmother never loved you."

"Hah! You been talkin' to that ol' dyke upstairs. Always was jealous of me. Wanted Becky all for herself. Probably did get her in the sack a few times." The words were tumbling from his mouth like rocks rolling in the surf. "Hell, Becky'd sleep with anybody. We got it on good before I banged up my knees—after that it was anybody *but* me."

He stopped abruptly as his finger found the hole near the bow stem where the bullet had gone through. Becky was forgotten. I didn't exist. His whole attention centered on the bullet hole. The discovery seemed to sober him. He stepped back and studied the hole, looking at it first from one direction and then another. Slowly he turned toward the workbench and let his gaze rove over and under it.

Fascinated, I watched him search for the same device Matthew had looked for to track the direction of the bullet into the hull. Then I realized the significance of what I was witnessing—proof he'd fired the shot. He had come into this basement knowing, or fearing, he'd find that bullet hole. For years he must have worried someone else would find it. If they did, the bullet would have been damning evidence that could be used against him. But nothing had happened. The boat sat there in Mom's garage collecting dust. Finally, he forgot about it. Until Matthew started restoring *White Wings*. His old fear had resurfaced. He had to know. I watched and waited.

Turning to the workbench, he laid both hands on its top to steady himself. He looked on the wall behind it and along its back in the clutter of tools and shavings accumulated there. For a moment, my fear was suspended and I was tempted to play the game I played as a child. "You're getting warmer, warmer," I wanted to say. He bent over and looked beneath the bench at the shelf that held miscellaneous pieces of boards, pipes, and rods. "You're hot, very hot," I screamed mentally. And then he found it. The same rod Matthew had used.

He pulled it out and returned to the bow, inserting the rod into the hole and shoving it several feet until it stopped. Then he went to the starboard side of the hull, laboriously bent down on one knee, and looked through the place where the planks hadn't been replaced. He tried to reach into the hull, but couldn't bend low enough or reach far enough to touch the end of the rod. Groaning with the strain this position put on his old knee injuries, he eased himself down onto the concrete floor, and sat facing the boat with his legs flat out in front of him. He began hunching forward so he could position himself to reach the end of the rod.

"What are you doing?" I demanded.

"None of your damn business."

"I wouldn't do that if I were you."

"Well, you're not me, so shut up." He grunted and pushed himself further under the boat.

"The keel's just propped in there. It's not bolted."

"I was workin' on boats 'fore you was born. Don't tell me about boats."

Now his lower body was fully under the hull, his legs stretched out in front of him. He twisted his shoulders and bent his head into the hole so he could reach all the way to the end of the rod with his left hand. With grunts and groans he ran the tips of his fingers over the frame the rod was touching. I had moved around the stern so I could watch. "Where are you, you little bugger?" His voice was hollow inside the hull. "Ahh, there." Pause. "Hey! What the hell? It's notched. It's cut out." He swore and, bucking his head and shoulders up, collided with the plank above him.

With a grinding sound, *White Wings* shifted slightly on its stand and the bracing holding the keel gave way. There was a heavy thud as a quarter ton of lead fell, and a scream of pain from Kramer as it landed on his left calf.

"Ohhh! Ohhh! My leg. It's crushed my leg. I can't move. Help me!"

The door to the kitchen opened and a shaft of light fell down the stairs. "You all right down there, Rebecca?" It was Aggie.

"It's not me. It's Kramer. We need help."

"Kramer? What's he doing in my basement?"

"He's under the boat. *White Wings* dropped her keel on him."

Aggie came down the stairs. "Well I'll be damned." Kramer was lying flat on his back with most of his body under the boat. Eyes watering, head turning from side to side, his whole face was wracked with pain. She looked down, smiling broadly. "I'll be damned." She laughed. "If this isn't the nicest thing I've ever seen."

"Help me, you bitch," he screamed.

"Help you? You're trespassing on my property. Get out from under there and get out of my garage."

"My leg's broken, for God's sake. I'm dyin' down here."

The outside door opened and a blast of cold air and rain came into the basement, Matthew with it, shaking like a wet dog. Seeing us standing beside the boat, he walked over, curiosity on his face. Then he saw Kramer on the floor.

"My God! What's happening?"

"*White Wings* nailed him," I said. "He was screwing around under the boat and she dropped her keel on him."

"Is he stuck?"

"You're damn right I'm stuck," Kramer yelled. "The keel's on my leg. I think it's broken."

Immediately Matthew knelt down beside the boat and grabbed the lever, already in place, which he had intended for me to use when he bolted the keel. "When I push down, Rebecca, you and Aggie pull him out."

"I don't want to," Aggie said, still fuming.

"Christ, Aggie! Just do it."

She bent down and got hold of his left arm while I took his right.

"Okay, now pull." Matthew pushed down on the lever and we tugged on Kramer's arms. "Again." Out he came, sliding on his back, five inches at a time, screaming and cussing all the way. "Again," Matthew ordered. And again we pulled. Finally, his leg free, he curled up in pain.

"Aggie, call for an ambulance," Matthew said. "We'd never get him into the car."

Reluctantly, Aggie climbed the stairs to her kitchen. Matthew took off his coat and folded it as a pillow to put under Kramer's head. His boots were still on, so there was no way we could determine the extent of his injuries, but it was apparent he was in severe pain.

"So what were you doing under the boat?"

He moaned but didn't answer. I spoke for him. "He was looking for the bullet and he found the empty notch."

Pain or no pain, Kramer's eyes flashed at me. "What're you talkin' about?"

"The bullet. You knew it was there. It was you who shot it."

"I was just curious about that hole. There's no bullet."

"You're right," Matthew said. "There's no bullet in there now, because I took it out."

"I don't know what the fuck you're talkin' about." And those were the last words he said until the ambulance arrived.

We went upstairs to Aggie's kitchen.

"Want a cup of tea or something stronger?"

"Tea would be fine." My voice was frail.

"Me too," Matthew said.

We were standing by the table when I began to shake. Matthew put his arm around me.

"Aggie, bring the tea into the living room. She needs to sit down." He led me to the sofa, his arm around my back and under my arm, supporting me. When we sat, the tension of the last several minutes was released, and I burst into tears. He held me, bringing my head down to the hollow of his neck. I felt his handkerchief wiping my face and his hand stroking the hair from my eyes. Eventually my convulsions calmed to an occasional shudder.

"I guess I . . . I was . . . more scared . . . than I realized."

"Easy, darling." He held me close, kissing the tears from my cheeks. I took his handkerchief and blew my nose.

"At first I thought he was coming for me—going to do what he tried to do to Grandmother." I shuddered.

"Did he touch you?"

"No. It looked like he was going to, but then I realized it was *White Wings* he was after."

"How did he find the bullet hole?"

"When he got to the boat, he started looking for it—forgot about me. Ran his hands over the hull and along the edge of the deck." I raised myself up so I could look at Matthew. "He knew there was a bullet hole there somewhere. Matthew, he must have been the one who fired the shot."

Aggie came in with the tea and sat down.

"And now he knows we know," Matthew said.

"Yeah," Aggie said. "That wasn't the wisest move, Matthew, telling him you've got the bullet."

We looked at her. "What do you think he'll do?" I asked.

"Who knows what he'll do?" Aggie said. "He's drinking too much and personally I think he's crazy. It's a dangerous combination. Now this, what happened today. That bullet you've got's a real threat. Better watch out."

"I guess you're right," Matthew said, and to me, "No more being alone in the basement without me there, too."

"Or you either," I said.

"For a while, if his leg really is broken, he'll be incapacitated. Even without a cast, he has trouble with his crippled knees."

"I wish he'd gone under there head first," Aggie snarled.

I cried and laughed at the same time.

"Yeah," Matthew said. "*White Wings* really got him, didn't she?"

I stayed upstairs while Matthew turned off the lights in the basement and locked the outside door. Neither of us now felt like working on the boat. I had walked to Aggie's that afternoon, so Matthew offered to drive me home. He parked on the street by the wrought iron gate in front of the inn. The storm wasn't over. Wind whipped the branches of the big oaks in our yard and drummed rain onto the roof of the Jeep. The porch light was on but the windows were dark. I shivered. It looked like a haunted house in a Disney movie.

"I know it sounds silly, but let me walk you to the door."

"It's not silly at all. I'm still shaking."

We sprinted through the rain to the porch. I unlocked the door and we entered, flipping on the hall light. In Mom's apartment I found a note.

Rebecca,
    Sam and I are working on wedding plans. See you in the morning.

Love, Mom

I held the note as if studying it, but actually I was stalling for time while I decided what to do. I was afraid to stay alone but I didn't want to send a message to Matthew he might misunderstand.

"Bad news?"

"Oh. No. Mom's spending the night at Sam's."

"Well, you're not spending the night alone. The thing with Kramer was too traumatic. If you don't mind, I'll just stay out here on the sofa if you've got a pillow and some blankets."

"I can't ask you to do that. You've got school tomorrow and things of your own to do."

"Rebecca. I want to stay here. You need to know someone's out here and you're not alone."

"Matthew, thank you. I want you to stay, too. I'm still terrified."

He went to lock his car while I moved my nightgown and tooth-brush into Mom's room so Matthew could have mine. I wasn't going to put him on the sofa. When he returned we made hot cocoa and split a slice of apple pie I found in the fridge. Then he kissed me on the cheek and went to my room and I to Mom's.

"Please leave your door ajar and I will too," I asked.

"Sure."

I turned out the light and a moment later saw his light, reflecting down the hall, go out.

"Sweet dreams," he called.

"Same to you."

I lay awake for what seemed like hours but was probably only minutes. Finally, when sleep came, it was filled with heavy, anxious dreams I can't recall. Except the last one in which my foot was caught in a line pulling me closer and closer to a pit filled with hissing, writhing snakes. I screamed for help again and again, but no one came. Then I awoke.

"Rebecca, it's all right. You're okay. I'm right here." He gripped my shoulders, easing them back onto the pillow. Then he rubbed my forehead, his hand slipping across my sweaty skin.

"Matthew. It was an awful dream. I was being pulled into a pit filled with snakes."

"There, there. That's all it was. A dream."

"Hold me for a bit. I'm still scared."

I rolled onto my stomach and he lay beside me with his arm over my back. After a while I could feel him moving his hand over my shoulder blades and down my back, circling up again to my shoulders. Then I slept.

When I awoke, I was lying on my back looking at the ceiling. The room was filled with the gray half-light of early dawn. Moving my head to the right, I saw Matthew lying next to me with his head propped on his elbow.

"Hi," I said sleepily. "How long have you been here?"

"All night." He had wrapped himself in a blanket like we used to do as children when we played Indian. He was gazing at me, smiling.

"What are you doing?"

"Looking at you."

"How long have you been doing that?"

"Not long."

I turned my head and squinted. "What for?"

"You are the most beautiful person I've ever seen. And I am the luckiest person in the world to be able to lie here next to you and look at you." His face was serious with a gentle smile.

"It embarrasses me to have you look at me so intently."

"Please get used to it, because I want to do it forever."

"Only if you let me fall in love with you," I murmured.

I was still in my nightgown, drinking coffee and reading the paper, when Mom arrived the next morning. Matthew had gone back to his apartment an hour before to get ready for school. She joined me for a cup.

"We had quite a time last night," I said.

"Really? What happened?"

I told her about Kramer coming into Aggie's basement and getting his leg crushed under the keel. She listened with concern. Then I added he'd come looking for the bullet, and she was alarmed. When I said we'd told him we'd already found it, she was hysterical.

"You told him you had it? My God, Rebecca, that man's insane. I'm not leaving you alone in this house again. Sam and I can just cancel our honeymoon and stay here."

"Mom, Mom. I wasn't alone last night."

"Oh!" The wind left her sails. Her voice died.

"Matthew spent the night."

"Oh?"

"That's why your bed isn't made. I slept there and he slept in my bed."

"Ohh," trailing off with a degree of disappointment.

"It was nice. I had a nightmare and he rushed in to take care of me."

"Don't say more."

"Mom, it wasn't like that. He was so sweet. Rubbed my back until I fell asleep. In the morning he was still there, wrapped in a blanket, looking at me. He thinks I'm beautiful." I pondered that memory for a moment, then added, "I love him, Mom."

"I've noticed. Well, he's one of the dearest young men I've met. How do you feel about having him here when I'm away?"

I sighed. "Like I'm driving with one foot on the accelerator and one on the brake."

"You *are* in love."

"I just want to keep it cool enough to see if this is the right thing for me."

"Matthew?"

"No. Marriage."

During the next two weeks, what with helping Mom prepare for the wedding and Matthew complete *White Wings*, I could have used another set of hands and a few more hours in the day. I decided to postpone my tourist project until July. The Japanese Holiday Tour program wouldn't begin until next year and the brochure wouldn't be printed until this September, so I had plenty of time to line up prospective inns during the summer.

The news via the town grapevine was that Captain Kramer had had an accident helping Matthew with his boat renovation and had broken his left leg. At least part of the rumor was true. He was to be operated on as soon as the swelling abated and would probably be in a cast for several weeks. I hadn't noticed it before, but the absent planking near *White Wings*'s bow looked decidedly like a smile. With Kramer out of the picture for a while, Mom's worry that he might seek some kind of crazy revenge gave way to thoughts of her wedding.

The common room of the inn was the perfect place for the big event with its new furniture and draperies and refinished floor. Mom and I sat at a table near the fireplace reviewing the wedding plans.

"There isn't that much to do," she said. "I've already lined up a caterer for the reception, a florist, and the minister from the Congregational Church. You'll be my maid of honor and Sam's oldest daughter will be his best person."

"What a good idea. Who'll give you away?"

"Hardly necessary, but I thought I'd ask Matthew if he'd do it, saying it's on behalf of my father."

"Without names?"

"I think so. Haven't decided yet."

"He'll like being asked. And music?"

"I haven't figured that one out yet. Thought I'd ask Matthew if he knows someone with an electronic keyboard. Maybe you and Matthew would choose the music?"

"Sure."

She flipped through the pages of her address book, saying barely audible yesses and noes and writing down the names and addresses of the yesses. "I'm inviting only local people. Time's too short for mailing out-of-towners."

"What are you wearing?"

"At first I thought I'd wear my light blue spring suit I bought two years ago," she said, marking her place in the address book with the pen, "until I realized that was the old Taylor talking." Her face broke into a smile. "What I really want to do is buy a new and *very* stylish cocktail dress that'll knock Sam's eyes out."

"May I help?"

"I'm counting on it."

I looked at her for a moment, the bright spring sunlight coming through the window silhouetting her gray hair, her half glasses set on the end of her nose so she could look over them at me, and a slight smile of anticipation always at the edge of her mouth. "Mom, I'm happy for you."

"Thanks. I *am* happy."

The following Saturday Matthew and I rented a U-Haul trailer and moved my remaining belongings from Back Bay to Marblehead. Until I could move into Mom's apartment in the inn, we stored several boxes plus the TV, VCR, CD player, and my few pieces of furniture in the garage. We finished a little after five and were too tired to work on the boat, so we went to the Sail Loft for a beer. The crowd, mainly our age or a little younger, was clustered around the bar. These were people who lived in Marblehead because of the sailing and got together evenings to talk sailboats and realign relationships. We found a table near the wall and put our heads together so we could hear each other above the noise.

Nodding toward the bar, I said in his ear, "Want to go over and check out the girls?"

He glanced over. "No. Do you? The guys, I mean."

"No."

He looked at me, shaking his head. "I can't believe you'd rather be sitting here with me now. Look at the guys sneaking peeks at you. You could have anybody you wanted."

"I know and I've done that a few times. Not now, though. I'm content."

Again he shook his head in amazement. "You mean that, don't you?"

"Yes."

"You know what this is beginning to sound like?"

"Yes, and it terrifies me." I actually shivered. "Matthew, promise me something. At least for a while, let's not say the M word. I need some time to get used to the idea."

He thought for a moment until he realized what I meant, then said, "I won't say it, but I'll think it." I could feel his breath in my ear as he spoke.

I leaned back in my chair, putting symbolic distance between us. "I'm famished. Let's finish our beer and go by Penni's Pantry. They're still open. We can get a couple of steaks and stuff for a salad, and take it back to the inn."

He agreed. We returned to the inn to find another note from Mom saying she was spending the night with Sam. Good. We had bought only two steaks. I rubbed garlic salt and pepper into the meat, heated the broiler, and made a tossed salad on which I dribbled balsamic vinegar and sesame oil. Matthew sauteed onions and mushrooms for the steaks. We put the meat into the broiler for a quick singe on each side and heated sourdough bread. As we prepared the meal we hardly spoke but, working side by side, playfully rubbed shoulders and jostled each other with our hips. Finally, the table was set and Matthew poured two glasses of cabernet sauvignon.

We sat on the same side of the table so our knees touched and my right elbow bumped his left arm as I cut my steak.

Every movement became an opportunity to be close. It felt good. Too good.

"Matthew. I have to back off or I'll be hauling you into the bedroom."

He sighed deeply. "I'd go, too."

"Let's wait on it." I moved back slightly and put my hand on his. "With Reggie, and with other guys, it all went so fast. Whatever we did—dinners, parties, playing tennis, going for a walk—it didn't matter—was just marking time until we got into bed. It burns out too quickly."

"I suppose so. It probably would have been that way with Miranda."

"I know it's hard, but—" He burst out laughing, and so did I. "But seriously, let's get to know each other a little more. Okay?"

"You mean actually get some work done on the boat without falling on the floor in lust?"

"Something like that. Speaking of the boat," I said as we got up to do the dishes, "there's something I want to do and I want your opinion. Remember the piece of line you found secured to the cleat on the bow? It was bent—is that right?—bent to the cleat?" He nodded, smiling at my growing knowledge of nautical terms. "Well, you told me it was put on backward," I said, relapsing into landlubber language.

"Yes."

"I want to see what the guys in the harbormaster's office say about that. Maybe it'll be more evidence against Kramer."

"You're taking a chance. What if he finds out you're trying to track him down?"

"I don't think he'd say anything, because he knows you have the bullet."

"But he might *do* something," Matthew insisted.

"That's just it. If he does, we need something to convince a judge to give us a restraining order so he'll stay away from me. And you too, of course. If he's the only one who cleats a line that way, it's pretty clear he had his hands on *White Wings* the night she was wrecked."

"Why not let it ride for a while and see what he does when he recovers?"

"Because I'm afraid, and I don't want to just sit back and let it happen."

"Well, all right," he said reluctantly. "Do you want me to come with you?"

"No. I'm going to play helpless female and you'd only get in the way. And don't worry. I won't tip our hand."

Monday morning I walked into the harbormaster's office and found him and two officers in the outer office where the receptionist was seated. I stopped at her desk.

"May I help you?"

"Yes. I'm Rebecca Hayakawa and I want to check on the mooring we requested for our boat on the western shore."

She looked up my name and said, "You're all set. Boat's name is *White Wings*, and Matthew Adams is co-owner. Right?"

"Good. We'll finish the renovation in a couple of months and should have it in the water by the end of June."

I turned to the men sitting at a nearby table looking at a chart spread out before them. I walked over. "Could I bother you for a minute?"

They leaned back in their chairs and looked up at me with avuncular smiles.

"Hi. You're Taylor Hayakawa's daughter, aren't you?" said the harbormaster. "What can we do for you?"

"Well, this is silly, but I've got a bet with a girlfriend about how you tie a rope to a cleat. I say one way and she says another."

"Wait a minute," one of the officers said. He reached to the desk behind him and picked up a cleat that was sitting on a stack of papers as a weight. He then produced a lanyard from his desk drawer and handed them to me. "Show us the two ways."

"Let me see if I remember this." I looked at the four-foot section of line with a puzzled expression, and handed one end to the officer. "You hold this end." I took about two feet of the other end and wound it in a figure eight onto the cleat until I reached the end where I reversed it so the line crossed under itself. "There. That's how she says you're supposed to do it. Now I'll show you what I think." I don't much like playing dumb, but I love the way it gets men to eat out of my hand. I started at the end of the line, sticking it into the hole beneath the cleat and winding a figure eight onto the cleat, ending as I had before with the line crossing under itself. "There. Which one of us is right?"

The three men smiled, condescendingly. "Sorry to tell you, Rebecca, but your girlfriend's right. The way you did it, if there was a strain on the line, you couldn't release it." Taking hold of the end of the line and pulling it firmly, he asked me to remove the line from the cleat. I tugged and tugged, then laughed and gave up.

"Guess you're right."

" 'Fraid so."

"Nuts. Now I'm out two dollars. I was so sure I was right."

"Don't feel bad. There's a lot to know about lines and bends. And now you know no one ever secures a line to a cleat that way."

"Almost no one," said the harbormaster. "Karl Kramer used to do it that way. If he stopped a boat for a violation and was towing it in, he'd use your method, Rebecca, so the party in the boat couldn't detach the line and get away."

"Then we're both right. I haven't lost my two dollars."

"He's the only person I've ever known to bend to a cleat that way, but I guess you're saved on a technicality."

"Thanks. I knew I could count on you guys."

The next two weeks I worked on the boat with Matthew in the evening, and with Mom during the day. In a shop on Atlantic Avenue we found the perfect dress for a May wedding. Yellow and white, it was a soft chiffon that looked angelic and, at the same time, fit her so well it was sexy. A wispy veil of a hat, gloves, and yellow shoes completed the outfit.

"What am I forgetting, Rebecca?" It was Monday morning, six days before the wedding. We'd finished breakfast and were having a second cup of coffee in Mom's apartment.

"You've got your plane and hotel reservations?" They were flying to Paris for a week-long honeymoon.

"Sam's taking care of that."

"Did you check with him to be sure he has?"

"I'm not going to start that. He said he'd do the honeymoon plans, so it's one less thing I have to worry about."

"But what if he forgets something?"

"Then he forgets. We'll have to do something else."

I sighed.

"What?" She looked at me, wrinkling her forehead.

"I don't think I could do that with Matthew. I'd want to be sure."

"You'd want to run things, huh?"

"No, just be sure everything's under control."

"Same thing. And if he'd forgotten something you'd tell him to get on the stick."

I looked down at my coffee cup. Suddenly I was on the brink of tears. "I don't know why I'm even thinking of getting married," I said forlornly. "I know I'd make a mess of it. I *would* try to run things. I'd drive him away."

"I doubt it."

"How can you say that? You know how controlling I can be."

"Oh, you're controlling all right, but I don't think you'd drive him away. In time, the two of you would work it out. It's obvious you love each other. I wish I had a video of you two. The way you look at each other."

"Is it that bad?"

"No. It's sweet."

"Ugh. Sweet?"

"Yes." She took my hands in hers. "Darling, you can't work it all out beforehand. That's what marriage is—a time for you and Matthew to grow up together." I looked at her, still feeling hopelessly incompetent. "Heck, Sam and I are twice your age and I'm sure we'll have to do some growing up together. Don't be afraid. Being together is what both of you want. You'll make it go."

She got up, took the dishes to the kitchenette, and rinsed them. I sat pondering what she'd said, feeling a hint of hope simmering in my brain. In a few minutes she returned to the table.

"Now, let's get busy on how to run an inn. You're taking over a week from today. It's not that hard—like a miniature hotel, and you know the hotel business."

She spent an hour showing me the ropes. At the end she said, "The difference between an inn and a hotel is the innkeeper. In an inn, people want to feel they're welcome guests in your home."

"I can do that."

"I'm not surprised. It's been in your blood for three generations."

I'd become fairly adept with the drawknife. The mast, extending the full length of the basement, sat on three sawhorses. It had taken two full weeks of shaving and sanding, but I had transformed the square timber into a round, tapered mast. Earlier, I had leveraged the lead keel against the boat's wooden backbone to hold it in place while Matthew tightened the nuts on the keel bolts from inside the hull. While I had been building my muscles with the drawknife, he had finished the cedar planks for the hull, steaming them in the steam box and clamping the still pliable boards against the frames, fixing them in place with bronze screws, and finally sanding and caulking them. *White Wings* was beginning to look like a boat again.

At ten to ten he came over and put his arm around me. I laid down the sander with which I had been doing the finishing touches on the mast and together we gazed at the boat.

"We're doing okay, aren't we?" he said proudly.

"Yeah. She looks so much better with those holes closed up. What's left?"

"We've got the gaff to make—you can do that—and the centerboard to shape and sand. The boom wasn't damaged but it needs sanding and refinishing. Then we'll paint the boat and redo the brightwork."

"Can we still launch in June?"

"I think we'll make it. We can step the mast and do the rigging down at the waterfront."

"How're the sails coming?" I asked.

"Don't know. Might be a good idea if I took a turn by the sailmaker tomorrow."

"I'd like to go with you," I said. "Pick me up after school."

"Sure." He started turning out the lights. "Oh, by the way. I hear Kramer's out of the hospital, but I can't imagine he's able to get around very well. Are you okay alone at night?"

"Oh." I pictured Kramer as he came through the basement door two weeks previously and shivered. After a deep breath, I said,

"This week I'm okay. Mom's staying home for a change. Bride-before-the-wedding bit, I think."

"After that?"

"We'll see."

The sailmaker said the main and jib would be finished by the middle of June and asked me to pay half the total cost now. Fair enough, I thought. He was going to have to purchase the sail canvas, so I wrote him the check.

As we headed for the door, Matthew said, "See why I wanted you with me?"

I laughed. "Okay, but I'm keeping the sails if you skip town."

We opened the door and started across the parking lot. There, ten feet in front of us, was Karl Kramer hunched over two crutches, his hawklike nose pointing at us. His left pant leg was slit, revealing a walking cast of heavy plaster, beginning at the ball of his foot and extending up to his knee. Five dirty toes poked out the bottom.

My heart went to my throat as the fear I'd experienced that night in the basement returned. Matthew took my arm and stepped slightly in front of me. We stood there saying nothing.

"It's you, huh?" His voice grated like gravel underfoot.

"Out of the hospital, I see." Matthew moved even further in front of me.

"You're lookin' at me, aren't you?"

"Come on, Rebecca. Let's go." We started to go around him.

"Wait a minute. What's the hurry? Now that I've run in to you I got a question for the little girl." We stopped and I glared at him around Matthew's shoulder. "Why were you askin' about me over at the harbormaster's office?"

"I don't know what you're talking about."

"Ahh, I think you do. Somethin' about how I belay to a cleat."

"Let's go," Matthew insisted, nudging me toward the car.

Awkwardly he turned on his crutches and shouted after us. "What are you two cookin' up behind my back?" We kept walking. "Hey! Little Jap girl. I'm talkin' to you. Did you think you could question the harbormaster about me and he wouldn't tell me? 'Course he told me."

Matthew opened my door. The last words I heard were, "You two better watch your butts. I'm not gonna let you bad-mouth me."

Matthew got in. We started the engine and left.

"So, that makes us even," I said.

"What do you mean?"

"Now we've both goofed. You told him we had the bullet, and I didn't realize the harbormaster would tell him about the cleat. Did you notice, though, he thought I'd asked about him, but it was the harbormaster who said Kramer cleated that way. The old boy's getting more and more paranoid."

48

The organist from St. Paul's Church played Mendelssohn's wedding march on the electronic keyboard as Mom and Matthew entered from the hall and walked between the rented chairs filled with guests. The room was festooned in white ribbons, and glittering candles with vases of jonquils adorned every available flat surface. I was wearing my mauve silk dress which I'd had made in Hong Kong, cut in the straight Eastern style with buttons from the collar down the right side to the knee-length hem. I stood to the right of the minister and Sam and his daughter to the left, waiting for the bride's arrival. Sam, beaming with joy, wore a black tuxedo and light green cummerbund, and his daughter Cynthia, standing tall and confident in her role as best person, a light blue suit. Matthew in his one and only dark blue suit approached with the stately grace of a king escorting his queen as he led Mom down the aisle, her right hand on his left arm. And Mom radiated loveliness, her eyes and smile fixed on Sam.

Matthew gave her away with the words, "I do, on behalf of her father," and the vows were exchanged.

It seemed we'd only begun when the minister said, "Those whom God hath joined together, let no one put asunder." He then pronounced them husband and wife. Sam kissed Mom, the gathering applauded, and Wagner's recessional march blasted forth from two large speakers hidden behind banks of flowers. Cynthia and I followed them quickly down the aisle and into the hall. They were married.

With the precision of a drill team, the caterers swept into the room, moving chairs against the wall and setting up a bar and hors d'oeurve table. As the organist turned down his volume and switched to Strauss waltzes, Mom and Sam came back into the room, where the guests crowded around them. Champagne was served, and soon the noise of animated conversation drowned out the music.

Matthew and I watched from a corner of the room. "Don't they look happy?" Matthew said.

"Completely." I watched Sam wave his hands up and down as he related some tale to another innkeeper. Mom looking on, broke into laughter from time to time.

"Did you ever think she'd marry again?" he asked.

"Never occurred to me. I knew her as a single mom for so long, I just assumed that was her natural state. Then, all of a sudden, she blossomed."

Aggie walked over to us. "Good job, don't you think?"

"Yes," I agreed. "It went very well."

"Never thought I'd see it happen. She was starting to look like an old maid till Sam came along. More power to 'em."

The organ stopped as Cynthia's voice rose above the talking. "As best person . . ." The noise rumbled to a stop. She began again. "As best person—that's like best man, only better. Or maybe I should be called 'best woman.' Hey, I like that even more." There's a woman I can relate to, I thought. "As best woman it is incumbent on me to propose a toast." Her voice was clear and strong.

"I hope she doesn't take after Sam and talk all afternoon," Aggie said just as the room fell silent.

"Don't worry, Aggie," Cynthia called across the room, "I'll keep it short." People chuckled quietly, Aggie among them.

Cynthia raised her glass. "To Taylor and Sam. Young in spirit. Adventurous. Vessels of a love which overflows to all of us. Examples of courage. To Sam and Taylor. May we all be here for their fiftieth wedding anniversary."

Hear-hear and applause.

Then Sam toasted Taylor against a chorus of "Keep it short, Sam," saying simply, "To my lovely wife, Taylor." Mom followed with "To Sam, the center of my life."

The reception continued for another forty-five minutes, then Taylor and Sam went to her apartment to change for their trip. They were flying to Paris that night and Matthew and I were driving them to Logan Airport. Matthew carried their bags to the car and returned in time to see Mom climb the stairs and throw her bouquet into the air. As it arched to its zenith, I glanced at Matthew to be sure he was watching. Then, leaping into the air, I snared it before my competitors had a chance. Proudly I held it up for all to see, then, looking around, discovered that Aggie was the only other single person there. Oh well, maybe Matthew got the message.

Mom and Sam dashed to the car through a shower of rice and we headed for Logan.

"Got the tickets?" I asked Sam playfully. Mom scowled.

"Right here."

"So there, smarty pants!" Mom said.

We left them at the curb of the international terminal with kisses and waves, returning to Marblehead at dusk. Everything was quiet. The people were gone and the caterers had cleaned up and left. Matthew went to the kitchen and brought an unopened bottle of champagne into the apartment. There was just enough chill in the air to justify the fire he built and lit. He popped the cork and poured the champagne.

"To us." The look in his eyes added the words "Alone at last."

"Yes, to us." We drank and, barely touching his arm, I drew him to the sofa in front of the fire.

Sitting down, I kicked off my shoes and stretched out my feet toward the fire. I undid a couple of buttons at the bottom of my narrow skirt and then, with a smile, undid several more. Matthew watched approvingly. Then I crossed my feet and let the dress fall open to reveal my right thigh. He sighed deeply and rolled his eyes. Putty in my hand, I thought, and we both laughed.

"How did you like my catch?" I asked.

"The bouquet?"

"Of course, the bouquet. Did you notice how I beat out all my competitors?"

"You were magnificent."

"You do know what that means?"

He knit his brow and looked upward, thinking. "You're going out for the NBA?"

"No, you idiot. It means . . ."

His left hand was emerging from his pocket with a small black box which he held out to me. Suddenly I could not breathe. I took the box and opened it. The diamond, catching the light of the fire, sparkled like a star on a clear night. It was about a quarter of a carat and mounted in a gold Tiffany setting.

I took it from the box, looking up at Matthew who was beaming proudly. Gently he took the ring from me and held it at the end of the third finger of my left hand.

"Rebecca," he said solemnly, "will you marry me?"

I was speechless. Gazing into his eyes, his face blurred through my tears, I slowly nodded and mumbled, "Un-huh." He slid the ring onto my finger, squeezing it over the knuckle.

"There. It won't come off easily."

"I don't want it to."

He took me in his arms and we kissed. I snuggled against his neck and for a long time we held each other without speaking.

"I took a chance," he said finally. "I was afraid you still might not want to hear the M word."

"It's okay. It's time."

"I love you so much I couldn't wait any longer."

"You did right. I needed the nudge."

"When I saw you go for the bouquet," he said, "I decided tonight's the night. I had the ring locked in my glove compartment."

"How long has it been there?"

"About a month."

"My poor dear."

"Yeah. You about drove me nuts with your vacillation. I almost took it back to the jeweler once."

"Well, it's where it belongs, now." I lifted my hand and, turning it, let the light of the fire sparkle through the diamond. "It's beautiful, Matthew. Thank you."

"What made you decide it was time?"

I thought for several moments as I lay with my head on his chest looking into the fire. "I had this idea that everything had to be settled, figured out, before we could get married. I had to know for sure it was the right thing."

"Don't you think it's the right thing?" he said, worried.

"I don't know if it's right or wrong. I don't care anymore. What's wrong we'll straighten out, and what's right we'll enjoy. What I do know is, you're a good guy and we can make it go together." Then I added, "And you got nice buns."

"Rebecca. I didn't think you noticed such things."

"It's something I inherited from Grandmother Becky." I brought my bare right leg into his lap and, with my ear pressed against his chest, heard him suck in a quick breath. "And there's another thing, the clincher. I don't want us to miss out like Becky and Taylor did. Starting right now I want us to be together, loving each other, forever."

"So do I."

I leaned over and kissed him again. Slowly he got up and, taking hold of my hands, pulled me to him. Together we walked to Mom's bedroom, which was now mine.

Later, we were lying side by side, our naked bodies moist with perspiration, our hands locked together. My right foot was stroking his left leg. Tipping my head to his, I nibbled his ear, saying, "We fit nice."

"Like a hand in a glove."

"Yeah." I giggled. "Like a wiener in a bun."

"Hmmm. Like a blimp in its hangar."

"Go on. Like a thread in the eye of a needle."

"Like an ICBM in its silo."

"Wow. Talk about ego. More like a sperm in an egg."

"What? You're kidding, aren't you? I thought you said you were okay."

I laughed. "Don't worry, I am. I'm on the pill."

"Whew!"

"Let's get married soon. I wanna have babies."

"All at once? Like a litter?"

"No, silly," I said. "One at a time."

"How many?"

"Two," I said thoughtfully. "Maybe three."

"It'd be nice to have at least one boy."

"Well, you got the Y's, buddy. Better sharpen 'em up."

He sat up on his elbow and began drawing circles around my eyes and down my nose.

"When shall we get hitched?"

"How about September? That'd give me time to get through most of the tourist season and line up my inns for the Japanese tourist program."

Matthew's finger was tracing the lines of my jaw and sliding down to my neck.

"That's a long time to wait."

"It won't be so bad. Come and live here with me."

He smiled. "I'll move in tomorrow."

The tip of his finger made trails through the sweat on my chest, climbing my breasts and rolling over my nipples.

"You can help me run the inn, change beds, fix breakfast."

"Make bread, knead the dough." His hand gently massaged and squeezed my breast, then dropped to my waist, his fingers working the soft flesh of my stomach.

"You're hired," I said, putting my arm around his shoulder and pulling him on top of me.

About eleven, we got up and made some cocoa. We brought the cups to the living room and sat in front of the fire.

"Oh, I forgot. Mom gave me a present as maid of honor."

"Same here. Where did we put them?"

"On the table by the door when we were getting ready to drive them to the airport."

I retrieved them and brought them to the sofa.

"You do yours first," Matthew said.

I unwrapped the long narrow box and opened the lid. It was a bracelet with several decorated gold pieces the size of nickels linked together with small gold rings. "It's beautiful. How could Mom ever afford something like this?" I laid it across the back of my hand and held it up. "Unless it's something she had, like a gift." I looked beneath the central gold piece and saw an engraving. I turned on the lamp beside the sofa and read "To Becky, love, Taylor." Stunned, I read it again, silently, hearing my grandfather's words across half a century. Like the letters he'd written Grandmother, his hands had touched this bracelet, probably placed it on her wrist, and now I was holding it in my hand. I leaned against Matthew and let him examine it.

"What a treasure. And from your grandmother, too."

"This is the most wonderful gift Mom's ever given me."

Matthew began unwrapping his, a small square box. Inside, sitting on a bed of cotton, was a brass compass which bore on its lid the engraving "To Taylor with love, Becky. To help you find your way home."

"Gosh," he said. "To think she gave me something of Taylor's."

"She likes you." Even as I said this I knew there was more. "Matthew, you're involved in this family in a strange way, drawn in by *White Wings* and your dream about the pictures Becky and Taylor took of each other. It's almost as if *White Wings* chose you to complete Becky's search for Taylor. Now you and I are launching *White Wings* again. I think Mom sees you and me like the completion of Becky's and Taylor's love for each other."

"If she does, she's reading too much into it. You are you and I am I. We're not somebody else. And *White Wings* is the same boat she's always been, only restored. I love you with my love. Not your grandfather's. We're not Becky and Taylor."

"I know. But it is strange how it's happened."

"Maybe good things go in circles."

"And this is one of the best." I put my arms around him and held him.

Raising my eyes, I happened to glance out the window. "Oh God. Look there, Matthew."

At the end of the front walk beyond the iron gate, standing in the glow of the street light, was a man, leaning on crutches, coat hanging loosely from his stooped shoulders, his left leg in a white cast. He stared at the house for a long time, then turned and hobbled away.

"And bad things go in circles, too," Matthew said.

After a month of working on the boat weekends and every evening, we finished the restoration and were ready to show *White Wings* the light of day. Mom and Sam had returned from their honeymoon and were living at his inn, leaving me to run Fair Winds Inn. With the tourist season not yet in full swing, I had extra time to sand and paint the boat and was not so tired that I couldn't enjoy curling up to Matthew each night.

White Wings's epiphany was scheduled for Saturday, June 17. We spent most of the day maneuvering her from the jack stands in Aggie's basement back onto her trailer, a task that required jacking up the hull and moving the trailer, hooked to Matthew's Jeep, under it a few inches at a time, then changing the location of the jacks and repeating the process. Finally it was on the trailer. We pulled onto the driveway and placed the mast and boom on a rack beside the hull. Driving as if carrying a load of eggs, we eased it down the street half a block to Parker's boatyard. Most of the boats stored in the yard during the winter had been returned to the water, so we had no trouble finding a spot near the launching crane. We blocked the trailer wheels, unhitched the Jeep, and moved it aside. Then Matthew and I sat down on a bench to observe our baby from a distance.

This was the first time I'd seen her outside the cramped quarters of Aggie's basement. She was beautiful and sleek. The long, slanting rays of the setting sun turned her white hull to gold. "Matthew, we've done a good job."

"I'll say. We're a pretty good team, too."

Gazing at our boat, I said, "She's about the same length as the others, maybe a little shorter, but she seems much smaller."

"They're more bulky and their keels are deeper, so they sit higher on their trailers. She's about twenty-five feet at the sheer line and only fifteen at the waterline."

"Matthew, just look at the way the bow and stern extend outward into the air. She's like a willowy young girl, long-legged, svelte."

"I know, I can hardly wait to sail her."

"Do you hear her?" I said, turning my ear to the boat, pretending to listen. "She's begging us to put her in the water."

Matthew laughed. "Well, she'll have to wait a week. For now, let's call it a day. Tomorrow we'll step the mast and begin the rigging. Then, first thing Monday morning I'd like you to start bugging the sail maker to finish the sails."

Sunday we spent all day stepping the mast, running and splicing the wire rope for the forestay and the four shrouds, and securing them to the chain plates with turnbuckles. For the next several days, until Friday, Matthew was in school making up for snow days the children had off during the winter storms. I picked up the sails on Wednesday and we were ready to launch on Saturday.

A bank of clouds covered the rising sun, and the night's chill lingered in the air. But our hearts were light as the five of us, Taylor, Sam, Aggie, Matthew, and I, trooped down to the yard to celebrate the launching. For the occasion, I wore the bracelet Taylor had given Becky, and Matthew carried the compass she had given Taylor. With all of us pushing and pulling, we moved the trailer beneath the crane arm, and Matthew and I placed the straps under her hull. Matthew pushed the "up" button that controlled the electric hoist and slowly *White Wings* rose into the air and off the trailer. When she was free, he swung the crane arm over the water and, pushing the "down" button, let the boat descend gradually toward her natural habitat. He stopped about a foot from the water and I opened a bottle of champagne.

"Since *White Wings* is already christened," I said, "we've decided simply to offer her a toast. Everyone take a glass. Are you ready, Matthew?"

"Wait. Let me lower her a little more." The motor buzzed again and the tip of *White Wings*'s keel touched the water, sending concentric rings outward across the still surface. "Now!"

I raised my glass. "To *White Wings* who brought us together. First Becky and Taylor, and now Matthew and me. May the five of us sail with fair winds and a following sea: *White Wings*, here in the waters of Marblehead, Matthew and I, soon to be husband and wife, and Becky and Taylor, wherever you are."

As the five of us cheered, *White Wings* settled comfortably into the water. We released the straps and hoisted them up and away from the boat. Matthew went aboard while I pulled a long line attached to the bow, bringing her around to the dock.

"When do you take her out?" Sam asked.

"Tomorrow," Matthew said. "Today we'll finish the running rigging—the two halyards for the gaff and the jib, attach the mainsail to the mast hoops and bend it to the boom and gaff, attach the sheets and run up the sails to make sure they fit properly. It'll take all day."

"So tomorrow is the maiden voyage?" Mom asked.

"If all goes well today."

"The twenty-fifth of June," she said, meaningfully.

"I guess it is," Matthew replied. Then, after a moment's thought, "Oh. Of course."

"Yeah," Aggie chorused.

"What's important about June twenty-fifth?" Sam asked, puzzled.

"For one thing," Taylor said, "it's nine months before I was born."

"Oh." Sam nodded. "Did *White Wings* have something to do with that?"

"Right there in the cockpit," Aggie said, pointing at the boat tied to the dock.

Sam laughed. "I guess you kids had better be careful, then."

"It's also the date Becky went out alone every year after Taylor was lost in the war," Mom continued.

"Oh," Sam said solemnly.

"And the date she was lost at sea, when *White Wings* was swept onto the rocks and wrecked."

"Mom! Enough. That's past history. It's a new day. A new twenty-fifth."

"I know," Mom said. "I need to let it go."

"Well, the twenty-fifth won't be the maiden voyage if we don't get to work," Matthew said, hoisting the sail bag onto his shoulder.

As he turned to descend the gangway, a cabin cruiser going too fast roared past, its wake rolling toward the dock. *White Wings* began bobbing up and down, banging against the bumpers on the side of the dock.

"Look at that fool," Matthew yelled. "No regard for anybody."

"That particular fool," Aggie snarled, "is Captain Kramer." As the boat pulled away we could see a man standing on the bridge looking back at us, his leg in a cast. On the stern was the name *My Turn*.

"Is he drunk?" Matthew said.

"Probably," she said with disgust.

The five of us watched the boat move out into the harbor and circle back toward the mouth.

Matthew said, as it disappeared, "So that's the boat he got Becky on and tried to rape her."

"The same one," Aggie said. "Twenty-some years old, now. A monster, isn't it?"

"It's got to be forty feet long," Matthew guessed.

"Diesel, too," Aggie added.

"And Becky accused him of getting the money to buy it from running drugs?" Matthew asked.

"That's what she told me she did. Of course, she was just repeating the rumors she'd heard, that he rendezvoused with boats from Colombia and brought the stuff ashore. She must have been right, though, because he threatened he'd kill her if she went to the police."

"Why didn't they arrest him?" I asked.

"They did stop him once, but didn't find a thing. Let him go. I think he stopped the drug business after that."

"Well, folks. Does anybody else want to rain on our parade?" I was annoyed. "Come on, Matthew. Let's get to work."

The others left and Matthew and I set to work with the remaining rigging. When we broke for lunch, Matthew looked out across the harbor.

"Do you see him?" I asked.

"No. But you know, he wasn't just out for a spin. He did that deliberately."

By six o'clock the next day we had completed the running rigging and run up the sails, letting them luff in the breeze. With the sound of the flapping sails and the whine of the shrouds, *White Wings* tugged at her lines, saying, "Let's go, let's go."

"What do you think?" Matthew asked. "Too late to go out?"

"How's the weather?" The wind had shifted during the day to the southeast, bringing with it warm, moist air and low-hanging clouds.

"There's a nice breeze, about fifteen knots. Perfect for a trial run."

"Let's do it. With all that talk about June twenty-fifth yesterday, I think we owe it to Becky and Taylor to begin *White Wings*'s new life on the day her old life ended."

"Sounds good to me."

We cast off and let the bow come around, picking up the southeast wind off her stern quarter. The sails filled and, like a greyhound released from the gate, she leaped forward. Instantly she became a living, breathing thing whose life force, so long shattered and dormant in Taylor's garage, surged through her frames and stringers, swept across her deck and planking, and billowed out through her sails. In the waters beneath, her keel and centerboard sliced smoothly, leaving hardly a trace of a wake. Above, like a banner pole, her mast swept the darkening sky with its pure white sail. She was happy, delighted, exuberant and showed us her thanks for our many hours of work by giving us one hell of a sail.

When we reached the mouth of the harbor, Matthew pointed with his head toward the open sea. I nodded and he brought her to a course due east past Cat Island. Soon we were in open water where long rolling swells moved beneath us, lifting us and gently setting us down again. The wind was steady, perfect for sailing. For a fleeting moment I was a little girl, holding on for dear life and watching Grandmother Becky laugh as she sailed her beloved *White Wings*.

"Let's put her through her paces," Matthew called to me.

"Do it." I was as excited as he.

He brought her in close-hauled and we cut into the wind off our starboard bow. *White Wings* heeled to port, further and further as Matthew tightened the mainsheet, but held steady and confident even as her toerail touched the water. I was hiked out on the starboard side as far as I could go when I realized I was shouting like a bronco rider in a rodeo. Matthew grinned and yelled, "Yahoo!"

We came about, reversing our course, and ran with the wind, climbing the swells and surfing down the other side.

"Want to take her?" Matthew called.

"Sure. But stay with me and tell me what to do."

I moved onto the bench by the tiller with Matthew just in front of me. I let her continue to run free for a while and then asked if we could jibe.

"You've got the conn. What do you want to do?"

"I want to jibe." And we did, allowing the wind to cross over the stern. We tried several other maneuvers around and beyond Cat Island, then headed toward the West Shore Harbor where our mooring was.

Matthew looked at his watch. "I can't believe it's eight already. We'd better head right in."

"It is getting dark."

"Want me to take over?" he asked.

"Sure." As we shifted places, I looked back beyond Lighthouse Point. "Over there," I said, pointing. "Looks like fog."

"Not surprised. Warm air and a cold ocean."

"Will we make it in okay?"

"We should. It's a ways out there."

As we crossed the mouth of the harbor heading toward Salem and the western shore of Marblehead, we saw a power boat coming out of the harbor. At first we thought nothing of it. It was early in the season but still there were boats coming and going out of Marblehead. Its course seemed steady, and its bearing off our port side constant. As it left the restricted speed area of the harbor it seemed to rise out of the water and come straight at us.

"Maybe it's the harbormaster wanting to warn us about the fog," I said hopefully.

"From the bow you can't tell whose boat it is, but it looks too big to be the harbormaster."

The distance between us was closing rapidly and still the bearing remained the same.

"If he stays on that course he's going to hit us," I yelled.

"You're right. Maybe he doesn't see us. Get ready. I'm going to jibe."

Matthew pulled the tiller to port and jibed. The wind had picked up and moved us quickly onto the new heading. The power boat, its engines roaring louder and louder, shifted its course too. Again it was headed straight at us.

"We've got trouble, Rebecca. Grab your life jacket, put it on." He did the same.

Oh God, I thought. It's going to hit us.

Now it was coming at us so fast it had practically no bow wave. It planed across the water with a rumbling roar so deep I could feel it in my stomach.

"Matthew! He's trying to hit us."

It was on us before I could scream. Then suddenly it swerved and passed to our stern.

"Aowww!" I wailed. For an instant there was calm and then its stern wake crashed over our side, dumping gallons of ocean into the boat. As it sped away I saw the name *My Turn* on the stern. "Oh God! It's Kramer."

"Yeah," Matthew called. "I think he's just trying to scare us."

The water that gushed into the boat had drenched me. "What are we going to do? Look, he's coming around again."

"Start bailing. Raise that floorboard and get rid of some of this water. I'm heading straight into Marblehead Harbor." He came about and hauled in on the mainsheet as we heeled to starboard. I bailed frantically, but our speed remained sluggish, no match for the power boat.

Kramer circled around us until he was in front and then bore down on our bow. Matthew let his bow fall off to starboard, hoping against hope that Kramer would pass us on his port, unless he did intend a collision. In seconds the powerful diesel engines drove the boat toward us and passed so close on the port side it scraped our hull. Hearing the terrible screeching of fiberglass against wood, I buried my head in my hands and felt *White Wings* heave to the right. This time we were so close to his boat we rode his stern wake as it surged beneath us.

"Rebecca, Rebecca! Look at me." I opened my eyes but leaned forward holding my stomach. "Rebecca! We'll never get past him into the harbor. See that fog bank over there? If we can make that, we can lose him. Keep bailing, darling."

My eyes a blur, I found the bailer sloshing about by the centerboard well and set to scooping water over the side. "Just get me out of here."

Matthew jibed to a starboard tack. The fog was creeping around Lighthouse Point. It looked miles away. I sank onto the floor of the boat into the water, feeling nauseous. In the distance I could hear the diesels. Instead of roaring, they were humming as the boat came up behind us. I turned to look. Kramer's boat was lying still in the water about fifty feet away, its engines idling.

Matthew looked back. "What's he doing now?"

Then, with a roar from hell, the big diesels in neutral gear shook his boat. He gunned them again and again, and each time I screamed louder and louder. Suddenly, silence, except for his laughter echoing across the darkening sea.

"We don't have far to the fog. Keep praying we make it."

Abruptly the silence was again broken by the roar of diesels. His bow lifted into the air and he came at us, pushing tons of foaming water ahead of him. Suddenly all I could see was a white fiberglass wall looming up behind us and waves of water rushing at us. Again he swung the boat to the side and sped away, and again we were engulfed in cold black water. Then, instantly, the world turned a fuzzy gray. We were in the fog bank.

"Oh, thank God! Thank God," I cried.

"We made it."

"Don't stop, for Christ's sake. Keep going, Matthew."

"I am, but I'm changing course some to see if I can lose him."

It was as if we'd entered another dimension. We could have

been floating in the air above the water. Sounds were muffled. The air was cooler. And there was nothing around us except gray fog.

"Matthew," I whispered. "Are we safe?"

"Well, we're safer than we were."

"Where're we headed?"

"I haven't the slightest idea. Away from him, I hope."

We continued sailing for several minutes unable to see more than a few feet into the fog. I stopped feeling sick but felt no less fearful. Then we heard it again off our starboard beam. Not a roar, but the gentle hum of well-tuned diesels. The sound grew closer but no louder. It seemed to be paralleling our course. Our eyes, peeled in the direction of the sounds, could see nothing.

Like a voice from a hollow tomb, we heard him call. "Hey, Jap girl! Hey, teacher! I know you're there. You can't get away."

My heart sank. Hope was gone.

"So you thought you'd get old Kramer? Thought you'd pin Becky's death on me, huh? You never will, 'cause you're never gonna make it back." His laughter echoed about us in the fog.

Matthew put his finger to his mouth telling me not to make a sound, whispering, "He can't see us." Carefully I set the bailer down. He eased the tiller to starboard and *White Wings* turned to port. The sound of Kramer's laughter grew faint. Again silence. Only the ripple of the water beneath the boat and the sighing of the mainsail and stays. We continued in the blessed fog.

Rumble. We heard it again, and again it was in the same relative location off our starboard beam.

Then his voice rattled over the water. He was using a megaphone. "You picked a good date. June twenty-fifth. Back in nineteen hundred and forty-one, that's the date your whore grandmother got fucked by her boyfriend the preacher. Yeah, I know all about it. I was lyin' up on the rock out there watchin' it all through my glasses." My stomach wrenched. "Good show, too, even if they were under the awning. But damn, it shoulda been me. Not that fuckin' preacher." The engines continued to hum through the fog. "Then she had the nerve to ask me to help her steal the boat. The boat you're in now. So I helped her and told her she owed me one. When I tried to collect, she cried rape, and threatened to report me to the police for running drugs. The bitch."

I watched Matthew let the sheet out as far as possible, slowing our boat, hoping Kramer would bypass us in the fog. We waited, then we heard his engines move to idle again until we caught up to him.

Matthew leaned forward and whispered. "He must have us on his radar. Shit, we might as well be out in the open."

Matthew pulled in the sheet and we picked up speed. Kramer's engines revved slightly.

His voice came again out of the fog. "Yeah, June twenty-fifth's the perfect day for you to be out here. She always went out the twenty-fifth. I'd follow sometimes and watch with my glasses. Couldn't make it in 1973, though, 'cause I had a business appointment out in the ocean. I futzed around out there all afternoon lookin' for my rendezvous but those fuckers didn't show and the weather was buildin' up. It started to get dark and rougher 'n all hell, so I headed in.

"Guess what? There's your little boat flounderin' around in the storm, the sails torn and havin' a hell of a time. So I figure here's my chance. I come alongside and yell to Becky, 'Want a tow?' She says yes, so I throw her a line and pull her up beside me. I tell her to hold tight to my boat so I can lash a line to her bow cleat. All of a sudden I get this big surprise. She's not alone. She's got the god-damn preacher in there with her. I'd thought he was dead. Well, fuck her. I bend the line like I do to the cleat so you can't get it loose, and I hauls away. She and her boyfriend get knocked back into the stern and sit there thinkin' I've saved 'em. Hah! Instead I'm pullin' 'em out into the storm where they've got no chance of survivin'. Hell, if I can't have her, let Davy Jones fuck her."

I sat with my head in my hands, weeping for Becky and Taylor and for Matthew and me. It was only a matter of time. There was nothing we could do. Nowhere to run. I eased myself back to the stern, into the waiting arms of Matthew. He held me close and we wept together.

Again, Kramer's voice. "I don't know how far out we got, but it started gettin' rougher'n hell. Becky's no dope. She sees what's happenin' and takes a knife from somewhere and climbs out on the bow. I yell at her to get back, but she keeps cuttin' away at the line. So I fire a warnin' shot, but she ignores it. So I let go a couple more rounds. She manages to cut the line but falls flat onto the deck. Then a wave catches her and over she goes. The preacher dives after her. Last I saw, they're cuddlin' up together in their life jackets floatin' off to England."

My head shot up as Matthew yelled into the fog, "Kramer! Don't do this! Leave us alone. Don't make it worse for yourself."

"No way, sonny boy. You brought this on yourself with your snoopin' around. Now, you're gonna get yours, just like Becky did. Nobody fucks with Kramer and gets away with it."

The engines roared, and their sound came toward us, louder and louder.

"This is it," Matthew screamed. "Hold on to me."

Pounding waves came out of the fog beneath the great white bow which, by the grace of God, passed two feet behind us, sending the wake splashing over our stern.

"He meant it that time," Matthew said, squeezing me tighter. "He just plain missed."

We could hear the boat circling, coming around for another pass.

"Matthew. I love you." I pressed against his chest.

"I love you, Rebecca."

First there was a scraping sound, then a crunch, and we stopped dead in the water. Matthew let go the sheet and the boom swung out, spilling the wind.

"We've hit something," he said, letting go of me. Reaching over the side, he ran his hand over something wet and cold. "It's a rock or part of an island. I can't see."

He had no more time to see. Kramer, his diesels screaming, was coming across the water at us. Miss us again, I prayed. Oh God, please let him miss us.

The noise was so loud, the flash of the hull so close and the deluge from the spray so blinding, that all I could see was a white mass hit the rock a few feet ahead of us and take off into the air like a rocket. The propellers left the water, screaming like a chainsaw, and then everything went to pieces. Fiberglass flew in all directions, diesel oil sprayed the rocks, and fragments of glass fell around us. As quickly as it happened, all was silent.

Matthew and I raised our heads and gazed in awe. Then he reached forward and pulled up the centerboard. Together we began pushing ourselves off the rock. When we were free he hauled in the sheet. *White Wings*, of her own accord, picked up a port tack.

Then we heard him.

"Help! Help me! Over here." We heard hands thrashing in the water. To reach him we had to jibe and circle back. "Don't leave me," he called. His voice began to sputter. He coughed. The fog parted its curtain slightly and, fifteen feet ahead, we saw his white face disappear beneath the surface as his plaster cast pulled him down. As we came to the spot, Matthew spilled the wind and slowed the boat. Jumping from one side of the boat to the other, we peered down into the black depths. He'd vanished. For the next few minutes we drifted in silence, looking vainly into the fog. Then Matthew caught hold of the sheet and we resumed our port tack. Still too much in shock to speak, I snuggled next to him with my head buried in his shoulder.

Finally I asked, "Where're we headed?"

Matthew reached into his pocket, taking out a small flashlight and the compass Becky had given Taylor engraved with the words "to help you find your way home." He held the light on the compass and pointed. "This way. Toward home."

50

August in the Caribbean is hot as hell, but with the ocean at your doorstep it's bearable. I was sitting with Matthew on the veranda of the Clifton Resort Hotel on Tortola having a second cup of coffee after our buffet breakfast of sliced fresh fruit, soft-boiled eggs, and toast. The sun, well up in the sky by ten, peeked at us through the fronds of a banana tree, and a colorful parrotlike bird squawked the island news. Fifty feet from our table, ocean waves broke in a line onto the white sand beach where a couple with their three children made sand castles. Beyond that, windsurfers skidded across waters so clear they seemed to be sailing on air.

We hadn't waited till September to be married. Matthew would have been back teaching by then and a honeymoon impossible. So he ran the inn during July and the first part of August, while I set up my Japanese tour program. We were learning to compromise, and we weren't even married. On Saturday, August 12, we were married in St. Paul's Church. Mom gave me away, and Matthew's father was best man. Friends of mine from the hotel (I still had a few) were bridesmaids, Aggie was my maid of honor, and friends of Matthew's from Amherst and Marblehead High were ushers. My father sent his best from Japan but was unable to come, much to Mom's relief. Sam and Mom gave us a grand reception in their inn and that night we spent in the Hyatt Hotel at Logan Airport. The next morning, only yesterday, although it's hard to believe, we flew to Puerto Rico, then island-hopped to British Tortola in the Lesser Antilles.

A breeze from the ocean rustled the palms and stirred the warm air around us. Wearing unbuttoned shirts hanging loosely over our bathing suits, we sat without speaking, watching the windsurfers. I think Matthew was as exhausted as I. From the night of June twenty-fifth, when we sailed back into Marblehead Harbor to report the wreck of *My Turn* and the drowning of Karl Kramer, we'd been going at full throttle. From the harbormaster's office, we had stumbled up the hill to Aggie's house and collapsed on her sofa. She called Mom and Sam, then poured each of us a stiff scotch and we told them what had happened.

"To think we had to learn it from Kramer," Mom said. "All these years of wondering what happened to Becky and my father, and Kramer knew it all the time."

"He wasn't about to tell," Matthew said.

"What a brutal, terrible way they were taken," she continued. "I shudder thinking about it."

"Please, I can't talk about that now," I said, cringing. "I'm still shaking. He almost killed us, too."

"By the grace of God he missed us," Matthew said.

"That and *White Wings*," I added. "She found that rock. We had no idea where we were."

Matthew thought for a moment and said, "I guess on the radar he couldn't tell us from the rock."

"Well, Kramer's dead and that's good," Aggie said.

"And you're alive." Mom sighed. "Thank God."

"Remember you said he might have been running drugs," Matthew said to Aggie. "That's what he was doing out there the night he found Becky and Taylor. He was supposed to have had a rendezvous with a ship but it never showed up. He was on his way in when he found *White Wings*."

"Unbelievable," Sam exclaimed. "What kind of man could find a boat in distress and pull it out into the storm?"

"Huh," Aggie muttered. "A man like Kramer."

In the days and weeks that followed, Matthew and I went over the experiences of that night until I could talk about it without being afraid. The harbormaster held a hearing at which we testified, showing them the bullet and the piece of line we'd taken from the cleat. There were enough people in town that had seen Kramer going off the deep end, so there was no doubt about us being cleared of wrongdoing.

Having the inn to run and setting up my new business was a challenge and occupied my time. But best of all was getting married. I was so sick and tired of uncertainty. I wanted to settle down.

Now we were here on Tortola, with our little cottage near the beach and someone to feed and entertain us.

We went back to our cottage, picked up our face masks, and snorkels and flippers, and went down to the beach. The water was cooler than the air but still like a lukewarm bath. We drifted along like two submarines, our snorkels sticking up and our eyes scanning the bottom. About a hundred yards offshore we found a coral reef and spent the rest of the morning marveling at brightly colored fish.

After lunch we went back to the cottage for a nap and some very restful lovemaking. A breeze danced with the curtains and moved across our naked bodies. I put my head on Matthew's shoulder and together we slept the rest of the afternoon.

At night, after a feast of three kinds of fish baked over an open fire, we went to the bar where a steel band was playing, and ordered piña coladas. A strong breeze from the ocean whipped the banana trees and a full moon poked in and out of clouds scudding across the sky. I closed my eyes and leaned against Matthew, twining my arm in his.

"Let's stay here forever," I whispered. "Away from everything. From people that are cruel and mean. Just the two of us."

"Okay by me."

I sipped my drink. "I'd miss *White Wings*. But I love the idea of a place like this."

"We could become beachcombers."

"Don't tempt me."

The steel band took a break and was replaced by a young woman with a guitar. Her voice was clear and delicate, hardly audible above the guitar. She sang a ballad about a young island girl who fell in love with a sailor who went away and never returned. The music was lilting and the words sad, reminding me of Becky and Taylor.

"I think I'd like to go," I said. Matthew nodded and we got up to leave just as the singer was starting another song.

"Wait," Matthew said, taking my arm. "Isn't that—"

The singer played through a theme that sounded familiar and then started the lyrics. We listened mesmerized.

> *White wings, they never grow weary,*
> *They carry me cheerily over the sea;*
> *Night comes, I long for my dearie,*
> *I'll spread out my white wings and sail home to thee!*

Astonished, we waited to the end of her set and introduced ourselves. She said her name was Ruth.

"The second song you sang, Ruth. Where did you learn it?"

"Oh, you mean 'White Wings.' "

"Yes."

"Did you like it?" she said with an island accent. "It's a beautiful little song. I learned it as a schoolgirl. When I added it to my repertoire, I researched it and found out it was popular in the United States back in the eighteen-nineties. Have you heard it before?"

"Yes," I said. "I know the words. My mother taught me, and my grandmother taught her."

"It's a nice tune, too."

"How did you learn it?" I said, controlling my eagerness.

"A priest taught me. It was a church school."

"Here on Tortola?"

"Yes. St. Barnabas. On the hill above the harbor."

"Is the priest still there?"

"There is a priest there, but not the one who taught me the song. He was visiting."

"How long ago did this happen?"

"About five years ago, when I was in my last year. Why? Is something wrong?"

"No. Not at all. What's the priest's name?"

"The rector of the church? He's Father Grafton. But he's not the one who taught us songs."

"Do you remember the name of that priest?" I asked.

"It was so long ago. I'm sorry. I don't remember."

"That's okay," I said. "We'll ask Father Grafton."

"May I ask why you're so interested in the name of the priest who taught me 'White Wings'?"

"Sure. I think I might know him."

As we walked back to our cottage, Matthew said, "Now take it easy, Rebecca. Don't let your imagination run away with you."

"Don't be so damned practical. I'll let it run if it wants to. The rational world isn't all that perfect."

Next morning we walked to the town, winding our way past shops and warehouses near the harbor, and ascended the hill. The church was a small white stucco building with a steeple and bell tower surmounted by a cross. Its door was painted bright red and there were four stained glass windows on each of the side walls. Behind the church, separated by a grove of trees, was a two-story building, probably the school Ruth had attended. A sign near the church door said "St. Barnabas Anglican Church" and gave the hours of services and the name of the rector, the Rev. Hubert G. Grafton. At the bottom of the sign was the word "office" and an arrow pointing toward a house to the left of the church. We followed a well-worn path to the house and knocked on the door.

An older black man, perhaps sixty, opened the door. He was short with wild gray hair and bushy eyebrows. He wore white slacks and a black clerical shirt with a round collar. Taking off his glasses, he tipped his head to the side and examined us carefully.

"Yes?"

"Father Grafton?"

"Yes?"

"We're visiting here from the States, staying at the Clifton Resort Hotel. Last night, a young woman named Ruth, who entertains there, said she had learned one of her songs while a student here at St. Barnabas."

"Oh yes," he said, relaxing. "Ruth Howard. Doesn't she have a fine voice? Sings in our choir."

"She has a beautiful voice. She sang a song she learned here at the school."

"I'm not surprised. We have a fine musical program for the children."

"This particular song was taught her by a visiting priest."

"That's possible," he said, rubbing his chin. "There's lots of visiting clergy, especially during winter. Like to come down here to get away from the cold."

"Do you remember the name of the priest who taught Ruth some songs? It would have been about five years ago, when she was in her last year."

"Oh yes. A man about fifteen years older than I. He gave an organ concert, too. His wife was with him."

"And his name?"

Wrinkling his brow and grasping his chin with his thumb and forefinger, he thought for several moments. "I can't remember his name. He was here just for a short time. In and out, you know."

"One of the songs he taught her was 'White wings, they never grow weary.' "

"That's it. Now I remember. 'White Wings.' He and his wife lived on a boat. I can't for the life of me remember his name, though."

"I can't, either." A voice came from inside the house. "And for goodness sake, Hubert, invite the poor people in out of the heat."

We entered a darkened living room, the shades drawn against the sun.

"I'm Mrs. Grafton. Please have a seat. I'll bring you some lemonade." She was a heavy-set woman her husband's age and wore a loose-fitting white housedress. In a minute she was back with two glasses.

"Maybe you heard what we were asking, about the priest who taught Ruth the song 'White Wings.' "

"I remember that the two of them lived on this boat," Mrs. Grafton said. "I saw it in the harbor. A two-masted schooner."

"And you don't remember their names?"

"Nooo," she said, shaking her head, "but I'll never forget the story the wife told me. Said years before, the two of them got swept overboard from their sailboat and were rescued by a boat off

New England. From what she implied, I got the idea the boat that picked them up might have been running drugs. It brought them down here and let them off on one of the islands. They never went back. Liked it here. They sail from island to island on this schooner, help out in churches or schools where they can. Lots of people come down here and don't go back."

Trying to hide my excitement, I asked Father Grafton, "Do you know where they are now?"

"No. Like I said, they were here only a short time and were off to someplace else. Who knows? There's a thousand islands, big and small, here in the Caribbean."

"You can't remember their names, but you remember they lived on a boat. How's that?"

"That song you mentioned. 'White Wings.' That was the name of their boat."

We left the Graftons and walked to the crest of the hill overlooking the harbor. Holding hands, we let our eyes wander over the panorama.

"It's a big ocean," Matthew said. "When do we start searching?"

In the distance we could see an island and beyond that to the right yet another. To the left an old fishing schooner was making its way around the point of still another island.

I said nothing for a long time. Just gazed at the sea. Putting my arm around Matthew, I pulled him close to me.

"Do you think they're out there?" I asked, more to myself than to Matthew. "If they are," I continued, "Becky's seventy-four and Taylor's about seventy-nine. Pretty old to be living on a schooner, but I know people that age that play tennis and go skiing."

Matthew was shaking his head. "I don't know. I think it's one huge coincidence: the song, the visiting priest, the name of the boat. If they survived and did get down here, surely they'd have kept in touch. Becky would have wanted to let your mother know she was all right. Aggie, too. And you, Rebecca. Think of the grief and sorrow that could have been avoided."

I didn't answer. I was watching the schooner moving quietly over the placid waters with hardly a breeze to fill its sails. The only sounds were the laughter of children playing in a yard below us and the chatter of birds in the trees beside the school. I sat down on the grass, propped my elbows on my knees, and continued to gaze at the water. Matthew joined me.

Slowly my thoughts took shape. "If you could, right now, disappear from all the demands people put on you, and do it in a way that no one could hold it against you, would you do it?" He started to speak. "Wait. Don't answer yet. And if you could do it in a place like this, with the person you love, namely me, and not have money worries, would you do it?"

"No," he said abruptly. "It wouldn't be fair to the other people I love: my folks, your mother, Sam, Aggie. Sounds great in a fantasy, but I'd never really do it."

I sighed. "Probably I wouldn't either. But it's tempting. And if I were Becky, with everything she went through to find Taylor, it would be very tempting. Maybe they got here and decided to take a few months off from life and spend it getting to know each other again. And maybe they liked it so much they stayed on, the two of them, traveling from island to island on their schooner, exploring, sharing adventures, helping out where they could, hauling a mattress onto the deck and making love when it's too hot in the cabin."

"At seventy?"

"Why not? I want to. Don't you?"

He laughed, slightly embarrassed. "Well, yeah."

We said nothing for a few moments. Then I said, "You know, don't you, that it's not a coincidence? It has to be Becky and Taylor who taught Ruth that song."

"I know," Matthew said with a sigh. "Maybe it's that I'm not willing to grant older people, like my parents, the right to do something just because *they* want to. Especially something bizarre like leaving everybody and everything to live on a boat in the Caribbean."

I laughed, knowing the feeling well. "Remember my toast when we launched *White Wings*? 'Fair winds and a following sea to Becky and Taylor, wherever you are.'"

"I remember. As if you knew they were still alive."

"They are alive, somewhere out there." I stood and pulled Matthew up. "Kiss me as a toast to Becky and Taylor."

He smiled and put his arms around me. We kissed, then turned toward the vast Caribbean Sea and shouted at the top of our lungs, "To Becky and Taylor, wherever you are!"

Suddenly, explosively, hundreds of birds in the trees by the school burst from their branches, flying upward into the blue sky and outward toward the many islands of the Caribbean.

The typeface used in this book is a version of Caslon, the first designed by an Englishman. (By the end of the seventeenth century France and the Netherlands had superseded Italy as centers of type production, but the British were still importing it from the continent.) William Caslon (1692–1766) began as an engraver and only became a typefounder and designer of roman typefaces after being asked by a group of missionaries to create a font for an Arabic translation of the New Testament. Purely for identification he printed his name on the proofs in roman capitals, but one of the sponsors was so impressed that he urged Caslon to start his own foundry and lent him the money to do so. Caslon's type was preeminent in the eighteenth-century English-speaking world, particularly in the American colonies, and the Declaration of Independence was one of many documents first printed with it.